A TRAMP ABROAD

MARK TWAIN

A Tramp Abroad

Abridged and Edited with
an Introduction by

CHARLES NEIDER

With Illustrations by the Author

PERENNIAL LIBRARY
Harper & Row, Publishers
New York, Hagerstown, San Francisco, London

A hardcover edition of this book is published by Harper & Row, Publishers, Inc.

First PERENNIAL LIBRARY edition published 1978

ISBN: 0-06-080453-X

Designed by Eve Callahan

78 79 80 81 82 10 9 8 7 6 5 4 3 2 1

To Susy Neider
with love and admiration

Contents

Introduction

by Charles Neider

I had long thought that Mark Twain's *A Tramp Abroad* was probably both his funniest and his most uneven work. In 1960, the 125th anniversary of Samuel Langhorne Clemens's birth, while I was rereading his works, I noted in the margins of my copy of the book both my delight and my disappointment with it. I felt that it was cluttered with irrelevant or mediocre detail that sadly detracted from the great bursts of comic genius it contained, and that an abridged edition might serve to restore its faded popularity. "Digressions, digressions at every turn," I wrote. "This is a padded book. Ought to be reissued in concised form. Then it might find the modern following it so richly deserves." But I did not then have the opportunity to make available such an edition. I am delighted to be able to do so now.

Mark Twain published five travel books in all: *The Innocents Abroad* (1869), *Roughing It* (1872), *A Tramp Abroad* (1880), *Life on the Mississippi* (1883) and *Following the Equator* (1897). Albert Bigelow Paine, his official biographer, wrote in 1912, "The sales of the *Innocents* during the earlier years more than doubled those of the *Tramp* during a similar period. The later ratio of popularity is more nearly three to one. It has been repeatedly stated that in England the *Tramp* has the greater popularity, an assertion not sustained by the publisher's accountings." Since then the sales disparity of the two books has increased greatly, and there have been numerous times when *A Tramp Abroad* has been out of print.

The Innocents Abroad reflected the author's joy in writing it, *A Tramp Abroad* his labors and uncertainty. His critical faculties seemed to be on vacation, his artistic conscience to be dozing more than usual. And he was pressed by the need to fill up space to meet the requirements of a large subscription book and was too tired and bored to meet them creatively. Perhaps he had temporarily and to some extent written himself out. Within a decade he had written in detail about his experiences in Europe and the Near East, in the West and the Sandwich Islands, and in the Mississippi basin. (He had published many of his Mississippi River recollections in the *Atlantic* in 1875.) In addition he had written *Tom Sawyer*, the river idyll, the work of nostalgia harking back to his Hannibal years. And so he had substantially drawn upon all the basic themes and materials of his creative life.

What was required to make *A Tramp Abroad* work was that he should go to Europe unencumbered by family, free to be fresh and impulsive, and committed to writing letters for a newspaper, preferably a Western one; free from the need to write long letters to his friend William Dean Howells complaining about the book's lack of progress; free from the necessity to try to impress Howells in one way or another (an inner pressure and expressed not without charm); free from the badgering he had begun undergoing in Hartford and which he himself in the last analysis was largely responsible for. The original edition of *A Tramp Abroad* lacks the tension, the fire, the brilliant detail, the vocabulary, the energy and the invective of *The Innocents Abroad*. But in terms of stretches of sustained humor, of heights of humor, of sustained virtuoso performance, *The Innocents Abroad* does not come near it. There is nothing in the earlier book as inspired as "The Awful German Language" or as funny as the ascent of the Riffelberg. If these are harsh strictures let us add that they are made in the context of Clemens's performance as a whole. It was not a question of his faculties being on the wane. *A Tramp Abroad* was essentially a failure of stance. In

The Innocents Abroad the text is serious, the embroidery is enlivened by jokes. In the original edition of *A Tramp Abroad* the text itself is often a series of jokes.

In May 1877 Clemens went to Bermuda with his close Hartford friend, Reverend Joseph Twichell, jotting in a notebook that it was "the first actual pleasure trip" he had ever taken. Meanwhile the complexity and expense of his Hartford way of life were beginning to tax his strength and optimism. In a letter to his mother written in February 1878 he wrote, "Life has come to be a very serious matter with me. I have a badgered, harassed feeling a good part of my time. It comes mainly of business responsibilities and annoyances, and the persecution of kindly letters from well meaning strangers—to whom I must be rudely silent or else put in the biggest half of my time bothering over answers. There are other things also that help to consume my time and defeat my projects. Well, the consequence is, I cannot write a book at home. This cuts my income down. Therefore, I have about made up my mind to take my tribe and fly to some little corner of Europe and budge no more until I shall have completed one of the half dozen books that lie begun, up stairs."

And in one of the notebooks of that time we find this: "To go abroad has something of the same sense that death brings —'I am no longer of ye; what ye say of me is now of no consequence—but of how much consequence when I am with ye and of ye.' I know you will refrain from saying harsh things *because* they cannot hurt me, since I am out of reach and cannot hear them. This is why we say no harsh things of the dead."

Clemens, in his forty-third year, sailed for Europe on April 11, 1878, with the plan of taking a walking tour with Twichell that would be the basis of a new book of travels that both he and his publisher believed it was time for him to give to his public. He was no carefree or still relatively unknown and poor bachelor now, as he had been in 1867 when he joined the *Quaker City* excursion that resulted in his writing *The Innocents Abroad*. He was well-to-do, money hungry, an authentic citizen of the Gilded Age, a pater familias who preferred the company of a minister to that of the irreverent, swearing, smelly characters he had known in the West, and he embraced the Victorianism of Germany and Switzerland, countries new to him but which he preferred now as against those of southern and Catholic Europe. He was no longer interested in roughing it. What he had in mind for his new book was a series of pseudo-pedestrian adventures done in high, fat style, and he would tramp with Twichell, whom he depended on to inspire him and who, in the published book, would be Harris in disguise. As Clemens himself knew, there was a good deal of the preacher in him, and he was prejudiced against the Roman church.

While waiting for Twichell, Clemens and his family—entourage is a better word, for Clemens had brought along with him, in addition to his wife and two young daughters, his wife's friend Clara Spaulding, and a nursemaid and a butler —settled down in Germany, where they continued their assiduous study of the German language, begun in the Hartford house. Twichell arrived early in August and he and Clemens set out for the Black Forest. Twichell remained in Europe for about six weeks, after which the Clemens family went down to Italy, staying three weeks in Venice, a week in Florence and a fortnight in Rome. Then they went to Munich, where Clemens resumed work on the *Tramp*, begun in Heidelberg, writing and destroying much in the winter of 1878–79. He could not seem to work up enthusiasm for the task as a whole.

At one point he couldn't find his Swiss notebook and for a while believed he had a good excuse for not being able to write the new book. But he was not to be let off that easily. As he wrote to Twichell, "I was about to write to my publisher and propose some other book, when the confounded thing turned up, and down went my heart into my boots. But there was now no excuse, so I went solidly to work, tore up a great part of the MS written in Heidelberg—wrote and tore up, continued to write and tear up—and at last, reward of patient and noble persistence, my pen got the old swing again! Since then I'm glad that Providence knew better what to do with the Swiss note-book than I did."

Paine writes in his biography, "Originally there was a good deal about Munich in the new book, and some of the discarded chapters might have been retained with advantage. They were ruled out in the final weeding as being too serious, along with the French chapters. Only a few Italian memories were left to follow the Switzerland wanderings." According to Paine, Clemens's tales "The Stolen White Elephant" and "The Invalid's Story," as well as his sketch "The Great Revolution in Pitcairn," were originally chapters in the *Tramp*. Howells printed "The Great Revolution in Pitcairn" and "The Great French Duel," the latter a chapter of the *Tramp*, in the *Atlantic*, of which he was editor.

In a letter to Howells from Munich dated January 30, 1879, Clemens wrote, "I have destroyed such lots of MS written for this book! And I suppose there are such lots left which ought to be destroyed. If it should be, it *shall* be—that is certain. . . . I wish I *could* give those sharp satires on European life which you mention, but of course a man can't write successful satire except he be in a calm judicial good-humor— whereas I *hate* travel, and I *hate* hotels, and I *hate* the opera, and I *hate* the Old Masters—in truth I don't ever seem to be in a good enough humor with *any*thing to *satirize* it; no, I want to stand up before it and *curse* it, and foam at the mouth —or take a club and pound it to rags and pulp. I have got in two or three chapters about Wagner's Operas, and managed to do it without showing temper—but the strain of another such effort would burst me. . . . I want to make a book which people will *read*—and I shall make it profitable reading in spots—in spots merely *because* there's not much material for a larger amount."

The Clemenses tried Paris at the end of February. They encountered a cold wet winter, and Clemens's work on the book continued to be heavy and plaguing. As usual, he found himself indulging in a good deal of social life. The summer arrived. It was cold. Clemens recorded in his notebook, "France has neither winter, nor summer, nor morals. Apart from these drawbacks it is a fine country." Work on the book was still a heavy chore for him. The Clemenses made their way to London via the Low Countries but London was no respite. It was as cold as Paris had been, and as full of socializing.

They returned to the States early in September 1879. Clemens wrote to Twichell, "I am revising my MS. I did not expect to like it, but I do. I have been knocking out early chapters for more than a year now, not because they had not merit, but merely because they hindered the flow of the narrative; it was a dredging process. Day before yesterday my shovel fetched up three more chapters and laid them, reeking, on the festering shore-pile of their predecessors, and now I think the yarn swims right along, without hitch or halt. I believe it will be a readable book of travels. I cannot see that it lacks anything but information."

But he was not finished with the book yet, or rather it was not finished with him. Paine writes, "He had thought it finished when he left [Quarry Farm in Elmira, New York], but discovered that he must add several hundred pages to complete its bulk. It seemed to him that he had been given a life-sentence. He wrote six hundred pages and tore up all but two hundred and eighty-eight." Clemens finally completed his task early in January 1880, having by his own count written almost four thousand paof manuscript and using only twenty-six hundred.

He had massive doubts about the quality of his latest literary work but Howells, to whom he sent proofs, liked it and wrote to him, "Well, you are a blessing. You ought to believe in God's goodness, since he has bestowed upon the world such a delightful genius as yours to lighten its troubles." This was heavenly music to Clemens, who replied, "Your and Mrs. Howells's praises have been the greatest uplift I ever had. When a body is not even remotely expecting such things, how the surprise takes the breath away! We had been interpreting your stillness to melancholy and depression caused by that book. This is honest. Why, *everything* looks brighter now. A check for untold cash could not have made our hearts sing as your letter has done."

A Tramp Abroad was published in mid-March 1880, with an advance sale of twenty-five thousand copies. Howells reviewed it in the May issue of the *Atlantic*. He commented, "His humor springs from a certain intensity of common sense, a passionate love of justice, and a generous scorn of what is petty and mean; and it is these qualities which his 'school' have not been able to 'convey.' They have never been more conspicuous than in this last book of his, to which they may be said to give its sole coherence. It may be claiming more than a humorist could wish to assert that he is always in earnest; but this strikes us as the paradoxical charm of Mr. Clemens's best humor. Its wildest extravagance is the break and fling from a deep feeling, a wrath with some folly which disquiets him worse than other men, a personal hatred for some humbug or pretension that embitters him beyond anything but laughter."

Howells's review was typical of the inability in serious American literary circles at the time to accept the fact that Clemens was able to indulge in humor purely for its own sake simply because it was an essential part of his genius. That is, when those same circles tolerated the view that he was anything more than an inspired clown, despite strong English beliefs to the contrary. Clemens's Anglomania was well justified. The English recognized his true stature long before most of his literary countrymen did. Clemens himself had bought the notion that in order to justify his play of humor or his humor of play he had to moralize, to be the "moralist of the Main," as he had been dubbed in his Western years. Among the major causes of his difficulty in writing the *Tramp* was this conflict in him between needing inwardly to be funny and feeling the outward pressure to be Serious. One suspects that he brought Twichell to Europe, paying for his passage and expenses, at least partly to stabilize and buttress his graver side.

The companionship of a minister now, not that of a miner

as in the silver country days of *Roughing It*. But paradoxi-
cally, Twichell was not your ordinary man of the cloth; he
could share with Mark (as he called Clemens) roars of laughter when Mark's bawdy "1601" was read aloud and he could
tolerate Mark's gift of inspired swearing in male company.
And so in addition to being a steadying influence and a reminder that there was a need for preaching in the world, his
presence excited Clemens's sense of laughter. Also, Twichell
was a friend, a walker, a talker—and an opportunity for
Clemens to escape temporarily from a household full of
females (wife, wife's friend, two daughters, nursemaid), the
butler excepted.

In his later years, while dictating his autobiography, Clemens denied that he had ever been a humorist of the "mere"
sort but his practice belied him. In a discussion of a pirated
edition of *Mark Twain's Library of Humor*, he said, "This
book is a very interesting curiosity, in one way. It reveals the
surprising fact that within the compass of these forty years
wherein I have been playing professional humorist before
the public, I have had for company seventy-eight other
American humorists. Each and every one of the seventy-
eight rose in my time, became conspicuous and popular, and
by and by vanished. A number of these names were as familiar in their day as are the names of George Ade and Dooley
today—yet they have all so completely passed from sight now
that there is probably not a youth of fifteen years of age in
the country whose eye would light with recognition at the
mention of any one of the seventy-eight names. . . . In this
mortuary volume I find Nasby, Artemus Ward, Yawcob
Strauss, Derby, Burdette, Eli Perkins, the 'Danbury News
Man,' Orpheus C. Kerr, Smith O'Brien, Josh Billings and a
score of others, maybe two score, whose writings and sayings
were once in everybody's mouth but are now heard of no
more and are no longer mentioned. . . . Why have they
perished? Because they were merely humorists. Humorists
of the 'mere' sort cannot survive. Humor is only a fragrance,
a decoration. Often it is merely an odd trick of speech and

of spelling, as in the case of Ward and Billings and Nasby and the 'Disbanded Volunteer,' and presently the fashion passes and the fame along with it. There are those who say a novel should be a work of art solely and you must not preach in it, you must not teach in it. That may be true as regards novels but it is not true as regards humor. Humor must not professedly teach and it must not professedly preach, but it must do both if it would live forever. By forever, I mean thirty years. . . . I have always preached. That is the reason that I have lasted thirty years. If the humor came of its own accord and uninvited I have allowed it a place in my sermon but I was not writing the sermon for the sake of the humor. I should have written the sermon just the same, whether any humor applied for admission or not."

We need only read large portions of the present volume to see that Clemens, fortunately, did not always consider it necessary to "preach." Some of his "merely" humorous things *have* survived "forever"—because of their play of fancy, their wit, their fresh and idiomatic prose. The fact is that the breadth of his comic genius was very great, greater than Howells was willing or able to acknowledge, at least publicly. Clemens was not only involved with fun for its own sweet sake but with a personal vision of life as a strange and comic affair. The vogue of coy illiteracy practiced by Ward and Billings was bound to die, if only because it represented not a way of seeing life but of exploiting tricks of style and manner. Howells recognized Clemens's greatness but he did not, perhaps, understand the rarity of his comic genius. He was correct in claiming that there was a moralist lurking in Clemens but he went too far in implying that that was the chief basis of Clemens's humor. However, he was too intelligent and perceptive to fail to sense the complexity of the matter. Also, he was a good friend of Clemens and as such knew the playful side of the man. And so he inserted an escape hatch in his review: "It may be claiming more than a humorist could wish to assert that he is always in earnest." In any event he was writing for the sober *Atlantic* audience and was intent on doing Clemens a service by insisting that Clemens was more than just an American jokester or writer of children's books, and that the *Tramp* was a success because it was serious.

It was a curious review. It strove to praise, and it praised in sober language and with some difficulty. Clearly its author was perplexed. And halfway through it he had a start of guilt that caused him to write, "Nevertheless, if we have been saying anything about the book or about the sources of Mr. Clemens's humor to lead the reader to suppose that it is not immensely amusing, we have done it a great wrong. It is delicious, whether you open it at the sojourn in Heidelberg, or the voyage down the Neckar on a raft, or the mountaineering in Switzerland, or the excursion beyond the Alps into Italy." But he felt there was too much about the ascent of the Riffelberg and he would have preferred to have another appendix in its stead. The ascent of the Riffelberg I consider to be one of the wildest and funniest things that Clemens ever wrote, but it patently lacks a sermon.

In his endeavor to emphasize the book's seriousness Howells managed to strain his argument. Having noted that the book "has not the fresh frolicsomeness of *The Innocents Abroad;* it is Europe revisited and seen through eyes saddened by much experience of tables d'hôte, old masters, and travelling Americans," he said of Clemens, "His opinions are no longer the opinions of the Western American newly amused and disgusted at the European difference, but the Western American's impressions on being a second time confronted with things he has had time to think over. This is the serious undercurrent of the book, to which we find ourselves reverting from its obvious comicality." He neglected to say that in his previous trips to Europe Clemens had not visited Germany and Switzerland, that these countries do not represent Europe as a whole and that consequently Clemens's impressions of them lack the perspective of a subsequent visit. Nor did he note the change that had come over Clemens in the eleven years between 1867, the year of the *Quaker*

City excursion, and 1878. If in 1867 Clemens could be realisti-
cally described as a "Western American," in 1878 he would
have to be described as an entrenched if naturalized East-
erner.

In a copy of the book presented to Twichell, Clemens
acknowledged the *Tramp*'s great debt to the minister. "Just
imagine it for a moment: I was collecting material in Europe
during fourteen months for a book, and now that the thing
is printed I find that you, who were with me only a month
and a half of the fourteen, are in *actual* presence (not imaginary) in 440 pages of the 631 the book contains! Hang it, if you
had stayed at home it would have taken me fourteen *years*
to get the material. You have saved me an intolerable whole
world of hated labor, and I'll not forget it, my boy. You'll find
reminders of things, all along, that happened to us, and of
others that didn't happen, but you'll remember the spot
where they were invented. . . . We had a mighty good time,
Joe, and the six weeks I would dearly like to repeat *any* time,
but the rest of the fourteen months—*never*."

If I may venture to say it myself, this edited version of the
Tramp is now a thoroughly delicious book free of the pad-
ding demands of subscription publishing of Clemens's day.
One need only glance at the table of contents to see what
wonderful things it contains. "The Castle" is a brilliant example of Clemens's ability to observe closely and to bring to
bear all the resources of his articulateness in order to project
what he sees. There are devastating and very funny portraits
of young Americans putting on the dog abroad, marvelous
observations on the ant, and moving descriptions of nature.
"The Great French Duel" allows him to divert his inclination
to invective about the French to flights of satire that by their
very extremes acquire an almost benign, even loving effect.
Almost everywhere the catharsis is two-sided: his and ours.
And he uses some of his past, American experiences very
fruitfully and powerfully, with his mastery of dialect and the
vernacular in the foreground, in giving us Jim Baker's extraordinary bluejay yarn, the Hannibal tale about Nicodemus

Dodge and the skeleton, the story about the man who put up at Gadsby's, and the yarn about the Arkansas bride, all done with a riot of humorous invention.

"The Awful German Language" is a comic masterpiece, a virtuoso performance that by itself almost justifies all the troubles he had in composing the book. The incredible invention, incredibly sustained, leaves us awestruck. And one is awed by the amount of energy and careful, cunning labor, by the degree of canny architecture, that he was willing and able to commit to create this most delicate and dangerous of tightrope walks, in which a couple of false notes could be disastrous. Unbelievably, he relegated the performance to an appendix. Which proves his critical confusion, his defensive stance, about the book as a whole. One is tempted to think, "God help all lesser mortals if the great ones are capable of such mistakes."

It is the wildness of his comic invention, the tremendously bold flights of exaggeration—the extremes that bothered less gifted men like Howells, who somehow failed to understand how cathartic they can be—that are so richly and abundantly and freely evidenced in this new version of the book. Clemens's comic extremes were too much for well-tamed spirits like Howells, who probably did not fully grasp that Clemens went to Europe for release from the deadening confines of his plush Hartford existence, that he needed to break out in the vein that still gave him rich ore: humor. Thoughts of Howells, the *Atlantic,* the ruling New England literary set, led him to believe he had to produce serious stuff just when such material was farthest from what he needed to deal with personally. It is hardly a wonder that he experienced something dangerously close to a writer's block. And, almost cruelly, one of the troubles with the original edition is that he tried at times to be funny in the professional way, forcing humor as if to balance out deliberately the serious chapters he had written and which troubled him so much that in many instances he discarded them. Fortunately for us, the wild stuff insisted on expressing itself.

Having worked with the *Tramp* intimately, having in a sense fallen in love with it, perhaps I may be forgiven when I predict for it a new life and a large audience that, like myself, will cherish its comic riches at a time when there cannot be too much profound, cathartic laughter, not only in our own troubled nation but in the world at large.

The original edition was in one volume consisting of fifty chapters and six appendixes. I have abridged it by approximately 25 percent. The following chapters were omitted in their entirety: 16, 17, 18, 30, 40, 41, 43, 44 and 45. Deletions of varying lengths were made in Chapters 1, 15, 19, 26, 31, 32, 34 and 36. Chapters 2 and 3 have been joined together.

In my opinion the omitted chapters are strained in their attempts at humor and contain much superfluous or irrelevant matter. For instance, in 16, which is concerned with the legend and song of the Lorelei, Clemens goes so far as to reprint sheet music in German. Chapter 30, in the form of an official report by Harris to Twain, is so replete with foreign words and phrases as to seem silly. At the chapter's conclusion Clemens excoriates this dependence on linguistic foreignisms but by now the chapter only proves that even he can't have his cake and eat it too. Chapter 40, about glaciers and their rates of travel, contains extensive quotations from books he read on the subject, as does 41, which is about Alpine catastrophes. Chapter 45 retells the story of a catastrophe that cost eleven lives and is presented so spiritlessly that it gives the impression of being little more than a filler.

What is true of the omitted chapters is true as well of the chapter portions deleted. Chapter 1 contained unfunny quotations; 15 was partially about a legend, "The Cave of the Specter," related in a bored manner; 19 contained another legend, "The Legend of Dilsberg Castle," which was distracting, irrelevant and not well done. Other chapters contained dispiriting ruminations on couriers, church bells, or quotations from books about the Alps, together with feeble attempts at humor.

In the original edition the appendixes are titled "The Portier Analyzed," "Heidelberg Castle Described," "The College Prison and Inmates," "The Awful German Language," "Legends of the Castle" and "The Journals of Germany." I have discarded four appendixes and kept "Heidelberg Castle Described" and "The Awful German Language," which I have incorporated as whole units into appropriate places in the text.

The table of contents of the original edition has chapter summaries in the style of the time but no chapter titles and, with six exceptions, there are no chapter titles elsewhere in the book. The chapter titles in the present edition are my own, as are a number of the chapter divisions. Wherever feasible, they were selected from phrases in the chapter summaries. It was possible to abridge the book without inserting any language of my own, not even the briefest of conjunctions—a fact that may say something about the degree to which the omitted matter was intrinsically extraneous.

As was the case in my edition of *The Autobiography of Mark Twain* and in my one-volume abridgment, *George Washington: A Biography*, of Washington Irving's five-volume *Life of George Washington*, I have modernized the punctuation. However, I have respected Clemens's predilection for the use of dashes in this book. I roughly estimate that there are between six thousand and seven thousand punctuation changes. Of course, one must be careful not to be mechanical, one must vary and modulate. And one must try to judge where the punctuation was the compositor's and where it was Clemens's. An interesting sidelight on this problem occurs in the margin of a typescript page of his autobiographical dictations. *"Private:* Discard the stupid Harper rule for once: don't put a comma after 'old'—I can't *have* it! S L C." The notation is in Clemens's hand. He was referring to a phrase: "beyond that old safe frontier." And at times, when one feels the old punctuation is specifically more suited to his voice, it should be allowed to stand.

The result, in its difference from the original text, is far from superficial. What amounts almost to a substantive, and certainly to a kinesthetic, change seems to take place. Removal of the vast thickets of commas and semicolons, the substitution of many commas and periods for semicolons, and the making into shorter units of unjustifiably long and complicated and therefore labored sentences created by the use of series of semicolons instead of periods, allows the text to be luminous, clutter-free and beautifully transparent. As a consequence, what were formerly halting, stumbling rhythms now flow more gracefully in tune with the thought.

Effects are swifter, more sudden, more economical. There is a sense of muscle and motion. And there are more delights for the reader, who is no longer constantly reminded that he is being exposed to a long-outmoded punctuation fashion that was more in keeping with the stays and bustles and Victorian bric-a-brac of the period than much of Clemens's thought and style actually was. Sometimes the thought and language seem to feel released and to soar, or there's an overarching effect, or the thought is sudden and the point deadly. The language breathes and so do we, and the unnecessary wall between us and Clemens comes down.

With regard to my modernizing the punctuation, it may be worth noting that I have worked in a tradition followed by Bernard DeVoto, literary editor of the Mark Twain Estate and editor of *Mark Twain in Eruption*, and by Douglas Southall Freeman, who wrote the modern, monumental life of Washington and who defended his position in the first volume of his work. I may add, too, that Washington Irving himself modernized Washington's punctuation in his life of Washington.

An examination of Clemens's and Irving's manuscripts indicates that neither author punctuated as heavily as the printed versions of their work often suggest. Both authors in their correspondence occasionally complained of the heavy hands of printers in punctuating their text. The effect of modernizing the punctuation is comparable to that of removing coats of discolored varnish from an old painting. The new punctuation lessens the distance between the modern reader and the intimacy of Clemens's imagination, intelligence, language and humor.

Princeton, New Jersey
December 6, 1976

A TRAMP ABROAD

1. Heidelberg

One day it occurred to me that it had been many years since the world had been afforded the spectacle of a man adventurous enough to undertake a journey through Europe on foot. After much thought I decided that I was a person fitted to furnish to mankind this spectacle. So I determined to do it. This was in March 1878.

I looked about me for the right sort of person to accompany me in the capacity of agent and finally hired a Mr. Harris for this service.

It was also my purpose to study art while in Europe. Mr. Harris was in sympathy with me in this. He was as much of an enthusiast in art as I was and not less anxious to learn to paint. I desired to learn the German language. So did Harris.

Toward the middle of April we sailed in the *Holsatia*, Captain Brandt, and had a very pleasant trip indeed.

After a brief rest at Hamburg we made preparations for a long pedestrian trip southward in the soft spring weather but at the last moment we changed the program for private reasons and took the express-train.

We made a short halt at Frankfort-on-the-Main and found it an interesting city. I would have liked to visit the birthplace of Gutenberg but it could not be done, as no memorandum of the site of the house has been kept. So we spent an hour in the Goethe mansion instead. The city permits this house to belong to private parties instead of gracing and dignifying herself with the honor of possessing and protecting it.

Frankfort is one of the sixteen cities which have the distinction of being the place where the following incident occurred. Charlemagne, while chasing the Saxons (as *he* said), or being chased by them (as *they* said), arrived at the bank of the river at dawn in a fog. The enemy were either before him or behind him but in any case he wanted to get across very badly. He would have given anything for a guide but none was to be had. Presently he saw a deer, followed by her young, approach the water. He watched her, judging that she would seek a ford, and he was right. She waded over and the army followed. So a great Frankish victory or defeat was gained or avoided, and in order to commemorate the episode Charlemagne commanded a city to be built there, which he named Frankfort—the ford of the Franks. None of the other cities where this event happened were named from it. This is good evidence that Frankfort was the first place it occurred at.

Frankfort has another distinction—it is the birth place of the German alphabet or at least of the German word for alphabet—*Buchstaben.* They say that the first movable types were made on birch sticks—*Buchstabe*—hence the name.

I was taught a lesson in political economy in Frankfort. I had brought from home a box containing a thousand very cheap cigars. By way of experiment I stepped into a little shop in a queer old back street, took four gaily decorated boxes of wax matches and three cigars, and laid down a silver piece worth 48 cents. The man gave me 43 cents change.

In Frankfort everybody wears clean clothes, and I think we noticed that this strange thing was the case in Hamburg too and in the villages along the road. Even in the narrowest and poorest and most ancient quarters of Frankfort neat and clean clothes were the rule. The little children of both sexes were nearly always nice enough to take into a body's lap. And as for the uniforms of the soldiers, they were newness and brightness carried to perfection. One could never detect a smirch or a grain of dust upon them. The street-car conductors and drivers wore pretty uniforms which seemed to be just out of the bandbox, and their manners were as fine as their clothes.

We stopped at a hotel by the railway-station. Next morning, as we sat in my room waiting for breakfast to come up, we got a good deal interested in something which was going on over the way in front of another hotel. First, the personage who is called the *portier* (who is not the *porter* but is a sort of first-mate of a hotel) appeared at the door in a spick-and-span new blue cloth uniform decorated with shining brass buttons and with bands of gold lace around his cap and wristbands; and he wore white gloves, too. He shed an official glance upon the situation and then began to give orders. Two women-servants came out with pails and brooms and brushes and gave the sidewalk a thorough scrubbing. Meanwhile two others scrubbed the four marble steps which led up to the door. Beyond these we could see some men-servants taking up the carpet of the grand staircase. This carpet was carried away and the last grain of dust beaten and banged and swept out of it, then brought back and put down again. The brass stair-rods received an exhaustive polishing and were returned to their places. Now a troop of servants brought pots and tubs of blooming plants and formed them into a beautiful jungle about the door and the base of the staircase. Other servants adorned all the balconies of the various stories with flowers and banners. Others ascended to the roof and hoisted a great flag on a staff there. Now came some more chambermaids and retouched the sidewalk and afterward wiped the marble steps with damp cloths and finished by dusting them off with feather brushes. Now a broad black carpet was brought out and laid down the marble steps and out across the sidewalk to the curbstone. The *portier* cast his eye along it and found it was not absolutely straight. He commanded it to be straightened. The servants made the effort—made several efforts, in fact—but the *portier* was not satisfied. He finally had it taken up, and then he put it down himself and got it right.

At this stage of the proceedings a narrow bright red carpet

was unrolled and stretched from the top of the marble steps to the curbstone, along the center of the black carpet. This red path cost the *portier* more trouble than even the black one had done. But he patiently fixed and refixed it until it was exactly right and lay precisely in the middle of the black carpet. In New York these performances would have gathered a mighty crowd of curious and intensely interested spectators but here it only captured an audience of half a dozen little boys who stood in a row across the pavement, some with their school-knapsacks on their backs and their hands in their pockets, others with arms full of bundles, and all absorbed in the show. Occasionally one of them skipped irreverently over the carpet and took up a position on the other side. This always visibly annoyed the *portier.*

Now came a waiting interval. The landlord, in plain clothes and bareheaded, placed himself on the bottom marble step, abreast the *portier,* who stood on the other end of the same steps. Six or eight waiters, gloved, bareheaded and wearing their whitest linen, their whitest cravats and their finest swallow-tails, grouped themselves about these chiefs, but leaving the carpetway clear. Nobody moved or spoke any more but only waited.

In a short time the shrill piping of a coming train was heard and immediately groups of people began to gather in the street. Two or three open carriages arrived and deposited some maids of honor and some male officials at the hotel. Presently another open carriage brought the Grand Duke of Baden, a stately man in uniform, who wore the handsome brass-mounted, steel-spiked helmet of the army on his head. Last came the Empress of Germany and the Grand Duchess of Baden in a closed carriage. These passed through the low-bowing groups of servants and disappeared in the hotel, exhibiting to us only the backs of their heads, and then the show was over.

It appears to be as difficult to land a monarch as it is to launch a ship.

But as to Heidelberg. The weather was growing pretty

warm—very warm, in fact. So we left the valley and took quarters at the Schloss Hotel on the hill above the Castle.

Heidelberg lies at the mouth of a narrow gorge—a gorge the shape of a shepherd's crook. If one looks up it he perceives that it is about straight for a mile and a half, then makes a sharp curve to the right and disappears. This gorge —along whose bottom pours the swift Neckar—is confined between (or cloven through) a couple of long, steep ridges, a thousand feet high and densely wooded clear to their summits, with the exception of one section which has been shaved and put under cultivation. These ridges are chopped off at the mouth of the gorge and form two bold and conspicuous headlands, with Heidelberg nestling between them. From their bases spreads away the vast dim expanse of the Rhine valley, and into this expanse the Neckar goes wandering in shining curves and is presently lost to view.

Now if one turns and looks up the gorge once more he will see the Schloss Hotel on the right, perched on a precipice overlooking the Neckar—a precipice which is so sumptuously cushioned and draped with foliage that no glimpse of the rock appears. The building seems very airily situated. It has the appearance of being on a shelf half-way up the wooded mountainside, and as it is remote and isolated and very white it makes a strong mark against the lofty leafy rampart at its back.

This hotel had a feature which was a decided novelty and one which might be adopted with advantage by any house which is perched in a commanding situation. This feature may be described as a series of glass-inclosed parlors *clinging to the outside of the house,* one against each and every bedchamber and drawing-room. They are like long, narrow, high-ceilinged bird-cages hung against the building. My room was a corner room and had two of these things, a north one and a west one.

From the north cage one looks up the Neckar gorge, from the west one he looks down it. This last affords the most extensive view and it is one of the loveliest that can be imag-

ined, too. Out of a billowy upheaval of vivid green foliage, a
rifle-shot removed, rises the huge ruin of Heidelberg Castle,
with empty window arches, ivy-mailed battlements, molder-
ing towers—the Lear of inanimate nature—deserted, dis-
crowned, beaten by the storms but royal still and beautiful.
It is a fine sight to see the evening sunlight suddenly strike
the leafy declivity at the Castle's base and dash up it and
drench it as with a luminous spray, while the adjacent groves
are in deep shadow.

Behind the Castle swells a great dome-shaped hill, forest-
clad, and beyond that a nobler and loftier one. The Castle
looks down upon the compact brown-roofed town, and from
the town two picturesque old bridges span the river. Now the
view broadens. Through the gateway of the sentinel headlands you gaze out over the wide Rhine plain, which stretches away, softly and richly tinted, grows gradually and
dreamily indistinct and finally melts imperceptibly into the
remote horizon.

I have never enjoyed a view which had such a serene and
satisfying charm about it as this one gives.

The first night we were there we went to bed and to sleep
early but I awoke at the end of two or three hours and lay
a comfortable while listening to the soothing patter of the
rain against the balcony windows. I took it to be rain but it
turned out to be only the murmur of the restless Neckar,
tumbling over her dikes and dams far below in the gorge. I
got up and went into the west balcony and saw a wonderful
sight. Away down on the level, under the black mass of the
Castle, the town lay, stretched along the river, its intricate
cobweb of streets jeweled with twinkling lights. There were
rows of lights on the bridges. These flung lances of light upon
the water in the black shadows of the arches. And away at the
extremity of all this fairy spectacle blinked and glowed a
massed multitude of gas-jets which seemed to cover acres of
ground. It was as if all the diamonds in the world had been
spread out there. I did not know before that a half-mile of
sextuple railway-tracks could be made such an adornment.

One thinks Heidelberg by day—with its surroundings—is the last possibility of the beautiful: but when he sees Heidelberg by night, a fallen Milky Way, with that glittering railway constellation pinned to the border, he requires time to consider upon the verdict.

2. The Castle

Heidelberg Castle must have been very beautiful before the French battered and bruised and scorched it two hundred years ago. The stone is brown with a pinkish tint and does not seem to stain easily. The dainty and elaborate ornamentation upon its two chief fronts is as delicately carved as if it had been intended for the interior of a drawing-room rather than for the outside of a house. Many fruit and flower clusters, human heads and grim projecting lions' heads are still as perfect in every detail as if they were new. But the statues which are ranked between the windows have suffered. These are life-size statutes of old-time emperors, electors and similar grandees, clad in mail and bearing ponderous swords. Some have lost an arm, some a head, and one poor fellow is chopped off at the middle. There is a saying that if a stranger will pass over the drawbridge and walk across the court to the castle front without saying anything, he can make a wish and it will be fulfilled. But they say that the truth of this thing has never had a chance to be proved, for the reason that before any stranger can walk from the drawbridge to the appointed place the beauty of the palace front will extort an exclamation of delight from him.

A ruin must be rightly situated to be effective. This one

could not have been better placed. It stands upon a commanding elevation, it is buried in green woods, there is no level ground about it, but, on the contrary, there are wooded terraces upon terraces, and one looks down through shining leaves into profound chasms and abysses where twilight reigns and the sun cannot intrude. Nature knows how to garnish a ruin to get the best effect. One of these old towers is split down the middle and one half has tumbled aside. It tumbled in such a way as to establish itself in a picturesque attitude. Then all it lacked was a fitting drapery, and Nature has furnished that. She has robed the rugged mass in flowers and verdure and made it a charm to the eye. The standing half exposes its arched and cavernous rooms to you like open, toothless mouths. There, too, the vines and flowers have done their work of grace. The rear portion of the tower has not been neglected either but is clothed with a clinging garment of polished ivy which hides the wounds and stains of time. Even the top is not left bare but is crowned with a flourishing group of trees and shrubs. Misfortune has done for this old tower what it has done for the human character sometimes —improved it.

A gentleman remarked one day that it might have been fine to live in the castle in the day of its prime but that we had one advantage which its vanished inhabitants lacked— the advantage of having a charming ruin to visit and muse over. But that was a hasty idea. Those people had the advantage of *us*. They had the fine castle to live in and they could cross the Rhine valley and muse over the stately ruin of Trifels besides. The Trifels people in their day, five hundred years ago, could go and muse over majestic ruins which have vanished, now, to the last stone. There have always been ruins, no doubt, and there have always been pensive people to sigh over them, and asses to scratch upon them their names and the important date of their visit. Within a hundred years after Adam left Eden the guide probably gave the usual general flourish with his hand and said: "Place where the animals were named, ladies and gentlemen. Place where the tree of the forbidden fruit stood. Exact spot where Adam and Eve first met. And here, ladies and gentlemen, adorned and hallowed by the names and addresses of three generations of tourists, we have the crumbling remains of Cain's altar—fine old ruin!" Then, no doubt, he taxed them a shekel apiece and let them go.

An illumination of Heidelberg Castle is one of the sights of Europe. The Castle's picturesque shape, its commanding situation midway up the steep and wooded mountainside, its vast size—these features combine to make an illumination a most effective spectacle. It is necessarily an expensive show and consequently rather infrequent. Therefore whenever one of these exhibitions is to take place the news goes about in the papers and Heidelberg is sure to be full of people on that night. I and my agent had one of these opportunities and improved it.

About half past seven on the appointed evening we crossed the lower bridge with some American students in a pouring rain and started up the road which borders the Neunheim side of the river. This roadway was densely packed with carriages and foot-passengers, the former of all ages and the latter of all ages and both sexes. This black and solid mass was struggling painfully onward through the slop, the darkness and the deluge. We waded along for three-quarters of a mile and finally took up a position in an unsheltered beer-garden directly opposite the Castle. We could not *see* the Castle—or anything else, for that matter—but we could dimly discern the outlines of the mountain over the way through the pervading blackness and knew whereabouts the Castle was located. We stood on one of the hundred benches in the garden, under our umbrellas. The other ninety-nine were occupied by standing men and women, and they also had umbrellas. All the region round about and up and down the river-road was a dense wilderness of humanity hidden under an unbroken pavement of carriage tops and umbrellas. Thus we stood during two drenching hours. No rain fell on my head but the converging whalebone points of a dozen neigh-

boring umbrellas poured little cooling streams of water down
my neck and sometimes into my ears and thus kept me from
getting hot and impatient. I had the rheumatism, too, and
had heard that this was good for it. Afterward, however, I was
led to believe that the water treatment is *not* good for rheumatism. There were even little girls in that dreadful place.
A man held one in his arms just in front of me for as much
as an hour, with umbrella-drippings soaking into her clothing
all the time.

In the circumstances two hours was a good while for us to
have to wait but when the illumination did at last come we
felt repaid. It came unexpectedly, of course—things always
do that have been long looked and longed for. With a perfectly breath-taking suddenness several vast sheaves of vari-
colored rockets were vomited skyward out of the black
throats of the Castle towers, accompanied by a thundering
crash of sound, and instantly every detail of the prodigious
ruin stood revealed against the mountainside and glowing
with an almost intolerable splendor of fire and color. For
some little time the whole building was a blinding crimson
mass, the towers continued to spout thick columns of rockets
aloft, and overhead the sky was radiant with arrowy bolts
which clove their way to the zenith, paused, curved gracefully downward, then burst into brilliant fountain-sprays of
richly colored sparks. The red fires died slowly down within
the Castle and presently the shell grew nearly black outside.
The angry glare that shone out through the broken arches
and innumerable sashless windows now reproduced the aspect which the Castle must have borne in the old time when
the French spoilers saw the monster bonfire which they had
made there fading and smoldering toward extinction.

While we still gazed and enjoyed, the ruin was suddenly
enveloped in rolling and rumbling volumes of vaporous
green fire, then in dazzling purple ones. Then a mixture of
many colors followed and drowned the great fabric in its
blended splendors. Meantime the nearest bridge had been
illuminated, and from several rafts anchored in the river,

meteor showers of rockets, Roman candles, bombs, serpents and Catharine wheels were being discharged in wasteful profusion into the sky—a marvelous sight indeed to a person as little used to such spectacles as I was. For a while the whole region about us seemed as bright as day and yet the rain was falling in torrents all the time. The evening's entertainment presently closed and we joined the innumerable caravan of half-drowned spectators and waded home again.

The Castle grounds are very ample and very beautiful, and as they joined the Hotel grounds, with no fences to climb but only some nobly shaded stone stairways to descend, we spent a part of nearly every day in idling through their smooth walks and leafy groves. There was an attractive spot among the trees where were a great many wooden tables and benches, and there one could sit in the shade and pretend to sip at his foamy beaker of beer while he inspected the crowd. I say pretend because I only pretended to sip, without really sipping. That is the polite way. But when you are ready to go you empty the beaker at a draught. There was a brass band and it furnished excellent music every afternoon. Sometimes so many people came that every seat was occupied, every table filled. And never a rough in the assemblage—all nicely dressed fathers and mothers, young gentlemen and ladies and children, and plenty of university students and glittering officers, with here and there a gray professor or a peaceful old lady with her knitting, and always a sprinkling of gawky foreigners. Everybody had his glass of beer before him or his cup of coffee or his bottle of wine or his hot cutlet and potatoes. Young ladies chatted, or fanned themselves, or wrought at their crocheting or embroidering. The students fed sugar to their dogs or discussed duels or illustrated new fencing tricks with their little canes. And everywhere was comfort and enjoyment and everywhere peace and good-will to men. The trees were jubilant with birds and the paths with rollicking children. One could have a seat in that place and plenty of music any afternoon for about eight cents, or a family ticket for the season for two dollars.

For a change, when you wanted one, you could stroll to the Castle and burrow among its dungeons or climb about its ruined towers or visit its interior shows—the great Heidelberg Tun, for instance. Everybody has heard of the great Heidelberg Tun and most people have seen it, no doubt. It is a wine-cask as big as a cottage, and some traditions say it holds eighteen hundred thousand bottles, and other traditions say it holds eighteen hundred million barrels. I think it likely that one of these statements is a mistake and the other one a lie. However, the mere matter of capacity is a thing of no sort of consequence, since the cask is empty, and indeed has always been empty, history says. An empty cask the size of a cathedral could excite but little emotion in me. I do not see any wisdom in building a monster cask to hoard up emptiness in, when you can get a better quality, outside, any day, free of expense. What could this cask have been built for? The more one studies over that the more uncertain and unhappy he becomes. Some historians say that thirty couples, some say thirty thousand couples, can dance on the head of this cask at the same time. Even this does not seem to me to account for the building of it. It does not even throw light on it. A profound and scholarly Englishman—a specialist—who had made the great Heidelberg Tun his sole study for fifteen years told me he had at last satisfied himself that the ancients built it to make German cream in. He said that the average German cow yielded from one to two and a half teaspoonfuls of milk when she was not worked in the plow or the hay-wagon more than eighteen or nineteen hours a day. This milk was very sweet and good and of a beautiful transparent bluish tint. But in order to get cream from it in the most economical way a peculiar process was necessary. Now he believed that the habit of the ancients was to collect several milkings in a teacup, pour it into the Great Tun, fill up with water and then skim off the cream from time to time as the needs of the German Empire demanded.

This began to look reasonable. It certainly began to account for the German cream which I had encountered and marveled over in so many hotels and restaurants. But a thought struck me—

"Why did not each ancient dairyman take his own teacup of milk and his own cask of water and mix them, without making a government matter of it?"

"Where could he get a cask large enough to contain the right proportion of water?"

Very true. It was plain that the Englishman had studied the matter from all sides. Still I thought I might catch him on one point, so I asked him why the modern empire did not make the nation's cream in the Heidelberg Tun instead of leaving it to rot away unused. But he answered as one prepared—

"A patient and diligent examination of the modern German cream has satisfied me that they do not use the Great Tun now because they have got a *bigger* one hid away somewhere. Either that is the case or they empty the spring milkings into the mountain torrents and then skim the Rhine all summer."

There is a museum of antiquities in the Castle, and among its most treasured relics are ancient manuscripts connected with German history. There are hundreds of these, and their dates stretch back through many centuries. One of them is a decree signed and sealed by the hand of a successor of Charlemagne in the year 896. A signature made by a hand which vanished out of this life near a thousand years ago is a more impressive thing than even a ruined castle. Luther's wedding-ring was shown me, also a fork belonging to a time anterior to our era, and an early bootjack. And there was a plaster cast of the head of a man who was assassinated about sixty years ago. The stab-wounds in the face were duplicated with unpleasant fidelity. One or two real hairs still remained sticking in the eyebrows of the cast. That trifle seemed to almost change the counterfeit into a corpse.

There are many aged portraits—some valuable, some worthless, some of great interest, some of none at all. I bought a couple—one a gorgeous duke of the olden time, and the other a comely blue-eyed damsel, a princess, maybe. I bought them to start a portrait-gallery of my ancestors with. I paid a dollar and a half for the duke and two and a half for the princess. One can lay in ancestors at even cheaper rates than these in Europe if he will mouse among old picture shops and look out for chances.

3. Jim Baker's Bluejay Yarn

One never tires of poking about in the dense woods that clothe all these lofty Neckar hills to their tops. The great deeps of a boundless forest have a beguiling and impressive charm in any country but German legends and fairy tales have given these an added charm. They have peopled all that region with gnomes and dwarfs and all sorts of mysterious and uncanny creatures. At the time I am writing of I had been reading so much of this literature that sometimes I was not sure but I was beginning to believe in the gnomes and fairies as realities.

One afternoon I got lost in the woods about a mile from the hotel and presently fell into a train of dreamy thought about animals which talk, and kobolds, and enchanted folk, and the rest of the pleasant legendary stuff. And so, by stimulating my fancy, I finally got to imagining I glimpsed small flitting shapes here and there down the columned aisles of the forest. It was a place which was peculiarly meet for the occasion. It was a pine wood with so thick and soft a carpet of brown needles that one's footfall made no more sound than if he were treading on wool. The tree-trunks were as round and straight and smooth as pillars and stood close together. They were bare of branches to a point about twenty-five feet above-ground and from there upward so thick with boughs that not a ray of sunlight could pierce through. The world was bright with sunshine outside, but a deep and mellow twilight reigned in there and also a silence so profound that I seemed to hear my own breathings.

When I had stood ten minutes, thinking and imagining and getting my spirit in tune with the place and in the right mood to enjoy the supernatural, a raven suddenly uttered a hoarse croak over my head. It made me start, and then I was angry because I started. I looked up and the creature was sitting on a limb right over me, looking down at me. I felt something of the same sense of humiliation and injury which one feels when he finds that a human stranger has been clandestinely inspecting him in his privacy and mentally commenting upon him. I eyed the raven and the raven eyed me. Nothing was said during some seconds. Then the bird stepped a little way along his limb to get a better point of observation, lifted his wings, stuck his head far down below his shoulders toward me and croaked again—a croak with a distinctly insulting expression about it. If he had spoken in English he could not have said any more plainly than he did say in raven, "Well, what do *you* want here?" I felt as foolish as if I had been caught in some mean act by a responsible being and reproved for it. However, I made no reply. I would not bandy words with a raven. The adversary waited a while with his shoulders still lifted, his head thrust down between them, and his keen bright eye fixed on me. Then he threw out two or three more insults which I could not understand further than that I knew a portion of them consisted of language not used in church.

I still made no reply. Now the adversary raised his head and called. There was an answering croak from a little distance in the wood—evidently a croak of inquiry. The adversary explained with enthusiasm and the other raven dropped

everything and came. The two sat side by side on the limb
and discussed me as freely and offensively as two great natu-
ralists might discuss a new kind of bug. The thing became
more and more embarrassing. They called in another friend.
This was too much. I saw that they had the advantage of me
and so I concluded to get out of the scrape by walking out of
it. They enjoyed my defeat as much as any low white people
could have done. They craned their necks and laughed at me
(for a raven *can* laugh, just like a man), they squalled insulting remarks after me as long as they could see me. They were
nothing but ravens—I knew that—what they thought about
me could be a matter of no consequence—and yet when
even a raven shouts after you, "What a hat!" "Oh, pull down
your vest!" and that sort of thing, it hurts you and humiliates
you and there is no getting around it with fine reasoning and
pretty arguments.

Animals talk to each other, of course. There can be no
question about that but I suppose there are very few people
who can understand them. I never knew but one man who
could. I knew he could, however, because he told me so
himself. He was a middle-aged, simple-hearted miner who
had lived in a lonely corner of California among the woods
and mountains a good many years and had studied the ways
of his only neighbors, the beasts and the birds, until he believed he could accurately translate any remark which they
made. This was Jim Baker. According to Jim Baker, some
animals have only a limited education and use only very
simple words and scarcely ever a comparison or a flowery
figure. Whereas certain other animals have a large vocabulary, a fine command of language and a ready and fluent
delivery. Consequently these latter talk a great deal. They
like it. They are conscious of their talent and they enjoy
"showing off." Baker said that after long and careful observation he had come to the conclusion that the bluejays were the
best talkers he had found among birds and beasts. Said he:

"There's more *to* a bluejay than any other creature. He has
got more moods and more different kinds of feelings than

other creatures. And, mind you, whatever a bluejay feels he
can put into language. And no mere commonplace language,
either, but rattling, out-and-out book-talk—and bristling
with metaphor, too—just bristling! And as for command of
language—why *you* never see a bluejay get stuck for a word.
No man ever did. They just boil out of him! And another
thing: I've noticed a good deal, and there's no bird or cow or
anything that uses as good grammar as a bluejay. You may say
a cat uses good grammar. Well, a cat does—but you let a cat
get excited once, you let a cat get to pulling fur with another
cat on a shed, nights, and you'll hear grammar that will give
you the lockjaw. Ignorant people think it's the *noise* which
fighting cats make that is so aggravating but it ain't so. It's the
sickening grammar they use. Now I've never heard a jay use
bad grammar but very seldom, and when they do they are
as ashamed as a human, they shut right down and leave.

"You may call a jay a bird. Well, so he is, in a measure—
because he's got feathers on him and don't belong to no
church, perhaps. But otherwise he is just as much a human
as you be. And I'll tell you for why. A jay's gifts and instincts
and feelings and interests cover the whole ground. A jay
hasn't got any more principle than a Congressman. A jay will
lie, a jay will steal, a jay will deceive, a jay will betray. And
four times out of five a jay will go back on his solemnest
promise. The sacredness of an obligation is a thing which you
can't cram into no bluejay's head. Now, on top of all this
there's another thing. A jay can outswear any gentleman in
the mines. You think a cat can swear. Well, a cat can. But you
give a bluejay a subject that calls for his reserve-powers and
where is your cat? Don't talk to *me*—I know too much about
this thing. And there's yet another thing. In the one little
particular of scolding—just good, clean, out-and-out scolding
—a bluejay can lay over anything, human or divine. Yes sir,
a jay is everything that a man is. A jay can cry, a jay can laugh,
a jay can feel shame, a jay can reason and plan and discuss,
a jay likes gossip and scandal, a jay has got a sense of humor,
a jay knows when he is an ass just as well as you do—maybe

better. If a jay ain't human he better take in his sign, that's all. Now I'm going to tell you a perfectly true fact about some bluejays.When I first begun to understand jay language correctly there was a little incident happened here. Seven years ago the last man in this region but me moved away. There stands his house—been empty ever since. A log house with a plank roof—just one big room and no more. No ceiling—nothing between the rafters and the floor. Well, one Sunday morning I was sitting out here in front of my cabin with my cat, taking the sun and looking at the blue hills and listening to the leaves rustling so lonely in the trees and thinking of the home away yonder in the states that I hadn't heard from in thirteen years, when a bluejay lit on that house, with an acorn in his mouth, and says, 'Hello, I reckon I've struck something.' When he spoke, the acorn dropped out of his mouth and rolled down the roof, of course, but he didn't care. His mind was all on the thing he had struck. It was a knot-hole in the roof. He cocked his head to one side, shut one eye and put the other one to the hole like a possum looking down a jug, then he glanced up with his bright eyes, gave a wink or two with his wings—which signifies gratification, you understand—and says, 'It looks like a hole, it's located like a hole—blamed if I don't believe it *is* a hole!'

"Then he cocked his head down and took another look. He glances up perfectly joyful this time, winks his wings and his tail both and says, 'Oh, no, this ain't no fat thing, I reckon! If I ain't in luck!—why it's a perfectly elegant hole!' So he flew down and got that acorn and fetched it up and dropped it in and was just tilting his head back with the heavenliest smile on his face when all of a sudden he was paralyzed into a listening attitude and that smile faded gradually out of his countenance like breath off'n a razor, and the queerest look of surprise took its place. Then he says, 'Why, I didn't hear it fall!' He cocked his eye at the hole again and took a long look, raised up and shook his head, stepped around to the other side of the hole and took another look from that side, shook his head again. He studied a while, then he just went into the *de*tails—walked round and round the hole and spied into it from every point of the compass. No use. Now he took a thinking attitude on the comb of the roof and scratched the back of his head with his right foot a minute and finally says, 'Well, it's too many for *me*, that's certain. Must be a mighty long hole. However, I ain't got no time to fool around here, I got to 'tend to business. I reckon it's all right—chance it, anyway.'

"So he flew off and fetched another acorn and dropped it in, and tried to flirt his eye to the hole quick enough to see what become of it, but he was too late. He held his eye there as much as a minute. Then he raised up and sighed and says, 'Confound it, I don't seem to understand this thing no way. However, I'll tackle her again.' He fetched another acorn and done his level best to see what become of it but he couldn't. He says, 'Well, *I* never struck no such a hole as this before. I'm of the opinion it's a totally new kind of a hole.' Then he begun to get mad. He held in for a spell, walking up and down the comb of the roof and shaking his head and muttering to himself but his feelings got the upper hand of him presently and he broke loose and cussed himself black in the face. I never see a bird take on so about a little thing. When he got through he walks to the hole and looks in again for half a minute, then he says, 'Well, you're a long hole and a deep hole and a mighty singular hole altogether—but I've started in to fill you and I'm d——d if I *don't* fill you if it takes a hundred years!'

"And with that away he went. You never see a bird work so since you was born. He laid into his work like a nigger, and the way he hove acorns into that hole for about two hours and a half was one of the most exciting and astonishing spectacles I ever struck. He never stopped to take a look any more—he just hove 'em in and went for more. Well, at last he could hardly flop his wings, he was so tuckered out. He comes a-drooping down once more, sweating like an ice-pitcher, drops his acorn in and says, '*Now* I guess I've got the bulge on you by this time!' So he bent down for a look. If you'll believe me, when his head come up again he was just pale with rage. He says, 'I've shoveled acorns enough in there to keep the family thirty years, and if I can see a sign of one of 'em I wish I may land in a museum with a belly full of sawdust in two minutes!'

"He just had strength enough to crawl up on to the comb and lean his back agin the chimbly, and then he collected his impressions and begun to free his mind. I see in a second that what I had mistook for profanity in the mines was only just the rudiments, as you may say.

"Another jay was going by and heard him doing his devotions and stops to inquire what was up. The sufferer told him the whole circumstance and says, 'Now yonder's the hole, and if you don't believe me go and look for yourself.' So this fellow went and looked and comes back and says, 'How many did you say you put in there?' 'Not any less than two tons,' says the sufferer. The other jay went and looked again. He couldn't seem to make it out, so he raised a yell and three more jays come. They all examined the hole, they all made the sufferer tell it over again, then they all discussed it and got off as many leather-headed opinions about it as an average crowd of humans could have done.

"They called in more jays, then more and more, till pretty soon this whole region 'peared to have a blue flush about it. There must have been five thousand of them, and such another jawing and disputing and ripping and cussing you never heard. Every jay in the whole lot put his eye to the hole and delivered a more chuckle-headed opinion about the mystery than the jay that went there before him. They examined the house all over, too. The door was standing half open and at last one old jay happened to go and light on it and look in. Of course, that knocked the mystery galley-west in a second. There lay the acorns, scattered all over the floor. He flopped his wings and raised a whoop. 'Come here!' he says. 'Come here, everybody. Hang'd if this fool hasn't been trying to fill up a house with acorns!' They all came a-swooping down like a blue cloud, and as each fellow lit on the door and

took a glance the whole absurdity of the contract that that
first jay had tackled hit him home and he fell over backward
suffocating with laughter, and the next jay took his place and
done the same.

"Well, sir, they roosted around here on the housetop and
the trees for an hour and guffawed over that thing like
human beings. It ain't any use to tell me a bluejay hasn't got
a sense of humor, because I know better. And memory, too.
They brought jays here from all over the United States to
look down that hole every summer for three years. Other
birds too. And they could all see the point except an owl that
come from Nova Scotia to visit the Yo Semite, and he took
this thing in on his way back. He said he couldn't see anything funny in it. But then he was a good deal disappointed
about Yo Semite too."

4. Student Life

The summer semester was in full tide, consequently the most
frequent figure in and about Heidelberg was the student.
Most of the students were Germans, of course, but the repre-
sentatives of foreign lands were very numerous. They hailed
from every corner of the globe—for instruction is cheap in
Heidelberg and so is living, too. The Anglo-American Club,
composed of British and American students, had twenty-five
members, and there was still much material left to draw
from.

Nine-tenths of the Heidelberg students wore no badge or
uniform. The other tenth wore caps of various colors and
belonged to social organizations called "corps." There were

five corps, each with a color of its own. There were white caps, blue caps, and red, yellow and green ones. The famous duel-fighting is confined to the "corps" boys. The *"kneip"* seems to be a specialty of theirs too. Kneips are held now and then to celebrate great occasions like the election of a beer king, for instance. The solemnity is simple. The five corps assemble at night, and at a signal they all fall to loading themselves with beer out of pint-mugs as fast as possible, and each man keeps his own count—usually by laying aside a lucifer match for each mug he empties. The election is soon decided. When the candidates can hold no more a count is instituted and the one who has drunk the greatest number of pints is proclaimed king. I was told that the last beer king elected by the corps—or by his own capabilities—emptied his mug seventy-five times. No stomach could hold all that quantity at one time, of course—but there are ways of frequently creating a vacuum, which those who have been much at sea will understand.

One sees so many students abroad at all hours that he presently begins to wonder if they ever have any working-hours. Some of them have, some of them haven't. Each can choose for himself whether he will work or play, for German university life is a very free life, it seems to have no restraints. The student does not live in the college buildings but hires his own lodgings in any locality he prefers and he takes his meals when and where he pleases. He goes to bed when it suits him and does not get up at all unless he wants to. He is not entered at the university for any particular length of time, so he is likely to change about. He passes no examination upon entering college. He merely pays a trifling fee of five or ten dollars, receives a card entitling him to the privileges of the university, and that is the end of it. He is now ready for business—or play, as he shall prefer. If he elects to work he finds a large list of lectures to choose from. He selects the subjects which he will study and enters his name for these studies but he can skip attendance.

The result of this system is that lecture-courses upon spe-

cialties of an unusual nature are often delivered to very slim
audiences, while those upon more practical and every-day
matters of education are delivered to very large ones. I heard
of one case where day after day the lecturer's audience consisted of three students—and always the same three. But
one day two of them remained away. The lecturer began as
usual—

> "Gentlemen,"—

—then, without a smile,
he corrected himself, saying—
> "Sir,"—

—and went on with his
discourse.

It is said that the vast majority of the Heidelberg students
are hard workers and make the most of their opportunities,
that they have no surplus means to spend in dissipation and
no time to spare for frolicking. One lecture follows right on
the heels of another with very little time for the student to
get out of one hall and into the next. But the industrious ones
manage it by going on a trot. The professors assist them in the
saving of their time by being promptly in their little boxed-
up pulpits when the hours strike and as promptly out again
when the hour finishes. I entered an empty lecture-room one
day just before the clock struck. The place had simple unpainted pine desks and benches for about two hundred persons.

About a minute before the clock struck a hundred and fifty
students swarmed in, rushed to their seats, immediately
spread open their note-books and dipped their pens in the
ink. When the clock began to strike, a burly professor entered, was received with a round of applause, moved swiftly
down the center aisle, said "Gentlemen," and began to talk
as he climbed his pulpit steps. And by the time he had arrived in his box and faced his audience his lecture was well
under way and all the pens were going. He had no notes, he
talked with prodigious rapidity and energy for an hour—
then the students began to remind him in certain well-
understood ways that his time was up. He seized his hat, still

talking, proceeded swiftly down his pulpit steps, got out the last word of his discourse as he struck the floor. Everybody rose respectfully and he swept rapidly down the aisle and disappeared. An instant rush for some other lecture-room followed and in a minute I was alone with the empty benches once more.

Yes, without doubt, idle students are not the rule. Out of eight hundred in the town, I knew the faces of only about fifty but these I saw everywhere and daily. They walked about the streets and the wooded hills, they drove in cabs, they boated on the river, they sipped beer and coffee, after-noons, in the Schloss gardens. A good many of them wore the colored caps of the corps. They were finely and fashionably dressed, their manners were quite superb and they led an easy, careless, comfortable life. If a dozen of them sat to-gether and a lady or a gentleman passed whom one of them knew and saluted they all rose to their feet and took off their caps. The members of a corps always received a fellow-mem-ber in this way too but they paid no attention to members of other corps. They did not seem to see them. This was not a discourtesy. It was only a part of the elaborate and rigid corps etiquette.

There seems to be no chilly distance existing between the German students and the professor but, on the contrary, a companionable intercourse, the opposite of chilliness and reserve. When the professor enters a beer-hall in the evening where students are gathered together these rise up and take off their caps and invite the old gentleman to sit with them and partake. He accepts and the pleasant talk and the beer flow for an hour or two, and by and by the professor, properly charged and comfortable, gives a cordial good night, while the students stand bowing and uncovered. And then he moves on his happy way homeward with all his vast cargo of learning afloat in his hold. Nobody finds fault or feels out-raged. No harm has been done.

It seemed to be a part of corps etiquette to keep a dog or so, too. I mean a corps dog—the common property of the organization, like the corps steward or head servant. Then there are other dogs, owned by individuals.

On a summer afternoon in the Castle gardens I have seen six students march solemnly into the grounds in single file, each carrying a bright Chinese parasol and leading a prodigious dog by a string. It was a very imposing spectacle. Sometimes there would be about as many dogs around the pavilion as students, and of all breeds and of all degrees of beauty and ugliness. These dogs had a rather dry time of it, for they were tied to the benches and had no amusement for an hour or two at a time except what they could get out of pawing at the gnats or trying to sleep and not succeeding. However, they got a lump of sugar occasionally—they were fond of that.

It seemed right and proper that students should indulge in dogs. But everybody else had them too—old men and young ones, old women and nice young ladies. If there is one spectacle that is unpleasanter than another it is that of an elegantly dressed young lady towing a dog by a string. It is said to be the sign and symbol of blighted love. It seems to me that some other way of advertising it might be devised, which would be just as conspicuous and yet not so trying to the proprieties.

It would be a mistake to suppose that the easy-going pleasure-seeking student carries an empty head. Just the contrary. He has spent nine years in the gymnasium under a system which allowed him no freedom but vigorously compelled him to work like a slave. Consequently he has left the gymnasium with an education which is so extensive and complete that the most a university can do for it is to perfect some of its profounder specialties. It is said that when a pupil leaves the gymnasium he not only has a comprehensive education but he *knows* what he knows—it is not befogged with uncertainty, it is burnt into him so that it will stay. For instance, he does not merely read and write Greek but speaks it; the same with the Latin. Foreign youth steer clear of the gymnasium. Its rules are too severe. They go to the university to put a mansard roof on their whole general education. But the

German student already has his mansard roof, so he goes there to add a steeple in the nature of some specialty, such as a particular branch of law or medicine or philology—like international law or diseases of the eye or special study of the ancient Gothic tongues. So this German attends only the lectures which belong to the chosen branch, and drinks his beer and tows his dog around and has a general good time the rest of the day. He has been in rigid bondage so long that the large liberty of university life is just what he needs and likes and thoroughly appreciates. And as it cannot last forever he makes the most of it while it does last, and so lays up a good rest against the day that must see him put on the chains once more and enter the slavery of official or professional life.

5. The Dueling Ground

One day in the interest of science my agent obtained permission to bring me to the students' dueling-place. We crossed the river and drove up the bank a few hundred yards, then turned to the left, entered a narrow alley, followed it a hundred yards and arrived at a two-story public house. We were acquainted with its outside aspect, for it was visible from the hotel. We went up-stairs and passed into a large whitewashed apartment which was perhaps fifty feet long by thirty feet wide and twenty or twenty-five high. It was a well-lighted place. There was no carpet. Across one end and down both sides of the room extended a row of tables, and at these tables some fifty or seventy-five students were sitting.

Some of them were sipping wine, others were playing

cards, others chess, other groups were chatting together, and many were smoking cigarettes while they waited for the coming duels. Nearly all of them wore colored caps. There were white caps, green caps, blue caps, red caps, and bright-yellow ones. So, all the five corps were present in strong force. In the windows at the vacant end of the room stood six or eight long, narrow-bladed swords with large protecting guards for the hand, and outside was a man at work sharpening others on a grindstone. He understood his business, for when a sword left his hand one could shave himself with it.

It was observable that the young gentlemen neither bowed to nor spoke with students whose caps differed in color from their own. This did not mean hostility but only an armed neutrality. It was considered that a person could strike harder in the duel and with a more earnest interest if he had never been in a condition of comradeship with his antagonist. Therefore comradeship between the corps was not permitted. At intervals the presidents of the five corps have a cold official intercourse with each other but nothing further. For example, when the regular dueling-day of one of the corps approaches, its president calls for volunteers from among the membership to offer battle. Three or more respond—but there must not be less than three. The president lays their names before the other presidents with the request that they furnish antagonists for these challengers from among their corps. This is promptly done. It chanced that the present occasion was the battle-day of the Red Cap Corps. They were the challengers, and certain caps of other colors had volunteered to meet them. The students fight duels in the room which I have described *two days in every week during seven and a half or eight months in every year.* This custom has continued in Germany two hundred and fifty years.

To return to my narrative. A student in a white cap met us and introduced us to six or eight friends of his who also wore white caps, and while we stood conversing two strange-looking figures were led in from another room. They were students panoplied for the duel. They were bareheaded. Their eyes were protected by iron goggles which projected an inch or more, the leather straps of which bound their ears flat against their heads. Their necks were wound around and around with thick wrappings which a sword could not cut through. From chin to ankle they were padded thoroughly against injury. Their arms were bandaged and rebandaged, lawyer upon layer, until they looked like solid black logs. These weird apparitions had been handsome youths clad in fashionable attire fifteen minutes before but now they did not resemble any beings one ever sees unless in nightmares. They strode along with their arms projecting straight out from their bodies. They did not hold them out themselves but fellow-students walked beside them and gave the needed support.

There was a rush for the vacant end of the room now and we followed and got good places. The combatants were placed face to face, each with several members of his own corps about him to assist. Two seconds, well padded and with swords in their hands, took near stations. A student belonging to neither of the opposing corps placed himself in a good position to umpire the combat. Another student stood by with a watch and a memorandum-book to keep record of the time and the number and nature of the wounds. A gray-haired surgeon was present with his lint, his bandages and his instruments. After a moment's pause the duelists saluted the umpire respectfully, then one after another the several officials stepped forward, gracefully removed their caps and saluted him also and returned to their places. Everything was ready now. Students stood crowded together in the foreground, and others stood behind them on chairs and tables. Every face was turned toward the center of attraction.

The combatants were watching each other with alert eyes. A perfect stillness, a breathless interest, reigned. I felt that I was going to see some wary work. But not so. The instant the word was given the two apparitions sprang forward and began to rain blows down upon each other with such lightning rapidity that I could not quite tell whether I saw the swords or only flashes they made in the air. The rattling din of these blows as they struck steel or paddings was something wonderfully stirring and they were struck with such terrific force that I could not understand why the opposing sword was not beaten down under the assault. Presently, in the midst of the sword-flashes, I saw a handful of hair skip into the air as if it had lain loose on the victim's head and a breath of wind had puffed it suddenly away.

The seconds cried "Halt!" and knocked up the combatants' swords with their own. The duelists sat down. A student official stepped forward, examined the wounded head and touched the place with a sponge once or twice. The surgeon came and turned back the hair from the wound—and revealed a crimson gash two or three inches long and proceeded to bind an oval piece of leather and a bunch of lint over it. The tally-keeper stepped up and tallied one for the opposition in his book.

Then the duelists took position again. A small stream of blood was flowing down the side of the injured man's head and over his shoulder and down his body to the floor but he did not seem to mind this. The word was given and they plunged at each other as fiercely as before. Once more the blows rained and rattled and flashed. Every few moments the quick-eyed seconds would notice that a sword was bent —then they called "Halt!" struck up the contending weapons, and an assisting student straightened the bent one.

The wonderful turmoil went on—presently a bright spark sprung from a blade, and that blade, broken in several pieces, sent one of its fragments flying to the ceiling. A new sword was provided and the fight proceeded. The exercise was tremendous, of course, and in time the fighters began to show great fatigue. They were allowed to rest a moment every little while. They got other rests by wounding each other, for then they could sit down while the doctor applied the lint and bandages. The law is that the battle must continue fifteen minutes if the men can hold out. And as the pauses do not count, this duel was protracted to twenty or thirty minutes, I judged. At last it was decided that the men were too much wearied to do battle longer. They were led away drenched with crimson from head to foot. That was a good fight but it could not count, partly because it did not last the lawful fifteen minutes (of actual fighting) and partly because neither man was disabled by his wounds. It was a drawn battle, and corps law requires that drawn battles shall be refought as soon as the adversaries are well of their hurts.

During the conflict I had talked a little now and then with a young gentleman of the White Cap Corps, and he had mentioned that he was to fight next—and had also pointed out his challenger, a young gentleman who was leaning against the opposite wall smoking a cigarette and restfully observing the duel then in progress.

My acquaintanceship with a party to the coming contest had the effect of giving me a kind of personal interest in it. I naturally wished he might win and it was the reverse of pleasant to learn that he probably would not because, although he was a notable swordsman, the challenger was held to be his superior.

The duel presently began and in the same furious way which had marked the previous one. I stood close by but could not tell which blows told and which did not, they fell and vanished so like flashes of light. They all seemed to tell. The swords always bent over the opponents' heads from the forehead back over the crown and seemed to touch, all the way. But it was not so—a protecting blade, invisible to me, was always interposed between. At the end of ten seconds each man had struck twelve or fifteen blows and warded off twelve or fifteen and no harm done. Then a sword became disabled and a short rest followed whilst a new one was brought. Early in the next round the White Corps student got an ugly wound on the side of his head and gave his opponent one like it. In the third round the latter received another bad wound in the head and the former had his under-lip divided. After that the White Corps student gave many severe wounds but got none of consequence in return. At the end of five minutes from the beginning of the duel the surgeon stopped it. The challenging party had suffered such injuries that any addition to them might be dangerous. These injuries were a fearful spectacle but are better left undescribed. So, against expectation, my acquaintance was the victor.

6. Fighting in Earnest

The third duel was brief and bloody. The surgeon stopped it when he saw that one of the men had received such bad wounds that he could not fight longer without endangering his life.

The fourth duel was a tremendous encounter but at the end of five or six minutes the surgeon interfered once more: another man so severely hurt as to render it unsafe to add to his harms. I watched this engagement as I had watched the others—with rapt interest and strong excitement and with a shrink and a shudder for every blow that laid open a cheek or a forehead and a conscious paling of my face when I occasionally saw a wound of a yet more shocking nature inflicted. My eyes were upon the loser of this duel when he got his last and vanquishing wound—it was in his face and it carried away his—but no matter, I must not enter into details. I had but a glance and then turned quickly away but I would not have been looking at all if I had known what was coming. No, that is probably not true. One thinks he would not look if he knew what was coming but the interest and the excitement are so powerful that they would doubtless conquer all other feelings, and so, under the fierce exhilaration of the clashing steel, he would yield and look after all. Sometimes spectators of these duels faint—and it does seem a very reasonable thing to do, too.

Both parties to this fourth duel were badly hurt, so much so that the surgeon was at work upon them nearly or quite an hour—a fact which is suggestive. But this waiting interval was not wasted in idleness by the assembled students. It was past noon, therefore they ordered their landlord, downstairs, to send up hot beefsteaks, chickens and such things, and these they ate, sitting comfortably at the several tables, whilst they chatted, disputed and laughed. The door to the surgeon's room stood open meantime but the cutting, sewing, splicing and bandaging going on in there in plain view did not seem to disturb anyone's appetite. I went in and saw the surgeon labor awhile but could not enjoy it. It was much less trying to see the wounds given and received than to see them mended. The stir and turmoil and the music of the steel were wanting here—one's nerves were wrung by this grisly spectacle, whilst the duel's compensating pleasurable thrill was lacking.

Finally the doctor finished and the men who were to fight the closing battle of the day came forth. A good many dinners were not completed yet but no matter, they could be eaten cold after the battle, therefore everybody crowded forward to see. This was not a love duel but a "satisfaction" affair. These two students had quarreled and were here to settle it. They did not belong to any of the corps but they were furnished with weapons and armor and permitted to fight here by the five corps as a courtesy. Evidently these two young men were unfamiliar with the dueling ceremonies though they were not unfamiliar with the sword. When they were placed in position they thought it was time to begin—and they did begin, too, and with a most impetuous energy, without waiting for anybody to give the word. This vastly amused the spectators and even broke down their studied and courtly gravity and surprised them into laughter. Of course the seconds struck up the swords and started the duel over again. At the word, the deluge of blows began but before long the surgeon once more interfered—for the only reason which ever permits him to interfere—and the day's war was over. It was now two in the afternoon and I had been present since half past nine in the morning. The field of battle was indeed a red one by this time but some sawdust soon righted that. There had been one duel before I arrived. In it one of the men received many injuries while the other one escaped without a scratch.

I had seen the heads and faces of ten youths gashed in every direction by the keen two-edged blades and yet had not seen a victim wince nor heard a moan or detected any fleeting expression which confessed the sharp pain the hurts were inflicting. This was good fortitude indeed. Such endurance is to be expected in savages and prize-fighters, for they are born and educated to it, but to find it in such perfection in these gently bred and kindly natured young fellows is matter for surprise. It was not merely under the excitement of the sword-play that this fortitude was shown. It was shown in the surgeon's room where an uninspiring quiet reigned and where there was no audience. The doctor's manipulations brought out neither grimaces nor moans. And in the fights it was observable that these lads hacked and slashed with the same tremendous spirit, after they were covered with streaming wounds, which they had shown in the beginning.

The world in general looks upon the college duels as very farcical affairs. True, but considering that the college duel is fought by boys, that the swords are real swords and that the head and face are exposed, it seems to me that it is a farce which has quite a grave side to it. People laugh at it mainly because they think the student is so covered up with armor that he cannot be hurt. But it is not so. His eyes and ears are protected but the rest of his face and head are bare. He can not only be badly wounded but his life is in danger and he would sometimes lose it but for the interference of the surgeon. It is not intended that his life shall be endangered.

Fatal accidents are possible, however. For instance, the student's sword may break and the end of it fly up behind his antagonist's ear and cut an artery which could not be reached if the sword remained whole. This has happened sometimes, and death has resulted on the spot. Formerly the student's armpits were not protected—and at that time the swords were pointed, whereas they are blunt now. So an artery in the armpit was sometimes cut and death followed. Then in the days of sharp-pointed swords a spectator was an occasional victim—the end of a broken sword flew five or ten feet and buried itself in his neck or his heart and death ensued instantly. The student duels in Germany occasion two or three deaths every year now but this arises only from the carelessness of the wounded men. They eat or drink imprudently or commit excesses in the way of over-exertion. Inflammation sets in and gets such a headway that it cannot be arrested. Indeed there is blood and pain and danger enough about the college duel to entitle it to a considerable degree of respect.

All the customs, all the laws, all the details pertaining to the student duel are quaint and naïve. The grave, precise and courtly ceremony with which the thing is conducted invests it with a sort of antique charm.

This dignity and these knightly graces suggest the tournament, not the prize-fight. The laws are as curious as they are strict. For instance, the duelist may step forward from the line he is placed upon, if he chooses, but never back of it. If he steps back of it or even leans back it is considered that he did it to avoid a blow or contrive an advantage, so he is dismissed from his corps in disgrace. It would seem but natural to step from under a descending sword unconsciously and against one's will and intent—yet this unconsciousness is not allowed. Again: if under the sudden anguish of a wound the receiver of it makes a grimace, he falls some degrees in the estimation of his fellows. His corps are ashamed of him. They call him "hare foot," which is the German equivalent for chicken-hearted.

7. Corps Laws and Usages

In addition to the corps laws there are some corps usages which have the force of laws.

Perhaps the president of a corps notices that one of the membership who is no longer an exempt—that is a freshman —has remained a sophomore some little time without volunteering to fight. Some day the president, instead of calling for volunteers, will *appoint* this sophomore to measure swords with a student of another corps. He is free to decline—everybody says so—there is no compulsion. This is all true—but I have not heard of any student who *did* decline. He would naturally rather retire from the corps than decline. To decline and still remain in the corps would make him unpleasantly conspicuous and properly so since he knew when he joined that his main business as a member would be to fight. No, there is no law against declining—except the law of custom, which is confessedly stronger than written law, everywhere.

The ten men whose duels I had witnessed did not go away when their hurts were dressed, as I had supposed they would, but came back one after another as soon as they were free of the surgeon, and mingled with the assemblage in the dueling-room. The white-cap student who won the second fight witnessed the remaining three and talked with us during the intermissions. He could not talk very well, because his opponent's sword had cut his under-lip in two, and then the surgeon had sewed it together and overlaid it with a profusion of white plaster patches. Neither could he eat easily. Still he contrived to accomplish a slow and troublesome luncheon while the last duel was preparing. The man who was the worst hurt of all played chess while waiting to see this engagement. A good part of his face was covered with patches and bandages, and all the rest of his head was covered and concealed by them. It is said that the student likes to appear on the street and in other public places in this kind of array and that this predilection often keeps him out when exposure to rain or sun is a positive danger for him. Newly bandaged students are a very common spectacle in the public gardens of Heidelberg. It is also said that the student is glad to get wounds in the face, because the scars they leave will show so well there. And it is also said that these face wounds are so prized that youths have even been known to pull them apart from time to time and put red wine in them to make them heal badly and leave as ugly a scar as possible. It does not look reasonable but it is roundly asserted and maintained nevertheless. I am sure of one thing—scars are plenty enough in Germany among the young men and very grim ones they are, too. They crisscross the face in angry red welts and are permanent and ineffaceable. Some of these scars are of a very strange and dreadful aspect and the effect is striking when several such accent the milder ones, which form a city map on a man's face. They suggest the "burned district" then. We had often noticed that many of the students wore a colored silk band or ribbon diagonally across their breasts. It transpired that this signifies that the wearer has fought three duels in which a decision was reached—duels in which he either whipped or was whipped—for drawn battles do not count.* After a student has received his ribbon he is "free"; he can cease from fighting, without reproach—except some-

---

*FROM MY DIARY—Dined in a hotel a few miles up the Neckar, in a room whose walls were hung all over with framed portrait-groups of the Five Corps. Some were recent, but many antedated photography and were pictured in lithography—the dates ranged back to forty or fifty years ago. Nearly every individual wore the ribbon across his breast. In one portrait-group representing (as each of these pictures did) an entire Corps I took pains to count the ribbons: there were twenty-seven members, and twenty-one of them wore that significant badge.

one insult him. His president cannot appoint him to fight. He can volunteer if he wants to or remain quiescent if he prefers to do so. Statistics show that he does *not* prefer to remain quiescent. They show that the duel has a singular fascination about it somewhere, for these free men, so far from resting upon the privilege of the badge, are always volunteering. A corps student told me it was of record that Prince Bismarck fought thirty-two of these duels in a single summer term when he was in college. So he fought twenty-nine after his badge had given him the right to retire from the field.

The statistics may be found to possess interest in several particulars. Two days in every week are devoted to dueling. The rule is rigid that there must be three duels on each of these days. There are generally more but there cannot be fewer. There were six the day I was present; sometimes there are seven or eight. It is insisted that eight duels a week—four for each of the two days—is too low an average to draw a calculation from but I will reckon from that basis, preferring an understatement to an overstatement of the case. This requires about four hundred and eighty or five hundred duelists in a year—for in summer the college term is about three and a half months, and in winter it is four months and sometimes longer. Of the seven hundred and fifty students in the university at the time I am writing of, only eighty belonged to the five corps, and it is only these corps that do the dueling. Occasionally other students borrow the arms and battleground of the five corps in order to settle a quarrel but this does not happen every dueling-day.* Consequently eighty youths furnish the material for some two hundred and fifty duels a year. This average gives six fights a year to each of the eighty. This large work could not be accomplished if the badge-holders stood upon their privilege and ceased to volunteer.

*They have to borrow the arms because they could not get them else-where or otherwise. As I understand it, the public authorities all over Germany allow the five Corps to keep swords but *do not allow them to use them.* This law is rigid. It is only the execution of it that is lax.

Of course, where there is so much fighting the students make it a point to keep themselves in constant practice with the foil. One often sees them, at the tables in the Castle grounds, using their whips or canes to illustrate some new sword trick which they have heard about, and between the duels, on the day whose history I have been writing, the swords were not always idle. Every now and then we heard a succession of the keen hissing sounds which the sword makes when it is being put through its paces in the air, and this informed us that a student was practicing. Necessarily this unceasing attention to the art develops an expert occasionally. He becomes famous in his own university, his renown spreads to other universities. He is invited to Göttingen to fight with a Göttingen expert. If he is victorious he will be invited to other colleges, or those colleges will send their experts to him. Americans and Englishmen often join one or another of the five corps. A year or two ago the principal Heidelberg expert was a big Kentuckian. He was invited to the various universities and left a wake of victory behind him all about Germany but at last a little student in Strasburg defeated him. There was formerly a student in Heidelberg who had picked up somewhere and mastered a peculiar trick of cutting up under instead of cleaving down from above. While the trick lasted he won in sixteen successive duels in his own university but by that time observers had discovered what his charm was and how to break it, therefore his championship ceased.

The rule which forbids social intercourse between members of different corps is strict. In the dueling-house, in the parks, on the street, and anywhere and everywhere that students go, caps of a color group themselves together. If all the tables in a public garden were crowded but one, and that one had two red-cap students at it and ten vacant places, the yellow caps, the blue caps, the white caps and the green caps, seeking seats, would go by that table and not seem to see it, nor seem to be aware that there was such a table in the grounds. The student by whose courtesy we had been en-

Piece of
Sword

abled to visit the dueling-place wore the white cap—Prussian Corps. He introduced us to many white caps but to none of another color. The corps etiquette extended even to us, who were strangers, and required us to group with the white corps only and speak only with the white corps while we were their guests, and keep aloof from caps of the other colors. Once I wished to examine some of the swords but an American student said, "It would not be quite polite. These now in the windows all have red hilts or blue. They will bring in some with white hilts presently, and those you can handle freely." When a sword was broken in the first duel I wanted a piece of it but its hilt was the wrong color, so it was considered best and politest to await a properer season. It was brought to me after the room was cleared and I will now make a "life-size" sketch of it by tracing a line around it with my pen to show the width of the weapon. The length of these swords is about three feet and they are quite heavy. One's disposition to cheer during the course of the duels or at their close was naturally strong but corps etiquette forbade any demonstrations of this sort. However brilliant a contest or a victory might be, no sign or sound betrayed that anyone was moved. A dignified gravity and repression were maintained at all times.

When the dueling was finished and we were ready to go the gentlemen of the Prussian Corps to whom we had been introduced took off their caps in the courteous German way, and also shook hands. Their brethren of the same order took off their caps and bowed but without shaking hands. The gentlemen of the other corps treated us just as they would have treated white caps—they fell apart, apparently unconsciously, and left us an unobstructed pathway but did not seem to see us or know we were there. If we had gone thither the following week as guests of another corps, the white caps, without meaning any offense, would have observed the etiquette of their order and ignored our presence.

How strangely are comedy and tragedy blended in this life! I had not been home a full half-hour, after witnessing those playful sham-duels, when circumstances made it necessary for me to get ready immediately to assist personally at a real one—a duel with no effeminate limitations in the matter of results, but a battle to the death. An account of it, in the next chapter, will show the reader that duels between boys, for fun, and duels between men in earnest, are very different affairs.

8. The Great French Duel

Much as the modern French duel is ridiculed by certain smart people, it is in reality one of the most dangerous institutions of our day. Since it is always fought in the open air the combatants are nearly sure to catch cold. M. Paul de Cassagnac, the most inveterate of the French duelists, had suffered so often in this way that he is at last a confirmed invalid, and the best physician in Paris has expressed the opinion that if he goes on dueling for fifteen or twenty years more—unless he forms the habit of fighting in a comfortable room where damps and draughts cannot intrude—he will eventually endanger his life. This ought to moderate the talk of those people who are so stubborn in maintaining that the French duel is the most health-giving of recreations because of the open-air exercise it affords. And it ought also to moderate that foolish talk about French duelists and socialist-hated monarchs being the only people who are immortal.

But it is time to get at my subject. As soon as I heard of the late fiery outbreak between M. Gambetta and M. Fourtou in the French Assembly I knew that trouble must follow. I knew it because a long personal friendship with M. Gambetta had revealed to me the desperate and implacable nature of the man. Vast as are his physical proportions, I knew that the thirst for revenge would penetrate to the remotest frontiers of his person.

I did not wait for him to call on me but went at once to him. As I had expected, I found the brave fellow steeped in a profound French calm. I say French calm because French calmness and English calmness have points of difference. He was moving swiftly back and forth among the debris of his furniture, now and then staving chance fragments of it across the room with his foot, grinding a constant grist of curses through his set teeth and halting every little while to deposit another handful of his hair on the pile which he had been building of it on the table.

He threw his arms around my neck, bent me over his stomach to his breast, kissed me on both cheeks, hugged me four or five times and then placed me in his own arm-chair. As soon as I had got well again we began business at once.

I said I supposed he would wish me to act as his second, and he said, "Of course." I said I must be allowed to act under a French name so that I might be shielded from obloquy in my country in case of fatal results. He winced here, probably at the suggestion that dueling was not regarded with respect in America. However, he agreed to my requirement. This accounts for the fact that in all the newspaper reports M. Gambetta's second was apparently a Frenchman.

First, we drew up my principal's will. I insisted upon this and stuck to my point. I said I had never heard of a man in his right mind going out to fight a duel without first making his will. He said he had never heard of a man in his right mind doing anything of the kind. When he had finished the will, he wished to proceed to a choice of his "last words." He wanted to know how the following words, as a dying exclamation, struck me:

"I die for my God, for my country, for freedom of speech, for progress, and the universal brotherhood of man!"

I objected that this would require too lingering a death. It was a good speech for a consumptive but not suited to the exigencies of the field of honor. We wrangled over a good many ante-mortem outbursts but I finally got him to cut his obituary down to this, which he copied into his memorandum-book, purposing to get it by heart:

"I DIE THAT FRANCE MAY LIVE."

I said that this remark seemed to lack relevancy but he said relevancy was a matter of no consequence in last words, what you wanted was thrill.

The next thing in order was the choice of weapons. My principal said he was not feeling well and would leave that and the other details of the proposed meeting to me. Therefore I wrote the following note and carried it to M. Fourtou's friend:

> SIR: M. Gambetta accepts M. Fourtou's challenge and authorizes me to propose Plessis-Piquet as the place of meeting; to-morrow morning at daybreak as the time; and axes as the weapons. I am, sir, with great respect,
> MARK TWAIN

M. Fourtou's friend read this note and shuddered. Then he turned to me and said with a suggestion of severity in his tone:

"Have you considered, sir, what would be the inevitable result of such a meeting as this?"

"Well, for instance, what *would* it be?"

"Bloodshed!"

"That's about the size of it," I said. "Now, if it is a fair question, what was your side proposing to shed?"

I had him there. He saw he had made a blunder, so he hastened to explain it away. He said he had spoken jestingly. Then he added that he and his principal would enjoy axes, and indeed prefer them, but such weapons were barred by the French code and so I must change my proposal.

I walked the floor, turning the thing over in my mind, and finally it occurred to me that Gatling-guns at fifteen paces would be a likely way to get a verdict on the field of honor. So I framed this idea into a proposition.

But it was not accepted. The code was in the way again. I proposed rifles, then double-barreled shotguns, then Colt's navy revolvers. These being all rejected, I reflected awhile and sarcastically suggested brickbats at three-quarters of a mile. I always hate to fool away a humorous thing on a person who has no perception of humor, and it filled me with bitterness when this man went soberly away to submit the last proposition to his principal.

He came back presently and said his principal was charmed with the idea of brickbats at three-quarters of a mile but must decline on account of the danger to disinterested parties passing between. Then I said:

"Well, I am at the end of my string now. Perhaps *you* would be good enough to suggest a weapon? Perhaps you have even had one in your mind all the time?"

His countenance brightened and he said with alacrity:

"Oh, without doubt, monsieur!"

So he fell to hunting in his pockets—pocket after pocket, and he had plenty of them—muttering all the while, "Now, what could I have done with them?"

At last he was successful. He fished out of his vest pocket a couple of little things which I carried to the light and ascertained to be pistols. They were single-barrelled and silver-mounted and very dainty and pretty. I was not able to speak for emotion. I silently hung one of them on my watch-chain and returned the other. My companion in crime now unrolled a postage-stamp containing several cartridges and gave me one of them. I asked if he meant to signify by this that our men were to be allowed but one shot apiece. He replied that the French code permitted no more. I then begged him to go on and suggest a distance, for my mind was growing weak and confused under the strain which had been put upon it. He named sixty-five yards. I nearly lost my patience. I said:

"Sixty-five yards, with these instruments? Squirt-guns would be deadlier at fifty. Consider, my friend, you and I are banded together to destroy life, not make it eternal."

But with all my persuasions, all my arguments, I was only able to get him to reduce the distance to thirty-five yards, and even this concession he made with reluctance, and said with a sigh, "I wash my hands of this slaughter. On your head be it."

There was nothing for me but to go home to my old lion-heart and tell my humiliating story. When I entered, M. Gambetta was laying his last lock of hair upon the altar. He sprang toward me, exclaiming:

"You have made the fatal arrangements—I see it in your eye!"

"I have."

His face paled a trifle and he leaned upon the table for support. He breathed thick and heavily for a moment or two, so tumultuous were his feelings, then he hoarsely whispered:

"The weapon, the weapon! Quick! What is the weapon?"

"This!" and I displayed that silver-mounted thing. He cast but one glance at it, then swooned ponderously to the floor.

When he came to he said mournfully:

"The unnatural calm to which I have subjected myself has told upon my nerves. But away with weakness! I will confront my fate like a man and a Frenchman."

He rose to his feet and assumed an attitude which for sublimity has never been approached by man and has seldom been surpassed by statutes. Then he said in his deep bass tones:

"Behold, I am calm, I am ready. Reveal to me the distance."

"Thirty-five yards."

I could not lift him up, of course, but I rolled him over and poured water down his back. He presently came to and said:

"Thirty-five yards—without a rest? But why ask? Since murder was that man's intention, why should he palter with small details? But mark you one thing: in my fall the world shall see how the chivalry of France meets death."

After a long silence he asked:

"Was nothing said about that man's family standing up with him, as an offset to my bulk? But no matter. I would not stoop to make such a suggestion. If he is not noble enough to suggest it himself he is welcome to this advantage, which no honorable man would take."

He now sank into a sort of stupor of reflection, which lasted some minutes, after which he broke silence with:

"The hour—what is the hour fixed for the collision?"

"Dawn, to-morrow."

He seemed greatly surprised and immediately said:

"Insanity! I never heard of such a thing. Nobody is abroad at such an hour."

"That is the reason I named it. Do you mean to say you want an audience?"

"It is no time to bandy words. I am astonished that M. Fourtou should ever have agreed to so strange an innovation. Go at once and require a later hour."

I ran down-stairs, threw open the front door and almost plunged into the arms of M. Fourtou's second. He said:

"I have the honor to say that my principal strenuously objects to the hour chosen and begs you will consent to change it to half-past nine."

"Any courtesy, sir, which it is in our power to extend is at the service of your excellent principal. We agree to the proposed change of time."

"I beg you to accept the thanks of my client." Then he turned to a person behind him and said, "You hear, M. Noir, the hour is altered to half-past nine." Whereupon M. Noir bowed, expressed his thanks and went away. My accomplice continued:

"If agreeable to you, your chief surgeons and ours shall proceed to the field in the same carriage, as is customary."

"It is entirely agreeable to me and I am obliged to you for mentioning the surgeons, for I am afraid I should not have thought of them. How many shall I want? I suppose two or three will be enough?"

"Two is the customary number for each party. I refer to 'chief' surgeons; but considering the exalted positions occupied by our clients, it will be well and decorous that each of us appoint several consulting surgeons, from among the highest in the profession. These will come in their own private carriages. Have you engaged a hearse?"

"Bless my stupidity, I never thought of it! I will attend to it right away. I must seem very ignorant to you but you must try to overlook that, because I have never had any experience of such a swell duel as this before. I have had a good deal to do with duels on the Pacific coast but I see now that they were crude affairs. A hearse—sho! We used to leave the elected lying around loose and let anybody cord them up and cart them off that wanted to. Have you anything further to suggest?"

"Nothing, except that the head undertakers shall ride together, as is usual. The subordinates and mutes will go on foot, as is also usual. I will see you at eight o'clock in the morning and we will then arrange the order of the procession. I have the honor to bid you a good day."

I returned to my client, who said, "Very well. At what hour is the engagement to begin?"

"Half past nine."

"Very good indeed. Have you sent the fact to the newspapers?"

"*Sir!* If after our long and intimate friendship you can for a moment deem me capable of so base a treachery—"

"Tut, tut! What words are these, my dear friend? Have I wounded you? Ah, forgive me. I am overloading you with labor. Therefore go on with the other details and drop this one from your list. The bloody-minded Fourtou will be sure to attend to it. Or I myself—yes, to make certain, I will drop a note to my journalistic friend, M. Noir—"

"Oh, come to think of it, you may save yourself the trouble. That other second has informed M. Noir."

"H'm! I might have known it. It is just like that Fourtou, who always wants to make a display."

At half-past nine in the morning the procession approached the field of Plessis-Piquet in the following order: First came our carriage—nobody in it but M. Gambetta and myself. Then a carriage containing M. Fourtou and his second. Then a carriage containing two poet-orators who did not believe in God, and these had MS. funeral orations projecting from their breast pockets. Then a carriage containing the head surgeons and their cases of instruments. Then eight private carriages containing consulting surgeon. Then a hack containing a coroner. Then the two hearses. Then a carriage containing the head undertakers. Then a train of assistants and mutes on foot. And after these came plodding through the fog a long procession of camp followers, police and citizens generally. It was a noble turnout and would have made a fine display if we had had thinner weather.

There was no conversation. I spoke several times to my principal but I judge he was not aware of it, for he always referred to his note-book and muttered absently, "I die that France may live."

Arrived on the field, my fellow-second and I paced off the thirty-five yards and then drew lots for choice of position. This latter was but an ornamental ceremony, for all the choices were alike in such weather. These preliminaries being ended, I went to my principal and asked him if he was ready. He spread himself out to his full width and said in a stern voice, "Ready! Let the batteries be charged."

The loading was done in the presence of duly constituted witnesses. We considered it best to perform this delicate service with the assistance of a lantern on account of the state of the weather. We now placed our men.

At this point the police noticed that the public had massed themselves together on the right and left of the field. They therefore begged a delay while they should put these poor people in a place of safety.

The request was granted.

The police having ordered the two multitudes to take positions behind the duelists, we were once more ready. The weather growing still more opaque, it was agreed between myself and the other second that before giving the fatal signal we should each deliver a loud whoop to enable the combatants to ascertain each other's whereabouts.

I now returned to my principal and was distressed to observe that he had lost a good deal of his spirit. I tried my best to hearten him. I said, "Indeed, sir, things are not as bad as they seem. Considering the character of the weapons, the limited number of shots allowed, the generous distance, the impenetrable solidity of the fog and the added fact that one of the combatants is one-eyed and the other cross-eyed and near-sighted, it seems to me that this conflict need not necessarily be fatal. There are chances that both of you may survive. Therefore cheer up. Do not be downhearted."

This speech had so good an effect that my principal immediately stretched forth his hand and said, "I am myself again. Give me the weapon."

I laid it, all lonely and forlorn, in the center of the vast solitude of his palm. He gazed at it and shuddered. And still mournfully contemplating it, he murmured in a broken voice:

"Alas, it is not death I dread but mutilation."

I heartened him once more, and with such success that he presently said, "Let the tragedy begin. Stand at my back. Do not desert me in this solemn hour, my friend."

I gave him my promise. I now assisted him to point his

pistol toward the spot where I judged his adversary to be standing, and cautioned him to listen well and further guide himself by my fellow-second's whoop. Then I propped myself against M. Gambetta's back and raised a rousing "Whoop-ee!" This was answered from out the far distances of the fog, and I immediately shouted:

"One—two—three—*fire!*"

Two little sounds like *spit! spit!* broke upon my ear, and in the same instant I was crushed to the earth under a mountain of flesh. Bruised as I was, I was still able to catch a faint accent from above, to this effect:

"I die for . . . for . . . perdition take it, what *is* it I die for? . . . oh, yes—FRANCE! I die that France may live!"

The surgeons swarmed around with their probes in their hands and applied their microscopes to the whole area of M. Gambetta's person, with the happy result of finding nothing in the nature of a wound. Then a scene ensued which was in every way gratifying and inspiring.

The two gladiators fell upon each other's neck with floods of proud and happy tears. That other second embraced me. The surgeons, the orators, the undertakers, the police, everybody embraced, everybody congratulated, everybody cried, and the whole atmosphere was filled with praise and with joy unspeakable.

It seemed to me then that I would rather be a hero of a French duel than a crowned and sceptered monarch.

When the commotion had somewhat subsided, the body of surgeons held a consultation, and after a good deal of debate decided that with proper care and nursing there was reason to believe that I would survive my injuries. My internal hurts were deemed the most serious, since it was apparent that a broken rib had penetrated my left lung and that many of my organs had been pressed out so far to one side or the other of where they belonged that it was doubtful if they would ever learn to perform their functions in such remote and unaccustomed localities. They then set my left arm in two places, pulled my right hip into its socket again and re-elevated my nose. I was an object of great interest and even admiration, and many sincere and warm-hearted persons had themselves introduced to me and said they were proud to know the only man who had been hurt in a French duel in forty years.

I was placed in an ambulance at the very head of the procession and thus with gratifying *éclat* I was marched into Paris, the most conspicuous figure in that great spectacle, and deposited at the hospital.

The cross of the Legion of Honor has been conferred upon me. However, few escape that distinction.

Such is the true version of the most memorable private conflict of the age.

I have no complaints to make against any one. I acted for myself and I can stand the consequences.

Without boasting I think I may say I am not afraid to stand before a modern French duelist, but as long as I keep in my right mind I will never consent to stand behind one again.

9. At the Opera

One day we took the train and went down to Mannheim to see *King Lear* played in German. It was a mistake. We sat in our seats three whole hours and never understood anything but the thunder and lightning, and even that was reversed to suit German ideas, for the thunder came first and the lightning followed after.

The behavior of the audience was perfect. There were no rustlings or whisperings or other little disturbances. Each act was listened to in silence, and the applauding was done after the curtain was down. The doors opened at half-past four, the play began promptly at half-past five, and within two minutes afterward all who were coming were in their seats and quiet reigned. A German gentleman in the train had said that a Shakespearian play was an appreciated treat in Germany and that we should find the house filled. It was true. All the six tiers were filled, and remained so to the end—which suggested that it is not only balcony people who like Shakespeare in Germany but those of the pit and the gallery too.

Another time we went to Mannheim and attended a shivaree—otherwise an opera—the one called *Lohengrin*. The banging and slamming and booming and crashing were something beyond belief. The racking and pitiless pain of it remains stored up in my memory alongside the memory of the time that I had my teeth fixed. There were circumstances which made it necessary for me to stay through the four hours to the end, and I stayed, but the recollection of that long, dragging, relentless season of suffering is indestructible. To have to endure it in silence, and sitting still, made it all the harder. I was in a railed compartment with eight or ten strangers of the two sexes and this compelled repression, yet at times the pain was so exquisite that I could hardly keep the tears back. At those times, as the howlings and wailings and shriekings of the singers, and the ragings and roarings and explosions of the vast orchestra rose higher and higher and wilder and wilder and fiercer and fiercer, I could have cried if I had been alone. Those strangers would not have been surprised to see a man do such a thing who was being gradually skinned but they would have marveled at it here and made remarks about it, no doubt, whereas there was nothing in the present case which was an advantage over being skinned. There was a wait of half an hour at the end of the first act, and I could have gone out and rested during that time but I could not trust myself to do it, for I felt that I should desert and stay out. There was another wait of half an hour toward nine o'clock but I had gone through so much by that time that I had no spirit left and so had no desire but to be let alone.

I do not wish to suggest that the rest of the people there

were like me, for indeed they were not. Whether it was that they naturally liked that noise or whether it was that they had learned to like it by getting used to it, I did not at that time know, but they did like it—this was plain enough. While it was going on they sat and looked as rapt and grateful as cats do when one strokes their backs, and whenever the curtain fell they rose to their feet in one solid mighty multitude and the air was snowed thick with waving handkerchiefs, and hurricanes of applause swept the place. This was not comprehensible to me. Of course, there were many people there who were not under compulsion to stay, yet the tiers were as full at the close as they had been at the beginning. This showed that the people liked it.

It was a curious sort of a play. In the matter of costumes and scenery it was fine and showy enough but there was not much action. That is to say, there was not much really done, it was only talked about and always violently. It was what one might call a narrative play. Everybody had a narrative and a grievance and none were reasonable about it, but all in an offensive and ungovernable state. There was little of that sort of customary thing where the tenor and the soprano stand down by the footlights, warbling with blended voices, and keep holding out their arms toward each other and drawing them back and spreading both hands over first one breast and then the other with a shake and a pressure—no, it was every rioter for himself and no blending. Each sang his indictive narrative in turn, accompanied by the whole orchestra of sixty instruments, and when this had continued for some time and one was hoping they might come to an understanding and modify the noise, a great chorus composed entirely of maniacs would suddenly break forth and then during two minutes and sometimes three I lived over again all that I had suffered the time the orphan asylum burned down.

We only had one brief little season of heaven and heaven's sweet ecstasy and peace during all this long and diligent and acrimonious reproduction of the other place. This was while a gorgeous procession of people marched around and around in the third act and sang the Wedding Chorus. To my untutored ear that was music—almost divine music. While my seared soul was steeped in the healing balm of those gracious sounds it seemed to me that I could almost resuffer the torments which had gone before, in order to be so healed again. There is where the deep ingenuity of the operatic idea is betrayed. It deals so largely in pain that its scattered delights are prodigiously augmented by the contrasts. A pretty air in an opera is prettier there than it could be anywhere else, I suppose, just as an honest man in politics shines more than he would elsewhere.

I have since found out that there is nothing the Germans like so much as an opera. They like it not in a mild and moderate way but with their whole hearts. This is a legitimate result of habit and education. Our nation will like the opera too, by and by, no doubt. One in fifty of those who attend our operas likes it already, perhaps, but I think a good many of the other forty-nine go in order to learn to like it, and the rest in order to be able to talk knowingly about it. The latter usually hum the airs while they are being sung, so that their neighbors may perceive that they have been to operas before. The funerals of these do not occur often enough.

A gentle, old-maidish person and a sweet young girl of seventeen sat right in front of us that night at the Mannheim opera. These people talked between the acts and I understood them, though I understood nothing that was uttered on the distant stage. At first they were guarded in their talk but after they had heard my agent and me conversing in English they dropped their reserve and I picked up many of their little confidences. No, I mean many of *her* little confidences —meaning the elder party—for the young girl only listened and gave assenting nods but never said a word. How pretty she was and how sweet she was! I wished she would speak. But evidently she was absorbed in her own thoughts, her own young-girl dreams, and found a dearer pleasure in silence. But she was not dreaming sleepy dreams—no, she was awake, alive, alert, she could not sit still a moment. She was an enchanting study. Her gown was of a soft white silky stuff that clung to her round young figure like a fish's skin and it was rippled over with the gracefulest little fringy films of lace. She had deep, tender eyes, with long, curved lashes, and she had peachy cheeks and a dimpled chin and such a dear little dewy rosebud of a mouth, and she was so dovelike, so pure and so gracious, so sweet and bewitching. For long hours I did mightily wish she would speak. And at last she did. The red lips parted, and out leaped her thought—and with such a guileless and pretty enthusiasm, too: "Auntie, I just *know* I've got five hundred fleas on me!"

That was probably over the average. Yes, it must have been very much over the average. The average at that time in the Grand Duchy of Baden was forty-five to a young person (when alone), according to the official estimate of the home secretary for that year. The average for older people was shifty and indeterminable, for whenever a wholesome young girl came into the presence of her elders she immediately lowered their average and raised her own. She became a sort of contribution-box. This dear young thing in the theater had been sitting there unconsciously taking up a collection. Many a skinny old being in our neighborhood was the happier and the restfuler for her coming.

In that large audience that night there were eight very conspicuous people. These were ladies who had their hats or bonnets on. What a blessed thing it would be if a lady could make herself conspicuous in our theaters by wearing her hat. It is not usual in Europe to allow ladies and gentlemen to take bonnets, hats, overcoats, canes or umbrellas into the auditorium, but in Mannheim this rule was not enforced because the audiences were largely made up of people from a distance, and among these were always a few timid ladies who were afraid that if they had to go into an anteroom to get their things when the play was over they would miss their train. But the great mass of those who came from a distance always ran the risk and took the chances, preferring the loss of the train to a breach of good manners and the discomfort of being unpleasantly conspicuous during a stretch of three or four hours.

10. Wagner and Related Matters

Three or four hours. That is a long time to sit in one place, whether one be conspicuous or not, yet some of Wagner's operas bang along for six whole hours on a stretch! But the people sit there and enjoy it all and wish it would last longer. A German lady in Munich told me that a person could not like Wagner's music at first but must go through the deliberate process of learning to like it—then he would have his sure reward, for when he had learned to like it he would hunger for it and never be able to get enough of it. She said that six hours of Wagner was by no means too much. She said that this composer had made a complete revolution in music and was burying the old masters one by one. And she said that Wagner's operas differed from all others in one notable respect and that was that they were not merely spotted with music here and there but were *all* music, from the first strain to the last. This surprised me. I said I had attended one of his insurrections and found hardly *any* music in it except the Wedding Chorus. She said *Lohengrin* was noisier than Wagner's other operas but that if I would keep on going to see it I would find by and by that it was all music and therefore would then enjoy it. I *could* have said, "But would you advise a person to deliberately practise having the toothache in the pit of his stomach for a couple of years in order that he might then come to enjoy it?" But I reserved that remark.

This lady was full of the praises of the head-tenor who had performed in a Wagner opera the night before, and went on to enlarge upon his old and prodigious fame and how many honors had been lavished upon him by the princely houses of Germany. Here was another surprise. I had attended that very opera in the person of my agent and had made close and accurate observations. So I said:

"Why, madam, *my* experience warrants me in stating that that tenor's voice is not a voice at all but only a shriek—the shriek of a hyena."

"That is very true," she said. "He cannot sing now. It is already many years that he has lost his voice, but in other times he sang, yes, divinely! So whenever he comes now, you shall see, yes, that the theater will not hold the people. *Jawohl bei Gott!* His voice is *wunderschön* in that past time."

I said she was discovering to me a kindly trait in the Germans which was worth emulating. I said that over the water we were not quite so generous; that with us, when a singer had lost his voice and a jumper had lost his legs, these parties ceased to draw. I said I had been to the opera in Hanover once and in Mannheim once and in Munich (through my authorized agent) once, and this large experience had nearly persuaded me that the Germans *preferred* singers who couldn't sing. This was not such a very extravagant speech, either, for that burly Mannheim tenor's praises had been the talk of all Heidelberg for a week before his performance took place—yet his voice was like the distressing noise which a nail makes when you screech it across a window-pane. I said so to Heidelberg friends the next day and they said in the calmest and simplest way that that was very true but that in earlier times his voice *had* been wonderfully fine. And the tenor in Hanover was just another example of this sort. The English-speaking German gentleman who went with me to the opera there was brimming with enthusiasm over that tenor. He said:

"*Ach Gott!* A great man! You shall see him. He is so celebrate in all Germany—and he has a pension, yes, from the government. He not obliged to sing now, only twice every year. But if he not sing twice each year they take him his pension away."

Very well, we went. When the renowned old tenor appeared I got a nudge and an excited whisper:

"Now you see him!"

But the "celebrate" was an astonishing disappointment to me. If he had been behind a screen I should have supposed they were performing a surgical operation on him. I looked at my friend—to my great surprise he seemed intoxicated with pleasure, his eyes were dancing with eager delight. When the curtain at last fell he burst into the stormiest applause, and kept it up—as did the whole house—until the afflictive tenor had come three times before the curtain to make his bow. While the glowing enthusiast was swabbing the perspiration from his face I said:

"I don't mean the least harm, but really, now, do you think he can sing?"

"Him?" *No! Gott im Himmel, aber,* how he has been able to sing twenty-five years ago?" [Then pensively.] "*Ach,* no, *now* he not sing any more, he only cry. When he think he sing, now, he not sing at all, no, he only make like a cat which is unwell."

Where and how did we get the idea that the Germans are a stolid, phlegmatic race? In truth, they are widely removed from that. They are warm-hearted, emotional, impulsive, enthusiastic, their tears come at the mildest touch, and it is not hard to move them to laughter. They are the very children of impulse. We are cold and self-contained, compared to the Germans. They hug and kiss and cry and shout and dance and sing. And where we use one loving, petting expression they pour out a score. Their language is full of endearing diminutives. Nothing that they love escapes the application of a petting diminutive—neither the house, nor the dog, nor the horse, nor the grandmother, nor any other creature, animate or inanimate.

In the theaters at Hanover, Hamburg and Mannheim they had a wise custom. The moment the curtain went up, the lights in the body of the house went down. The audience sat in the cool gloom of a deep twilight, which greatly enhanced the glowing splendors of the stage. It saved gas, too, and people were not sweated to death.

When I saw *King Lear* played, nobody was allowed to see a scene shifted. If there was nothing to be done but slide a forest out of the way and expose a temple beyond, one did not see that forest split itself in the middle and go shrieking away, with the accompanying disenchanting spectacle of the hands and heels of the impelling impulse—no, the curtain was always dropped for an instant—one heard not the least movement behind it—but when it went up, the next instant, the forest was gone. Even when the stage was being entirely reset, one heard no noise. During the whole time that *King Lear* was playing the curtain was never down two minutes at any one time. The orchestra played until the curtain was ready to go up for the first time, then they departed for the evening. Where the stage-waits never reach two minutes there is no occasion for music. I had never seen this two-minute business between acts but once before, and that was when the "Shaughraun" was played at Wallack's.

I was at a concert in Munich one night, the people were streaming in, the clock-hand pointed to seven, the music struck up, and instantly all movement in the body of the house ceased—nobody was standing or walking up the aisles or fumbling with a seat, the stream of incomers had suddenly dried up at its source. I listened undisturbed to a piece of music that was fifteen minutes long—always expecting some tardy ticket-holders to come crowding past my knees, and being continuously and pleasantly disappointed—but when the last note was struck, here came the stream again. You see, they had made those late comers wait in the comfortable waiting-parlor from the time the music had begun until it was ended.

It was the first time I had ever seen this sort of criminals denied the privilege of destroying the comfort of a house full of their betters. Some of these were pretty fine birds, but no matter, they had to tarry outside in the long parlor under the inspection of a double rank of liveried footmen and waiting-maids who supported the two walls with their backs and held the wraps and traps of their masters and mistresses on their arms.

We had no footmen to hold our things and it was not permissible to take them into the concert-room but there were some men and women to take charge of them for us. They gave us checks for them and charged a fixed price, payable in advance—five cents.

In Germany they always hear one thing at an opera which has never yet been heard in America, perhaps—I mean the closing strain of a fine solo or duet. We always smash into it with an earthquake of applause. The result is that we rob ourselves of the sweetest part of the treat. We get the whisky but we don't get the sugar in the bottom of the glass.

Our way of scattering applause along through an act seems to me to be better than the Mannheim way of saving it all up till the act is ended. I do not see how an actor can forget himself and portray hot passion before a cold still audience. I should think he would feel foolish. It is a pain to me to this day to remember how that old German Lear raged and wept and howled around the stage with never a response from that hushed house, never a single outburst till the act was ended. To me there was something unspeakably uncomfortable in the solemn dead silences that always followed this old person's tremendous outpourings of his feelings. I could not help putting myself in his place—I thought I knew how sick and flat he felt during those silences, because I remembered a case which came under my observation once and which—but I will tell the incident:

One evening on board a Mississippi steamboat a boy of ten

years lay asleep in a berth—a long, slim-legged boy, he was, encased in quite a short shirt. It was the first time he had ever made a trip on a steamboat and so he was troubled and scared and had gone to bed with his head filled with impending snaggings and explosions and conflagrations and sudden death. About ten o'clock some twenty ladies were sitting around about the ladies' saloon, quietly reading, sewing, embroidering and so on, and among them sat a sweet, benignant old dame with round spectacles on her nose and her busy knitting-needles in her hands. Now all of a sudden, into the midst of this peaceful scene burst that slim-shanked boy in the brief shirt, wild-eyed, erect-haired, and shouting, "Fire, fire! *jump and run, the boat's afire and there ain't a minute to lose!*" All those ladies looked sweetly up and smiled, nobody stirred, the old lady pulled her spectacles down, looked over them and said gently:

"But you mustn't catch cold, child. Run and put on your breastpin and then come and tell us all about it."

It was a cruel chill to give to a poor little devil's gushing vehemence. He was expecting to be a sort of hero—the creator of a wild panic—and here everybody sat and smiled a mocking smile, and an old woman made fun of his bugbear. I turned and crept humbly away—for I was that boy—and never even cared to discover whether I had dreamed the fire or actually seen it.

I am told that in a German concert or opera they hardly ever encore a song; that though they may be dying to hear it again, their good breeding usually preserves them against requiring the repetition.

Kings may encore. That is quite another matter. It delights everybody to see that the King is pleased. And as to the actor encored, his pride and gratification are simply boundless. Still, there are circumstances in which even a royal encore—

But it is better to illustrate. The King of Bavaria is a poet and has a poet's eccentricities—with the advantage over all other poets of being able to gratify them, no matter what form they may take. He is fond of the opera but not fond of sitting in the presence of an audience. Therefore it has sometimes occurred in Munich that when an opera has been concluded and the players were getting off their paint and finery a command has come to them to get their paint and finery on again. Presently the King would arrive, solitary and alone, and the players would begin at the beginning and do the entire opera over again with only that one individual in the vast solemn theater for audience. Once he took an odd freak into his head. High up and out of sight, over the prodigious stage of the court theater, is a maze of interlacing waterpipes so pierced that in case of fire innumerable little threadlike streams of water can be caused to descend, and in case of need this discharge can be augmented to a pouring flood. American managers might make a note of that. The King was sole audience. The opera proceeded; it was a piece with a storm in it. The mimic thunder began to mutter, the mimic wind began to wail and sough, and the mimic rain to patter. The King's interest rose higher and higher. It developed into enthusiasm. He cried out:

"It is good, very good, indeed! But I will have real rain! Turn on the water!"

The manager pleaded for a reversal of the command. Said it would ruin the costly scenery and the splendid costumes. But the King cried:

"No matter, no matter, I will have real rain! Turn on the water!"

So the real rain was turned on and began to descend in gossamer lances to the mimic flower-beds and gravel walks of the stage. The richly dressed actresses and actors tripped about singing bravely and pretending not to mind it. The King was delighted—his enthusiasm grew higher. He cried out:

"Bravo, bravo! More thunder! more lightning! Turn on more rain!"

The thunder boomed, the lightning glared, the stormwinds raged, the deluge poured down. The mimic royalty on the stage, with their soaked satins clinging to their bodies, slopped around ankle-deep in water, warbling their sweetest and best. The fiddlers under the eaves of the stage sawed away for dear life, with the cold overflow spouting down the backs of their necks. And the dry and happy King sat in his lofty box and wore his gloves to ribbons applauding.

"More yet!" cried the King. "More yet—let loose all the thunder, turn on all the water! I will hang the man that raises an umbrella!"

When this most tremendous and effective storm that had ever been produced in any theater was at last over, the King's approbation was measureless. He cried:

"Magnificent, magnificent! *Encore!* Do it again!"

But the manager succeeded in persuading him to recall the encore, and said the company would feel sufficiently rewarded and complimented in the mere fact that the encore was desired by his Majesty, without fatiguing him with a repetition to gratify their own vanity.

During the remainder of the act the lucky performers were those whose parts required changes of dress. The others were a soaked, bedraggled and uncomfortable lot but in the last degree picturesque. The stage scenery was ruined, trapdoors were so swollen that they wouldn't work for a week afterward, the fine costumes were spoiled, and no end of minor damages were done by that remarkable storm.

It was a royal idea—that storm—and royally carried out. But observe the moderation of the King. He did not insist upon his encore. If he had been a gladsome, unreflecting American opera-audience he probably would have had his storm repeated and repeated until he drowned all those people.

11. The Awful German Language

The summer days passed pleasantly in Heidelberg. We had a skilled trainer, and under his instructions we were getting our legs in the right condition for the contemplated pedestrian tours. We were well satisfied with the progress which we had made in the German language and more than satisfied with what we had accomplished in art.

I went often to look at the collection of curiosities in Heidelberg Castle, and one day I surprised the keeper of it with my German. I spoke entirely in that language. He was greatly interested and after I had talked a while he said my German was very rare, possibly a "unique," and wanted to add it to his museum.

If he had known what it had cost me to acquire my art he would also have known that it would break any collector to buy it. Harris and I had been hard at work on our German during several weeks at that time, and although we had made good progress it had been accomplished under great difficulty and annoyance, for three of our teachers had died in the meantime. A person who has not studied German can form no idea of what a perplexing language it is.

Surely there is not another language that is so slipshod and systemless and so slippery and elusive to the grasp. One is washed about in it hither and thither in the most helpless way and when at last he thinks he has captured a rule which offers firm ground to take a rest on amid the general rage and turmoil of the ten parts of speech, he turns over the page and reads, "Let the pupil make careful note of the following *exceptions.*" He runs his eye down and finds that there are more exceptions to the rule than instances of it. So overboard he goes again to hunt for another Ararat and find another quicksand. Such has been and continues to be my experience. Every time I think I have got one of these four confusing "cases" where I am master of it, a seemingly insignificant preposition intrudes itself into my sentence, clothed with an awful and unsuspected power, and crumbles the ground from under me. For instance, my book inquires after a certain bird—(it is always inquiring after things which are of no sort of consequence to anybody): "Where is the bird?" Now the answer to this question—according to the book—is that the bird is waiting in the blacksmith shop on account of the rain. Of course no bird would do that, but then you must stick to the book. Very well, I begin to cipher out the German for that answer. I begin at the wrong end, necessarily, for that is the German idea. I say to myself, "*Regen* (rain) is masculine —or maybe it is feminine—or possibly neuter—it is too much trouble to look now. Therefore, it is either *der* (the) Regen, or *die* (the) Regen, or *das* (the) Regen, according to which gender it may turn out to be when I look. In the interest of science, I will cipher it out on the hypothesis that it is masculine. Very well—then *the* rain is *der* Regen, if it is simply in the quiescent state of being *mentioned,* without enlargement or discussion—Nominative case. But if this rain is lying around in a kind of a general way on the ground, it is then definitely located, it is *doing something*—that is, *resting* (which is one of the German grammar's ideas of doing something), and this throws the rain into the Dative case and makes it *dem* Regen. However, this rain is not resting but is doing something *actively*—it is falling—to interfere with the bird, likely—and this indicates *movement,* which has the effect of sliding it into the Accusative case and changing *dem* Regen into *den* Regen." Having completed the grammatical horoscope of this matter, I answer up confidently and state in German that the bird is staying in the blacksmith shop "wegen (on account of) *den* Regen." Then the teacher lets me softly down with the remark that whenever the word "wegen" drops into a sentence it *always* throws that subject into the *Genitive* case, regardless of consequences—and that therefore this bird stayed in the blacksmith shop "wegen *des* Regens."

N. B.—I was informed, later, by a higher authority, that there was an "exception" which permits one to say "wegen *den* Regen" in certain peculiar and complex circumstances but that this exception is not extended to anything *but* rain.

There are ten parts of speech and they are all troublesome. An average sentence in a German newspaper is a sublime and impressive curiosity. It occupies a quarter of a column. It contains all the ten parts of speech—not in regular order but mixed. It is built mainly of compound words constructed by the writer on the spot and not to be found in any dictionary—six or seven words compacted into one, without joint or seam—that is, without hyphens. It treats of fourteen or fifteen different subjects, each inclosed in a parenthesis of its own, with here and there extra parentheses which reinclose three or four of the minor parentheses, making pens within pens. Finally, all the parentheses and reparentheses are massed together between a couple of king-parentheses, one of which is placed in the first line of it—*after which comes the* VERB, and you find out for the first time what the man has been talking about. And after the verb—merely by way of ornament, as far as I can make out—the writer shovels in *"haben sind gewesen gehabt haben geworden sein,"* or words to that effect, and the monument is finished. I suppose that this closing hurrah is in the nature of the flourish to a man's signature—not necessary, but pretty. German books are easy enough to read when you hold them before the looking-glass or stand on your head—so as to reverse the construction—but I think that to learn to read and understand a German newspaper is a thing which must always remain an impossibility to a foreigner.

Yet even the German books are not entirely free from attacks of the Parenthesis distemper—though they are usually so mild as to cover only a few lines, and therefore when you at last get down to the verb it carries some meaning to your mind because you are able to remember a good deal of what has gone before.

Now here is a sentence from a popular and excellent German novel—with a slight parenthesis in it. I will make a perfectly literal translation and throw in the parenthesis-marks and some hyphens for the assistance of the reader—though in the original there are no parentheses-marks or hyphens, and the reader is left to flounder through to the remote verb the best way he can:

"But when he, upon the street, the (in-satin-and-silk-covered-now-very-unconstrainedly-after-the-newest-fashion-dressed) government counselor's wife *met*," etc., etc.*

That is from *The Old Mamselle's Secret,* by Mrs. Marlitt. And that sentence is constructed upon the most approved German model. You observe how far that verb is from the reader's base of operations. Well, in a German newspaper they put their verb away over on the next page and I have heard that sometimes after stringing along on exciting preliminaries and parentheses for a column or two they get in a hurry and have to go to press without getting to the verb at all. Of course, then the reader is left in a very exhausted and ignorant state.

We have the Parenthesis disease in our literature too and one may see cases of it every day in our books and newspapers but with us it is the mark and sign of an unpractised writer or a cloudy intellect, whereas with the Germans it is doubtless the mark and sign of a practised pen and of the presence of that sort of luminous intellectual fog which stands for clearness among these people. For surely it is *not* clearness—it necessarily can't be clearness. Even a jury

---

* *Wenn er aber auf der Strasse der in Sammt und Seide gehüllten jetz sehr ungenirt nach der neusten mode gekleideten Regierungsrathin begegnet.*

would have penetration enough to discover that. A writer's ideas must be a good deal confused, a good deal out of line and sequence, when he starts out to say that a man met a counselor's wife in the street, and then right in the midst of this so simple undertaking halts these approaching people and makes them stand still until he jots down an inventory of the woman's dress. That is manifestly absurd. It reminds a person of those dentists who secure your instant and breathless interest in a tooth by taking a grip on it with the forceps and then stand there and drawl through a tedious anecdote before they give the dreaded jerk. Parentheses in literature and dentistry are in bad taste.

The Germans have another kind of parenthesis, which they make by splitting a verb in two and putting half of it at the beginning of an exciting chapter and the *other half* at the end of it. Can any one conceive of anything more confusing than that? These things are called "separable verbs." The German grammar is blistered all over with separable verbs and the wider the two portions of one of them are spread apart the better the author of the crime is pleased with his performance. A favorite one is *reiste ab*—which means *departed*. Here is an example which I culled from a novel and reduced to English:

"The trunks being now ready, the DE- after kissing his mother and sisters, and once more pressing to his bosom his adored Gretchen, who, dressed in simple white muslin, with a single tuberose in the ample folds of her rich brown hair, had tottered feebly down the stairs, still pale from the terror and excitement of the past evening, but longing to lay her poor aching head yet once again upon the breast of him whom she loved more dearly than life itself, PARTED."

However, it is not well to dwell too much on the separable verbs. One is sure to lose his temper early and if he sticks to the subject and will not be warned, it will at last either soften his brain or petrify it. Personal pronouns and adjectives are a fruitful nuisance in this language and should have been left out. For instance, the same sound, *sie,* means *you* and it means *she* and it means *her* and it means *it* and it means *they* and it means *them*. Think of the ragged poverty of a language which has to make one word do the work of six—and a poor little weak thing of only three letters at that. But mainly think of the exasperation of never knowing which of these meanings the speaker is trying to convey. This explains why, whenever a person says *sie* to me, I generally try to kill him, if a stranger.

Now observe the Adjective. Here was a case where simplicity would have been an advantage. Therefore, for no other reason, the inventor of this language complicated it all he could. When we wish to speak of our "good friend or friends" in our enlightened tongue we stick to the one form and have no trouble or hard feeling about it but with the German tongue it is different. When a German gets his hands on an adjective he declines it and keeps on declining it until the common sense is all declined out of it. It is as bad as Latin. He says, for instance:

SINGULAR

Nominative—Mein gut*er* Freund, my good friend.
Genitive—Mein*es* gut*en* Freund*es*, of my good friend.
Dative—Mein*em* gut*en* Freund, to my good friend.
Accusative—Mein*en* gut*en* Freund, my good friend.

PLURAL

N.—Mein*e* gut*en* Freund*e*, my good friends.
G.—Mein*er* gut*en* Freund*e*, of my good friends.
D.—Mein*en* gut*en* Freund*en*, to my good friends.
A.—Mein*e* gut*en* Freund*e*, my good friends.

Now let the candidate for the asylum try to memorize those variations and see how soon he will be elected. One might better go without friends in Germany than take all this trouble about them. I have shown what a bother it is to decline a good (male) friend. Well, this is only a third of the work, for there is a variety of new distortions of the adjective to be learned when the object is feminine, and still another when the object is neuter. Now there are more adjectives in this language than there are black cats in Switzerland and they must all be as elaborately declined as the examples above suggested. Difficult?—troublesome?—these words cannot describe it. I heard a Californian student in Heidelberg say in one of his calmest moods that he would rather decline two drinks than one German adjective.

The inventor of the language seems to have taken pleasure in complicating it in every way he could think of. For instance, if one is casually referring to a house, *Haus,* or a horse, *Pferd,* or a dog, *Hund,* he spells these words as I have indicated but if he is referring to them in the Dative case he sticks on a foolish and unnecessary *e* and spells them *Hause, Pferde, Hunde.* So, as an added *e* often signifies the plural, as the *s* does with us, the new student is likely to go on for a month making twins out of a Dative dog before he discovers his mistake. And on the other hand, many a new student who could ill afford loss has bought and paid for two dogs and only got one of them, because he ignorantly bought that dog in the Dative singular when he really supposed he was talking plural—which left the law on the seller's side, of course, by the strict rules of grammar, and therefore a suit for recovery could not lie.

In German all the Nouns begin with a capital letter. Now that is a good idea, and a good idea in this language is necessarily conspicuous from its lonesomeness. I consider this capitalizing of nouns a good idea because by reason of it you are almost always able to tell a noun the minute you see it. You fall into error occasionally because you mistake the name of a person for the name of a thing and waste a good deal of time trying to dig a meaning out of it. German names almost always do mean something and this helps to deceive the student. I translated a passage one day, which said that "the infuriated tigress broke loose and utterly ate up the unfortunate fir forest" *(Tannenwald).* When I was girding up my loins to doubt this, I found out that Tannenwald in this instance was a man's name.

Every noun has a gender and there is no sense or system in the distribution, so the gender of each must be learned separately and by heart. There is no other way. To do this one has to have a memory like a memorandum-book. In German a young lady has no sex, while a turnip has. Think what overwrought reverence that shows for the turnip and what callous disrespect for the girl. See how it looks in print—I translate this from a conversation in one of the best of the German Sunday-school books:

"*Gretchen.*—Wilhelm, where is the turnip?

"*Wilhelm.*—She has gone to the kitchen.

"*Gretchen.*—Where is the accomplished and beautiful English maiden?

"*Wilhelm*—It has gone to the opera."

To continue with the German genders: a tree is male, its buds are female, its leaves are neuter. Horses are sexless, dogs are male, cats are female—tomcats included, of course. A person's mouth, neck, bosom, elbows, fingers, nails, feet and body are of the male sex, and his head is male or neuter according to the word selected to signify it and *not* according to the sex of the individual who wears it—for in Germany all the women wear either male heads or sexless ones. A person's nose, lips, shoulders, breast, hands and toes are of the female sex and his hair, ears, eyes, chin, legs, knees, heart and conscience haven't any sex at all. The inventor of the language probably got what he knew about a conscience from hearsay.

Now, by the above dissection the reader will see that in Germany a man may *think* he is a man but when he comes to look into the matter closely he is bound to have his doubts. He finds that in sober truth he is a most ridiculous mixture. And if he ends by trying to comfort himself with the thought that he can at least depend on a third of this mess as being manly and masculine the humiliating second thought will quickly remind him that in this respect he is no better off than any woman or cow in the land.

In the German it is true that by some oversight of the

inventor of the language a Woman is a female but a Wife *(Weib)* is not—which is unfortunate. A Wife here has no sex. She is neuter. So, according to the grammar, a fish is *he,* his scales are *she* but a fishwife is neither. To describe a wife as sexless may be called under-description. That is bad enough, but over-description is surely worse. A German speaks of an Englishman as the *Engländer.* To change the sex he adds *inn,* and that stands for Englishwoman—*Engländerinn.* That seems descriptive enough but still it is not exact enough for a German, so he precedes the word with that article which indicates that the creature to follow is feminine, and writes it down thus: *"die* Engländer*inn,"*—which means "the *she-Englishwoman."* I consider that that person is over-described.

Well, after the student has learned the sex of a great number of nouns he is still in a difficulty because he finds it impossible to persuade his tongue to refer to things as *"he"* and *"she"* and *"him"* and *"her,"* which it has been always accustomed to refer to as *"it."* When he even frames a German sentence in his mind, with the hims and hers in the right places, and then works up his courage to the utterance-point, it is no use—the moment he begins to speak his tongue flies the track and all those labored males and females come out as *"its."* And even when he is reading German to himself he always calls those things *"it,"* whereas he ought to read in this way:

Tale of the Fishwife and Its Sad Fate*

It is a bleak Day. Hear the Rain, how he pours, and the Hail, how he rattles, and see the Snow, how he drifts along, and oh the Mud, how deep he is! Ah the poor Fishwife, it is stuck fast in the Mire, it has dropped its Basket of Fishes, and its Hands have been cut by the Scales as it seized some of the falling Creatures, and one Scale has even got into its Eye, and it cannot get her out.

*I capitalize the nouns in the German (and ancient English) fashion.

It opens its Mouth to cry for Help but if any Sound comes out of him, alas he is drowned by the raging of the Storm. And now a Tomcat has got one of the Fishes and she will surely escape with him. No, she bites off a Fin, she holds her in her Mouth—will she swallow her? No, the Fish-wife's brave Mother-dog deserts his Puppies and rescues the Fin—which he eats, himself, as his Reward. O, horror, the Lightning has struck the Fish-basket. He sets him on Fire. See the Flame, how she licks the doomed Utensil with her red and angry Tongue. Now she attacks the helpless Fishwife's Foot—she burns him up, all but the big Toe, and even *she* is partly consumed. And still she spreads, still she waves her fiery Tongues. She attacks the Fishwife's Leg and destroys *it*. She attacks its Hand and destroys *her*. She attacks its poor worn Garment and destroys *her* also. She attacks its Body and consumes *him*. She wreathes herself about its Heart and *it* is consumed. Next about its Breast, and in a Moment *she* is a Cinder. Now she reaches its Neck—*he* goes. Now its Chin—*it* goes. Now its Nose—*she* goes. In another Moment, except Help come, the Fishwife will be no more. Time presses—is there none to succor and save? Yes! Joy, joy, with flying Feet the she-Englishwoman comes! But alas, the generous she-Female is too late: where now is the fated Fishwife? It has ceased from its Sufferings, it has gone to a better Land. All that is left of it for its loved Ones to lament over is this poor smoldering Ash-heap. Ah, woeful, woeful Ash-heap! Let us take him up tenderly, reverently, upon the lowly Shovel and bear him to his long Rest, with the Prayer that when he rises again it will be in a Realm where he will have one good square responsible Sex and have it all to himself instead of having a mangy lot of assorted Sexes scattered all over him in Spots.

There, now, the reader can see for himself that this pronoun business is a very awkward thing for the unaccustomed tongue.

I suppose that in all languages the similarities of look and sound between words which have no similarity in meaning are a fruitful source of perplexity to the foreigner. It is so in our tongue and it is notably the case in the German. Now there is that troublesome word *vermählt:* to me it has so close a resemblance—either real or fancied—to three or four other words that I never know whether it means despised, painted, suspected or married; until I look in the dictionary and then I find it means the latter. There are lots of such words and they are a great torment. To increase the difficulty there are words which *seem* to resemble each other and yet do not but they make just as much trouble as if they did. For instance, there is the word *vermiethen* (to let, to lease, to hire) and the word *verheirathen* (another way of saying to *marry*). I heard of an Englishman who knocked at a man's door in Heidelberg and proposed, in the best German he could command, to *"verheirathen"* that house. Then there are some words which mean one thing when you emphasize the first syllable but mean something very different if you throw the emphasis on the last syllable. For instance, there is a word which means a runaway, or the act of glancing through a book, according to the placing of the emphasis, and another word which signifies to *associate* with a man or to *avoid* him, according to where you put the emphasis—and you can generally depend on putting it in the wrong place and getting into trouble.

There are some exceedingly useful words in this language. *Schlag,* for example, and *Zug.* There are three-quarters of a column of *Schlags* in the dictionary and a column and a half of *Zugs.* The word *Schlag* means Blow, Stroke, Dash, Hit, Shock, Clap, Slap, Time, Bar, Coin, Stamp, Kind, Sort, Manner, Way, Apoplexy, Wood-cutting, Inclosure, Field, Forest-clearing. This is its simple and *exact* meaning—that is to say, its restricted, its fettered meaning. But there are ways by which you can set it free so that it can soar away, as on the wings of the morning, and never be at rest. You can hang any word you please to its tail, and make it mean anything you want to. You can begin with *Schlag-ader,* which means artery, and you can hang on the whole dictionary, word by word, clear through the alphabet to *Schlag-wasser*, which means bilge-water—and including *Schlag-mutter*, which means mother-in-law.

Just the same with *Zug*. Strictly speaking, *Zug* means Pull, Tug, Draught, Procession, March, Progress, Flight, Direction, Expedition, Train, Caravan, Passage, Stroke, Touch, Line, Flourish, Trait of Character, Feature, Lineament, Chess-move, Organ-stop, Team, Whiff, Bias, Drawer, Propensity, Inhalation, Disposition. But that thing which it does *not* mean—when all its legitimate pennants have been hung on—has not been discovered yet.

One cannot overestimate the usefulness of *Schlag* and *Zug*. Armed just with these two and the word *Also*, what cannot the foreigner on German soil accomplish? The German word *Also* is the equivalent of the English phrase "You know" and does not mean anything at all—in *talk*, though it sometimes does in print. Every time a German opens his mouth an *Also* falls out and every time he shuts it he bites one in two that was trying to *get* out.

Now, the foreigner, equipped with these three noble words, is master of the situation. Let him talk right along, fearlessly. Let him pour his indifferent German forth, and when he lacks for a word let him heave a *Schlag* into the vacuum. All the chances are that it fits it like a plug but if it doesn't, let him promptly heave a *Zug* after it. The two together can hardly fail to bung the hole. But if, by a miracle, they *should* fail, let him simply say *Also!* and this will give him a moment's chance to think of the needful word. In Germany, when you load your conversational gun it is always best to throw in a *Schlag* or two and a *Zug* or two, because it doesn't make any difference how much the rest of the charge may scatter, you are bound to bag something with *them*. Then you blandly say *Also* and load up again. Nothing gives such an air of grace and elegance and unconstraint to a German or an English conversation as to scatter it full of "Also's" or "You-knows."

In my note-book I find this entry:

July I.—In the hospital yesterday a word of thirteen syllables was successfully removed from a patient—a North-German from near Hamburg. But as most unfortunately the surgeons had opened him in the wrong place, under the impression that he contained a panorama, he died. The sad event has cast a gloom over the whole community.

That paragraph furnishes a text for a few remarks about one of the most curious and notable features of my subject —the length of German words. Some German words are so long that they have a perspective. Observe these examples:

FREUNDSCHAFTSBEZEIGUNGEN.

DILETTANTENAUFDRINGLICHKEITEN.

STADTVERORDNETENVERSAMMLUNGEN.

These things are not words, they are alphabetical processions. And they are not rare. One can open a German newspaper any time and see them marching majestically across the page—and if he has any imagination he can see the banners and hear the music, too. They impart a martial thrill to the meekest subject. I take a great interest in these curiosities. Whenever I come across a good one I stuff it and put it in my museum. In this way I have made quite a valuable collection. When I get duplicates, I exchange with other collectors and thus increase the variety of my stock. Here are some specimens which I lately bought at an auction sale of the effects of a bankrupt bric-à-brac hunter:

GENERALSTAATSVERORDNETENVERSAMMLUNGEN.

ALTERTHUMSWISSENSCHAFTEN.

KINDERBEWAHRUNGSANSTALTEN.

UNABHAENGIGKEITSERKLAERUNGEN.

WIEDERERSTELLUNGSBESTREBUNGEN.

WAFFENSTILLSTANDSUNTERHANDLUNGEN.

Of course when one of these grand mountain ranges goes stretching across the printed page, it adorns and ennobles that literary landscape—but at the same time it is a great distress to the new student, for it blocks up his way. He cannot crawl under it or climb over it or tunnel through it.

So he resorts to the dictionary for help, but there is no help there. The dictionary must draw the line somewhere—so it leaves this sort of words out. And it is right, because these long things are hardly legitimate words but are rather combinations of words, and the inventor of them ought to have been killed. They are compound words with the hyphens left out. The various words used in building them are in the dictionary but in a very scattered condition. So you can hunt the materials out one by one and get at the meaning at last but it is a tedious and harassing business. I have tried this process upon some of the above examples. *"Freundschafts-bezeigungen"* seems to be "Friendship demonstrations," which is only a foolish and clumsy way of saying "demonstrations of friendship." *"Unabhaengigkeitserklaerungen"* seems to be "Independencedeclarations," which is no improvement upon "Declarations of Independence," so far as I can see. *"Generalstaatsverordnetenversammlungen"* seems to be "Generalstatesrepresentativesmeetings," as nearly as I can get at it—a mere rhythmical, gushy euphuism for "meetings of the legislature," I judge. We used to have a good deal of this sort of crime in our literature but it has gone out now. We used to speak of a thing as a "never-to-be-forgotten" circumstance, instead of cramping it into the simple and sufficient word "memorable" and then going calmly about our business as if nothing had happened. In those days we were not content to embalm the thing and bury it decently, we wanted to build a monument over it.

But in our newspapers the compounding-disease lingers a little to the present day, but with the hyphens left out, in the German fashion. This is the shape it takes: instead of saying "Mr. Simmons, clerk of the county and district courts, was in town yesterday," the new form puts it thus: "Clerk of the County and District Courts Simmons was in town yesterday." This saves neither time nor ink and has an awkward sound besides. One often sees a remark like this in our papers: *"Mrs.* Assistant District Attorney Johnson returned to her city residence yesterday for the season." That is a case of

really unjustifiable compounding, because it not only saves
no time or trouble but confers a title on Mrs. Johnson which
she has no right to. But these little instances are trifles indeed
contrasted with the ponderous and dismal German system of
piling jumbled compounds together. I wish to submit the
following local item from a Mannheim journal by way of
illustration:

"In the daybeforeyesterdayshortlyaftereleveno'clock
Night, the inthistownstandingtavern called 'The Wagoner'
was down-burnt. When the fire to the onthedownburning-
houseresting Stork's Nest reached, flew the parent Storks
away. But when the bytheraging, firesurrounded Nest *itself*
caught Fire, straightway plunged the quickreturning Moth-
er-stork into the Flames and died, her Wings over her young
ones outspread."

Even the cumbersome German construction is not able to
take the pathos out of that picture—indeed it somehow
seems to strengthen it. This item is dated away back yonder
months ago. I could have used it sooner but I was waiting to
hear from the Father-stork. I am still waiting.

"Also!" If I have not shown that the German is a difficult
language, I have at least intended to do it. I have heard of an
American student who was asked how he was getting along
with his German and who answered promptly: "I am not
getting along at all. I have worked at it hard for three level
months and all I have got to show for it is one solitary German
phrase—*'Zwei glas'* " (two glasses of beer). He paused a moment, reflectively, then added with feeling: "But I've got
that *solid!*"

And if I have not also shown that German is a harassing and
infuriating study, my execution has been at fault, and not my
intent. I heard lately of a worn and sorely tried American
student who used to fly to a certain German word for relief
when he could bear up under his aggravations no longer—
the only word in the whole language whose sound was sweet
and precious to his ear and healing to his lacerated spirit. This
was the word *Damit.* It was only the *sound* that helped him,

not the meaning.* And so, at last, when he learned that the emphasis was not on the first syllable, his only stay and support was gone and he faded away and died.

I think that a description of any loud, stirring, tumultuous episode must be tamer in German than in English. Our descriptive words of this character have such a deep, strong, resonant sound, while their German equivalents do seem so thin and mild and energyless. Boom, burst, crash, roar, storm, bellow, blow, thunder, explosion; howl, cry, shout, yell, groan; battle, hell. These are magnificent words. They have a force and magnitude of sound befitting the things which they describe. But their German equivalents would be ever so nice to sing the children to sleep with, or else my awe-inspiring ears were made for display and not for superior usefulness in analyzing sounds. Would any man want to die in a battle which was called by so tame a term as a *Schlacht?* Or would not a consumptive feel too much bundled up, who was about to go out, in a shirt-collar and a seal-ring, into a storm which the bird-song word *Gewitter* was employed to describe? And observe the strongest of the several German equivalents for explosion—*Ausbruch.* Our word Toothbrush is more powerful than that. It seems to me that the Germans could do worse than import it into their language to describe particularly tremendous explosions with. The German word for hell—*Hölle*—sounds more like *helly* than anything else. Therefore, how necessarily chipper, frivolous and unimpressive it is. If a man were told in German to go there, could he really rise to the dignity of feeling insulted?

Having pointed out in detail the several vices of this language, I now come to the brief and pleasant task of pointing out its virtues. The capitalizing of the nouns I have already mentioned. But far before this virtue stands another—that of spelling a word according to the sound of it. After one short lesson in the alphabet the student can tell how any German word is pronounced without having to ask, whereas in our

---

*It merely means, in its general sense, *"herewith."*

language if a student should inquire of us, "What does B, O, W, spell?" we should be obliged to reply, "Nobody can tell what it spells when you set it off by itself. You can only tell by referring to the context and finding out what it signifies —whether it is a thing to shoot arrows with, or a nod of one's head, or the forward end of a boat."

There are some German words which are singularly and powerfully effective. For instance, those which describe lowly, peaceful and affectionate home life. Those which deal with love in any and all forms, from mere kindly feeling and honest good will toward the passing stranger, clear up to courtship. Those which deal with outdoor Nature in its softest and loveliest aspects—with meadows and forests and birds and flowers, the fragrance and sunshine of summer, and the moonlight of peaceful winter nights. In a word, those which deal with any and all forms of rest, repose and peace. Those also which deal with the creatures and marvels of fairyland. And lastly and chiefly, in those words which express pathos is the language surpassingly rich and effective. There are German songs which can make a stranger to the language cry. That shows that the *sound* of the words is correct—it interprets the meanings with truth and with exactness, and so the ear is informed, and through the ear the heart.

The Germans do not seem to be afraid to repeat a word when it is the right one. They repeat it several times if they choose. That is wise. But in English, when we have used a word a couple of times in a paragraph we imagine we are growing tautological and so we are weak enough to exchange it for some other word which only approximates exactness, to escape what we wrongly fancy is a greater blemish. Repetition may be bad but surely inexactness is worse.

There are people in the world who will take a great deal of trouble to point out the faults in a religion or a language and then go blandly about their business without suggesting any remedy. I am not that kind of a person. I have shown that the German language needs reforming. Very well, I am ready to reform it. At least I am ready to make the proper suggestions. Such a course as this might be immodest in another. But I have devoted upward of nine full weeks, first and last, to a careful and critical study of this tongue and thus have acquired a confidence in my ability to reform it which no mere superficial culture could have conferred upon me.

In the first place I would leave out the Dative case. It confuses the plurals. And, besides, nobody ever knows when he is in the Dative case except he discover it by accident—and then he does not know when or where it was that he got into it or how long he has been in it or how he is ever going to get out of it again. The Dative case is but an ornamental folly—it is better to discard it.

In the next place I would move the Verb further up to the front. You may load up with ever so good a Verb but I notice that you never really bring down a subject with it at the present German range—you only cripple it. So I insist that this important part of speech should be brought forward to a position where it may be easily seen with the naked eye.

Thirdly, I would import some strong words from the English tongue—to swear with and also to use in describing all sorts of vigorous things in a vigorous way.*

Fourthly, I would reorganize the sexes and distribute them according to the will of the Creator. This as a tribute of respect, if nothing else.

Fifthly, I would do away with those great long com-

---

* *"Verdammt"* and its variations and enlargements are words which have plenty of meaning, but the *sounds* are so mild and ineffectual that German ladies can use them without sin. German ladies who could not be induced to commit a sin by any persuasion or compulsion promptly rip out one of these harmless little words when they tear their dresses or don't like the soup. It sounds about as wicked as our "My gracious." German ladies are constantly saying, *"Ach! Gott!" "Mein Gott!" "Gott in Himmel!" "Herr Gott!" "Der Herr Jesus!"* etc. They think our ladies have the same custom, perhaps, for I once heard a gentle and lovely old German lady say to a sweet young American girl: "The two languages are so alike—how pleasant that is. We say *'Ach! Gott!'* you say 'Goddam.' "

pounded words or require the speaker to deliver them in sections, with intermissions for refreshments. To wholly do away with them would be best, for ideas are more easily received and digested when they come one at a time than when they come in bulk. Intellectual food is like any other. It is pleasanter and more beneficial to take it with a spoon than with a shovel.

Sixthly, I would require a speaker to stop when he is done and not hang a string of those useless *"haben sind gewesen gehabt haben geworden seins"* to the end of his oration. This sort of gewgaws undignify a speech instead of adding a grace. They are therefore an offense and should be discarded.

Seventhly, I would discard the Parenthesis. Also the reparenthesis, the re-reparenthesis and the re-re-re-re-re-reparenthesis, and likewise the final wide-reaching all-inclosing king-parenthesis. I would require every individual, be he high or low, to unfold a plain straightforward tale or else coil it and sit on it and hold his peace. Infractions of this law should be punishable with death.

And eighthly, and last, I would retain *Zug* and *Schlag* with their pendants and discard the rest of the vocabulary. This would simplify the language.

I have now named what I regard as the most necessary and important changes. These are perhaps all I could be expected to name for nothing. But there are other suggestions which I can and will make in case my proposed application shall result in my being formally employed by the government in the work of reforming the language.

My philological studies have satisfied me that a gifted person ought to learn English (barring spelling and pronouncing) in thirty hours, French in thirty days and German in thirty years. It seems manifest, then, that the latter tongue ought to be trimmed down and repaired. If it is to remain as it is it ought to be gently and reverently set aside among the dead languages, for only the dead have time to learn it.

A Fourth of July Oration in the German Tongue, Delivered at a Banquet of the Anglo-American Club of Students by the Author of this Book

GENTLEMEN: Since I arrived, a month ago, in this old wonderland, this vast garden of Germany, my English tongue has so often proved a useless piece of baggage to me and so troublesome to carry around in a country where they haven't the checking system for luggage, that I finally set to work last week and learned the German language. Also! Es freut mich dass dies so ist, denn es muss, in ein hauptsächlich degree, höflich sein, dass man auf ein occasion like this, sein Rede in die Sprache des Landes worin he boards, aussprechen soll. Dafür habe ich, aus reinische Verlegenheit—no, Vergangenheit—no, I mean Höflichkeit—aus reinische Höflichkeit habe ich resolved to tackle this business in the German language, um Gottes willen! Also! Sie müssen so freundlich sein, and verzeih mich die interlarding von ein oder zwei Englischer Worte, hie und da, denn ich finde dass die deutsche is not a very copious language, and so when you've really got anything to say, you've got to draw on a language that can stand the strain.

Wenn aber man kann nicht meinem Rede verstehen, so werde ich ihm später dasselbe übersetz, wenn er solche Dienst verlangen wollen haben werden sollen sein hätte. (I don't know what wollen haben werden sollen sein hätte means but I notice they always put it at the end of a German sentence—merely for general literary gorgeousness, I suppose.)

This is a great and justly honored day—a day which is worthy of the veneration in which it is held by the true patriots of all climes and nationalities—a day which offers a fruitful theme for thought and speech. Und meinem Freunde—no, meinen Freunden—meines Freundes—well, take your choice, they're all the same price, I don't know which one is right—also! ich habe gehabt haben worden gewesen sein, as Goethe says in his Paradise Lost—ich—ich—that is to say—ich—but let us change cars.

Also! Die Anblick so viele Grossbrittanischer und Amerikanischer hier zusammengetroffen in Bruderliche concord, ist zwar a welcome and inspiriting spectacle. And what has moved you to it? Can the terse German tongue rise to the expression of this impulse? Is it Freundschaftsbezeigungenstadtverordnetenversammlungenfamilieneigenthümlichkeiten? Nein, o nein! This is a crisp and noble word but it fails to pierce the marrow of the impulse which has gathered this friendly meeting and produced diese Anblick—eine Anblick welche ist gut zu sehen—gut für die Augen in a foreign land and a far country—eine Anblick solche als in die gewöhnliche Heidelberger phrase nennt man ein "schönes Aussicht!" Ja, freilich natürlich wahrscheinlich ebensowohl! Also! Die Aussicht auf dem Königsstuhl mehr grösserer ist, aber geistlische sprechend nicht so schön, lob'Gott! Because sie sind hier zusammengetroffen, in Bruderlichem concord, ein grossen Tag zu feiern, whose high benefits were not for one land and one locality only, but have conferred a measure of good upon all lands that know liberty to-day and love it. Hundert Jahre vorüber, waren die Engländer und die Amerikaner Feinde. Aber heute sind sie herzlichen Freunde, Gott sei Dank! May this good-fellowship endure. May these banners here blended in amity so remain. May they never any more wave over opposing hosts or be stained with blood which was kindred, is kindred and always will be kindred, until a line drawn upon a map shall be able to say: *"This* bars the ancestral blood from flowing in the veins of the descendant!"

12. Lessons in Art

We had had the best instructors in drawing and painting in Germany—Hämmerling, Vogel, Müller, Dietz and Schumann. Hämmerling taught us landscape-painting, Vogel taught us figure-drawing, Müller taught us to do still-life, and Dietz and Schumann gave us a finishing course in two specialties—battle-pieces and shipwrecks. Whatever I am in Art I owe to these men. I have something of the manner of each and all of them but they all said that I had also a manner of my own and that it was conspicuous. They said there was a marked individuality about my style—insomuch that if I ever painted the commonest type of a dog, I should be sure to throw a something into the aspect of that dog which would keep him from being mistaken for the creation of any other artist. Secretly I wanted to believe all these kind sayings but I could not. I was afraid that my masters' partiality for me and pride in me biased their judgment. So I resolved to make a test. Privately and unknown to anyone, I painted my great picture, "Heidelberg Castle Illuminated"—my first really important work in oils—and had it hung up in the midst of a wilderness of oil-pictures in the Art Exhibition, with no name attached to it. To my great gratification it was instantly recognized as mine. All the town flocked to see it, and people even came from neighboring localities to visit it. It made more stir than any other work in the Exhibition. But the most gratifying thing of all was that chance strangers, passing through, who had not heard of my picture, were not only drawn to it, as by a lodestone, the moment they entered the gallery but always took it for a "Turner."

Mr. Harris was graduated in Art about the same time with myself and we took a studio together. We waited awhile for some orders. Then, as time began to drag a little, we concluded to make a pedestrian tour. After much consideration we determined on a trip up the shores of the beautiful Neckar to Heilbronn. Apparently nobody had ever done that. There were ruined castles on the overhanging cliffs and crags all the way. These were said to have their legends, like those on the Rhine, and what was better still, they had never been in print. There was nothing in the books about that lovely region. It had been neglected by the tourist, it was virgin soil for the literary pioneer.

Meantime the knapsacks, the rough walking-suits and the stout walking-shoes which we had ordered were finished and brought to us. A Mr. X and a young Mr. Z had agreed to go with us. We went around one evening and bade good-by to our friends, and afterward had a little farewell banquet at the hotel. We got to bed early, for we wanted to make an early start so as to take advantage of the cool of the morning.

We were out of bed at break of day, feeling fresh and vigorous, and took a hearty breakfast, then plunged down through the leafy arcades of the Castle grounds, toward the town. What a glorious summer morning it was and how the flowers did pour out their fragrance and how the birds did sing! It was just the time for a tramp through the woods and mountains.

We were all dressed alike: broad slouch hats to keep the sun off, gray knapsacks, blue army shirts, blue overalls, leathern gaiters buttoned tight from knee down to ankle, high-quarter coarse shoes snugly laced. Each man had an opera-glass, a canteen and a guide-book case slung over his shoulder, and carried an alpenstock in one hand and a sun-umbrella in the other. Around our hats were wound many folds of soft white muslin, with the ends hanging and flapping down our backs—an idea brought from the Orient and used by tourists all over Europe. Harris carried the little watchlike

machine called a "pedometer," whose office is to keep count
of a man's steps and tell how far he has walked. Everybody
stopped to admire our costumes and give us a hearty "Pleasant march to you!"

When we got down-town I found that we could go by rail
to within five miles of Heilbronn. The train was just starting,
so we jumped aboard and went tearing away in splendid
spirits. It was agreed all around that we had done wisely,
because it would be just as enjoyable to walk *down* the Neckar as up it, and it could not be needful to walk both ways.
There were some nice German people in our compartment.
I got to talking some pretty private matters presently and
Harris became nervous, so he nudged me and said:

"Speak in German—these Germans may understand English."

I did so and it was well I did, for it turned out that there
was not a German in that party who did not understand
English perfectly. It is curious how wide-spread our language
is in Germany. After a while some of those folks got out and
a German gentleman and his two young daughters got in. I
spoke in German to one of the latter several times but without result. Finally she said:

"Ich verstehe nur Deutch und Englishe"—or words to that
effect. That is, "I don't understand any language but German
and English."

And sure enough, not only she but her father and sister
spoke English. So after that we had all the talk we wanted,
and we wanted a good deal, for they were very agreeable
people. They were greatly interested in our costumes, especially the alpenstocks, for they had not seen any before. They
said that the Neckar road was perfectly level, so we must be
going to Switzerland or some other rugged country, and
asked us if we did not find the walking pretty fatiguing in
such warm weather. But we said no.

We reached Wimpfen—I think it was Wimpfen—in about
three hours, and got out, not the least tired; found a good
hotel and ordered beer and dinner—then took a stroll

The Tower

through the venerable old village. It was very picturesque
and tumble-down, and dirty and interesting. It had queer
houses five hundred years old in it, and a military tower, 115
feet high, which had stood there more than ten centuries. I
made a little sketch of it. I kept a copy but gave the original
to the Burgomaster. I think the original was better than the
copy, because it had more windows in it and the grass stood
up better and had a brisker look. There was none around the
tower, though. I composed the grass myself from studies I
made in a field by Heidelberg in Hämmerling's time. The
man on top, looking at the view, is apparently too large but

I found he could not be made smaller conveniently. I wanted
him there and I wanted him visible, so I thought out a way
to manage it. I composed the picture from two points of
view. The spectator is to observe the man from about where
that flag is and he must observe the tower itself from the
ground. This harmonizes the seeming discrepancy.

Near an old cathedral, under a shed, were three crosses of
stone—moldy and damaged things, bearing life-size stone
figures. The two thieves were dressed in the fanciful court
costumes of the middle of the sixteenth century, while the
Saviour was nude, with the exception of a cloth around the
loins.

We had dinner under the green trees in a garden belonging to the hotel and overlooking the Neckar. Then, after a
smoke, we went to bed. We had a refreshing nap, then got
up about three in the afternoon and put on our panoply. As
we tramped gaily out at the gate of the town, we overtook
a peasant's cart, partly laden with odds and ends of cabbages
and similar vegetable rubbish, and drawn by a small cow and
a smaller donkey yoked together. It was a pretty slow concern but it got us into Heilbronn before dark—five miles, or
possibly it was seven.

We stopped at the very same inn which the famous old
robber-knight and rough fighter, Götz von Berlichingen,
abode in after he got out of captivity in the Square Tower of
Heilbronn between three hundred and fifty and four hundred years ago. Harris and I occupied the same room which
he had occupied and the same paper had not all peeled off
the walls yet. The furniture was quaint old carved stuff, full
four hundred years old, and some of the smells were over a
thousand. There was a hook in the wall, which the landlord
said the terrific old Götz used to hang his iron hand on when
he took it off to go to bed. This room was very large—it might
be called immense—and it was on the first floor, which means
it was in the second story, for in Europe the houses are so
high that they do not count the first story, else they would get
tired climbing before they got to the top. The wall-paper was

a fiery red with huge gold figures in it, well smirched by time, and it covered all the doors. These doors fitted so snugly and continued the figures of the paper so unbrokenly that when they were closed one had to go feeling and searching along the wall to find them. There was a stove in the corner—one of those tall, square, stately white porcelain things that looks like a monument and keeps you thinking of death when you ought to be enjoying your travels. The windows looked out on a little alley, and over that into a stable and some poultry and pig yards in the rear of some tenement-houses. There were the customary two beds in the room, one in one end of it, the other in the other, about an old-fashioned brass-mounted, single-barreled pistol-shot apart. They were fully as narrow as the usual German bed, too, and had the German bed's ineradicable habit of spilling the blankets on the floor every time you forgot yourself and went to sleep.

A round table as large as King Arthur's stood in the center of the room. While the waiters were getting ready to serve our dinner on it we all went out to see the renowned clock on the front of the municipal buildings.

13. The Wives' Treasures

The *Rathhaus,* or municipal building, is of the quaintest and most picturesque Middle-Age architecture. It has a massive portico and steps before it, heavily balustraded and adorned with life-size rusty iron knights in complete armor. The clock-face on the front of the building is very large and of curious pattern. Ordinarily a gilded angel strikes the hour on a big bell with a hammer. As the striking ceases a life-size figure of Time raises its hour-glass and turns it. Two golden rams advance and butt each other. A gilded cock lifts its wings. But the main features are two great angels who stand on each side of the dial with long horns at their lips. It was said that they blew melodious blasts on these horns every hour—but they did not do it for us. We were told later that they blew only at night, when the town was still.

Within the *Rathhaus* were a number of huge wild boars' heads, preserved, and mounted on brackets along the wall. They bore inscriptions telling who killed them and how many hundred years ago it was done. One room in the building was devoted to the preservation of ancient archives. There they showed us no end of aged documents. Some were signed by Popes, some by Tilly and other great generals, and one was a letter written and subscribed by Götz von Berlichingen in Heilbronn in 1519 just after his release from the Square Tower.

This fine old robber-knight was a devoutly and sincerely religious man, hospitable, charitable to the poor, fearless in fight, active, enterprising, and possessed of a large and generous nature. He had in him a quality which was rare in that rough time—the quality of being able to overlook moderate injuries and of being able to forgive and forget mortal ones as soon as he had soundly trounced the authors of them. He was prompt to take up any poor devil's quarrel and risk his neck to right him. The common folk held him dear, and his memory is still green in ballad and tradition. He used to go on the highway and rob rich wayfarers. And other times he would swoop down from his high castle on the hills of the Neckar and capture passing cargoes of merchandise. In his memoirs he piously thanks the Giver of all Good for remembering him in his needs and delivering sundry such cargoes into his hands at times when only special providences could have relieved him. He was a doughty warrior and found a deep joy in battle. In an assault upon a stronghold in Bavaria when he was only twenty-three years old, his right hand was shot away but he was so interested in the fight that he did not observe it for a while. He said that the iron hand which was made for him afterward and which he wore for more than half a century was nearly as clever a member as the fleshy one had been. I was glad to get a facsimile of the letter written by this fine old German Robin Hood, though I was not able to read it. He was a better artist with his sword than with his pen.

We went down by the river and saw the Square Tower. It was a very venerable structure, very strong and very ornamental. There was no opening near the ground. They had to use a ladder to get into it, no doubt.

We visited the principal church, also—a curious old structure, with a towerlike spire adorned with all sorts of grotesque images. The inner walls of the church were placarded with large mural tablets of copper bearing engraved inscriptions celebrating the merits of old Heilbronn worthies of two or three centuries ago, and also bearing rudely painted effigies of themselves and their families tricked out in the queer costumes of those days. The head of the family sat in the foreground, and beyond him extended a sharply receding and diminishing row of sons. Facing him sat his wife, and beyond her extended a long row of diminishing daughters. The family was usually large but the perspective bad.

Then we hired the hack and the horse which Götz von Berlichingen used to use, and drove several miles into the country to visit the place called *Weibertreu*—Wife's Fidelity I suppose it means. It was a feudal castle of the Middle Ages. When we reached its neighborhood we found it was beautifully situated but on top of a mound or hill, round and tolerably steep and about two hundred feet high. Therefore, as the sun was blazing hot, we did not climb up there but took the place on trust and observed it from a distance while the horse leaned up against a fence and rested. The place has no interest except that which is lent it by its legend, which is a very pretty one—to this effect:

The Legend

In the Middle Ages a couple of young dukes, brothers, took opposite sides in one of the wars, the one fighting for the Emperor, the other against him. One of them owned the castle and village on top of the mound which I have been speaking of, and in his absence his brother came with his knights and soldiers and began a siege. It was a long and tedious business, for the people made a stubborn and faithful defense. But at last their supplies ran out and starvation began its work. More fell by hunger than by the missiles of the enemy. They by and by surrendered and begged for charitable terms. But the beleaguering prince was so incensed against them for their long resistance that he said he would spare none but the women and children—all the men should be put to the sword without exception and all their goods destroyed. Then the women came and fell on their knees and begged for the lives of their husbands.

"No," said the prince, "not a man of them shall escape alive. You yourselves shall go with your children into houseless and friendless banishment. But that you may not starve I grant you this one grace, that each woman may bear with her from this place as much of her most valuable property as she is able to carry."

Very well, presently the gates swung open and out filed those women carrying their *husbands* on their shoulders. The besiegers, furious at the trick, rushed forward to slaughter the men, but the Duke stepped between and said:

"No, put up your swords—a prince's word is inviolable."

When we got back to the hotel, King Arthur's Round Table was ready for us in its white drapery, and the head waiter and his first assistant, in swallowtails and white cravats, brought in the soup and the hot plates at once.

Mr. X had ordered the dinner, and when the wine came on, he picked up a bottle, glanced at the label and then turned to the grave, the melancholy, the sepulchral head waiter and said it was not the sort of wine he had asked for. The head waiter picked up the bottle, cast his undertaker-eye on it and said:

"It is true. I beg pardon." Then he turned on his subordinate and calmly said, "Bring another label."

At the same time he slid the present label off with his hand and laid it aside. It had been newly put on, its paste was still wet. When the new label came he put it on. Our French wine being now turned into German wine, according to desire, the head waiter went blandly about his other duties as if the working of this sort of miracle was a common and easy thing to him.

Mr. X said he had not known before that there were people honest enough to do this miracle in public but he was aware that thousands upon thousands of labels were imported into America from Europe every year to enable dealers to furnish to their customers in a quiet and inexpensive way all the different kinds of foreign wines they might require.

We took a turn around the town after dinner and found it fully as interesting in the moonlight as it had been in the daytime. The streets were narrow and roughly paved and there was not a sidewalk or a street-lamp anywhere. The dwellings were centuries old and vast enough for hotels. They widened all the way up. The stories projected further and further forward and aside as they ascended, and the long rows of lighted windows, filled with little bits of panes, cur-tained with figured white muslin and adorned outside with boxes of flowers, made a pretty effect. The moon was bright, and the light and shadow very strong, and nothing could be more picturesque than those curving streets with their rows of huge high gables leaning far over toward each other in a friendly gossiping way, and the crowds below drifting through the alternating blots of gloom and mellow bars of moonlight. Nearly everybody was abroad, chatting, singing, romping, or massed in lazy comfortable attitudes in the door-ways.

In one place there was a public building which was fenced

about with a thick, rusty chain which sagged from post to post in a succession of low swings. The pavement here was made of heavy blocks of stone. In the glare of the moon a party of barefooted children were swinging on those chains and having a noisy good time. They were not the first ones who had done that. Even their great-great-grandfathers had not been the first to do it when they were children. The strokes of the bare feet had worn grooves inches deep in the stone flags. It had taken many generations of swinging children to accomplish that. Everywhere in the town were the mold and decay that go with antiquity and evidence it but I do not know that anything else gave us so vivid a sense of the old age of Heilbronn as those footworn grooves in the paving-stones.

14. A Cruise in the Dark

When we got back to the hotel I wound and set the pedometer and put it in my pocket, for I was to carry it next day and keep record of the miles we made. The work which we had given the instrument to do during the day which had just closed had not fatigued it perceptibly.

We were in bed by ten, for we wanted to be up and away on our tramp homeward with the dawn. I hung fire but Harris went to sleep at once. I hate a man who goes to sleep at once. There is a sort of indefinable something about it which is not exactly an insult and yet is an insolence and one which is hard to bear, too. I lay there fretting over this injury and trying to go to sleep but the harder I tried the wider awake I grew. I got to feeling very lonely in the dark, with no company but an undigested dinner. My mind got a start by and by and began to consider the beginning of every subject which has ever been thought of but it never went further than the beginning. It was touch and go. It fled from topic to topic with a frantic speed. At the end of an hour my head was in a perfect whirl and I was dead tired, fagged out.

The fatigue was so great that it presently began to make some head against the nervous excitement. While imagining myself wide awake I would really doze into momentary unconsciousness and come suddenly out of it with a physical jerk which nearly wrenched my joints apart—the delusion of the instant being that I was tumbling backward over a precipice. After I had fallen over eight or nine precipices and thus found out that one half of my brain had been asleep eight or nine times without the wide-awake, hard-working other half suspecting it, the periodical unconsciousnesses began to extend their spell gradually over more of my brain-territory and at last I sank into a drowse which grew deeper and deeper and was doubtless just on the very point of becoming a solid, blessed dreamless stupor, when—what was that?

My dulled faculties dragged themselves partly back to life and took a receptive attitude. Now out of an immense, a limitless distance, came a something which grew and grew, and approached, and presently was recognizable as a sound —it had rather seemed to be a feeling before. This sound was a mile away now—perhaps it was the murmur of a storm. And now it was nearer—not a quarter of a mile away. Was it the muffled rasping and grinding of distant machinery? No, it came still nearer. Was it the measured tramp of a marching troop? But it came nearer still, and still nearer—and at last it was right in the room: it was merely a mouse gnawing the woodwork. So I had held my breath all that time for such a trifle.

Well, what was done could not be helped. I would go to sleep at once and make up the lost time. That was a thoughtless thought. Without intending it—hardly knowing it—I fell to listening intently to that sound and even unconsciously counting the strokes of the mouse's nutmeg-grater. Presently I was deriving exquisite suffering from this employment, yet maybe I could have endured it if the mouse had attended steadily to his work. But he did not do that. He stopped every now and then and I suffered more while waiting and listening for him to begin again than I did while he was gnawing. Along at first I was mentally offering a reward of five—six—seven—ten—dollars for that mouse but toward the last I was offering rewards which were entirely beyond my means. I close-reefed my ears—that is to say, I bent the flaps of them down and furled them into five or six folds and pressed them against the hearing-orifice—but it did no good: the faculty was so sharpened by nervous excitement that it was become a microphone and could hear through the overlays without trouble.

My anger grew to a frenzy. I finally did what all persons before me have done, clear back to Adam—resolved to throw something. I reached down and got my walking-shoes, then sat up in bed and listened in order to exactly locate the noise. But I couldn't do it. It was as unlocatable as a cricket's noise. And where one thinks that that is, is always the very place where it isn't. So I presently hurled a shoe at random and with a vicious vigor. It struck the wall over Harris's head and fell down on him. I had not imagined I could throw so far. It woke Harris and I was glad of it until I found he was not angry. Then I was sorry. He soon went to sleep again, which pleased me. But straightway the mouse began again, which roused my temper once more. I did not want to wake Harris a second time, but the gnawing continued until I was compelled to throw the other shoe. This time I broke a mirror—there were two in the room—I got the largest one, of course. Harris woke again but did not complain, and I was sorrier than ever. I resolved that I would suffer all possible torture before I would disturb him a third time.

The mouse eventually retired, and by and by I was sinking to sleep, when a clock began to strike. I counted till it was done, and was about to drowse again when another clock began. I counted. Then the two great *Rathhaus* clock angels began to send forth soft, rich, melodious blasts from their long trumpets. I had never heard anything that was so lovely or weird or mysterious—but when they got to blowing the quarter-hours, they seemed to me to be overdoing the thing. Every time I dropped off for a moment a new noise woke me. Each time I woke I missed my coverlet and had to reach down to the floor and get it again.

At last all sleepiness forsook me. I recognized the fact that I was hopelessly and permanently wide awake. Wide awake and feverish and thirsty. When I had lain tossing there as long as I could endure it, it occurred to me that it would be a good idea to dress and go out in the great square and take a re-freshing wash in the fountain and smoke and reflect there until the remnant of the night was gone.

I believed I could dress in the dark without waking Harris. I had banished my shoes after the mouse but my slippers would do for a summer night. So I rose softly, and gradually got on everything—down to one sock. I couldn't seem to get on the track of that sock, any way I could fix it. But I had to have it. So I went down on my hands and knees, with one slipper on and the other in my hand, and began to paw gently around and rake the floor but with no success. I enlarged my circle and went on pawing and raking. With every pressure of my knee, how the floor creaked! And every time I chanced to rake against any article, it seemed to give out thirty-five or thirty-six times more noise than it would have done in the daytime. In those cases I always stopped and held my breath till I was sure Harris had not awakened—then I crept along again. I moved on and on but I could not find the sock. I could not seem to find anything but furniture. I could not remem-ber that there was much furniture in the room when I went to bed, but the place was alive with it now—especially chairs —chairs everywhere—had a couple of families moved in in the mean time? And I never could seem to *glance* on one of those chairs but always struck it full and square with my head. My temper rose by steady and sure degrees and as I pawed on and on I fell to making vicious comments under my breath.

Finally, with a venomous access of irritation, I said I would leave without the sock, so I rose up and made straight for the door—as I supposed—and suddenly confronted my dim spectral image in the unbroken mirror. It startled the breath out of me for an instant. It also showed me that I was lost and had no sort of idea where I was. When I realized this I was so angry that I had to sit down on the floor and take hold of something to keep from lifting the roof off with an explosion of opinion. If there had been only one mirror it might possibly have helped to locate me but there were two, and two were as bad as a thousand. Besides, these were on opposite sides of the room. I could see the dim blur of the windows but in my turned-around condition they were exactly where they ought not to be and so they only confused me instead of helping me.

I started to get up, and knocked down an umbrella. It made a noise like a pistol-shot when it struck that hard, slick, carpetless floor. I grated my teeth and held my breath— Harris did not stir. I set the umbrella slowly and carefully on end against the wall but as soon as I took my hand away its heel slipped from under it and down it came again with another bang. I shrunk together and listened a moment in silent fury—no harm done, everything quiet. With the most painstaking care and nicety I stood the umbrella up once more, took my hand away, and down it came again.

I have been strictly reared but if it had not been so dark and solemn and awful there in that lonely, vast room, I do believe I should have said something then which could not be put into a Sunday-school book without injuring the sale of it. If my reasoning powers had not been already sapped dry by my harassments I would have known better than to try to set an umbrella on end on one of those glassy German floors in the dark. It can't be done in the daytime without four failures to one success. I had one comfort, though—Harris was yet still and silent—he had not stirred.

The umbrella could not locate me—there were four standing around the room, and all alike. I thought I would feel along the wall and find the door in that way. I rose up and began this operation but raked down a picture. It was not a large one but it made noise enough for a panorama. Harris gave out no sound but I felt that if I experimented any further with the pictures I should be sure to wake him. Better give up trying to get out. Yes, I would find King Arthur's Round Table once more—I had already found it several times—and use it for a base of departure on an exploring tour for my bed. If I could find my bed I could then find my water pitcher. I would quench my raging thirst and turn in. So I started on my hands and knees, because I could go faster that way, and with more confidence, too, and not knock down things. By and by I found the table—with my head—rubbed the bruise a little, then rose up and started, with hands abroad and fingers spread, to balance myself. I found a chair, then the wall, then another chair, then a sofa, then an alpenstock, then another sofa. This confounded me, for I had thought there was only one sofa. I hunted up the table again and took a fresh start; found some more chairs.

It occurred to me now, as it ought to have done before, that as the table was round it was therefore of no value as a base to aim from, so I moved off once more and at random among the wilderness of chairs and sofas—wandered off into unfamiliar regions and presently knocked a candlestick off a mantelpiece, grabbed at the candlestick and knocked off a lamp, grabbed at the lamp and knocked off a water pitcher with a rattling crash, and thought to myself, "I've found you at last—I judged I was close upon you." Harris shouted "murder," and "thieves," and finished with "I'm absolutely drowned."

The crash had roused the house. Mr. X pranced in in his long night-garment, with a candle, young Z after him with another candle. A procession swept in at another door, with candles and lanterns—landlord and two German guests in their nightgowns, and a chambermaid in hers.

I looked around. I was at Harris's bed, a Sabbath-day's journey from my own. There was only one sofa. It was against

Leaving Heilbronn

the wall. There was only one chair where a body could get at it—I had been revolving around it like a planet and colliding with it like a comet half the night.

I explained how I had been employing myself and why. Then the landlord's party left, and the rest of us set about our preparations for breakfast, for the dawn was ready to break. I glanced furtively at my pedometer and found I had made 47 miles. But I did not care, for I had come out for a pedestrian tour anyway.

15. Raftsmen on the Neckar

When the landlord learned that I and my agents were artists our party rose perceptibly in his esteem. We rose still higher when he learned that we were making a pedestrian tour of Europe.

Leaving Heilbronn

He told us all about the Heidelberg road and which were the best places to avoid and which the best ones to tarry at. He charged me less than cost for the things I broke in the night. He put up a fine luncheon for us and added to it a quantity of great light-green plums, the pleasantest fruit in Germany. He was so anxious to do us honor that he would not allow us to walk out of Heilbronn but called up Götz von Berlichingen's horse and cab and made us ride.

I made a sketch of the turnout. It is not a Work, it is only what artists call a "study"—a thing to make a finished picture from. This sketch has several blemishes in it. For instance, the wagon is not traveling as fast as the horse is. This is wrong. Again, the person trying to get out of the way is too small. He is out of perspective, as we say. The two upper lines are not the horse's back, they are the reins. There seems to be a wheel missing—this would be corrected in a finished Work, of course. That thing flying out behind is not a flag, it is a curtain. That other thing up there is the sun but I didn't get enough distance on it. I do not remember now what that thing is that is in front of the man who is running but I think it is a haystack or a woman. This study was exhibited in the Paris Salon of 1879 but did not take any medal. They do not give medals for studies.

We discharged the carriage at the bridge. The river was full of logs—long, slender, barkless pine logs—and we leaned on the rails of the bridge and watched the men put them together into rafts. These rafts were of a shape and construction to suit the crookedness and extreme narrowness of the Neckar. They were from fifty to one hundred yards long and they gradually tapered from a nine-log breadth at their sterns to a three-log breadth at their bow-ends. The main part of the steering is done at the bow, with a pole. The three-log breadth there furnishes room for only the steersman, for these little logs are not larger around than an average young lady's waist. The connections of the several sections of the raft are slack and pliant, so that the raft may be readily bent into any sort of curve required by the shape of the river.

The Neckar is in many places so narrow that a person can throw a dog across it, if he has one. When it is also sharply curved in such places the raftsman has to do some pretty nice snug piloting to make the turns. The river is not always allowed to spread over its whole bed—which is as much as thirty and sometimes forty yards wide—but is split into three equal bodies of water by stone dikes which throw the main volume, depth and current into the central one. In low water these neat narrow-edged dikes project four or five inches above the surface, like the comb of a submerged roof, but in high water they are overflowed. A hatful of rain makes high water in the Neckar, and a basketful produces an overflow.

There are dikes abreast the Schloss Hotel, and the current is violently swift at that point. I used to sit for hours in my glass cage, watching the long, narrow rafts slip along through the central channel, grazing the right-bank dike and aiming carefully for the middle arch of the stone bridge below. I watched them in this way and lost all this time hoping to see one of them hit the bridge-pier and wreck itself sometime or other but was always disappointed. One was smashed there one morning but I had just stepped into my room a moment to light a pipe, so I lost it.

While I was looking down upon the rafts that morning in Heilbronn the daredevil spirit of adventure came suddenly upon me and I said to my comrades:

"*I* am going to Heidelberg on a raft. Will you venture with me?"

Their faces paled a little but they assented with as good a grace as they could. Harris wanted to cable his mother— thought it his duty to do that, as he was all she had in this world—so, while he attended to this I went down to the longest and finest raft and hailed the captain with a hearty "Ahoy, shipmate!" which put us upon pleasant terms at once, and we entered upon business. I said we were on a pedestrian tour to Heidelberg and would like to take passage with him. I said this partly through young Z, who spoke German very well, and partly through Mr. X, who spoke it peculiarly. I can *understand* German as well as the maniac that invented it but I *talk* it best through an interpreter.

The captain hitched up his trousers, then shifted his quid thoughtfully. Presently he said just what I was expecting he would say—that he had no license to carry passengers and therefore was afraid the law would be after him in case the matter got noised about or any accident happened. So I *chartered* the raft and the crew and took all the responsibilities on myself.

With a rattling song the starboard watch bent to their work and hove the cable short, then got the anchor home, and our bark moved off with a stately stride and soon was bowling along at about two knots an hour.

Our party were grouped amidships. At first the talk was a little gloomy and ran mainly upon the shortness of life, the uncertainty of it, the perils which beset it, and the need and wisdom of being always prepared for the worst. This shaded off into low-voiced references to the dangers of the deep and kindred matters. But as the gray east began to redden and the mysterious solemnity and silence of the dawn to give place to the joy-songs of the birds, the talk took a cheerier tone and our spirits began to rise steadily.

Germany in the summer is the perfection of the beautiful

but nobody has understood and realized and enjoyed the utmost possibilities of this soft and peaceful beauty unless he has voyaged down the Neckar on a raft. The motion of a raft is the needful motion. It is gentle and gliding and smooth and noiseless, it calms down all feverish activities, it soothes to sleep all nervous hurry and impatience. Under its restful influence all the troubles and vexations and sorrows that harass the mind vanish away, and existence becomes a dream, a charm, a deep and tranquil ecstasy. How it contrasts with hot and perspiring pedestrianism, and dusty and deafening railroad rush, and tedious jolting behind tired horses over blinding white roads!

We went slipping silently along between the green and fragrant banks, with a sense of pleasure and contentment that grew and grew all the time. Sometimes the banks were overhung with thick masses of willows that wholly hid the ground behind. Sometimes we had noble hills on one hand, clothed densely with foliage to their tops, and on the other hand open levels blazing with poppies or clothed in the rich blue of the corn-flower. Sometimes we drifted in the shadow of forests and sometimes along the margin of long stretches of velvety grass, fresh and green and bright, a tireless charm to the eye. And the birds!—they were everywhere. They swept back and forth across the river constantly, and their jubilant music was never stilled.

It was a deep and satisfying pleasure to see the sun create the new morning, and gradually, patiently, lovingly clothe it on with splendor after splendor and glory after glory till the miracle was complete. How different is this marvel observed from a raft from what it is when one observes it through the dingy windows of a railway-station in some wretched village while he munches a petrified sandwich and waits for the train.

16. Down the River

Men and women and cattle were at work in the dewy fields by this time. The people often stepped aboard the raft as we glided along the grassy shores and gossiped with us and with the crew for a hundred yards or so, then stepped ashore again, refreshed by the ride.

Only the men did this. The women were too busy. The women do all kinds of work on the continent. They dig, they hoe, they reap, they sow, they bear monstrous burdens on their backs, they shove similar ones long distances on wheelbarrows, they drag the cart when there is no dog or lean cow to drag it—and when there is, they assist the dog or cow. Age is no matter—the older the woman the stronger she is, apparently. On the farm a woman's duties are not defined—she does a little of everything. But in the towns it is different, there she only does certain things, the men do the rest. For instance, a hotel chambermaid has nothing to do but make beds and fires in fifty or sixty rooms, bring towels and candles and fetch several tons of water up several flights of stairs, a hundred pounds at a time, in prodigious metal pitchers. She does not have to work more than eighteen or twenty hours a day and she can always get down on her knees and scrub the floors of halls and closets when she is tired and needs a rest.

As the morning advanced and the weather grew hot we took off our outside clothing and sat in a row along the edge of the raft and enjoyed the scenery, with our sun-umbrellas over our heads and our legs dangling in the water. Every now and then we plunged in and had a swim. Every projecting grassy cape had its joyous group of naked children, the boys to themselves and the girls to themselves, the latter usually in care of some motherly dame who sat in the shade of a tree with her knitting. The little boys swam out to us sometimes but the little maids stood knee-deep in the water and stopped their splashing and frolicking to inspect the raft with their innocent eyes as it drifted by. Once we turned a corner suddenly and surprised a slender girl of twelve years or upward, just stepping into the water. She had not time to run but she did what answered just as well. She promptly drew a lithe young willow bough athwart her white body with one hand and then contemplated us with a simple and untroubled interest. Thus she stood while we glided by. She was a pretty creature, and she and her willow bough made a very pretty picture and one which could not offend the modesty of the most fastidious spectator. Her white skin had a low bank of fresh green willows for background and effective contrast—for she stood against them—and above and out of them projected the eager faces and white shoulders of two smaller girls.

Toward noon we heard the inspiriting cry:

"Sail ho!"

"Where away?" shouted the captain.

"Three points off the weather bow!"

We ran forward to see the vessel. It proved to be a steamboat—for they had begun to run a steamer up the Neckar for the first time in May. She was a tug and one of very peculiar build and aspect. I had often watched her from the hotel and wondered how she propelled herself, for apparently she had no propeller or paddles. She came churning along now, making a deal of noise of one kind and another and aggravating it every now and then by blowing a hoarse whistle. She had nine keel-boats hitched on behind and following after her in a long, slender rank. We met her in a narrow place between dikes, and there was hardly room for us both in the cramped passage. As she went grinding and groaning by we perceived the secret of her moving impulse. She did not drive herself up the river with paddles or propeller, she pulled herself by hauling on a great chain. This chain is laid in the bed of the river and is only fastened at the two ends. It is seventy miles long. It comes in over the boat's bow, passes around a drum and is payed out astern. She pulls on that chain and so drags herself up the river or down it. She has neither bow nor stern, strictly speaking, for she has a long-bladed rudder on each end and she never turns around. She uses both rudders all the time, and they are powerful enough to enable her to turn to the right or the left and steer around curves in spite of the strong resistance of the chain. I would not have believed that that impossible thing could be done but I saw it done and therefore I know that there is one impossible thing which *can* be done. What miracle will man attempt next?

We met many big keel-boats on their way up, using sails, mule power and profanity—a tedious and laborious business. A wire rope led from the foretopmast to the file of mules on the tow-path a hundred yards ahead, and by dint of much banging and swearing and urging, the detachment of drivers managed to get a speed of two or three miles an hour out of the mules against the stiff current. The Neckar has always been used as a canal and thus has given employment to a great many men and animals. But now that this steamboat is able, with a small crew and a bushel or so of coal, to take nine keel-boats farther up the river in one hour than thirty men and thirty mules can do it in two, it is believed that the old-fashioned towing industry is on its death-bed. A second steamboat began work in the Neckar three months after the first one was put in service.

At noon we stepped ashore and bought some bottled beer and got some chickens cooked while the raft waited. Then we immediately put to sea again and had our dinner while the beer was cold and the chickens hot. There is no pleasanter place for such a meal than a raft that is gliding down the winding Neckar past green meadows and wooded hills and slumbering villages and craggy heights graced with crumbling towers and battlements.

We made the port of Neckarsteinach in good season and

Bird waiting for a Fish, a
Common Spectacle.
(Perspective of Bird not Correct.)

Raft coming down between Stone Dikes.

Raft curving itself through
Crooked piece of River. (Merely
a Study not a finished
picture)

Rafting on the Neckar

went to the hotel and ordered a trout dinner, the same to be ready against our return from a two-hour pedestrian excursion to the village and castle of Dilsberg, a mile distant, on the other side of the river. I do not mean that we proposed to be two hours making two miles—no, we meant to employ most of the time in inspecting Dilsberg.

For Dilsberg is a quaint place. It is most quaintly and picturesquely situated, too. Imagine the beautiful river before you. Then a few rods of brilliant green sward on its opposite shore. Then a sudden hill—no preparatory gently rising slopes but a sort of instantaneous hill—a hill two hundred and fifty or three hundred feet high, as round as a bowl, with the same taper upward that an inverted bowl has and with about the same relation of height to diameter that distinguishes a bowl of good honest depth—a hill which is thickly clothed with green bushes—a comely, shapely hill rising abruptly out of the dead level of the surrounding green plains, visible from a great distance down the bends of the river, and with just exactly room on the top of its head for its steepled and turreted and roof-clustered cap of architecture, which same is tightly jammed and compacted within the perfectly round hoop of the ancient village wall.

There is no house outside the wall on the whole hill, or any vestige of a former house. All the houses are inside the wall but there isn't room for another one. It is really a finished town and has been finished a very long time. There is no space between the wall and the first circle of buildings. No, the village wall is itself the rear wall of the first circle of buildings, and the roofs jut a little over the wall and thus furnish it with eaves. The general level of the massed roofs is gracefully broken and relieved by the dominating towers of the ruined castle and the tall spires of a couple of churches. So, from a distance Dilsberg has rather more the look of a king's crown than a cap. That lofty green eminence and its quaint coronet form quite a striking picture, you may be sure, in the flush of the evening sun.

We crossed over in a boat and began the ascent by a narrow, steep path which plunged us at once into the leafy deeps of the bushes. But they were not cool deeps by any means, for the sun's rays were weltering hot and there was little or no breeze to temper them. As we panted up the sharp ascent we met brown, bareheaded and barefooted boys and girls occasionally and sometimes men. They came upon us without warning, they gave us good day, flashed out of sight in the bushes and were gone as suddenly and mysteriously as they had come. They were bound for the other side of the river to work. This path had been traveled by many generations of these people. They have always gone down to the valley to earn their bread but they have always climbed their hill again to eat it and to sleep in their snug town.

It is said that the Dilsbergers do not emigrate much. They find that living up there above the world in their peaceful nest is pleasanter than living down in the troublous world. The seven hundred inhabitants are all blood-kin to each other, too. They have always been blood-kin to each other for fifteen hundred years. They are simply one large family, and they like the home folks better than they like strangers, hence they persistently stay at home. It has been said that for ages Dilsberg has been merely a thriving and diligent idiot-factory. I saw no idiots there, but the captain said, "Because of late years the government has taken to lugging them off to asylums and otherwheres. And government wants to cripple the factory, too, and is trying to get these Dilsbergers to marry out of the family, but they don't like to."

The captain probably imagined all this, as modern science denies that the intermarrying of relatives deteriorates the stock.

Arrived within the wall, we found the usual village sights and life. We moved along a narrow, crooked lane which had been paved in the Middle Ages. A strapping, ruddy girl was beating flax or some such stuff in a little bit of a goods-box of a barn, and she swung her flail with a will—if it was a flail. I was not farmer enough to know what she was at. A frowsy, barelegged girl was herding half a dozen geese with a stick

—driving them along the lane and keeping them out of the dwellings. A cooper was at work in a shop which I know he did not make so large a thing as a hogshead in, for there was not room. In the front rooms of dwellings girls and women were cooking or spinning, and ducks and chickens were waddling in and out over the threshold, picking up chance crumbs and holding pleasant converse. A very old and wrinkled man sat asleep before his door, with his chin upon his breast and his extinguished pipe in his lap. Soiled children were playing in the dirt everywhere along the lane, unmindful of the sun.

Except the sleeping old man, everybody was at work, but the place was very still and peaceful nevertheless, so still that the distant cackle of the successful hen smote upon the ear but little dulled by intervening sounds. That commonest of village sights was lacking here—the public pump, with its great stone tank or trough of limpid water and its group of gossiping pitcher-bearers, for there is no well or fountain or spring on this tall hill. Cisterns of rain-water are used.

Our alpenstocks and muslin tails compelled attention, and as we moved through the village we gathered a considerable procession of little boys and girls and so went in some state to the castle. It proved to be an extensive pile of crumbling walls, arches and towers, massive, properly grouped for picturesque effect, weedy, grass-grown and satisfactory. The children acted as guides. They walked us along the top of the highest wall, then took us up into a high tower and showed us a wide and beautiful landscape made up of wavy distances of woody hills, and a nearer prospect of undulating expanses of green lowlands, on the one hand, and castle-graced crags and ridges on the other, with the shining curves of the Neckar flowing between. But the principal show, the chief pride of the children, was the ancient and empty well in the grass-grown court of the castle. Its massive stone curb stands up three or four feet above-ground and is whole and uninjured. The children said that in the Middle Ages this well was four hundred feet deep and furnished all the village with an abundant supply of water in war and peace. They said that in that old day its bottom was below the level of the Neckar, hence the water-supply was inexhaustible.

But there were some who believed it had never been a well at all and was never deeper than it is now—eighty feet; that at that depth a subterranean passage branched from it and descended gradually to a remote place in the valley, where it opened into somebody's cellar or other hidden recess, and that the secret of this locality is now lost. Those who hold this belief say that herein lies the explanation that Dilsberg, besieged by Tilly and many a soldier before him, was never taken: after the longest and closest sieges the besiegers were astonished to perceive that the besieged were as fat and hearty as ever, and as well furnished with munitions of war —therefore it must be that the Dilsbergers had been bringing these things in through the subterranean passage all the time.

The children said that there was in truth a subterranean outlet down there, and they would prove it. So they set a great truss of straw on fire and threw it down the well while we leaned on the curb and watched the glowing mass descend. It struck bottom and gradually burned out. No smoke came up. The children clapped their hands and said:

"You see! Nothing makes so much smoke as burning straw —now where did the smoke go to, if there is no subterranean outlet?"

So it seemed quite evident that the subterranean outlet indeed existed. But the finest thing within the ruin's limits was a noble linden which the children said was four hundred years old, and no doubt it was. It had a mighty trunk and a mighty spread of limb and foliage. The limbs near the ground were nearly the thickness of a barrel.

That tree had witnessed the assaults of men in mail—how remote such a time seems, and how ungraspable is the fact that real men ever did fight in real armor!—and it had seen the time when these broken arches and crumbling battlements were a trim and strong and stately fortress, fluttering

its gay banners in the sun, and peopled with vigorous humanity—how impossibly long ago that seems!—and here it stands
yet and possibly may still be standing here, sunning itself and
dreaming its historical dreams, when to-day shall have been
joined to the days called "ancient."

We returned to Neckarsteinach, plunged our hot heads
into the trough at the town pump and then went to the
hotel and ate our trout dinner in leisurely comfort in the
garden, with the beautiful Neckar flowing at our feet, the
quaint Dilsberg looming beyond and the graceful towers
and battlements of a couple of medieval castles (called the
"Swallow's Nest" and "The Brothers") assisting the rugged
scenery of a bend of the river down to our right. We got to
sea in season to make the eight-mile run to Heidelberg before the night shut down. We sailed by the hotel in the
mellow glow of sunset and came slashing down with the
mad current into the narrow passage between the dikes. I
believed I could shoot the bridge myself, so I went to the
forward triplet of logs and relieved the pilot of his pole and
his responsibility.

We went tearing along in a most exhilarating way and I
performed the delicate duties of my office very well indeed
for a first attempt. But perceiving, presently, that I really was
going to shoot the bridge itself instead of the archway under
it, I judiciously stepped ashore. The next moment I had my
longcoveted desire: I saw a raft wrecked. It hit the pier in the
center and went all to smash and scatteration like a box of
matches struck by lightning.

I was the only one of our party who saw this grand sight.
The others were attitudinizing for the benefit of the long
rank of young ladies who were promenading on the bank and
so they lost it. But I helped to fish them out of the river down
below the bridge and then described it to them as well as I
could.

They were not interested, though. They said they were
wet and felt ridiculous and did not care anything for descriptions of scenery. The young ladies and other people crowded

around and showed a great deal of sympathy but that did not help matters, for my friends said they did not want sympathy, they wanted a back alley and solitude.

17. Cholley Adams

Next morning brought good news—our trunks had arrived from Hamburg at last. Let this be a warning to the reader. The Germans are very conscientious, and this trait makes them very particular. Therefore if you tell a German you want a thing done immediately he takes you at your word. He thinks you mean what you say. So he does that thing immediately—according to his idea of immediately—which is about a week. That is, it is a week if it refers to the building of a garment, or it is an hour and a half if it refers to the cooking of a trout. Very well. If you tell a German to send your trunk to you by "slow freight" he takes you at your word, he sends it by "slow freight," and you cannot imagine how long you will go on enlarging your admiration of the expressiveness of that phrase in the German tongue before you get that trunk. The hair on my trunk was soft and thick and youthful when I got it ready for shipment in Hamburg. It was baldheaded when it reached Heidelberg. However, it was still sound, that was a comfort, it was not battered in the least. The baggagemen seemed to be conscientiously careful, in Germany, of the baggage intrusted to their hands. There was nothing now in the way of our departure, therefore we set about our preparations.

Naturally my chief solicitude was about my collection of Ceramics. Of course I could not take it with me, that would be inconvenient, and dangerous besides. I took advice, but the best brick-a-brackers were divided as to the wisest course to pursue. Some said pack the collection and warehouse it. Others said try to get it into the Grand Ducal Museum at Mannheim for safe keeping. So I divided the collection and followed the advice of both parties. I set aside for the Museum those articles which were the most frail and precious.

Among these was my Etruscan tear-jug. I have made a little sketch of it here. That thing creeping up the side is not a bug, it is a hole. I bought this tear-jug of a dealer in antiquities for four hundred and fifty dollars. It is very rare. The man said the Etruscans used to keep tears or something in these things and that it was very hard to get hold of a broken one now. I also set aside my Henri II plate. See sketch from my pencil. It is in the main correct, though I think I have foreshortened one end of it a little too much, perhaps. This is very fine and rare. The shape is exceedingly beautiful and unusual. It has wonderful decorations on it but I am not able to reproduce them. It cost more than the tear-jug, as the dealer said there was not another plate just like it in the world. He said there was much false Henri II ware around but that the genuineness of this piece was unquestionable. He showed me its pedigree or its history, if you please. It was a document which traced this plate's movements all the way down from its birth—showed who bought it from whom and what he paid for it—from the first buyer down to me,

Henri II Plate

Etruscan Tear-Jug

whereby I saw that it had gone steadily up from thirty-five cents to seven hundred dollars. He said that the whole Ceramic world would be informed that it was now in my possession and would make a note of it, with the price paid.

There were Masters in those days, but, alas—it is not so now. Of course the main preciousness of this piece lies in its color. It is that old sensuous, pervading, ramifying, interpolating, transboreal blue which is the despair of modern art. The little sketch which I have made of this gem cannot and does not do it justice, since I have been obliged to leave out the color. But I've got the expression, though.

However, I must not be frittering away the reader's time with these details. I did not intend to go into any detail at all at first but it is the failing of the true ceramiker or the true devotee in any department of brick-a-brackery, that once he gets his tongue or his pen started on his darling theme he cannot well stop until he drops from exhaustion. He has no more sense of the flight of time than has any other lover when talking of his sweetheart. The very "marks" on the bottom of a piece of rare crockery are able to throw me into a gibbering ecstasy and I could forsake a drowning relative to help dispute about whether the stopple of a departed Buon Retiro scent-bottle was genuine or spurious.

Many people say that for a male person, bric-a-brac hunting is about as robust a business as making doll-clothes or decorating Japanese pots with decal-comanie butterflies would be, and these people fling mud at that elegant Englishman, Byng, who wrote a book called *The Bric-a-Brac Hunter*, and make fun of him for chasing around after what they choose to call "his despicable trifles" and for "gushing" over these trifles and for exhibiting his "deep infantile delight" in what they call his "tuppenny collection of beggarly trivialities" and for beginning his book with a picture of himself seated in a "sappy, self-complacent attitude in the midst of his poor little ridiculous bric-a-brac junk shop."

It is easy to say these things, it is easy to revile us, easy to despise us, therefore let these people rail on, they cannot feel

Old Blue China.

I also set apart my exquisite specimen of Old Blue China

This is considered to be the finest example of Chinese art now in existence; I do not refer to the bastard Chinese art of modern times but that noble & pure & genuine art which flourished under the fostering & appreciative care of the Emperors of the Chung-a Lung-Fung dynasty. -

Old Blue China

as Byng and I feel—it is their loss, not ours. For my part I am content to be a brick-a-bracker and a ceramiker—more, I am proud to be so named. I am proud to know that I lose my reason as immediately in the presence of a rare jug with an illustrious mark on the bottom of it as if I had just emptied that jug. Very well. I packed and stored a part of my collection, and the rest of it I placed in the care of the Grand Ducal Museum in Mannheim, by permission. My Old Blue China Cat remains there yet. I presented it to that excellent institution.

I had but one misfortune with my things. An egg which I had kept back from breakfast that morning was broken in packing. It was a great pity. I had shown it to the best connoisseurs in Heidelberg and they all said it was an antique. We spent a day or two in farewell visits and then left for Baden-Baden. We had a pleasant trip of it, for the Rhine valley is always lovely. The only trouble was that the trip was too short. If I remember rightly it only occupied a couple of hours, therefore I judge that the distance was very little, if any, over fifty miles. We quitted the train at Oos and walked the entire remaining distance to Baden-Baden, with the exception of a lift of less than an hour which we got on a passing wagon, the weather being exhaustingly warm. We came into town on foot.

One of the first persons we encountered as we walked up the street was the Rev. Mr.——, an old friend from America —a lucky encounter, indeed, for his is a most gentle, refined and sensitive nature and his company and companionship are a genuine refreshment. We knew he had been in Europe some time but were not at all expecting to run across him. Both parties burst forth into loving enthusiasms, and Rev. Mr.——said:

"I have got a brimful reservoir of talk to pour out on you and an empty one ready and thirsting to receive what you have got. We will sit up till midnight and have a good satisfying interchange, for I leave here early in the morning." We agreed to that, of course.

I had been vaguely conscious for a while of a person who was walking in the street abreast of us. I had glanced furtively at him once or twice, and noticed that he was a fine, large, vigorous young fellow with an open, independent countenance, faintly shaded with a pale and even almost imperceptible crop of early down, and that he was clothed from head to heel in cool and enviable snow-white linen. I thought I had also noticed that his head had a sort of listening tilt to it. Now about this time the Rev. Mr.——said:

"The sidewalk is hardly wide enough for three, so I will walk behind, but keep the talk going, keep the talk going, there's no time to lose, and you may be sure I will do my share." He ranged himself behind us, and straightway that stately snow-white young fellow closed up to the sidewalk alongside him, fetched him a cordial slap on the shoulder with his broad palm and sung out with a hearty cheeriness:

"Americans for two-and-a-half and the money up! *Hey?"*

The Reverend winced, but said mildly:

"Yes—we are Americans."

"Lord love you, you can just bet that's what *I* am, every time! Put it there!"

He held out his Sahara of a palm, and the Reverend laid his diminutive hand in it and got so cordial a shake that we heard his glove burst under it.

"Say, didn't I put you up right?"

"Oh yes."

"Sho! I spotted you for *my* kind the minute I heard your clack. You been over here long?"

"About four months. Have you been over long?"

"Long? Well, I should say so! Going on two *years,* by geeminy! Say, are you homesick?"

"No, I can't say that I am. Are you?"

"Oh, *hell* yes!" This with immense enthusiasm.

The Reverend shrunk a little in his clothes, and we were aware, rather by instinct than otherwise, that he was throwing out signals of distress to us. But we did not interfere or try to succor him, for we were quite happy.

The young fellow hooked his arm into the Reverend's now with the confiding and grateful air of a waif who has been longing for a friend and a sympathetic ear and a chance to lisp once more the sweet accents of the mother-tongue—and then he limbered up the muscles of his mouth and turned himself loose—and with such a relish! Some of his words were not Sunday-school words, so I am obliged to put blanks where they occur.

"Yes indeed! If *I* ain't an American there *ain't* any Americans, that's all. And when I heard you fellows gassing away in the good old American language, I'm ——— if it wasn't all I could do to keep from hugging you! My tongue's all warped with trying to curl it around these ——— forsaken wind-galled nine-jointed German words here. Now I *tell* you it's awful good to lay it over a Christian word once more and kind of let the old taste soak in. I'm from western New York. My name is Cholley Adams. I'm a student, you know. Been here going on two years. I'm learning to be a horse-doctor! I *like* that part of it, you know, but ——— these people, they won't learn a fellow in his own language, they make him learn in German. So before I could tackle the horse-doctoring I had to tackle this miserable language.

"First off, I thought it would certainly give me the botts but I don't mind it now. I've got it where the hair's short, I think. And dontchuknow, they made me learn Latin too. Now between you and me, I wouldn't give a ——— for all the Latin that was ever jabbered. And the first thing I calculate to do when I get through, is to just sit down and forget it. 'Twon't take me long and I don't mind the time anyway. And I tell you what! The difference between school-teaching over yonder and school-teaching over here—sho! *We* don't know anything about it! Here you've got to peg and peg and peg and there just ain't any let-up—and what you learn here, you've got to *know*, dontchuknow—or else you'll have one of these ——— spavined, spectacled, ring-boned, knock-kneed old professors in your hair. I've been here long *enough* and I'm

getting blessed tired of it, mind I *tell* you. The old man wrote
me that he was coming over in June and said he'd take me
home in August whether I was done with my education or
not, but durn him, he didn't come. Never said why. Just sent
me a hamper of Sunday-school books and told me to be good
and hold on a while. I don't take to Sunday-school books,
dontchuknow—I don't hanker after them when I can get pie
—but I *read* them anyway because whatever the old man
tells me to do, that's the thing that I'm a-going to *do,* or tear
something, you know. I buckled in and read all of those books
because he wanted me to but that kind of thing don't excite
me, I like something *hearty.* But I'm awful homesick. I'm
homesick from ear-socket to crupper and from crupper to
hock-joint but it ain't any use, I've got to stay here til the old
man drops the rag and gives the word—yes, *sir,* right here
in this ——— country I've got to linger till the old man says
Come!—and you bet your bottom dollar, Johnny, it *ain't* just
as easy as it is for a cat to have twins!"

At the end of this profane and cordial explosion he fetched
a prodigious *"Whoosh!"* to relieve his lungs and make recognition of the heat and then he straightway dived into
his narrative again for "Johnny's" benefit, beginning, "Well,
——— it ain't any use talking, some of those old American
words *do* have a kind of a bully swing to them, a man can
express himself with 'em—a man can get at what he wants
to *say,* dontchuknow."

When we reached our hotel and it seemed that he was
about to lose the Reverend he showed so much sorrow and
begged so hard and so earnestly that the Reverend's heart
was not hard enough to hold out against the pleadings—so he
went away with the parent-honoring student like a right
Christian and took supper with him in his lodgings and sat in
the surf-beat of his slang and profanity till near midnight and
then left him—left him pretty well talked out but grateful
"clear down to his frogs," as he expressed it. The Reverend
said it had transpired during the interview that "Cholley"
Adams's father was an extensive dealer in horses in western

New York. This accounted for Cholley's choice of a profession. The Reverend brought away a pretty high opinion of Cholley as a manly young fellow, with stuff in him for a useful citizen. He considered him rather a rough gem but a gem nevertheless.

18. Baden-Baden

Baden-Baden sits in the lap of the hills, and the natural and artificial beauties of the surroundings are combined effectively and charmingly. The level strip of ground which stretches through and beyond the town is laid out in handsome pleasure grounds shaded by noble trees and adorned at intervals with lofty and sparkling fountain-jets. Thrice a day a fine band makes music in the public promenade before the Conversation House, and in the afternoon and evening that locality is populous with fashionably dressed people of both sexes who march back and forth past the great music-stand and look very much bored though they make a show of feeling otherwise. It seems like a rather aimless and stupid existence. A good many of these people are there for a real purpose, however. They are racked with rheumatism and they are there to stew it out in the hot baths. These invalids looked melancholy enough, limping about on their canes and crutches and apparently brooding over all sorts of cheerless things. People say that Germany, with her damp stone houses, is the home of rheumatism. If that is so, Providence must have foreseen that it would be so and therefore filled the land with these healing baths. Perhaps no other country is so generously supplied with medicinal springs as Germany.

Some of these baths are good for one ailment, some for another. And again, peculiar ailments are conquered by combining the individual virtues of several different baths. For instance, for some forms of disease, the patient drinks the native hot water of Baden-Baden with a spoonful of salt from the Carlsbad springs dissolved in it. That is not a dose to be forgotten right away.

They don't *sell* this hot water. No, you go into the great Trinkhalle and stand around, first on one foot and then on the other, while two or three young girls sit pottering at some sort of ladylike sewing-work in your neighborhood and can't seem to see you—polite as three-dollar clerks in government offices.

By and by one of these rises painfully and "stretches"— stretches fists and body heavenward till she raises her heels from the floor, at the same time refreshing herself with a yawn of such comprehensiveness that the bulk of her face disappears behind her upper lip and one is able to see how she is constructed inside—then she slowly closes her cavern, brings down her fists and her heels, comes languidly forward, contemplates you contemptuously, draws you a glass of hot water and sets it down where you can get it by reaching for it. You take it and say:

"How much?"—and she returns you, with elaborate indifference, a beggar's answer:

"Nach Beliebe." (What you please.)

This thing of using the common beggar's trick and the common beggar's shibboleth to put you on your liberality when you were expecting a simple straightforward commercial transaction adds a little to your prospering sense of irritation. You ignore her reply and ask again:

"How much?"

—and she calmly, indifferently, repeats:

"Nach Beliebe."

You are getting angry but you are trying not to show it. You resolve to keep on asking your question till she changes her answer, or at least her annoyingly indifferent manner. Therefore, if your case be like mine, you two fools stand there, and without perceptible emotion of any kind or any emphasis on any syllable you look blandly into each other's eyes and hold the following idiotic conversation:

"How much?"

"Nach Beliebe."

"How much?"

"Nach Beliebe."

"How much?"

"Nach Beliebe."

"How much?"

"Nach Beliebe."

"How much?"

"Nach Beliebe."

"How much?"

"Nach Beliebe."

I do not know what another person would have done but at this point I gave it up. That cast-iron indifference, that tranquil contemptuousness conquered me and I struck my colors. Now I knew she was used to receiving about a penny from manly people who care nothing about the opinions of scullery-maids, and about tuppence from moral cowards. But I laid a silver twenty-five cent piece within her reach and tried to shrivel her up with this sarcastic speech:

"If it isn't enough will you stoop sufficiently from your official dignity to say so?"

She did not shrivel. Without deigning to look at me at all, she languidly lifted the coin and bit it!—to see if it was good. Then she turned her back and placidly waddled to her former roost again, tossing the money into an open till as she went along. She was victor to the last, you see.

I have enlarged upon the ways of this girl because they are typical. Her manners are the manners of a goodly number of the Baden-Baden shopkeepers. The shopkeeper there swindles you if he can and insults you whether he succeeds in swindling you or not. The keepers of baths also take great and patient pains to insult you. The frowsy woman who sat at the desk in the lobby of the great Friederichsbad and sold bath

tickets not only insulted me twice every day with rigid
fidelity to her great trust but she took trouble enough to
cheat me out of a shilling, one day, to have fairly entitled her
to ten. Baden-Baden's splendid gamblers are gone, only her
microscopic knaves remain.

An English gentleman who had been living there several
years said:

"If you could disguise your nationality you would not find
any insolence here. These shopkeepers detest the English
and despise the Americans. They are rude to both, more
especially to ladies of your nationality and mine. If these go
shopping without a gentleman or a man-servant they are
tolerably sure to be subjected to petty insolences—insolences
of manner and tone rather than word, though words that are
hard to bear are not always wanting. I know of an instance
where a shopkeeper tossed a coin back to an American lady
with the remark, snappishly uttered, 'We don't take French
money here.' And I know of a case where an English lady said
to one of these shopkeepers, 'Don't you think you ask too
much for this article?' and he replied with the question, 'Do
you think you are obliged to buy it?' However, these people
are not impolite to Russians or Germans. And as to rank, they
worship that, for they have long been used to generals and
nobles. If you wish to see to what abysses servility can descend, present yourself before a Baden-Baden shopkeeper in
the character of a Russian prince."

It is an inane town filled with sham and petty fraud and
snobbery, but the baths are good. I spoke with many people and they were all agreed in that. I had had twinges of
rheumatism unceasingly during three years, but the last
one departed after a fortnight's bathing there and I have
never had one since. I fully believe I left my rheumatism
in Baden-Baden. Baden-Baden is welcome to it. It was little but it was all I had to give. I would have preferred to
leave something that was catching but it was not in my
power.

There are several hot springs there and during two thousand years they have poured forth a never-diminishing abun-

dance of the healing water. This water is conducted in pipes to the numerous bath-houses and is reduced to an endurable temperature by the addition of cold water. The new Friederichsbad is a very large and beautiful building, and in it one may have any sort of bath that has ever been invented, and with all the additions of herbs and drugs that his ailment may need or that the physician of the establishment may consider a useful thing to put into the water. You go there, enter the great door, get a bow graduated to your style and clothes from the gorgeous portier, and a bath ticket and an insult from the frowsy woman for a quarter. She strikes a bell and a serving-man conducts you down a long hall and shuts you into a commodious room which has a washstand, a mirror, a bootjack and a sofa in it, and there you undress at your leisure.

The room is divided by a great curtain. You draw this curtain aside and find a large white marble bathtub with its rim sunk to the level of the floor and with three white marble steps leading down into it. This tub is full of water which is as clear as crystal, and is tempered to 28 degrees Réaumur (about 95 degrees Fahrenheit). Sunk into the floor, by the tub, is a covered copper box which contains some warm towels and a sheet. You look fully as white as an angel when you are stretched out in that limpid bath. You remain in it ten minutes the first time and afterward increase the duration from day to day till you reach twenty-five or thirty minutes. There you stop. The appointments of the place are so luxurious, the benefit so marked, the price so moderate and the insults so sure that you very soon find yourself adoring the Friederichsbad and infesting it.

We had a plain, simple, unpretending, good hotel in Baden-Baden—the Hôtel de France—and alongside my room I had a giggling, cackling, chattering family who always went to bed just two hours after me and always got up just two hours ahead of me. But that is common in German hotels. The people generally go to bed long after eleven and get up long before eight. The partitions convey sound like a drumhead and everybody knows it. But no matter, a German family who are all kindness and consideration in the daytime make apparently no effort to moderate their noises for your benefit at night. They will sing, laugh and talk loudly and bang furniture around in the most pitiless way. If you knock on your wall appealingly they will quiet down and discuss the matter softly among themselves for a moment—then, like the mice, they fall to persecuting you again and as vigorously as before. They keep cruelly late and early hours for such noisy folk.

Of course, when one begins to find fault with foreign people's ways he is very likely to get a reminder to look nearer home before he gets far with it. I open my note-book to see if I can find some more information of a valuable nature about Baden-Baden, and the first thing I fall upon is this:

"*Baden-Baden* (no date). Lot of vociferous Americans at breakfast this morning. Talking *at* everybody while pretending to talk among themselves. On their first travels, manifestly. Showing off. The usual signs—airy, easy-going references to grand distances and foreign places. 'Well, *good*-by, old fellow—if I don't run across you in Italy, you hunt me up in London before you sail.' "

The next item which I find in my note-book is this one:

"The fact that a band of 6,000 Indians are now murdering our frontiersmen at their impudent leisure and that we are only able to send 1,200 soldiers against them is utilized here to discourage emigration to America. The common people think the Indians are in New Jersey."

This is a new and peculiar argument against keeping our army down to a ridiculous figure in the matter of numbers. It is rather a striking one, too. I have not distorted the truth in saying that the facts in the above item, about the army and the Indians, are made use of to discourage emigration to America. That the common people should be rather foggy in their geography and foggy as to the location of the Indians is matter for amusement, maybe, but not of surprise.

There is an interesting old cemetery in Baden-Baden and

we spent several pleasant hours in wandering through it and spelling out the inscriptions on the aged tombstones. Apparently after a man has lain there a century or two and has had a good many people buried on top of him it is considered that his tombstone is not needed by him any longer. I judge so from the fact that hundreds of old gravestones have been removed from the graves and placed against the inner walls of the cemetery. What artists they had in the old times! They chiseled angels and cherubs and devils and skeletons on the tombstones in the most lavish and generous way—as to supply—but curiously grotesque and outlandish as to form. It is not always easy to tell which of the figures belong among the blest and which of them among the opposite party. But there was an inscription in French on one of those old stones which was quaint and pretty and was plainly not the work of any other than a poet. It was to this effect:

HERE
REPOSES IN GOD,
CAROLINE DE CLERY,
A RELIGIEUSE OF ST. DENIS,
AGED 83 YEARS—AND BLIND.
THE LIGHT WAS RESTORED TO HER
IN BADEN THE 5TH OF JANUARY,
1839.

We made several excursions on foot to the neighboring villages, over winding and beautiful roads and through enchanting woodland scenery. The woods and roads were similar to those at Heidelberg but not so bewitching. I suppose that roads and woods which are up to the Heidelberg mark are rare in the world.

Once we wandered clear away to La Favorita Palace, which is several miles from Baden-Baden. The grounds about the palace were fine. The palace was a curiosity. It was built by a Margravine in 1725 and remains as she left it at her death. We wandered through a great many of its rooms, and they all had striking peculiarities of decoration. For instance, the walls of one room were pretty completely covered with small pictures of the Margravine in all conceivable varieties of fanciful costumes, some of them male.

The walls of another room were covered with grotesquely and elaborately figured hand-wrought tapestry. The musty ancient beds remained in the chambers, and their quilts and curtains and canopies were decorated with curious hand-work, and the walls and ceilings frescoed with historical and mythological scenes in glaring colors. There was enough crazy and rotten rubbish in the building to make the true brick-a-bracker green with envy. A painting in the dining-hall verged upon the indelicate—but then the Margravine was herself a trifle indelicate.

It is in every way a wildly and picturesquely decorated house and brimful of interest as a reflection of the character and tastes of that rude bygone time.

In the grounds a few rods from the palace stands the Margravine's chapel just as she left it—a coarse wooden structure wholly barren of ornament. It is said that the Margravine would give herself up to debauchery and exceedingly fast living for several months at a time and then retire to this miserable wooden den and spend a few months in repenting and getting ready for another good time. She was a devoted Catholic and was perhaps quite a model sort of a Christian as Christians went then, in high life.

Tradition says she spent the last two years of her life in the strange den I have been speaking of after having indulged herself in one final, triumphant and satisfying spree. She shut herself up there without company and without even a servant, and so abjured and forsook the world. In her little bit of a kitchen she did her own cooking. She wore a hair shirt next the skin and castigated herself with whips—these aids to grace are exhibited there yet. She prayed and told her beads in another little room before a waxen Virgin niched in a little box against the wall. She bedded herself like a slave.

In another small room is an unpainted wooden table, and behind it sit half-life-size waxen figures of the Holy Family

made by the very worst artist that ever lived, perhaps, and
clothed in gaudy, flimsy drapery.* The Margravine used to
bring her meals to this table and *dine with the Holy Family.*
What an idea that was! What a grisly spectacle it must have
been! Imagine it: Those rigid, shock-headed figures, with
corpsy complexions and fishy glass eyes, occupying one side
of the table in the constrained attitudes and dead fixedness
that distinguish all men that are born of wax, and this wrinkled, smoldering old fire-eater occupying the other side,
mumbling her prayers and munching her sausages in the
ghostly stillness and shadowy indistinctness of a winter twilight. It makes one feel crawly even to think of it.

In this sordid place, and clothed, bedded and fed like a
pauper, this strange princess lived and worshiped during two
years, and in it she died. Two or three hundred years ago this
would have made the poor den holy ground and the church
would have set up a miracle-factory there and made plenty
of money out of it. The den could be moved into some portions of France and made a good property even now.

19. The Black Forest

From Baden-Baden we made the customary trip into the
Black Forest. We were on foot most of the time. One cannot
describe those noble woods, nor the feeling with which they
inspire him. A feature of the feeling, however, is a deep sense
of contentment. Another feature of it is a buoyant, boyish

---

*The Saviour was represented as a lad of about fifteen years of age. This
figure had lost one eye.

gladness. And a third and very conspicuous feature of it is one's sense of the remoteness of the work-day world and his entire emancipation from it and its affairs.

Those woods stretch unbroken over a vast region, and everywhere they are such dense woods and so still and so piney and fragrant. The stems of the trees are trim and straight, and in many places all the ground is hidden for miles under a thick cushion of moss of a vivid green color, with not a decayed or ragged spot in its surface and not a fallen leaf or twig to mar its immaculate tidiness. A rich cathedral gloom pervades the pillared aisles, so the stray flecks of sunlight that strike a trunk here and a bough yonder are strongly accented, and when they strike the moss they fairly seem to burn. But the weirdest effect and the most enchanting is that produced by the diffused light of the low afternoon sun. No single ray is able to pierce its way in then, but the diffused light takes color from moss and foliage and pervades the place like a faint, green-tinted mist, the theatrical fire of fairyland. The suggestion of mystery and the supernatural which haunts the forest at all times is intensified by this unearthly glow.

We found the Black Forest farmhouses and villages all that the Black Forest stories have pictured them. The first genuine specimen which we came upon was the mansion of a rich farmer and member of the Common Council of the parish or district. He was an important personage in the land and so was his wife also, of course. His daughter was the "catch" of the region and she may be already entering into immortality as the heroine of one of Auerbach's novels, for all I know. We shall see, for if he puts her in I shall recognize her by her Black Forest clothes and her burned complexion, her plump figure, her fat hands, her dull expression, her gentle spirit, her generous feet, her bonnetless head, and the plaited tails of hemp-colored hair hanging down her back.

The house was big enough for a hotel. It was a hundred feet long and fifty wide, and ten feet high from ground to eaves, but from the eaves to the comb of the mighty roof was as much as forty feet or maybe even more. This roof was of ancient mud-colored straw thatch a foot thick and was covered all over, except in a few trifling spots, with a thriving and luxurious growth of green vegetation, mainly moss. The mossless spots were places where repairs had been made by the insertion of bright new masses of yellow straw. The eaves projected far down like sheltering, hospitable wings. Across the gable that fronted the road, and about ten feet above the ground, ran a narrow porch with a wooden railing. A row of small windows filled with very small panes looked upon the porch. Above were two or three other little windows, one clear up under the sharp apex of the roof. Before the ground-floor door was a huge pile of manure. The door of a second-story room on the side of the house was open, and occupied by the rear elevation of a cow. Was this probably the drawing-room? All of the front half of the house from the ground up seemed to be occupied by the people, the cows and the chickens, and all the rear half by draught-animals and hay. But the chief feature all around this house was the big heaps of manure.

We became very familiar with the fertilizer in the Forest. We fell unconsciously into the habit of judging of a man's station in life by this outward and eloquent sign. Sometimes we said, "Here is a poor devil, this is manifest." When we saw a stately accumulation we said, "Here is a banker." When we encountered a country-seat surrounded by an Alpine pomp of manure we said, "Doubtless a duke lives here."

The importance of this feature has not been properly magnified in the Black Forest stories. Manure is evidently the Black-Forester's main treasure—his coin, his jewel, his pride, his Old Master, his ceramics, his bric-a-brac, his darling, his title to public consideration, envy, veneration, and his first solicitude when he gets ready to make his will. The true Black Forest novel, if it is ever written, will be skeletoned somewhat in this way:

Skeleton for Black Forest Novel

Rich old farmer, named Huss. Has inherited great wealth of manure, and by diligence has added to it. It is double-starred in Baedeker.* The Black Forest artist paints it—his masterpiece. The king comes to see it. Gretchen Huss, daughter and heiress. Paul Hoch, young neighbor, suitor for Gretchen's hand—ostensibly. He really wants the manure. Hoch has a good many cart-loads of the Black Forest currency himself and therefore is a good catch but he is sordid, mean and without sentiment, whereas Gretchen is all sentiment and poetry. Hans Schmidt, young neighbor, full of sentiment, full of poetry, loves Gretchen, Gretchen loves him. But he has no manure. Old Huss forbids him the house. His heart breaks, he goes away to die in the woods, far from the cruel world—for he says bitterly, "What is man without manure?"

[Interval of six months.]

Paul Hoch comes to old Huss and says, "I am at last as rich as you required—come and view the pile." Old Huss views it and says, "It is sufficient—take her and be happy"—meaning Gretchen.

[Interval of two weeks.]

Wedding party assembled in old Huss's drawing-room. Hoch placid and content, Gretchen weeping over her hard fate. Enter old Huss's head bookkeeper. Huss says fiercely, "I gave you three weeks to find out why your books don't balance and to prove that you are not a defaulter. The time is up—find me the missing property or you go to prison as a thief." Bookkeeper: "I have found it." "Where?" Bookkeeper (sternly—tragically): "In the bridegroom's pile!—behold the thief—see him blench and tremble!" [Sensation.] Paul Hoch: "Lost, lost!"—falls over the cow in a swoon and is handcuffed.

*When Baedeker's guide-books mention a thing and put two stars (**) after it, it means well worth visiting.

Gretchen: "Saved!" Falls over the calf in a swoon of joy but is caught in the arms of Hans Schmidt, who springs in at that moment. Old Huss: "What, you here, varlet? Unhand the maid and quit the place." Hans (still supporting the insensible girl): "Never! Cruel old man, know that I come with claims which even you cannot despise."

Huss: "What, *you?* name them."

Hans: "Then listen. The world had forsaken me, I forsook the world, I wandered in the solitude of the forest, longing for death but finding none. I fed upon roots, and in my bitterness I dug for the bitterest, loathing the sweeter kind. Digging, three days agone, I struck a manure mine!—a Golconda, a limitless Bonanza, of solid manure! I can buy you *all* and have mountain ranges of manure left! Ha-ha, *now* thou smilest a smile!" [Immense sensation.] Exhibition of specimens from the mine. Old Huss (enthusiastically): "Wake her up, shake her up, noble young man, she is yours!" Wedding takes place on the spot. Bookkeeper restored to his office and emoluments. Paul Hoch led off to jail. The Bonanza king of the Black Forest lives to a good old age, blessed with the love of his wife and of his twenty-seven children, and the still sweeter envy of everybody around.

We took our noon meal of fried trout one day at the Plow Inn in a very pretty village (Ottenhöfen), and then went into the public room to rest and smoke. There we found nine or ten Black Forest grandees assembled around a table. They were the Common Council of the parish. They had gathered there at eight o'clock that morning to elect a new member and they had now been drinking beer four hours at the new member's expense. They were men of fifty or sixty years of age, with grave good-natured faces, and were all dressed in the costume made familiar to us by the Black Forest stories. Broad, round-topped black felt hats with the brims curled up all round. Long red waistcoats with large metal buttons, black alpaca coats with the waists up between the shoulders. There were no speeches, there was but little talk, there were

no frivolities. The Council filled themselves gradually, steadily, but surely, with beer and conducted themselves with
sedate decorum, as became men of position, men of influence, men of manure.

We had a hot afternoon tramp up the valley along the
grassy bank of a rushing stream of clear water, past farmhouses, water-mills and no end of wayside crucifixes and
saints and Virgins. These crucifixes, etc., are set up in memory of departed friends by survivors and are almost as frequent as telegraph-poles are in other lands.

We followed the carriage-road and had our usual luck. We
traveled under a beating sun and always saw the shade leave
the shady places before we could get to them. In all our
wanderings we seldom managed to strike a piece of road at
its time for being shady. We had a particularly hot time of it
on that particular afternoon, and with no comfort but what
we could get out of the fact that the peasants at work away
up on the steep mountainsides above our heads were even
worse off than we were. By and by it became impossible to
endure the intolerable glare and heat any longer, so we
struck across the ravine and entered the deep cool twilight
of the forest to hunt for what the guide-book called the "old
road."

We found an old road and it proved eventually to be the
right one, though we followed it at the time with the conviction that it was the wrong one. If it was the wrong one there
could be no use in hurrying, therefore we did not hurry, but
sat down frequently on the soft moss and enjoyed the restful
quiet and shade of the forest solitudes. There had been distractions in the carriage-road—school-children, peasants,
wagons, troops of pedestrianizing students from all over Germany—but we had the old road to ourselves.

Now and then, while we rested, we watched the laborious
ant at his work. I found nothing new in him—certainly nothing to change my opinion of him. It seems to me that in the
matter of intellect the ant must be a strangely overrated bird.
During many summers now I have watched him when I

ought to have been in better business, and I have not yet come across a living ant that seemed to have any more sense than a dead one. I refer to the ordinary ant, of course. I have had no experience of those wonderful Swiss and African ones which vote, keep drilled armies, hold slaves and dispute about religion. Those particular ants may be all that the naturalist paints them but I am persuaded that the average ant is a sham. I admit his industry, of course. He is the hardest-working creature in the world—when anybody is looking—but his leather-headedness is the point I make against him. He goes out foraging, he makes a capture and then what does he do? Go home? No—he goes anywhere but home. He doesn't know where home is. His home may be only three feet away—no matter, he can't find it. He makes his capture, as I have said. It is generally something which can be of no sort of use to himself or anybody else. It is usually seven times bigger than it ought to be. He hunts out the awkwardest place to take hold of it. He lifts it bodily up in the air by main force and starts not toward home but in the opposite direction, not calmly and wisely but with a frantic haste which is wasteful of his strength. He fetches up against a pebble and instead of going around it he climbs over it backward dragging his booty after him, tumbles down on the other side, jumps up in a passion, kicks the dust off his clothes, moistens his hands, grabs his property viciously, yanks it this way, then that, shoves it ahead of him a moment, turns tail and lugs it after him another moment, gets madder and madder, then presently hoists it into the air and goes tearing away in an entirely new direction. Comes to a weed. It never occurs to him to go around it. No, he must climb it. And he does climb it, dragging his worthless property to the top—which is as bright a thing to do as it would be for me to carry a sack of flour from Heidelberg to Paris by way of Strasburg steeple. When he gets up there he finds that that is not the place. Takes a cursory glance at the scenery and either climbs down again or tumbles down and starts off once more—as usual, in a new direction. At the end of half an hour he fetches up within six inches of the place he started from and lays his burden down. Meantime he has been over all the ground for two yards around and climbed all the weeds and pebbles he came across. Now he wipes the sweat from his brow, strokes his limbs and then marches aimlessly off, in as violent a hurry as ever. He traverses a good deal of zigzag country and by and by stumbles on his same booty again. He does not remember to have ever seen it before. He looks around to see which is not the way home, grabs his bundle and starts. He goes through the same adventures he had before. Finally stops to rest, and a friend comes along. Evidently the friend remarks that a last year's grasshopper leg is a very noble acquisition and inquires where he got it. Evidently the proprietor does not remember exactly where he did get it, but thinks he got it "around here somewhere." Evidently the friend contracts to help him freight it home. Then, with a judgment peculiarly antic (pun not intentional), they take hold of opposite ends of that grasshopper leg and begin to tug with all their might in opposite directions. Presently they take a rest and confer together. They decide that something is wrong, they can't make out what. Then they go at it again, just as before. Same result. Mutual recriminations follow. Evidently each accuses the other of being an obstructionist. They warm up, and the dispute ends in a fight. They lock themselves together and chew each other's jaws for a while. Then they roll and tumble on the ground till one loses a horn or a leg and has to haul off for repairs. They make up and go to work again in the same old insane way but the crippled ant is at a disadvantage. Tug as he may, the other one drags off the booty and him at the end of it. Instead of giving up, he hangs on and gets his shins bruised against every obstruction that comes in the way. By and by, when that grasshopper leg has been dragged all over the same old ground once more, it is finally dumped at about the spot where it originally lay. The two perspiring ants inspect it thoughtfully and decide that dried grasshopper legs are a poor sort of property after all. And then each starts off in a different direction to see if

he can't find an old nail or something else that is heavy
enough to afford entertainment and at the same time value-
less enough to make an ant want to own it.

There in the Black Forest, on the mountainside, I saw an
ant go through with such a performance as this with a dead
spider of fully ten times his own weight. The spider was not
quite dead but too far gone to resist. He had a round body
the size of a pea. The little ant—observing that I was noticing
—turned him on his back, sank his fangs into his throat, lifted
him into the air and started vigorously off with him, stumbling over little pebbles, stepping on the spider's legs and
tripping himself up, dragging him backward, shoving him
bodily ahead, dragging him up stones six inches high instead
of going around them, climbing weeds twenty times his own
height and jumping from their summits—and finally leaving
him in the middle of the road to be confiscated by any other
fool of an ant that wanted him. I measured the ground which
this ass traversed, and arrived at the conclusion that what he
had accomplished inside of twenty minutes would constitute
some such job as this—relatively speaking—for a man. To
wit: to strap two eight-hundred-pound horses together, carry
them eighteen hundred feet, mainly over (not around) boulders averaging six feet high, and in the course of the journey
climb up and jump from the top of one precipice like
Niagara, and three steeples, each a hundred and twenty feet
high. And then put the horses down in an exposed place
without anybody to watch them, and go off to indulge in
some other idiotic miracle for vanity's sake.

Science has recently discovered that the ant does not lay
up anything for winter use. This will knock him out of literature, to some extent. He does not work except when people
are looking, and only then when the observer has a green,
naturalistic look and seems to be taking notes. This amounts
to deception and will injure him for the Sunday-schools. He
has not judgment enough to know what is good to eat from
what isn't. This amounts to ignorance and will impair the
world's respect for him. He cannot stroll around a stump and

find his way home again. This amounts to idiocy, and once the damaging fact is established, thoughtful people will cease to look up to him, the sentimental will cease to fondle him. His vaunted industry is but a vanity and of no effect, since he never gets home with anything he starts with. This disposes of the last remnant of his reputation and wholly destroys his main usefulness as a moral agent, since it will make the sluggard hesitate to go to him any more. It is strange, beyond comprehension, that so manifest a humbug as the ant has been able to fool so many nations and keep it up so many ages without being found out.

The ant is strong but we saw another strong thing where we had not suspected the presence of much muscular power before. A toadstool—that vegetable which springs to full growth in a single night—had torn loose and lifted a matted mass of pine needles and dirt of twice its own bulk into the air and supported it there like a column supporting a shed. Ten thousand toadstools with the right purchase could lift a man, I suppose. But what good would it do?

All our afternoon's progress had been uphill. About five or half past we reached the summit, and all of a sudden the dense curtain of the forest parted and we looked down into a deep and beautiful gorge and out over a wide panorama of wooded mountains with their summits shining in the sun and their glade-furrowed sides dimmed with purple shade. The gorge under our feet—called Allerheiligen—afforded room in the grassy level at its head for a cozy and delightful human nest, shut away from the world and its botherations, and consequently the monks of the old times had not failed to spy it out, and here were the brown and comely ruins of their church and convent to prove that priests had as fine an instinct seven hundred years ago in ferreting out 'he choicest nooks and corners in a land as priests have to-day.

A big hotel crowds the ruins a little now and drives a brisk trade with summer tourists. We descended into the gorge and had a supper which would have been very satisfactory if the trout had not been boiled. The Germans are pretty sure

to boil a trout or anything else if left to their own devices.
This is an argument of some value in support of the theory
that they were the original colonists of the wild islands off the
coast of Scotland. A schooner laden with oranges was
wrecked upon one of those islands a few years ago and the
gentle savages rendered the captain such willing assistance
that he gave them as many oranges as they wanted. Next day
he asked them how they liked them.

They shook their heads and said:

"Baked, they were tough. And even boiled they warn't
things for a hungry man to hanker after."

We went down the glen after supper. It is beautiful—a
mixture of sylvan loveliness and craggy wildness. A limpid
torrent goes whistling down the glen, and toward the foot of
it winds through a narrow cleft between lofty precipices and
hurls itself over a succession of falls. After one passes the last
of these he has a backward glimpse at the falls which is very
pleasing—they rise in a seven-stepped stairway of foamy and
glittering cascades and make a picture which is as charming
as it is unusual.

20. Nicodemus Dodge

We were satisfied that we could walk to Oppenau in one day
now that we were in practice, so we set out next morning
after breakfast determined to do it. It was all the way downhill and we had the loveliest summer weather for it. So we
set the pedometer and then stretched away on an easy, regular stride down through the cloven forest, drawing in the
fragrant breath of the morning in deep refreshing draughts
and wishing we might never have anything to do forever but

walk to Oppenau and keep on doing it and then doing it over again.

Now the true charm of pedestrianism does not lie in the walking or in the scenery but in the talking. The walking is good to time the movement of the tongue by and to keep the blood and the brain stirred up and active. The scenery and the woodsy smells are good to bear in upon a man an unconscious and unobtrusive charm and solace to eye and soul and sense. But the supreme pleasure comes from the talk. It is no matter whether one talks wisdom or nonsense, the case is the same, the bulk of the enjoyment lies in the wagging of the gladsome jaw and the flapping of the sympathetic ear.

And what a motley variety of subjects a couple of people will casually rake over in the course of a day's tramp! There being no constraint, a change of subject is always in order and so a body is not likely to keep pegging at a single topic until it grows tiresome. We discussed everything we knew, during the first fifteen or twenty minutes that morning, and then branched out into the glad, free, boundless realm of the things we were not certain about.

Harris said that if the best writer in the world once got the slovenly habit of doubling up his "haves" he could never get rid of it while he lived. That is to say, if a man gets the habit of saying "I should have liked to have known more about it" instead of saying simply and sensibly, "I should have liked to know more about it," that man's disease is incurable. Harris said that this sort of lapse is to be found in every copy of every newspaper that has ever been printed in English, and in almost all of our books. He said he had observed it in Kirkham's grammar and in Macaulay. Harris believed that milk-teeth are commoner in men's mouths than those "doubled-up haves."*

That changed the subject to dentistry. I said I believed the

*I do not know that there have not been moments in the course of the present session when I should have been very glad to have accepted the proposal of my noble friend, and to have exchanged parts in some of our evenings of work.—[From a Speech of the English Chancellor of the Exchequer, August 1879.]

average man dreaded tooth-pulling more than amputation and that he would yell quicker under the former operation than he would under the latter. The philosopher Harris said that the average man would not yell in either case if he had an audience. Then he continued:

"When our brigade first went into camp on the Potomac we used to be brought up standing, occasionally, by an ear-splitting howl of anguish. That meant that a soldier was getting a tooth pulled in a tent. But the surgeons soon changed that. They instituted open-air dentistry. There never was a howl afterward—that is, from the man who was having the tooth pulled. At the daily dental hour there would always be about five hundred soldiers gathered together in the neighborhood of that dental chair waiting to see the performance —and help. And the moment the surgeon took a grip on the candidate's tooth and began to lift, every one of those five hundred rascals would clap his hand to his jaw and begin to hop around on one leg and howl with all the lungs he had! It was enough to raise your hair to hear that variegated and enormous unanimous caterwaul burst out! With so big and so derisive an audience as that, a sufferer wouldn't emit a sound though you pulled his head off. The surgeons said that pretty often a patient was compelled to laugh in the midst of his pangs but that they had never caught one crying out after the open-air exhibition was instituted."

Dental surgeons suggested doctors, doctors suggested death, death suggested skeletons—and so, by a logical process the conversation melted out of one of these subjects and into the next until the topic of skeletons raised up Nicodemus Dodge out of the deep grave in my memory where he had lain buried and forgotten for twenty-five years. When I was a boy in a printing-office in Missouri, a loose-jointed, long-legged, tow-headed, jeans-clad, countrified cub of about sixteen lounged in one day, and without removing his hands from the depths of his trousers pockets or taking off his faded ruin of a slouch hat, whose broken rim hung limp and ragged about his eyes and ears like a bug-eaten cabbage leaf, stared indifferently around, then leaned his hip against the editor's table, crossed his mighty brogans, aimed at a distant fly from a crevice in his upper teeth, laid him low and said with composure:

"Whar's the boss?"

"I am the boss," said the editor, following this curious bit of architecture wonderingly along up to its clock-face with his eye.

"Don't want anybody fur to learn the business, 'tain't likely?"

"Well, I don't know. Would you like to learn it?"

"Pap's so po' he cain't run me no mo', so I want to git a show somers if I kin, 'tain't no diffunce what—I'm strong and hearty and I don't turn my back on no kind of work, hard nur soft."

"Do you think you would like to learn the printing business?"

"Well, I don't re'ly k'yer a durn what I *do* learn, so's I git a chance fur to make my way. I'd jist as soon learn print'n's anything."

"Can you read?"

"Yes—middlin'."

"Write?"

"Well, I've seed people could lay over me thar."

"Cipher?"

"Not good enough to keep store, I don't reckon, but up as fur as twelve-times-twelve I ain't no slouch. 'Tother side of that is what gits me."

"Where is your home?"

"I'm f'm old Shelby."

"What's your father's religious denomination?"

"Him? Oh, he's a blacksmith."

"No, no—I don't mean his trade. What's his *religious* denomination?"

"*Oh*—I didn't understand you befo'. He's a Freemason."

"No, no, you don't get my meaning yet. What I mean is, does he belong to any *church?*"

"*Now* you're talkin'! Couldn't make out what you was a-
tryin' to git through yo' head no way. B'long to a *church!*
Why, boss, he's ben the pizenest kind of a Free-will Babtis'
for forty year. They ain't no pizener ones 'n what *he* is.
Mighty good man, pap is. Everybody says that. If they said
any diffrunt they wouldn't say it whar *I* wuz—not *much* they
wouldn't."

"What is your own religion?"

"Well, boss, you've kind o' got me, thar—and yit you hain't
got me so mighty much, nuther. I think 't if a feller he'ps
another feller when he's in trouble, and don't cuss, and don't
do no mean things, nur noth'n' he ain' no business to do, and
don't spell the Saviour's name with a little g, he ain't runnin'
no resks—he's about as saift as if he b'longed to a church."

"But suppose he did spell it with a little g—what then?"

"Well, if he done it a-purpose, I reckon he wouldn't stand
no chance—he *oughtn't* to have no chance, anyway, I'm
most rotten certain 'bout that."

"What is your name?"

"Nicodemus Dodge."

"I think maybe you'll do, Nicodemus. We'll give you a trial,
anyway."

"All right."

"When would you like to begin?"

"Now."

So, within ten minutes after we had first glimpsed this
nondescript he was one of us, and with his coat off and hard
at it.

Beyond that end of our establishment which was furthest
from the street was a deserted garden, pathless, and thickly
grown with the bloomy and villainous "jimpson" weed and
its common friend the stately sunflower. In the midst of this
mournful spot was a decayed and aged little "frame" house
with but one room, one window and no ceiling—it had been
a smoke-house a generation before. Nicodemus was given
this lonely and ghostly den as a bedchamber.

The village smarties recognized a treasure in Nicodemus

right away—a butt to play jokes on. It was easy to see that he was inconceivably green and confiding. George Jones had the glory of perpetrating the first joke on him. He gave him a cigar with a firecracker in it and winked to the crowd to come. The thing exploded presently and swept away the bulk of Nicodemus's eyebrows and eyelashes. He simply said:

"I consider them kind of seeg'yars dangersome"—and seemed to suspect nothing. The next evening Nicodemus waylaid George and poured a bucket of ice-water over him.

One day while Nicodemus was in swimming, Tom McElroy "tied" his clothes. Nicodemus made a bonfire of Tom's by way of retaliation.

A third joke was played upon Nicodemus a day or two later —he walked up the middle aisle of the village church, Sunday night, with a staring hand-bill pinned between his shoulders. The joker spent the remainder of the night, after church, in the cellar of a deserted house, and Nicodemus sat on the cellar door till toward breakfast-time to make sure that the prisoner remembered that if any noise was made, some rough treatment would be the consequence. The cellar had two feet of stagnant water in it and was bottomed with six inches of soft mud.

But I wander from the point. It was the subject of skeletons that brought this boy back to my recollection. Before a very long time had elapsed, the village smarties began to feel an uncomfortable consciousness of not having made a very shining success out of their attempts on the simpleton from "old Shelby." Experimenters grew scarce and chary. Now the young doctor came to the rescue. There was delight and applause when he proposed to scare Nicodemus to death, and explained how he was going to do it. He had a noble new skeleton—the skeleton of the late and only local celebrity, Jimmy Finn, the village drunkard—a grisly piece of property which he had bought of Jimmy Finn himself at auction for fifty dollars under great competition when Jimmy lay very sick in the tanyard a fortnight before his death. The fifty dollars had gone promptly for whisky and had considerably hurried up the change of ownership in the skeleton. The doctor would put Jimmy Finn's skeleton in Nicodemus's bed!

This was done—about half past ten in the evening. About Nicodemus's usual bedtime—midnight—the village jokers came creeping stealthily through the jimpson weeds and sunflowers toward the lonely frame den. They reached the window and peeped in. There sat the long-legged pauper on his bed, in a very short shirt and nothing more. He was dangling his legs contentedly back and forth and wheezing the music of "Camptown Races" out of a paper-overlaid comb which he was pressing against his mouth. By him lay a new jewsharp, a new top, a solid india-rubber ball, a handful of painted marbles, five pounds of "store" candy and a well-gnawed slab of gingerbread as big and as thick as a volume of sheet-music. He had sold the skeleton to a traveling quack for three dollars and was enjoying the result!

Just as we had finished talking about skeletons and were drifting into the subject of fossils, Harris and I heard a shout and glanced up the steep hillside. We saw men and women standing away up there looking frightened, and there was a bulky object tumbling and floundering down the steep slope toward us. We got out of the way, and when the object landed in the road it proved to be a boy. He had tripped and fallen, and there was nothing for him to do but trust to luck and take what might come.

When one starts to roll down a place like that there is no stopping till the bottom is reached. Think of people *farming* on a slant which is so steep that the best you can say of it— if you want to be fastidiously accurate—is that it is a little steeper than a ladder and not quite so steep as a mansard roof. But that is what they do. Some of the little farms on the hillside opposite Heidelberg were stood up "edgeways." The boy was wonderfully jolted up, and his head was bleeding from cuts which it had got from small stones on the way.

Harris and I gathered him up and set him on a stone, and by that time the men and women had scampered down and brought his cap.

Men, women and children flocked out from neighboring cottages and joined the crowd. The pale boy was petted and stared at and commiserated, and water was brought for him to drink and bathe his bruises in. And such another clatter of tongues! All who had seen the catastrophe were describing it at once, and each trying to talk louder than his neighbor. And one youth of a superior genius ran a little way up the hill, called attention, tripped, fell, rolled down among us and thus triumphantly showed exactly how the thing had been done.

Harris and I were included in all the descriptions. How we were coming along. How Hans Gross shouted. How we looked up startled. How we saw Peter coming like a cannon-shot. How judiciously we got out of the way and let him come. And with what presence of mind we picked him up and brushed him off and set him on a rock when the performance was over. We were as much heroes as anybody else except Peter, and were so recognized. We were taken with Peter and the populace to Peter's mother's cottage and there we ate bread and cheese and drank milk and beer with everybody and had a most sociable good time. And when we left we had a hand-shake all around and were receiving and shouting back *Leb' wohl's* until a turn in the road separated us from our cordial and kindly new friends forever.

We accomplished our undertaking. At half past eight in the evening we stepped into Oppenau, just eleven hours and a half out from Allerheiligen—one hundred and forty-six miles. This is the distance by pedometer. The guide-book and the Imperial Ordnance maps make it only ten and a quarter—a surprising blunder, for these two authorities are usually singularly accurate in the matter of distances.

21. Sunday on the Continent

That was a thoroughly satisfactory walk—and the only one we were ever to have which was all the way downhill. We took the train next morning and returned to Baden-Baden through fearful fogs of dust. Every seat was crowded, too, for it was Sunday and consequently everybody was taking a "pleasure" excursion. Hot! The sky was an oven—and a sound one, too, with no cracks in it to let in any air. An odd time for a pleasure excursion, certainly!

Sunday is the great day on the continent—the free day, the happy day. One can break the Sabbath in a hundred ways without committing any sin.

We do not work on Sunday, because the commandment forbids it. The Germans do not work on Sunday, because the commandment forbids it. We rest on Sunday, because the commandment requires it. The Germans rest on Sunday, because the commandment requires it. But in the definition of the word "rest" lies all the difference. With us its Sunday meaning is, stay in the house and keep still. With the Germans its Sunday and week-day meanings seem to be the same—rest the *tired part* and never mind the other parts of the frame. Rest the tired part and use the means best calculated to rest that particular part. Thus: If one's duties have kept him in the house all the week, it will rest him to be out on Sunday. If his duties have required him to read weighty and serious matter all the week, it will rest him to read light matter on Sunday. If his occupation has busied him with death and funerals all the week, it will rest him to go to the theater Sunday night and put in two or three hours laughing at a comedy. If he is tired with digging ditches or felling trees all the week, it will rest him to lie quiet in the house on Sunday. If the hand, the arm, the brain, the tongue or any other member is fatigued with inanition, it is not to be rested by adding a day's inanition. But if a member is fatigued with exertion, inanition is the right rest for it. Such is the way in which the Germans seem to define the word "rest." That is to say, they rest a member by recreating, recuperating, restoring its forces. But our definition is less broad. We all rest alike on Sunday—by secluding ourselves and keeping still, whether that is the surest way to rest the most of us or not. The Germans make the actors, the preachers, etc., work on Sunday. We encourage the preachers, the editors, the printers, etc., to work on Sunday, and imagine that none of the sin of it falls upon us. But I do not know how we are going to get around the fact that if it is wrong for the printer to work at his trade on Sunday it must be equally wrong for the preacher to work at his, since the commandment has made no exception in his favor. We buy Monday morning's paper and read it and thus encourage Sunday printing. But I shall never do it again.

The Germans remember the Sabbath-day to keep it holy by abstaining from work, as commanded. We keep it holy by abstaining from work, as commanded, and by also abstaining from play, which is not commanded. Perhaps we constructively *break* the command to rest, because the resting we do is in most cases only a name and not a fact.

These reasonings have sufficed in a measure to mend the rent in my conscience which I made by traveling to Baden-Baden that Sunday. We arrived in time to furbish up and get to the English church before services began. We arrived in considerable style, too, for the landlord had ordered the first carriage that could be found, since there was no time to lose, and our coachman was so splendidly liveried that we were

probably mistaken for a brace of stray dukes. Else why were
we honored with a pew all to ourselves, away up among the
very elect at the left of the chancel? That was my first
thought. In the pew directly in front of us sat an elderly lady,
plainly and cheaply dressed. At her side sat a young lady with
a very sweet face, and she also was quite simply dressed. But
around us and about us were clothes and jewels which it
would do anybody's heart good to worship in.

I thought it was pretty manifest that the elderly lady was
embarrassed at finding herself in such a conspicuous place
arrayed in such cheap apparel. I began to feel sorry for her
and troubled about her. She tried to seem very busy with her
prayer-book and her responses, and unconscious that she was
out of place, but I said to myself, "She is not succeeding—
there is a distressed tremulousness in her voice which betrays
increasing embarrassment." Presently the Saviour's name
was mentioned, and in her flurry she lost her head completely and rose and courtesied instead of making a slight
nod as everybody else did. The sympathetic blood surged to
my temples and I turned and gave those fine birds what I
intended to be a beseeching look, but my feelings got the
better of me and changed it into a look which said, "If any
of you pets of fortune laugh at this poor soul you will deserve
to be flayed for it." Things went from bad to worse and I
shortly found myself mentally taking the unfriended lady
under my protection. My mind was wholly upon her. I forgot
all about the sermon. Her embarrassment took stronger and
stronger hold upon her. She got to snapping the lid of her
smelling-bottle—it made a loud, sharp sound but in her trouble she snapped and snapped away, unconscious of what she
was doing. The last extremity was reached when the collec-
tion-plate began its rounds. The moderate people threw in
pennies, the nobles and the rich contributed silver, but she
laid a twenty-mark gold piece upon the book-rest before her
with a sounding slap! I said to myself, "She has parted with
all her little hoard to buy the consideration of these unpitying
people—it is a sorrowful spectacle." I did not venture to look

around this time, but as the service closed I said to myself, "Let them laugh, it is their opportunity. But at the door of this church they shall see her step into our fine carriage with us, and our gaudy coachman shall drive her home."

Then she rose—and all the congregation stood while she walked down the aisle. She was the Empress of Germany!

No—she had not been so much embarrassed as I had supposed. My imagination had got started on the wrong scent and that is always hopeless. One is sure then to go straight on misinterpreting everything, clear through to the end. The young lady with her imperial Majesty was a maid of honor— and I had been taking her for one of her boarders, all the time.

This is the only time I have ever had an Empress under my personal protection. And considering my inexperience, I wonder I got through with it so well. I should have been a little embarrassed myself if I had known earlier what sort of a contract I had on my hands.

We found that the Empress had been in Baden-Baden several days. It is said that she never attends any but the English form of church service.

I lay abed and read and rested from my journey's fatigues the remainder of that Sunday but I sent my agent to represent me at the afternoon service, for I never allow anything to interfere with my habit of attending church twice every Sunday.

There was a vast crowd in the public grounds that night to hear the band play the "Fremersberg." This piece tells one of the old legends of the region: how a great noble of the Middle Ages got lost in the mountains and wandered about with his dogs in a violent storm until at last the faint tones of a monastery bell, calling the monks to a midnight service, caught his ear and he followed the direction the sounds came from and was saved. A beautiful air ran through the music without ceasing, sometimes loud and strong, sometimes so soft that it could hardly be distinguished—but it was always there. It swung grandly along through the shrill whistling of the storm-wind, the rattling patter of the rain and the boom and crash of the thunder. It wound soft and low through the lesser sounds, the distant ones, such as the throbbing of the convent bell, the melodious winding of the hunter's horn, the distressed bayings of his dogs and the solemn chanting of the monks. It rose again with a jubilant ring and mingled itself with the country songs and dances of the peasants assembled in the convent hall to cheer up the rescued huntsman while he ate his supper. The instruments imitated all these sounds with a marvelous exactness. More than one man started to raise his umbrella when the storm burst forth and the sheets of mimic rain came driving by. It was hardly possible to keep from putting your hand to your hat when the fierce wind began to rage and shriek and it was *not* possible to refrain from starting when those sudden and charmingly real thunder-crashes were let loose.

I suppose the "Fremersberg" is very low-grade music. I know, indeed, that it *must* be low-grade music, because it so delighted me, warmed me, moved me, stirred me, uplifted me, enraptured me, that I was full of cry all the time, and mad with enthusiasm. My soul had never had such a scouring out since I was born. The solemn and majestic chanting of the monks was not done by instruments but by men's voices, and it rose and fell and rose again in that rich confusion of warring sounds and pulsing bells and the stately swing of that ever-present enchanting air, and it seemed to me that nothing but the very lowest of low-grade music *could* be so divinely beautiful. The great crowd which the "Fremersberg" had called out was another evidence that it was low-grade music, for only the few are educated up to a point where high-grade music gives pleasure. I have never heard enough classic music to be able to enjoy it. I dislike the opera because I want to love it and can't.

I suppose there are two kinds of music—one kind which one feels, just as an oyster might, and another sort which requires a higher faculty, a faculty which must be assisted and developed by teaching. Yet if base music gives certain of us wings, why should we want any other? But we do. We want it because the higher and better like it. We want it without giving it the necessary time and trouble, so we climb into that upper tier, that dress-circle, by a lie. We *pretend* we like it. I know several of that sort of people—and I propose to be one of them myself when I get home with my fine European education.

And then there is painting. What a red rag is to a bull, Turner's "Slave Ship" was to me before I studied art. Mr. Ruskin is educated in art up to a point where that picture throws him into as mad an ecstasy of pleasure as it used to throw me into one of rage, last year, when I was ignorant. His cultivation enables him—and me, now—to see water in that glaring yellow mud, and natural effects in those lurid explosions of mixed smoke and flame, and crimson sunset glories. It reconciles him—and me, now—to the floating of iron cable-chains and other unfloatable things. It reconciles us to fishes swimming around on top of the mud—I mean the water. The most of the picture is a manifest impossibility— that is to say, a lie. And only rigid cultivation can enable a man to find truth in a lie. But it enabled Mr. Ruskin to do it, and it has enabled me to do it, and I am thankful for it. A Boston newspaper reporter went and took a look at the Slave Ship floundering about in that fierce conflagration of reds and yellows and said it reminded him of a tortoise-shell cat having a fit in a platter of tomatoes. In my then uneducated state that went home to my non-cultivation and I thought here is a man with an unobstructed eye. Mr. Ruskin would have said: This person is an ass. That is what I would say, now.*

However, our business in Baden-Baden this time was to

---

*Months after this was written I happened into the National Gallery in London and soon became so fascinated with the Turner pictures that I could hardly get away from the place. I went there often afterward, meaning to see the rest of the gallery, but the Turner spell was too strong, it could not be shaken off. However, the Turners which attracted me most did not remind me of the Slave Ship.

join our courier. I had thought it best to hire one, as we should be in Italy by and by and we did not know that language. Neither did he. We found him at the hotel, ready to take charge of us. I asked him if he was "all fixed." He said he was. That was very true. He had a trunk, two small satchels and an umbrella. I was to pay him fifty-five dollars a month and railway fares. On the continent the railway fare on a trunk is about the same it is on a man. Couriers do not have to pay any board and lodging. This seems a great saving to the tourist—at first. It does not occur to the tourist that *somebody* pays that man's board and lodging. It occurs to him by and by, however, in one of his lucid moments.

22. An American Party

Next morning we left in the train for Switzerland and reached Lucerne about ten o'clock at night. The first discovery I made was that the beauty of the lake had not been exaggerated. Within a day or two I made another discovery. This was that the lauded chamois is not a wild goat, that it is not a horned animal, that it is not shy, that it does not avoid human society and that there is no peril in hunting it. The chamois is a black or brown creature no bigger than a mustard seed. You do not have to go after it, it comes after you. It arrives in vast herds and skips and scampers all over your body, inside your clothes. Thus it is not shy but extremely sociable. It is not afraid of man. On the contrary, it will attack him. Its bite is not dangerous but neither is it pleasant. Its activity has not been overstated—if you try to put your finger on it it will skip a thousand times its own length at one jump, and no eye is sharp enough to see where it lights. A great deal of romantic nonsense has been written about the Swiss chamois and the perils of hunting it, whereas the truth is that even women and children hunt it and fearlessly. Indeed, everybody hunts it. The hunting is going on all the time, day and night, in bed and out of it. It is poetic foolishness to hunt it with a gun. Very few people do that. There is not one man in a million who can hit it with a gun. It is much easier to catch it than it is to shoot it, and only the experienced chamois-hunter can do either. Another common piece of exaggeration is that about the "scarcity" of the chamois. It is the reverse of scarce. Droves of one hundred million chamois are not unusual in the Swiss hotels. Indeed, they are so numerous as to be a great pest. The romancers always dress up the chamois-hunter in a fanciful and picturesque costume, whereas the best way to hunt this game is to do it without any costume at all. The article of commerce called chamois-skin is another fraud. Nobody could skin a chamois, it is too small. The creature is a humbug in every way, and everything which has been written about it is sentimental exaggeration. It was no pleasure to me to find the chamois out, for he had been one of my pet illusions. All my life it had been my dream to see him in his native wilds some day and engage in the adventurous sport of chasing him from cliff to cliff. It is no pleasure to me to expose him now and destroy the reader's delight in him and respect for him but still it must be done, for when an honest writer discovers an imposition it is his simple duty to strip it bare and hurl it down from its place of honor, no matter who suffers by it. Any other course would render him unworthy of the public confidence.

Lucerne is a charming place. It begins at the water's edge, with a fringe of hotels, and scrambles up and spreads itself over two or three sharp hills in a crowded, disorderly but picturesque way, offering to the eye a heaped-up confusion of red roofs, quaint gables, dormer windows, toothpick steeples, with here and there a bit of ancient embattled wall bending itself over the ridges, worm-fashion, and here and there an old square tower of heavy masonry. And also here and there a town clock with only one hand—a hand which stretches straight across the dial and has no joint in it. Such a clock helps out the picture but you cannot tell the time of day by it. Between the curving line of hotels and the lake is a broad avenue with lamps and a double rank of low shade trees. The lake-front is walled with masonry like a pier and has a railing to keep people from walking overboard. All day long the vehicles dash along the avenue, and nurses, children and tourists sit in the shade of the trees or lean on the railing and watch the schools of fishes darting about in the clear water or gaze out over the lake at the stately border of snow-hooded mountain peaks. Little pleasure steamers black with people are coming and going all the time, and everywhere one sees young girls and young men paddling about in fanciful rowboats or skimming along by the help of sails when there is any wind. The front rooms of the hotels have little railed balconies where one may take his private luncheon in calm, cool comfort and look down upon this busy and pretty scene and enjoy it without having to do any of the work connected with it.

Most of the people, both male and female, are in walking costume and carry alpenstocks. Evidently it is not considered safe to go about in Switzerland, even in town, without an alpenstock. If the tourist forgets and comes down to breakfast without his alpenstock he goes back and gets it and stands it up in the corner. When his touring in Switzerland is finished, he does not throw that broomstick away but lugs it home with him to the far corners of the earth, although this costs him more trouble and bother than a baby or a courier could. You see, the alpenstock is his trophy. His name is burned upon it. And if he has climbed a hill or jumped a brook or traversed a brickyard with it, he has the names of those places burned upon it too. Thus it is his regimental flag, so to speak, and bears the record of his achievements. It is worth three francs when he buys it, but a bonanza could not purchase it after his great deeds have been inscribed upon it. There are artisans all about Switzerland whose trade it is to burn these things upon the alpenstock of the tourist. And observe, a man is respected in Switzerland according to his alpenstock. I found I could get no attention there while I carried an unbranded one. However, branding is not expensive, so I soon remedied that. The effect upon the next detachment of tourists was very marked. I felt repaid for my trouble.

Half of the summer horde in Switzerland is made up of English people. The other half is made up of many nationalities, the Germans leading and the Americans coming next. The Americans were not as numerous as I had expected they would be.

The seven-thirty table d'hôte at the great Schweitzerhof furnished a mighty array and variety of nationalities but it offered a better opportunity to observe costumes than people, for the multitude sat at immensely long tables and therefore the faces were mainly seen in perspective. But the breakfasts were served at small round tables, and then if one had the fortune to get a table in the midst of the assemblage he could have as many faces to study as he could desire. We used to try to guess out the nationalities and generally succeeded tolerably well. Sometimes we tried to guess people's names but that was a failure, that is a thing which probably requires a good deal of practice. We presently dropped it and gave our efforts to less difficult particulars. One morning I said:

"There is an American party."

Harris said:

"Yes—but name the state."

I named one state, Harris named another. We agreed upon one thing, however—that the young girl with the party was very beautiful and very tastefully dressed. But we disagreed as to her age. I said she was eighteen, Harris said she was twenty. The dispute between us waxed warm, and I finally said, with a pretense of being in earnest:

"Well, there is one way to settle the matter—I will go and ask her."

Harris said sarcastically, "Certainly, that is the thing to do.

All you need to do is to use the common formula over here: go and say, 'I'm an American!' Of course she will be glad to see you."

Then he hinted that perhaps there was no great danger of my venturing to speak to her.

I said, "I was only talking—I didn't intend to approach her, but I see that you do not know what an intrepid person I am. I am not afraid of any woman that walks. I will go and speak to this young girl."

The thing I had in my mind was not difficult. I meant to address her in the most respectful way and ask her to pardon me if her strong resemblance to a former acquaintance of mine was deceiving me. And when she should reply that the name I mentioned was not the name she bore, I meant to beg pardon again, most respectfully, and retire. There would be no harm done. I walked to her table, bowed to the gentleman, then turned to her and was about to begin my little speech when she exclaimed: "I *knew* I wasn't mistaken—I told John it was you! John said it probably wasn't but I knew I was right. I said you would recognize me presently and come over. And I'm glad you did, for I shouldn't have felt much flattered if you had gone out of this room without recognizing me. Sit down, sit down—how odd it is—you are the last person I was ever expecting to see again."

This was a stupefying surprise. It took my wits clear away for an instant. However, we shook hands cordially all around and I sat down. But truly this was the tightest place I ever was in. I seemed to vaguely remember the girl's face now but I had no idea where I had seen it before or what name belonged with it. I immediately tried to get up a diversion about Swiss scenery to keep her from launching into topics that might betray that I did not know her but it was of no use, she went right along upon matters which interested her more:

"Oh dear, what a night that was when the sea washed the forward boats away—do you remember it?"

"Oh, *don't* I!" said I—but I didn't. I wished the sea had

washed the rudder and the smoke-stack and the captain away—then I could have located this questioner.

"And don't you remember how frightened poor Mary was and how she cried?"

"Indeed I do!" said I. "Dear me, how it all comes back!"

I fervently wished it *would* come back—but my memory was a blank. The wise way would have been to frankly own up but I could not bring myself to do that after the young girl had praised me so for recognizing her, so I went on deeper and deeper into the mire, hoping for a chance clue but never getting one. The Unrecognizable continued with vivacity:

"Do you know George married Mary, after all?"

"Why, no! Did he?"

"Indeed he did. He said he did not believe she was half as much to blame as her father was, and I thought he was right. Didn't you?"

"Of course he was. It was a perfectly plain case. I always said so."

"Why, no you didn't!—at least that summer."

"Oh, no, not that summer. No, you are perfectly right about that. It was the following winter that I said it."

"Well, as it turned out, Mary was not in the least to blame —it was all her father's fault—at least his and old Darley's."

It was necessary to say something—so I said:

"I always regarded Darley as a troublesome old thing."

"So he was, but then they always had a great affection for him, although he had so many eccentricities. You remember that when the weather was the least cold he would try to come into the house."

I was rather afraid to proceed. Evidently Darley was not a man—he must be some other kind of animal—possibly a dog, maybe an elephant. However, tails are common to all animals, so I ventured to say:

"And what a tail he had!"

"*One!* He had a thousand!"

This was bewildering. I did not quite know what to say, so I only said:

"Yes, he *was* rather well fixed in the matter of tails."

"For a negro, and a crazy one at that, I should say he was," said she.

It was getting pretty sultry for me. I said to myself, "Is it possible she is going to stop there and wait for me to speak? If she does, the conversation is blocked. A negro with a thousand tails is a topic which a person cannot talk upon fluently and instructively without more or less preparation. As to diving rashly into such a vast subject—"

But here, to my gratitude, she interrupted my thoughts by saying:

"Yes, when it came to tales of his crazy woes, there was simply no end to them if anybody would listen. His own quarters were comfortable enough but when the weather was cold the family were sure to have his company—nothing could keep him out of the house. But they always bore it kindly because he had saved Tom's life years before. You remember Tom?"

"Oh, perfectly. Fine fellow he was, too."

"Yes he was. And what a pretty little thing his child was!"

"You may well say that. I never saw a prettier child."

"I used to delight to pet it and handle it and play with it."

"So did I."

"You named it. What *was* that name? I can't call it to mind."

It appeared to me that the ice was getting pretty thin here. I would have given something to know what the child's sex was. However, I had the good luck to think of a name that would fit either sex—so I brought it out:

"I named it Frances."

"From a relative, I suppose? But you named the one that died, too—one that I never saw. What did you call that one?"

I was out of neutral names, but as the child was dead and she had never seen it, I thought I might risk a name for it and trust to luck. Therefore I said:

"I called that one Thomas Henry."

She said musingly:

"That is very singular . . . very singular."

I sat still and let the cold sweat run down. I was in a good deal of trouble but I believed I could worry through if she wouldn't ask me to name any more children. I wondered where the lightning was going to strike next. She was still ruminating over that last child's title, but presently she said:

"I have always been sorry you were away at the time—I would have had you name my child."

"*Your* child! Are you married?"

"I have been married thirteen years."

"Christened, you mean."

"No, married. The youth by your side is my son."

"It seems incredible—even impossible. I do not mean any harm by it, but would you mind telling me if you are any over eighteen?—that is to say, will you tell me how old you are?"

"I was just nineteen the day of the storm we were talking about. That was my birthday."

That did not help matters much, as I did not know the date of the storm. I tried to think of some non-committal thing to say to keep up my end of the talk and render my poverty in the matter of reminiscences as little noticeable as possible, but I seemed to be about out of non-committal things. I was about to say, "You haven't changed a bit since then"—but that was risky. I thought of saying, "You have improved ever so much since then"—but that wouldn't answer, of course. I was about to try a shy at the weather for a saving change, when the girl slipped in ahead of me and said:

"How I have enjoyed this talk over those happy old times —haven't you?"

"I never have spent such a half-hour in all my life before!" said I with emotion. And I could have added, with a near approach to truth, "And I would rather be scalped than spend another one like it." I was holily grateful to be through with the ordeal and was about to make my good-bys and get out when the girl said:

"But there is one thing that is ever so puzzling to me."

"Why, what is that?"

"That dead child's name. What did you say it was?"

Here was another balmy place to be in. I had forgotten the child's name. I hadn't imagined it would be needed again. However, I had to pretend to know anyway, so I said:

"Joseph William."

The youth at my side corrected me and said:

"No, Thomas Henry."

I thanked him—in words—and said with trepidation:

"O yes—I was thinking of another child that I named—I have named a great many and I get them confused—this one *was* named Henry Thompson—"

"Thomas Henry," calmly interposed the boy.

I thanked him again—strictly in words—and stammered out:

"Thomas Henry—yes, Thomas Henry was the poor child's name. I named him for Thomas—er—Thomas Carlyle, the great author, you know—and Henry—er—er—Henry the Eighth. The parents were very grateful to have a child named Thomas Henry."

"That makes it more singular than ever," murmured my beautiful friend.

"Does it? Why?"

"Because when the parents speak of that child now they always call it Susan Amelia."

That spiked my gun. I could not say anything. I was entirely out of verbal obliquities. To go further would be to lie and that I would not do. So I simply sat still and suffered—sat mutely and resignedly there and sizzled—for I was being slowly fried to death in my own blushes. Presently the enemy laughed a happy laugh and said:

"I *have* enjoyed this talk over old times, but you have not. I saw very soon that you were only pretending to know me and so as I had wasted a compliment on you in the beginning I made up my mind to punish you. And I have succeeded pretty well. I was glad to see that you knew George and Tom and Darley, for I had never heard of them before and therefore could not be sure that you had. And I was glad to learn the names of those imaginary children, too. One can get quite a fund of information out of you if one goes at it cleverly. Mary and the storm and the sweeping away of the forward boats were facts—all the rest was fiction. Mary was my sister. Her full name was Mary——. *Now* do you remember me?"

"Yes," I said, "I do remember you now, and you are as hard-hearted as you were thirteen years ago in that ship, else you wouldn't have punished me so. You haven't changed your nature nor your person in any way at all. You look just as young as you did then, you are just as beautiful as you were then, and you have transmitted a deal of your comeliness to this fine boy. There—if that speech moves you any, let's fly the flag of truce, with the understanding that I am conquered and confess it."

All of which was agreed to and accomplished on the spot. When I went back to Harris I said:

"Now you see what a person with talent and address can do."

"Excuse me, I see what a person of colossal ignorance and simplicity can do. The idea of your going and intruding on a party of strangers that way and talking for half an hour. Why, I never heard of a man in his right mind doing such a thing before. What did you say to them?"

"I never said any harm. I merely asked the girl what her name was."

"I don't doubt it. Upon my word I don't. I think you were capable of it. It was stupid in me to let you go over there and make such an exhibition of yourself. But you know I couldn't really believe you would do such an inexcusable thing. What will those people think of us? But how did you say it?—I mean the manner of it. I hope you were not abrupt."

"No, I was careful about that. I said 'My friend and I would like to know what your name is, if you don't mind.'"

"No, that was not abrupt. There is a polish about it that does you infinite credit. And I am glad you put me in. That was a delicate attention which I appreciate at its full value. What did she do?"

"She didn't do anything in particular. She told me her name."

"Simply told you her name. Do you mean to say she did not show any surprise?"

"Well, now I come to think, she did show something. Maybe it was surprise. I hadn't thought of that—I took it for gratification."

"Oh, undoubtedly you were right. It must have been gratification. It could not be otherwise than gratifying to be assaulted by a stranger with such a question as that. Then what did you do?"

"I offered my hand and the party gave me a shake."

"I saw it! I did not believe my own eyes at the time. Did the gentlemen say anything about cutting your throat?"

"No, they all seemed glad to see me, as far as I could judge."

"And do you know, I believe they were. I think they said to themselves, 'Doubtless this curiosity has got away from his keeper—let us amuse ourselves with him.' There is no other way of accounting for their facile docility. You sat down. Did they *ask* you to sit down?"

"No, they did not ask me, but I suppose they did not think of it."

"You have an unerring instinct. What else did you do? What did you talk about?"

"Well, I asked the girl how old she was."

"*Un*doubtedly. Your delicacy is beyond praise. Go on, go on—don't mind my apparent misery—I always look so when I am steeped in a profound and reverent joy. Go on—she told you her age?"

"Yes, she told me her age, and all about her mother and her grandmother and her other relations and all about herself."

"Did she volunteer these statistics?"

"No, not exactly that. I asked the questions and she answered them."

"This is divine. Go on—it is not possible that you forgot to inquire into her politics?"

"No, I thought of that. She is a democrat, her husband is a republican, and both of them are Baptists."

"Her husband? Is that child married?"

"She is not a child. She is married, and that is her husband who is there with her."

"Has she any children?"

"Yes—seven and a half."

"That is impossible."

"No, she has them. She told me herself."

"Well, but seven and a *half*? How do you make out the half? Where does the half come in?"

"There is a child which she had by another husband—not this one but another one—so it is a stepchild, and they do not count it full measure."

"Another husband? Has she had another husband?"

"Yes, four. This one is number four."

"I don't believe a word of it. It is impossible upon its face. Is that boy there her brother?"

"No, that is her son. He is her youngest. He is not as old as he looks. He is only eleven and a half."

"These things are all manifestly impossible. This is a wretched business. It is a plain case: they simply took your measure and concluded to fill you up. They seem to have succeeded. I am glad I am not in the mess. They may at least be charitable enough to think there ain't a pair of us. Are they going to stay here long?"

"No, they leave before noon."

"There is one man who is deeply grateful for that. How did you find out? You asked, I suppose?"

"No, along at first I inquired into their plans in a general way, and they said they were going to be here a week and make trips round about. But toward the end of the interview, when I said you and I would tour around with them with pleasure and offered to bring you over and introduce you, they hesitated a little and asked if you were from the same establishment that I was. I said you were, and then they said they had changed their mind and considered it necessary to start at once and visit a sick relative in Siberia."

"Ah me, you struck the summit! You struck the loftiest altitude of stupidity that human effort has ever reached. You shall have a monument of jackasses' skulls as high as the Strasburg spire if you die before I do. They wanted to know if I was from the same 'establishment' that you hailed from, did they? What did they mean by 'establishment'?"

"I don't know. It never occurred to me to ask."

"Well *I* know. They meant an asylum—an *idiot* asylum, do you understand? So they *do* think there's a pair of us, after all. Now what do you think of yourself?"

"Well, I don't know. I didn't know I was doing any harm. I didn't *mean* to do any harm. They were very nice people and they seemed to like me."

Harris made some rude remarks and left for his bedroom —to break some furniture, he said. He was a singularly irascible man. Any little thing would disturb his temper.

I had been well scorched by the young woman, but no matter, I took it out of Harris. One should always "get even" in some way, else the sore place will go on hurting.

23. The Man Who Put Up at Gadsby's

The Hofkirche is celebrated for its organ concerts. All summer long the tourists flock to that church about six o'clock in the evening and pay their franc and listen to the noise. They don't stay to hear all of it but get up and tramp out over the sounding stone floor, meeting late comers who tramp in in a sounding and vigorous way. This tramping back and forth is kept up nearly all the time and is accented by the continuous slamming of the door and the coughing and barking and sneezing of the crowd. Meantime the big organ is booming and crashing and thundering away, doing its best to prove that it is the biggest and loudest organ in Europe and that a tight little box of a church is the most favorable place to average and appreciate its powers in. It is true there were some soft and merciful passages occasionally but the tramp-tramp of the tourists only allowed one to get fitful glimpses of them, so to speak. Then right away the organist would let go another avalanche.

The commerce of Lucerne consists mainly in gimcrackery of the souvenir sort. The shops are packed with Alpine crystals, photographs of scenery, and wooden and ivory carvings. I will not conceal the fact that miniature figures of the Lion of Lucerne are to be had in them. Millions of them. But they are libels upon him, every one of them. There is a subtle something about the majestic pathos of the original which the copyist cannot get. Even the sun fails to get it. Both the photographer and the carver give you a dying lion and that is all. The shape is right, the attitude is right, the proportions are right, but that indescribable something which makes the Lion of Lucerne the most mournful and moving piece of stone in the world is wanting.

The Lion lies in his lair in the perpendicular face of a low cliff—for he is carved from the living rock of the cliff. His size is colossal, his attitude is noble. His head is bowed, the broken spear is sticking in his shoulder, his protecting paw rests upon the lilies of France. Vines hang down the cliff and wave in the wind, and a clear stream trickles from above and empties into a pond at the base, and in the smooth surface of the pond the lion is mirrored among the water-lilies.

Around about are green trees and grass. The place is a sheltered, reposeful woodland nook remote from noise and stir and confusion—and all this is fitting, for lions do die in such places and not on granite pedestals in public squares fenced with fancy iron railings. The Lion of Lucerne would be impressive anywhere, but nowhere so impressive as where he is.

We did not buy any wooden images of the Lion, nor any ivory or ebony or marble or chalk or sugar or chocolate ones, or even any photographic slanders of him. The truth is these copies were so common, so universal in the shops and everywhere that they presently became as intolerable to the wearied eye as the latest popular melody usually becomes to the harassed ear. In Lucerne, too, the wood carvings of other sorts, which had been so pleasant to look upon when one saw them occasionally at home, soon began to fatigue us. We grew very tired of seeing wooden quails and chickens picking and strutting around clock-faces, and still more tired of seeing wooden images of the alleged chamois skipping about wooden rocks or lying upon them in family groups or peering alertly up from behind them. The first day, I would have bought a hundred and fifty of these clocks if I had had the money—and I did buy three—but on the third day the disease had run its course, I had convalesced and was in the market once more—trying to sell. However, I had no luck, which was just as well, for the things will be pretty enough, no doubt, when I get them home.

For years my pet aversion had been the cuckoo clock. Now here I was, at last, right in the creature's home. So wherever I went that distressing *"hoo* 'hoo! *hoo* 'hoo! *hoo* 'hoo!" was always in my ears. For a nervous man this was a fine state of things. Some sounds are hatefuler than others but no sound is quite so inane and silly and aggravating as the *"hoo* 'hoo" of a cuckoo clock, I think. I bought one and am carrying it home to a certain person, for I have always said that if the opportunity ever happened, I would do that man an ill turn. What I meant was that I would break one of his legs or something of that sort but in Lucerne I instantly saw that I could impair his mind. That would be more lasting and more satisfactory every way. So I bought the cukoo clock and if I ever get home with it he is "my meat," as they say in the mines. I thought of another candidate—a book-reviewer whom I could name if I wanted to—but after thinking it over I didn't buy him a clock. I couldn't injure his mind.

We visited the two long, covered wooden bridges which span the green and brilliant Reuss just below where it goes plunging and hurrahing out of the lake. These rambling, sway-backed tunnels are very attractive things with their alcoved outlooks upon the lovely and inspiriting water. They contain two or three hundred queer old pictures by old Swiss masters—old boss sign-painters who flourished before the decadence of art.

The lake is alive with fishes plainly visible to the eye, for the water is very clear. The parapets in front of the hotels were usually fringed with fishers of all ages. One day I thought I would stop and see a fish caught. The result brought back to my mind very forcibly a circumstance which I had not thought of before for twelve years. This one:

The Man Who Put Up at Gadsby's

When my odd friend Riley and I were newspaper correspondents in Washington in the winter of '67 we were coming down Pennsylvania Avenue one night near midnight in a driving storm of snow, when the flash of a street-lamp fell upon a man who was eagerly tearing along in the opposite direction. This man instantly stopped and exclaimed:

"This is lucky! You are Mr. Riley, ain't you?"

Riley was the most self-possessed and solemnly deliberate person in the republic. He stopped, looked his man over from head to foot, and finally said:

"I am Mr. Riley. Did you happen to be looking for me?"

"That's just what I was doing," said the man joyously, "and it's the biggest luck in the world that I've found you. My name is Lykins. I'm one of the teachers of the high school—

San Francisco. As soon as I heard the San Francisco postmastership was vacant I made up my mind to get it—and here I am."

"Yes," said Riley slowly, "as you have remarked . . . Mr. Lykins . . . here you are. And have you got it?"

"Well, not exactly *got* it, but the next thing to it. I've brought a petition, signed by the Superintendent of Public Instruction and all the teachers and by more than two hundred other people. Now I want you, if you'll be so good, to go around with me to the Pacific delegation, for I want to rush this thing through and get along home."

"If the matter is so pressing, you will prefer that we visit the delegation to-night," said Riley in a voice which had nothing mocking in it—to an unaccustomed ear.

"Oh, to-night, by all means! I haven't got any time to fool around. I want their promise before I go to bed—I ain't the talking kind, I'm the *doing* kind!"

"Yes . . . you've come to the right place for that. When did you arrive?"

"Just an hour ago."

"When are you intending to leave?"

"For New York to-morrow evening—for San Francisco next morning."

"Just so. . . . What are you going to do tomorrow?"

"*Do!* Why, I've got to go to the President with the petition and the delegation and get the appointment, haven't I?"

"Yes . . . very true . . . that is correct. And then what?"

"Executive session of the Senate at 2 P.M.—got to get the appointment confirmed—I reckon you'll grant that?"

"Yes . . . yes," said Riley meditatively, "you are right again. Then you take the train for New York in the evening, and the steamer for San Francisco next morning?"

"That's it—that's the way I map it out!"

Riley considered a while, and then said:

"You couldn't stay . . . a day . . . well, say two days longer?"

"Bless your soul, no! It's not my style. I ain't a man to go fooling around—I'm a man that *does* things, I tell you."

The storm was raging, the thick snow blowing in gusts. Riley stood silent, apparently deep in a reverie, during a minute or more, then he looked up and said:

"Have you ever heard about that man who put up at Gadsby's, once? . . . But I see you haven't."

He backed Mr. Lykins against an iron fence, buttonholed him, fastened him with his eye like the Ancient Mariner, and proceeded to unfold his narrative as placidly and peacefully as if we were all stretched comfortably in a blossomy summer meadow instead of being persecuted by a wintry midnight tempest:

"I will tell you about that man. It was in Jackson's time. Gadsby's was the principal hotel then. Well, this man arrived from Tennessee about nine o'clock one morning with a black coachman and a splendid four-horse carriage and an elegant dog, which he was evidently fond and proud of. He drove up before Gadsby's, and the clerk and the landlord and everybody rushed out to take charge of him but he said, 'Never mind,' and jumped out and told the coachman to wait—said he hadn't time to take anything to eat, he only had a little claim against the government to collect, would run across the way to the Treasury and fetch the money and then get right along back to Tennessee, for he was in considerable of a hurry.

"Well, about eleven o'clock that night he came back and ordered a bed and told them to put the horses up—said he would collect the claim in the morning. This was in January, you understand—January 1834—the 3d of January—Wednesday.

"Well, on the 5th of February he sold the fine carriage and bought a cheap second-hand one—said it would answer just as well to take the money home in, and he didn't care for style.

"On the 11th of August he sold a pair of the fine horses— said he'd often thought a pair was better than four to go over the rough mountain roads with where a body had to be careful about his driving—and there wasn't so much of his claim but he could lug the money home with a pair easy enough.

"On the 13th of December he sold another horse—said two warn't necessary to drag that old light vehicle with—in fact, one could snatch it along faster than was absolutely necessary now that it was good solid winter weather and the roads in splendid condition.

"On the 17th of February 1835 he sold the old carriage and bought a cheap second-hand buggy—said a buggy was just the trick to skim along mushy, slushy early spring roads with, and he had always wanted to try a buggy on those mountain roads, anyway.

"On the 1st of August he sold the buggy and bought the remains of an old sulky—said he just wanted to see those green Tennesseans stare and gawk when they saw him come a-ripping along in a sulky—didn't believe they'd ever heard of a sulky in their lives.

"Well, on the 29th of August he sold his colored coachman —said he didn't need a coachman for a sulky—wouldn't be room enough for two in it anyway—and besides, it wasn't every day that Providence sent a man a fool who was willing to pay nine hundred dollars for such a third-rate negro as that —been wanting to get rid of the creature for years but didn't like to *throw* him away.

"Eighteen months later—that is to say, on the 15th of February 1837—he sold the sulky and bought a saddle—said horseback-riding was what the doctor had always recommended *him* to take, and dog'd if he wanted to risk *his* neck going over those mountain roads on wheels in the dead of winter, not if he knew himself.

"On the 9th of April he sold the saddle—said he wasn't going to risk *his* life with any perishable saddle-girth that ever was made, over a rainy, miry April road, while he could ride bareback and know and feel he was safe—always *had* despised to ride on a saddle, anyway.

"On the 24th of April he sold his horse—said, 'I'm just fifty-seven to-day, hale and hearty—it would be a *pretty* howdy-do for me to be wasting such a trip as that and such weather as this on a horse when there ain't anything in the world so splendid as a tramp on foot through the fresh spring woods and over the cheery mountains to a man that *is* a man —and I can make my dog carry my claim in a little bundle, anyway, when it's collected. So to-morrow I'll be up bright and early, make my little old collection and mosey off to Tennessee on my own hind legs, with a rousing good-by to Gadsby's.'

"On the 22d of June he sold his dog—said, 'Dern a dog, anyway, where you're just starting off on a rattling bully pleasure tramp through the summer woods and hills—perfect nuisance—chases the squirrels, barks at everything, goes a-capering and splattering around in the fords—man can't get any chance to reflect and enjoy nature—and I'd a blamed sight ruther carry the claim myself, it's a mighty sight safer. A dog's mighty uncertain in a financial way—always noticed it—well, *good*-by, boys—last call—I'm off for Tennessee with a good leg and a gay heart early in the morning.' "

There was a pause and a silence—except the noise of the wind and the pelting snow. Mr. Lykins said impatiently:

"Well?"

Riley said:

"Well—that was thirty years ago."

"Very well, very well—what of it?"

"I'm great friends with that old patriarch. He comes every evening to tell me good-by. I saw him an hour ago—he's off for Tennessee early tomorrow morning—as usual. Said he calculated to get his claim through and be off before night-owls like me have turned out of bed. The tears were in his eyes, he was so glad he was going to see his old Tennessee and his friends once more."

Another silent pause. The stranger broke it:

"Is that all?"

"That is all."

"Well, for the *time* of night and the *kind* of night it seems to me the story was full long enough. But what's it all *for?*"

"Oh, nothing in particular."

"Well, where's the point of it?"

"Oh, there isn't any particular point to it. Only, if you are not in *too* much of a hurry to rush off to San Francisco with that post-office appointment, Mr. Lykins, I'd advise you to *'put up at Gadsby's'* for a spell and take it easy. Good-by. *God* bless you!"

So saying, Riley blandly turned on his heel and left the astonished school-teacher standing there, a musing and motionless snow image shining in the broad glow of the streetlamp.

He never got that post-office.

To go back to Lucerne and its fishers, I concluded after about nine hours' waiting that the man who proposes to tarry till he sees somebody hook one of those well-fed and experienced fishes will find it wisdom to "put up at Gadsby's" and take it easy. It is likely that a fish has not been caught on that lake pier for forty years. But no matter, the patient fisher watches his cork there all the day long just the same and seems to enjoy it. One may see the fisher-loafers just as thick and contented and happy and patient all along the Seine at Paris but tradition says that the only thing ever caught there in modern times is a thing they don't fish for at all—the recent dog and the translated cat.

24. A Specimen Tourist

Close by the Lion of Lucerne is what they call the "Glacier Garden"—and it is the only one in the world. It is on high ground. Four or five years ago some workmen who were digging foundations for a house came upon this interesting relic of a long-departed age. Scientific men perceived in it a confirmation of their theories concerning the glacial period, so through their persuasions the little tract of ground was bought and permanently protected against being built upon. The soil was removed, and there lay the rasped and guttered track which the ancient glacier had made as it moved along upon its slow and tedious journey. This track was perforated by huge pot-shaped holes in the bed-rock, formed by the furious washing-around in them of boulders by the turbulent torrent which flows beneath all glaciers. These huge round boulders still remain in the holes. They and the walls of the holes are worn smooth by the long-continued chafing which they gave each other in those old days. It took a mighty force to churn these big lumps of stone around in that vigorous way. The neighboring country had a very different shape at that time—the valleys have risen up and become hills since, and the hills have become valleys. The boulders discovered in the pots had traveled a great distance, for there is no rock like them nearer than the distant Rhone Glacier.

For some days we were content to enjoy looking at the blue Lake Lucerne and at the piled-up masses of snow-mountains that border it all around—an enticing spectacle, this last, for there is a strange and fascinating beauty and charm about a majestic snow-peak with the sun blazing upon it or the moonlight softly enriching it—but finally we concluded to try a bit of excursioning around on a steamboat, and a dash on foot at the Rigi. Very well, we had a delightful trip to Fluelen on a breezy, sunny day. Everybody sat on the upper deck on benches under an awning. Everybody talked, laughed and exclaimed at the wonderful scenery. In truth, a trip on that lake is almost the perfection of pleasuring. The mountains were a never-ceasing marvel. Sometimes they rose straight up out of the lake and towered aloft and overshadowed our pygmy steamer with their prodigious bulk in the most impressive way. Not snow-clad mountains, these, yet they climbed high enough toward the sky to meet the clouds and veil their foreheads in them. They were not barren and repulsive but clothed in green, and restful and pleasant to the eye. And they were so almost straight-up-and-down, sometimes, that one could not imagine a man being able to keep his footing upon such a surface, yet there are paths, and the Swiss people go up and down them every day.

Sometimes one of these monster precipices had the slight inclination of the huge ship-houses in dockyards—then high aloft, toward the sky, it took a little stronger inclination, like that of a mansard roof—and perched on this dizzy mansard one's eye detected little things like martin boxes and presently perceived that these were the dwellings of peasants— an airy place for a home, truly. And suppose a peasant should walk in his sleep, or his child should fall out of the front yard? —the friends would have a tedious long journey down out of those cloud-heights before they found the remains. And yet those far-away homes looked ever so seductive, they were so remote from the troubled world, they dozed in such an atmosphere of peace and dreams—surely no one who had learned to live up there would ever want to live on a meaner level.

We swept through the prettiest little curving arms of the lake among these colossal green walls, enjoying new delights always as the stately panorama unfolded itself before us and rerolled and hid itself behind us. And now and then we had the thrilling surprise of bursting suddenly upon a tremendous white mass like the distant and dominating Jungfrau or some kindred giant looming head and shoulders above a tumbled waste of lesser Alps.

Once, while I was hungrily taking in one of these surprises and doing my best to get all I possibly could of it while it should last, I was interrupted by a young and care-free voice:

"You're an American, I think—so'm I."

He was about eighteen or possibly nineteen. Slender and of medium height. Open, frank, happy face. A restless but independent eye. A snub nose, which had the air of drawing back with a decent reserve from the silky new-born mustache below it until it should be introduced. A loosely hung jaw calculated to work easily in the sockets. He wore a low-crowned, narrow-brimmed straw hat with a broad blue ribbon around it which had a white anchor embroidered on it in front. Nobby short-tailed coat, pantaloons, vest, all trim and neat and up with the fashion. Red-striped stockings, very low-quarter patent-leather shoes tied with black ribbon. Blue ribbon around his neck, wide-open collar. Tiny diamond studs. Wrinkleless kids. Projecting cuffs fastened with large oxydized silver sleeve-buttons bearing the device of a dog's face—English pug. He carried a slim cane surmounted with an English pug's head with red glass eyes. Under his arm he carried a German grammar—Otto's. His hair was short, straight and smooth, and presently when he turned his head a moment I saw that it was nicely parted behind. He took a cigarette out of a dainty box, stuck it into a meerschaum holder which he carried in a morocco case, and reached for my cigar. While he was lighting I said:

"Yes—I am an American."

"I knew it—I can always tell them. What ship did you come over in?"

"Holsatia."

"We came in the *Batavia*—Cunard, you know. What kind of a passage did you have?"

"Tolerably rough."

"So did we. Captain said he'd hardly ever seen it rougher. Where are you from?"

"New England."

"So'm I. I'm from New Bloomfield. Anybody with you?"

"Yes—a friend."

"Our whole family's along. It's awful slow going around alone—don't you think so?"

"Rather slow."

"Ever been over here before?"

"Yes."

"I haven't. My first trip. But we've been all around—Paris and everywhere. I'm to enter Harvard next year. Studying German all the time now. Can't enter till I know German. I know considerable French—I get along pretty well in Paris or anywhere where they speak French. What hotel are you stopping at?"

"Schweitzerhof."

"No! is that so? I never see you in the reception-room. I go to the reception-room a good deal of the time, because there's so many Americans there. I make lots of acquaintances. I know an American as soon as I see him—and so I speak to him and make his acquaintance. I like to be always making acquaintances—don't you?"

"Lord, yes!"

"You see it breaks up a trip like this, first rate. I never get bored on a trip like this if I can make acquaintances and have somebody to talk to. But I think a trip like this would be an awful bore if a body couldn't find anybody to get acquainted with and talk to on a trip like this. I'm fond of talking, ain't you?"

"Passionately."

"Have you felt bored on this trip?"

"Not all the time, part of it."

"That's it!—you see you ought to go around and get acquainted and talk. That's my way. That's the way I always do —I just go 'round, 'round, 'round and talk, talk, talk—I never get bored. You been up the Rigi yet?"

"No."

"Going?"

"I think so."

"What hotel you going to stop at?"

"I don't know. Is there more than one?"

"Three. You stop at the Schreiber—you'll find it full of Americans. What ship did you say you came over in?"

"*City of Anterp.*"

"German, I guess. You going to Geneva?"

"Yes."

"What hotel you going to stop at?"

"Hotel de l'Écu de Génève."

"Don't you do it! No Americans there! You stop at one of

those big hotels over the bridge—they're packed full of Americans."

"But I want to practice my Arabic."

"Good gracious, do you speak Arabic?"

"Yes—well enough to get along."

"Why, hang it, you won't get along in Geneva—*they* don't speak Arabic, they speak French. What hotel are you stopping at here?"

"Hotel Pension-Beaurivage."

"Sho, you ought to stop at the Schweitzerhof. Didn't you know the Schweitzerhof was the best hotel in Switzerland? —look at your Baedeker."

"Yes, I know—but I had an idea there warn't any Americans there."

"No Americans! Why, bless your soul, it's just alive with them! I'm in the great reception-room most all the time. I make lots of acquaintances there. Not as many as I did at first, because now only the new ones stop in there—the others go right along through. Where are you from?"

"Arkansaw."

"Is that so? I'm from New England—New Bloomfield's my town when I'm at home. I'm having a mighty good time to-day, ain't you?"

"Divine."

"That's what I call it. I like this knocking around loose and easy and making acquaintances and talking. I know an American soon as I see him, so I go and speak to him and make his acquaintance. I ain't ever bored on a trip like this if I can make new acquaintances and talk. I'm awful fond of talking when I can get hold of the right kind of a person, ain't you?"

"I prefer it to any other dissipation."

"That's my notion too. Now some people like to take a book and sit down and read and read and read or moon around yawping at the lake or these mountains and things but that ain't my way. No sir, if they like it let 'em do it, I don't object. But as for me, talking's what *I* like. You been up the Rigi?"

"Yes."

"What hotel did you stop at?"

"Schreiber."

"That's the place!—I stopped there too. *Full* of Americans, *wasn't* it? It always is—always is. That's what they say. Everybody says that. What ship did you come over in?"

"*Ville de Paris.*"

"French, I reckon. What kind of a passage did . . . excuse me a minute, there's some Americans I haven't seen before."

And away he went. He went uninjured, too—I had the murderous impulse to harpoon him in the back with my alpenstock but as I raised the weapon the disposition left me. I found I hadn't the heart to kill him, he was such a joyous, innocent, good-natured numbskull.

Half an hour later I was sitting on a bench inspecting with strong interest a noble monolith which we were skimming by —a monolith not shaped by man but by Nature's free great hand—a massy pyramidal rock eighty feet high devised by Nature ten million years ago against the day when a man worthy of it should need it for his monument. The time came at last and now this grand remembrancer bears Schiller's name in huge letters upon its face. Curiously enough, this rock was not degraded or defiled in any way. It is said that two years ago a stranger let himself down from the top of it with ropes and pulleys and painted all over it in blue letters bigger than those in Schiller's name these words:

"Try Sozodont"
"Buy Sun Stove Polish"
"Helmbold's Buchu"
"Try Benzaline for the Blood"

He was captured, and it turned out that he was an American. Upon his trial the judge said to him:

"You are from a land where any insolent that wants to is privileged to profane and insult Nature and, through her, Nature's God, if by so doing he can put a sordid penny in his pocket. But here the case is different. Because you are a foreigner and ignorant I will make your sentence light. If you were a native I would deal strenuously with you. Hear and obey: You will immediately remove every trace of your offensive work from the Schiller monument. You pay a fine of ten thousand francs. You will suffer two years' imprisonment at hard labor. You will then be horsewhipped, tarred and feathered, deprived of your ears, ridden on a rail to the confines of the canton and banished forever. The severest penalties are omitted in your case—not as a grace to you but to that great republic which had the misfortune to give you birth."

The steamer's benches were ranged back to back across the deck. My back hair was mingling innocently with the back hair of a couple of ladies. Presently they were addressed by someone and I overheard this conversation:

"You are Americans, I think? So'm I."

"Yes—we are Americans."

"I knew it—I can always tell them. What ship did you come over in?"

"*City of Chester.*"

"Oh yes—Inman line. We came in the *Batavia*—Cunard, you know. What kind of a passage did you have?"

"Pretty fair."

"That was luck. We had it awful rough. Captain said he'd hardly ever seen it rougher. Where are you from?"

"New Jersey."

"So'm I. No—I didn't mean that. I'm from New England. New Bloomfield's my place. These your children?—belong to both of you?"

"Only to one of us. They are mine. My friend is not married."

"Single, I reckon? So'm I. Are you two ladies traveling alone?"

"No—my husband is with us."

"Our whole family's along. It's awful slow going around alone—don't you think so?"

"I suppose it must be."

"Hi, there's Mount Pilatus coming in sight again. Named after Pontius Pilate, you know, that shot the apple off of William Tell's head. Guide-book tells all about it, they say. I didn't read it—an American told me. I don't read when I'm knocking around like this, having a good time. Did you ever see the chapel where William Tell used to preach?"

"I did not know he ever preached there."

"Oh yes he did. That American told me so. He don't ever shut up his guide-book. He knows more about this lake than the fishes in it. Besides, they *call* it 'Tell's Chapel'—you know that yourself. You ever been over here before?"

"Yes."

"I haven't. It's my first trip. But we've been all around— Paris and everywhere. I'm to enter Harvard next year. Studying German all the time now. Can't enter till I know German. This book's Otto's grammar. It's a mighty good book to get the *ich habe gehabt haben's* out of. But I don't really study when I'm knocking around this way. If the notion takes me I just run over my little old *ich habe gehabt, du hast gehabt, er hat gehabt, wir haben gehabt, ihr haben gehabt, sie haben gehabt*—kind of 'Now-I-lay-me-down-to-sleep' fashion, you know, and after that maybe I don't buckle to it again for three days. It's awful undermining to the intellect, German is. You want to take it in small doses, or first you know your brains all run together and you feel them sloshing around in your head same as so much drawn butter. But French is different. *French* ain't anything. I ain't any more afraid of French than a tramp's afraid of pie. I can rattle off my little *j'ai, tu as, il a* and the rest of it just as easy as a-b-c. I get along pretty well in Paris or anywhere where they speak French. What hotel are you stopping at?"

"The Schweitzerhof."

"No! Is that so? I never see you in the big reception-room. I go in there a good deal of the time, because there's so many Americans there. I make lots of acquaintances. You been up the Rigi yet?"

"No."

"Going?"

"We think of it."

"What hotel you going to stop at?"

"I don't know."

"Well, then, you stop at the Schreiber—it's full of Americans. What ship did you come over in?"

"City of Chester."

"Oh yes, I remember I asked you that before. But I always ask everybody what ship they came over in, and so sometimes I forget and ask again. You going to Geneva?"

"Yes."

"What hotel you going to stop at?"

"We expect to stop in a pension."

"I don't hardly believe you'll like that. There's very few Americans in the pensions. What hotel are you stopping at here?"

"The Schweitzerhof."

"Oh yes, I asked you that before too. But I always ask everybody what hotel they're stopping at, and so I've got my head all mixed up with hotels. But it makes talk, and I love to talk. It refreshes me up so—don't it you—on a trip like this?"

"Yes—sometimes."

"Well, it does me too. As long as I'm talking I never feel bored—ain't that the way with you?"

"Yes—generally. But there are exceptions to the rule."

"Oh, of course. *I* don't care to talk to everybody, *myself.* If a person starts in to jabber-jabber-jabber about scenery and history and pictures and all sorts of tiresome things I get the fan-tods mighty soon. I say 'Well, I must be going now— hope I'll see you again'—and then I take a walk. Where you from?"

"New Jersey."

"Why, bother it all, I asked you *that* before too. Have you seen the Lion of Lucerne?"

"Not yet."

"Nor I, either. But the man who told me about Mount

Pilatus says it's one of the things to see. It's twenty-eight feet long. It don't seem reasonable but he said so, anyway. He saw it yesterday. Said it was dying, then, so I reckon it's dead by this time. But that ain't any matter, of course they'll stuff it. Did you say the children are yours—or *hers?*"

"Mine."

"Oh, so you did. Are you going up the . . . no, I asked you that. What ship . . . no, I asked you that too. What hotel are you . . . no, you told me that. Let me see . . . um. . . . Oh, what kind of a voy . . . no, we've been over that ground too. Um . . . um . . . well, I believe that is all. *Bonjour*—I am very glad to have made your acquaintance, ladies. *Guten Tag.*"

25. The Jodel in Its Native Wilds

The Rigi-Kulm is an imposing Alpine mass, six thousand feet high, which stands by itself and commands a mighty prospect of blue lakes, green valleys and snowy mountains—a compact and magnificent picture three hundred miles in circumference. The ascent is made by rail or horseback or on foot, as one may prefer. I and my agent panoplied ourselves in walking-costume one bright morning and started down the lake on the steamboat. We got ashore at the village of Wäggis, three-quarters of an hour distant from Lucerne. This village is at the foot of the mountain.

We were soon tramping leisurely up the leafy mule-path, and then the talk began to flow, as usual. It was twelve o'clock noon, and a breezy, cloudless day. The ascent was gradual

and the glimpses, from under the curtaining boughs, of blue
water and tiny sailboats and beetling cliffs, were as charming
as glimpses of dreamland. All the circumstances were perfect
—and the anticipations too, for we should soon be enjoying
for the first time that wonderful spectacle, an Alpine sunrise
—the object of our journey. There was (apparently) no real
need to hurry, for the guide-book made the walking-distance
from Wäggis to the summit only three hours and a quarter.
I say "apparently," because the guide-book had already
fooled us once—about the distance from Allerheiligen to Oppenau—and for aught I knew it might be getting ready to
fool us again. We were only certain as to the altitudes—we
calculated to find out for ourselves how many hours it is from
the bottom to the top. The summit is six thousand feet above
the sea but only forty-five hundred feet above the lake. When
we had walked half an hour we were fairly into the swing and
humor of the undertaking, so we cleared for action. That is
to say, we got a boy whom we met to carry our alpenstocks
and satchels and overcoats and things for us. That left us free
for business. I suppose we must have stopped oftener to
stretch out on the grass in the shade and take a bit of a smoke
than this boy was used to, for presently he asked if it had been
our idea to hire him by the job or by the year? We told him
he could move along if he was in a hurry. He said he wasn't
in such a very particular hurry, but he wanted to get to the
top while he was young. We told him to clear out then and
leave the things at the uppermost hotel and say we should be
along presently. He said he would secure us a hotel if he
could but if they were all full he would ask them to build
another one and hurry up and get the paint and plaster dry
against we arrived. Still gently chaffing us, he pushed ahead
up the trail and soon disappeared. By six o'clock we were
pretty high up in the air, and the view of lake and mountains
had greatly grown in breadth and interest. We halted awhile
at a little public house, where we had bread and cheese and
a quart or two of fresh milk, out on the porch, with the big
panorama all before us—and then moved on again.

Ten minutes afterward we met a hot, red-faced man plunging down the mountain with mighty strides, swinging his alpenstock ahead of him and taking a grip on the ground with its iron point to support these big strides. He stopped, fanned himself with his hat, swabbed the perspiration from his face and neck with a red handkerchief, panted a moment or two and asked how far it was to Wäggis. I said three hours. He looked surprised and said:

"Why, it seems as if I could toss a biscuit into the lake from here, it's so close by. Is that an inn there?"

I said it was.

"Well," said he, "I can't stand another three hours, I've had enough for to-day. I'll take a bed there."

I asked:

"Are we nearly to the top?"

"Nearly to the *top!* Why, bless your soul, you haven't really started yet."

I said we would put up at the inn too. So we turned back and ordered a hot supper and had quite a jolly evening of it with this Englishman.

The German landlady gave us neat rooms and nice beds, and when I and my agent turned in it was with the resolution to be up early and make the utmost of our first Alpine sunrise. But of course we were dead tired and slept like policemen. So when we awoke in the morning and ran to the window it was already too late, because it was half past eleven. It was a sharp disappointment. However, we ordered breakfast and told the landlady to call the Englishman but she said he was already up and off at daybreak—and swearing mad about something or other. We could not find out what the matter was. He had asked the landlady the altitude of her place above the level of the lake and she had told him fourteen hundred and ninety-five feet. That was all that was said. Then he lost his temper. He said that between —— fools and guide-books a man could acquire ignorance enough in twenty-four hours in a country like this to last him a year. Harris believed our boy had been loading him up with misinformation and this was probably the case, for his epithet described that boy to a dot.

We got under way about the turn of noon and pulled out for the summit again with a fresh and vigorous step. When we had gone about two hundred yards and stopped to rest I glanced to the left while I was lighting my pipe, and in the distance detected a long worm of black smoke crawling lazily up the steep mountain. Of course that was the locomotive. We propped ourselves on our elbows at once to gaze, for we had never seen a mountain railway yet. Presently we could make out the train. It seemed incredible that that thing should creep straight up a sharp slant like the roof of a house —but there it was, and it was doing that very miracle.

In the course of a couple of hours we reached a fine breezy altitude where the little shepherd huts had big stones all over their roofs to hold them down to the earth when the great storms rage. The country was wild and rocky about here but there were plenty of trees, plenty of moss, and grass.

Away off on the opposite shore of the lake we could see some villages, and now for the first time we could observe the real difference between their proportions and those of the giant mountains at whose feet they slept. When one is in one of those villages it seems spacious and its houses seem high and not out of proportion to the mountain that overhangs them—but from our altitude, what a change! The mountains were bigger and grander than ever as they stood there thinking their solemn thoughts with their heads in the drifting clouds, but the villages at their feet—when the painstaking eye could trace them up and find them—were so reduced, so almost invisible and lay so flat against the ground that the exactest simile I can devise is to compare them to ant-deposits of granulated dirt overshadowed by the huge bulk of a cathedral. The steamboats skimming along under the stupendous precipices were diminished by distance to the daintiest little toys, the sailboats and rowboats to shallops proper for fairies that keep house in the cups of lilies and ride to court on the backs of bumblebees.

Presently we came upon half a dozen sheep nibbling grass in the spray of a stream of clear water that sprang from a rock wall a hundred feet high, and all at once our ears were startled with a melodious "Lul . . . l . . . l . . . lul-lul-*la*hee-o-o-o!" pealing joyously from a near but invisible source, and recognized that we were hearing for the first time the famous Alpine *jodel* in its own native wilds. And we recognized also that it was that sort of quaint commingling of barytone and falsetto which at home we call "Tyrolese warbling."

The jodeling (pronounced y*o*dling—emphasis on the *o*) continued and was very pleasant and inspiriting to hear. Now the jodeler appeared—a shepherd boy of sixteen—and in our gladness and gratitude we gave him a franc to jodel some more. So he jodeled and we listened. We moved on presently and he generously jodeled us out of sight. After about fifteen minutes we came across another shepherd boy who was jodeling, and gave him half a franc to keep it up. He also jodeled us out of sight. After that we found a jodeler every ten minutes. We gave the first one eight cents, the second one six cents, the third one four, the fourth one a penny, contributed nothing to Nos. 5, 6 and 7, and during the remainder of the day hired the rest of the jodelers, at a franc apiece, not to jodel any more. There is somewhat too much of this jodeling in the Alps.

About the middle of the afternoon we passed through a prodigious natural gateway called the Felsenthor, formed by two enormous upright rocks, with a third lying across the top. There was a very attractive little hotel close by but our energies were not conquered yet, so we went on.

Three hours afterward we came to the railway-track. It was planted straight up the mountain with the slant of a ladder that leans against a house, and it seemed to us that a man would need good nerves who proposed to travel up it or down it either.

During the latter part of the afternoon we cooled our roasting interiors with ice-cold water from clear streams, the only really satisfying water we had tasted since we left home, for at the hotels on the continent they merely give you a tumbler of ice to soak your water in and that only modifies its hotness, doesn't make it cold. Water can only be made cold enough for summer comfort by being prepared in a refrigerator or a closed ice-pitcher. Europeans say ice-water impairs digestion. How do they know?—they never drink any.

At ten minutes past six we reached the Kaltbad station, where there is a spacious hotel with great verandas which command a majestic expanse of lake and mountain scenery. We were pretty well fagged out now but as we did not wish to miss the Alpine sunrise we got through with our dinner as quickly as possible and hurried off to bed. It was unspeakably comfortable to stretch our weary limbs between the cold, damp sheets. And how we did sleep!—for there is no opiate like Alpine pedestrianism.

In the morning we both awoke and leaped out of bed at the same instant and ran and stripped aside the window-curtains but we suffered a bitter disappointment again: it was already half past three in the afternoon.

We dressed sullenly and in ill spirits, each accusing the other of oversleeping. Harris said if we had brought the courier along, as we ought to have done, we should not have missed these sunrises. I said he knew very well that one of us would have had to sit up and wake the courier. And I added that we were having trouble enough to take care of ourselves on this climb, without having to take care of a courier besides.

During breakfast our spirits came up a little, since we found by the guide-book that in the hotels on the summit the tourist is not left to trust to luck for his sunrise but is roused betimes by a man who goes through the halls with a great Alpine horn, blowing blasts that would raise the dead. And there was another consoling thing: the guide-book said that up there on the summit the guests did not wait to dress much but seized a red bed blanket and sailed out arrayed like an Indian. This was good. This would be romantic. Two hundred and fifty people grouped on the windy summit with their hair flying and their red blankets flapping in the solemn presence of the snowy ranges and the messenger splendors of the coming sun would be a striking and memorable spectacle. So it was good luck, not ill luck, that we had missed those other sunrises.

We were informed by the guide-book that we were now 3,228 feet above the level of the lake—therefore full two-thirds of our journey had been accomplished. We got away at a quarter past four, P.M. A hundred yards above the hotel the railway divided. One track went straight up the steep hill, the other one turned square off to the right, with a very slight grade. We took the latter and followed it more than a mile, turned a rocky corner and came in sight of a handsome new hotel. If we had gone on we should have arrived at the summit but Harris preferred to ask a lot of questions—as usual, of a man who didn't know anything—and he told us to go back and follow the other route. We did so. We could ill afford this loss of time.

We climbed and climbed and we kept on climbing. We reached about forty summits but there was always another one just ahead. It came on to rain and it rained in dead earnest. We were soaked through and it was bitter cold. Next a smoky fog of clouds covered the whole region densely and we took to the railway-ties to keep from getting lost. Sometimes we sloped along in a narrow path on the left-hand side of the track but by and by when the fog blew aside a little and we saw that we were treading the rampart of a precipice and that our left elbows were projecting over a perfectly boundless and bottomless vacancy, we gasped, and jumped for the ties again.

The night shut down, dark and drizzly and cold. About eight in the evening the fog lifted and showed us a well-worn path which led up a very steep rise to the left. We took it, and as soon as we had got far enough from the railway to render the finding it again an impossibility, the fog shut down on us once more.

We were in a bleak unsheltered place now and had to

trudge right along in order to keep warm, though we rather expected to go over a precipice sooner or later. About nine o'clock we made an important discovery—that we were not in any path. We groped around a while on our hands and knees but could not find it, so we sat down in the mud and the wet scant grass to wait.

We were terrified into this by being suddenly confronted with a vast body which showed itself vaguely for an instant and in the next instant was smothered in the fog again. It was really the hotel we were after, monstrously magnified by the fog, but we took it for the face of a precipice and decided not to try to claw up it.

We sat there an hour with chattering teeth and quivering bodies, and quarreled over all sorts of trifles, but gave most of our attention to abusing each other for the stupidity of deserting the railway-track. We sat with our backs to that precipice because what little wind there was came from that quarter. At some time or other the fog thinned a little. We did not know when, for we were facing the empty universe and the thinness could not show, but at last Harris happened to look around and there stood a huge, dim, spectral hotel where the precipice had been. One could faintly discern the windows and chimneys and a dull blur of lights. Our first emotion was deep, unutterable gratitude, our next was a foolish rage born of the suspicion that possibly the hotel had been visible three-quarters of an hour while we sat there in those cold puddles quarreling.

Yes, it was the Rigi-Kulm hotel—the one that occupies the extreme summit and whose remote little sparkle of lights we had often seen glinting high aloft among the stars from our balcony away down yonder in Lucerne. The crusty portier and the crusty clerks gave us the surly reception which their kind deal in in prosperous times, but by mollifying them with an extra display of obsequiousness and servility we finally got them to show us to the room which our boy had engaged for us.

We got into some dry clothing, and while our supper was

preparing we loafed forsakenly through a couple of vast cavernous drawing-rooms, one of which had a stove in it. This stove was in a corner, and densely walled around with people. We could not get near the fire, so we moved at large in the arctic spaces among a multitude of people who sat silent, smileless, forlorn and shivering—thinking what fools they were to come, perhaps. There were some Americans and some Germans but one could see that the great majority were English.

We lounged into an apartment where there was a great crowd, to see what was going on. It was a memento-magazine. The tourists were eagerly buying all sorts and styles of paper-cutters marked "Souvenir of the Rigi," with handles made of the little curved horn of the ostensible chamois. There were all manner of wooden goblets and such things, similarly marked. I was going to buy a paper-cutter but I believed I could remember the cold comfort of the Rigi-Kulm without it, so I smothered the impulse.

Supper warmed us and we went immediately to bed—but first, as Mr. Baedeker requests all tourists to call his attention to any errors which they may find in his guide-books, I dropped him a line to inform him that when he said the foot journey from Wäggis to the summit was only three hours and a quarter, he missed it by just about three days. I had previously informed him of his mistake about the distance from Allerheiligen to Oppenau, and had also informed the Ordnance Department of the German government of the same error in the imperial maps. I will add here that I never got any answer to these letters or any thanks from either of those sources. And, what is still more discourteous, these corrections have not been made either in the maps or the guide-books. But I will write again when I get time, for my letters may have miscarried.

We curled up in the clammy beds and went to sleep without rocking. We were so sodden with fatigue that we never stirred nor turned over till the blooming blasts of the Alpine horn aroused us. It may well be imagined that we did not lose any time. We snatched on a few odds and ends of clothing, cocooned ourselves in the proper red blankets and plunged along the halls and out into the whistling wind bareheaded. We saw a tall wooden scaffolding on the very peak of the summit a hundred yards away and made for it. We rushed up the stairs to the top of this scaffolding and stood there above the vast outlying world with hair flying and ruddy blankets waving and cracking in the fierce breeze.

"Fifteen minutes too late, at last!" said Harris in a vexed voice. "The sun is clear above the horizon."

"No matter," I said, "it is a most magnificent spectacle and we will see it do the rest of its rising, anyway."

In a moment we were deeply absorbed in the marvel before us and dead to everything else. The great cloud-barred disk of the sun stood just above a limitless expanse of tossing white-caps—so to speak—a billowy chaos of massy mountain domes and peaks draped in imperishable snow and flooded with an opaline glory of changing and dissolving splendors, while through rifts in a black cloud-bank above the sun, radiating lances of diamond dust shot to the zenith. The cloven valleys of the lower world swam in a tinted mist which veiled the ruggedness of their crags and ribs and ragged forests and turned all the forbidding region into a soft and rich and sensuous paradise.

We could not speak. We could hardly breathe. We could only gaze in drunken ecstasy and drink it in. Presently Harris exclaimed:

"Why—nation, it's going *down!*"

Perfectly true. We had missed the *morning* hornblow and slept all day. This was stupefying.

Harris said:

"Look here, the sun isn't the spectacle—it's *us*—stacked up here on top of this gallows in these idiotic blankets, and two hundred and fifty well-dressed men and women down here gawking up at us and not caring a straw whether the sun rises or sets as long as they've got such a ridiculous spectacle as this to set down in their memorandum-books. They seem to be laughing their ribs loose and there's one girl there that appears to be going all to pieces. I never saw such a man as you before. I think you are the very last possibility in the way of an ass."

"What have *I* done?" I answered with heat.

"What have you done? You've got up at half past seven o'clock in the evening to see the sun rise, that's what you've done."

"And have you done any better, I'd like to know? I always used to get up with the lark till I came under the petrifying influence of your turgid intellect."

"*You* used to get up with the lark—oh, no doubt—you'll get up with the hangman one of these days. But you ought to be ashamed to be jawing here like this in a red blanket on a forty-foot scaffold on top of the Alps. And no end of people down here to boot. This isn't any place for an exhibition of temper."

And so the customary quarrel went on. When the sun was fairly down, we slipped back to the hotel in the charitable gloaming and went to bed again. We had encountered the hornblower on the way and he had tried to collect compensation not only for announcing the sunset, which we did see, but for the sunrise, which we had totally missed. But we said no, we only took our solar rations on the "European plan"— pay for what you get. He promised to make us hear his horn in the morning if we were alive.

26. Looking for a Western Sunrise

He kept his word. We heard his horn and instantly got up. It was dark and cold and wretched. As I fumbled around for the matches, knocking things down with my quaking hands, I wished the sun would rise in the middle of the day when it was warm and bright and cheerful and one wasn't sleepy. We proceeded to dress by the gloom of a couple of sickly candles but we could hardly button anything, our hands shook so. I thought of how many happy people there were in Europe, Asia and America and everywhere who were sleeping peacefully in their beds and did not have to get up and see the Rigi sunrise—people who did not appreciate their advantage, as like as not, but would get up in the morning wanting more boons of Providence. While thinking these thoughts I yawned in a rather ample way and my upper teeth got hitched on a nail over the door and while I was mounting a chair to free myself, Harris drew the window-curtain and said:

"Oh, this is luck! We sha'n't have to go out at all—yonder are the mountains, in full view."

That was glad news indeed. It made us cheerful right away. One could see the grand Alpine masses dimly outlined against the black firmament, and one or two faint stars blinking through rifts in the night. Fully clothed, and wrapped in blankets, we huddled ourselves up by the window with lighted pipes and fell into chat while we waited in exceeding comfort to see how an Alpine sunrise was going to look by candlelight. By and by a delicate, spiritual sort of effulgence spread itself by imperceptible degrees over the loftiest altitudes of the snowy wastes—but there the effort seemed to stop. I said presently:

"There is a hitch about this sunrise somewhere. It doesn't seem to go. What do you reckon is the matter with it?"

"I don't know. It appears to hang fire somewhere. I never saw a sunrise act like that before. Can it be that the hotel is playing anything on us?"

"Of course not. The hotel merely has a property interest in the sun, it has nothing to do with the management of it. It is a precarious kind of property, too. A succession of total eclipses would probably ruin this tavern. Now what can be the matter with this sunrise?"

Harris jumped up and said:

"I've got it! I know what's the matter with it! We've been looking at the place where the sun *set* last night!"

"It is perfectly true! Why couldn't you have thought of that sooner? Now we've lost another one! And all through your blundering. It was exactly like you to light a pipe and sit down to wait for the sun to rise in the west."

"It was exactly like me to find out the mistake, too. You never would have found it out. I find out all the mistakes."

"You make them all, too, else your most valuable faculty would be wasted on you. But don't stop to quarrel now— maybe we are not too late yet."

But we were. The sun was well up when we got to the exhibition-ground.

On our way up we met the crowd returning—men and women dressed in all sorts of queer costumes and exhibiting all degrees of cold and wretchedness in their gaits and countenances. A dozen still remained on the ground when we reached there, huddled together about the scaffold with their backs to the bitter wind. They had their red guidebooks open at the diagram of the view and were painfully picking out the several mountains and trying to impress their names and positions on their memories. It was one of the saddest sights I ever saw.

Two sides of this place were guarded by railings to keep people from being blown over the precipices. The view, looking sheer down into the broad valley eastward from this great elevation—almost a perpendicular mile—was very quaint and curious. Counties, towns, hilly ribs and ridges, wide stretches of green meadow, great forest tracts, winding streams, a dozen blue lakes, a flock of busy steamboats—we saw all this little world in unique circumstantiality of detail —saw it just as the birds see it—and all reduced to the smallest of scales and as sharply worked out and finished as a steel engraving. The numerous toy villages with tiny spires projecting out of them were just as the children might have left them when done with play the day before. The forest tracts were diminished to cushions of moss. One or two big lakes were dwarfed to ponds, the smaller ones to puddles—though they did not look like puddles but like blue eardrops which had fallen and lodged in slight depressions conformable to their shapes among the moss-beds and the smooth levels of dainty green farm-land. The microscopic steamboats glided along as in a city reservoir, taking a mighty time to cover the distance between ports which seemed only a yard apart. And the isthmus which separated two lakes looked as if one might stretch out on it and lie with both elbows in the water, yet we knew invisible wagons were toiling across it and finding the distance a tedious one. This beautiful miniature world had exactly the appearance of those "relief maps" which reproduce nature precisely, with the heights and depressions and other details graduated to a reduced scale and with the rocks, trees, lakes, etc., colored after nature.

I believed we could walk down to Wäggis or Vitznau in a day but I knew we could go down by rail in about an hour, so I chose the latter method. I wanted to see what it was like, anyway. The train came along about the middle of the afternoon, and an odd thing it was. The locomotive-boiler stood on end and it and the whole locomotive were tilted sharply backward. There were two passenger-cars, roofed, but wide open all around. These cars were not tilted back, but the seats were. This enables the passenger to sit level while going down a steep incline.

There are three railway-tracks. The central one is cogged. The "lantern wheel" of the engine grips its way along these cogs and pulls the train up the hill or retards its motion on the down trip. About the same speed—three miles an hour —is maintained both ways. Whether going up or down, the locomotive is always at the lower end of the train. It pushes in the one case, braces back in the other. The passenger rides backward going up and faces forward going down.

We got front seats, and while the train moved along about fifty yards on level ground I was not the least frightened. But now it started abruptly down-stairs, and I caught my breath. And I, like my neighbors, unconsciously held back all I could and threw my weight to the rear, but of course that did no particular good. I had slidden down the balusters when I was a boy and thought nothing of it but to slide down the balusters in a railway-train is a thing to make one's flesh creep. Sometimes we had as much as ten yards of almost level ground, and this gave us a few full breaths in comfort. But straightway we would turn a corner and see a long steep line of rails stretching down below us, and the comfort was at an end. One expected to see the locomotive pause or slack up a little and approach this plunge cautiously but it did nothing of the kind. It went calmly on, and when it reached the jumping-off place it made a sudden bow, and went gliding smoothly downstairs untroubled by the circumstances.

It was wildly exhilarating to slide along the edge of the precipices after this grisly fashion and look straight down upon that far-off valley which I was describing a while ago.

There was no level ground at the Kaltbad station. The railbed was as steep as a roof. I was curious to see how the stop was going to be managed. But it was very simple. The train came sliding down, and when it reached the right spot it just stopped—that was all there was "to it"—stopped on the steep incline, and when the exchange of passengers and baggage had been made it moved off and went sliding down again. The train can be stopped anywhere at a moment's notice.

There was one curious effect which I need not take the trouble to describe—because I can scissor a description of it out of the railway company's advertising pamphlet and save my ink:

"On the whole tour, particularly at the Descent, we undergo an optical illusion which often seems to be incredible. All the shrubs, fir trees, stables, houses, etc., seem to be bent in a slanting direction as by an immense pressure of air. They are all standing awry, so much awry that the chalets and cottages of the peasants seem to be tumbling down. It is the consequence of the steep inclination of the line. Those who are seated in the carriage do not observe that they are going down a declivity of twenty to twenty-five degrees (their seats being adapted to this course of proceeding and being bent down at their backs). They mistake their carriage and its horizontal lines for a proper measure of the normal plain, and therefore all the objects outside which really are in a horizontal position must show a disproportion of twenty to twenty-five degrees declivity in regard to the mountain."

By the time one reaches Kaltbad he has acquired confidence in the railway, and he now ceases to try to ease the locomotive by holding back. Thenceforward he smokes his pipe in serenity and gazes out upon the magnificent picture below and about him with unfettered enjoyment. There is nothing to interrupt the view or the breeze. It is like inspecting the world on the wing. However—to be exact—there is one place where the serenity lapses for a while. This is while one is crossing the Schnurrtobel Bridge, a frail structure which swings its gossamer frame down through the dizzy air, over a gorge, like a vagrant spider-strand.

One has no difficulty in remembering his sins while the train is creeping down this bridge. And he repents of them, too. Though he sees, when he gets to Vitznau, that he need not have done it, the bridge was perfectly safe.

So ends the eventful trip which we made to the Rigi-Kulm to see an Alpine sunrise.

27. From Lucerne to Interlaken

An hour's sail brought us to Lucerne again. We now prepared for a considerable walk—from Lucerne to Interlaken over the Brünig Pass. But at the last moment the weather was so good that I changed my mind and hired a four-horse carriage. It was a huge vehicle, roomy, as easy in its motion as a palanquin, and exceedingly comfortable.

We got away pretty early in the morning after a hot breakfast and went bowling along over a. hard, smooth road through the summer loveliness of Switzerland, with near and distant lakes and mountains before and about us for the entertainment of the eye, and the music of multitudinous birds to charm the ear. Sometimes there was only the width of the road between the imposing precipices on the right and the clear cool water on the left with its shoals of uncatchable fishes skimming about through the bars of sun and shadow. And sometimes, in place of the precipices, the grassy land stretched away in an apparently endless upward slant and was dotted everywhere with snug little chalets, the peculiarly captivating cottage of Switzerland.

The ordinary chalet turns a broad, honest gable end to the road, and its ample roof hovers over the home in a protecting, caressing way, projecting its sheltering eaves far outward. The quaint windows are filled with little panes and garnished with white muslin curtains and brightened with boxes of blooming flowers. Across the front of the house and up the spreading eaves and along the fanciful railings of the shallow porch are elaborate carvings—wreaths, fruits, arabesques, verses from Scripture, names, dates, etc. The building is wholly of wood, reddish brown in tint, a very pleasing color. It generally has vines climbing over it. Set such a house against the fresh green of the hillside and it looks ever so cozy and inviting and picturesque and is a decidedly graceful addition to the landscape.

We had such a beautiful day and such endless pictures of limpid lakes and green hills and valleys and majestic mountains and milky cataracts dancing down the steeps and gleaming in the sun that we could not help feeling sweet toward all the world. So we tried to drink all the milk and eat all the grapes and apricots and berries and buy all the bouquets of wild flowers which the little peasant boys and girls offered for sale. But we had to retire from this contract, for it was too heavy. At short distances—and they were entirely too short—all along the road were groups of neat and comely children with their wares nicely and temptingly set forth in the grass under the shade trees, and as soon as we approached they swarmed into the road, holding out their baskets and milk bottles, and ran beside the carriage barefoot and bareheaded and importuned us to buy. They seldom desisted early but continued to run and insist—beside the wagon while they could and behind it until they lost breath. Then they turned and chased a returning carriage back to their trading-post again. After several hours of this without any intermission it becomes almost annoying. I do not know what we should have done without the returning carriages to draw off the pursuit. However, there were plenty of these, loaded with dusty tourists and piled high with luggage. Indeed, from Lucerne to Interlaken we had the spectacle, among other scenery, of an unbroken procession of fruit-peddlers and tourist carriages.

Our talk was mostly anticipatory of what we should see on the down-grade of the Brünig by and by after we should pass the summit. All our friends in Lucerne had said that to look down upon Meiringen and the rushing blue-gray river Aar and the broad level green valley and across at the mighty Alpine precipices that rise straight up to the clouds out of that valley, and up at the microscopic chalets perched upon the dizzy eaves of those precipices and winking dimly and fitfully through the drifting veil of vapor, and still up and up at the superb Oltschibach and the other beautiful cascades that leap from those rugged heights, robed in powdery spray, ruffled with foam and girdled with rainbows—to look upon these things, they said, was to look upon the last possibility of the sublime and the enchanting. Therefore, as I say, we talked mainly of these coming wonders. If we were conscious of any impatience it was to get there in favorable season. If we felt any anxiety it was that the day might remain perfect and enable us to see those marvels at their best.

As we approached the Kaiserstuhl a part of the harness gave way. We were in distress for a moment, but only a moment. It was the fore-and-aft gear that was broken—the thing that leads aft from the forward part of the horse and is made fast to the thing that pulls the wagon. In America this would have been a heavy leathern strap but all over the continent it is nothing but a piece of rope the size of your little finger—clothes-line is what it is. Cabs use it, private carriages, freight-carts and wagons, all sorts of vehicles have it. In Munich I afterward saw it used on a long wagon laden with fifty-four half-barrels of beer. I had before noticed that the cabs in Heidelberg used it—not new rope but rope that had been in use since Abraham's time—and I had felt nervous sometimes behind it when the cab was tearing down a hill. But I had long been accustomed to it now and had even become afraid of the leather strap which belonged in its place. Our driver got a fresh piece of clothes-line out of his locker and repaired the break in two minutes.

We had four very handsome horses, and the driver was

very proud of his turnout. He would bowl along on a reasonable trot on the highway but when he entered a village he did it on a furious run and accompanied it with a frenzy of ceaseless whip-crackings that sounded like volleys of musketry. He tore through the narrow streets and around the sharp curves like a moving earthquake, showering his volleys as he went, and before him swept a continuous tidal wave of scampering children, ducks, cats, and mothers clasping babies which they had snatched out of the way of the coming destruction. And as this living wave washed aside along the walls its elements, being safe, forgot their fears and turned their admiring gaze upon that gallant driver till he thundered around the next curve and was lost to sight.

He was a great man to those villagers, with his gaudy clothes and his terrific ways. Whenever he stopped to have his cattle watered and fed with loaves of bread, the villagers stood around admiring him while he swaggered about, the little boys gazed up at his face with humble homage, and the landlord brought out foaming mugs of beer and conversed proudly with him while he drank. Then he mounted his lofty box, swung his explosive whip and away he went again, like a storm. I had not seen anything like this before since I was a boy and the stage used to flourish through the village with the dust flying and the horn tooting.

When we reached the base of the Kaiserstuhl we took two more horses. We had to toil along with difficulty for an hour and a half or two hours, for the ascent was not very gradual, but when we passed the backbone and approached the station the driver surpassed all his previous efforts in the way of rush and clatter. He could not have six horses all the time, so he made the most of his chance while he had it.

Up to this point we had been in the heart of the William Tell region. The hero is not forgotten, by any means, or held in doubtful veneration. His wooden image, with his bow drawn, above the doors of taverns was a frequent feature of the scenery.

About noon we arrived at the foot of the Brünig Pass and

made a two-hour stop at the village hotel, another of those clean, pretty and thoroughly well-kept inns which are such an astonishment to people who are accustomed to hotels of a dismally different pattern in remote country-towns. There was a lake here in the lap of the great mountains. The green slopes that rose toward the lower crags were graced with scattered Swiss cottages nestling among miniature farms and gardens, and from out a leafy ambuscade in the upper heights tumbled a brawling cataract.

After dinner we talked with several Englishmen and they inflamed our desire to a hotter degree than ever to see the sights of Meiringen from the heights of the Brünig Pass. They said the view was marvelous and that one who had seen it once could never forget it. They also spoke of the romantic nature of the road over the pass and how in one place it had been cut through a flank of the solid rock in such a way that the mountain overhung the tourist as he passed by. And they furthermore said that the sharp turns in the road and the abruptness of the descent would afford us a thrilling experience, for we should go down in a flying gallop and seem to be spinning around the rings of a whirlwind like a drop of whisky descending the spirals of a corkscrew. I got all the information out of these gentlemen that we could need. And then, to make everything complete, I asked them if a body could get hold of a little fruit and milk here and there in case of necessity. They threw up their hands in speechless intimation that the road was simply paved with refreshment-peddlers. We were impatient to get away now, and the rest of our two-hour stop rather dragged. But finally the set time arrived and we began the ascent. Indeed it was a wonderful road. It was smooth and compact and clean, and the side next the precipices was guarded all along by dressed stone posts about three feet high, placed at short distances apart. The road could not have been better built if Napoleon the First had built it. He seems to have been the introducer of the sort of roads which Europe now uses. All literature which describes life as it existed in England, France and Germany up to the close of the last century is filled with pictures of coaches and carriages wallowing through these three countries in mud and slush half-wheel deep. But after Napoleon had floundered through a conquered kingdom he generally arranged things so that the rest of the world could follow dryshod.

We went on climbing higher and higher and curving hither and thither in the shade of noble woods, and with a rich variety and profusion of wild flowers all about us, and glimpses of rounded grassy backbones below us occupied by trim chalets and nibbling sheep, and other glimpses of far lower altitudes where distance diminished the chalets to toys and obliterated the sheep altogether. And every now and then some ermined monarch of the Alps swung magnificently into view for a moment, then drifted past an intervening spur and disappeared again.

It was an intoxicating trip altogether. The exceeding sense of satisfaction that follows a good dinner added largely to the enjoyment. The having something especial to look forward to and muse about, like the approaching grandeurs of Meiringen, sharpened the zest. Smoking was never so good before, solid comfort was never solider. We lay back against the thick cushions, silent, meditative, steeped in felicity.

I rubbed my eyes, opened them, and started. I had been dreaming I was at sea, and it was a thrilling surprise to wake up and find land all around me. It took me a couple of seconds to "come to," as you may say. Then I took in the situation. The horses were drinking at a trough in the edge of a town, the driver was taking beer, Harris was snoring at my side, the courier, with folded arms and bowed head, was sleeping on the box, two dozen barefooted and bareheaded children were gathered about the carriage with their hands crossed behind, gazing up with serious and innocent admiration at the dozing tourists baking there in the sun. Several small girls held night-capped babies nearly as big as themselves in their arms, and even these fat babies seemed to take a sort of sluggish interest in us.

We had slept an hour and a half and missed all the scenery!

I did not need anybody to tell me that. If I had been a girl I could have cursed for vexation. As it was, I woke up the agent and gave him a piece of my mind. Instead of being humiliated he only upbraided me for being so wanting in vigilance. He said he had expected to improve his mind by coming to Europe, but a man might travel to the ends of the earth with me and never see anything, for I was manifestly endowed with the very genius of ill luck. He even tried to get up some emotion about that poor courier, who never got a chance to see anything on account of my heedlessness. But when I thought I had borne about enough of this kind of talk I threatened to make Harris tramp back to the summit and make a report on that scenery, and this suggestion spiked his battery.

We drove sullenly through Brienz, dead to the seductions of its bewildering array of Swiss carvings and the clamorous *hoo*-hooing of its cuckoo clocks, and had not entirely recovered our spirits when we rattled across the bridge over the rushing blue river and entered the pretty town of Interlaken. It was just about sunset, and we had made the trip from Lucerne in ten hours.

28. An Arkansas Bride

We located ourselves at the Jungfrau Hotel, one of those huge establishments which the needs of modern travel have created in every attractive spot on the continent. There was a great gathering at dinner and, as usual, one heard all sorts of languages.

The table d'hôte was served by waitresses dressed in the

quaint and comely costume of the Swiss peasants. This consists of a simple gros de laine trimmed with ashes of roses with overskirt of sacre bleu ventre saint gris, cut bias on the off-side, with facings of petit polonaise and narrow insertions of pâté de foie gras backstitched to the mise en scène in the form of a jeu d'esprit. It gives to the wearer a singularly piquant and alluring aspect.

One of these waitresses, a woman of forty, had side-whiskers reaching half-way down her jaw. They were two fingers broad, dark in color, pretty thick, and the hairs were an inch long. One sees many women on the continent with quite conspicuous mustaches but this was the only woman I saw who had reached the dignity of whiskers.

After dinner the guests of both sexes distributed themselves about the front porches and the ornamental grounds belonging to the hotel to enjoy the cool air but, as the twilight deepened toward darkness, they gathered themselves together in that saddest and solemnest and most constrained of all places, the great blank drawing-room which is the chief feature of all continental summer hotels. There they grouped themselves about in couples and threes and mumbled in bated voices and looked timid and homeless and forlorn.

There was a small piano in this room, a clattery, wheezy, asthmatic thing, certainly the very worst miscarriage in the way of a piano that the world has seen. In turn, five or six dejected and homesick ladies approached it doubtingly, gave it a single inquiring thump and retired with the lockjaw. But the boss of that instrument was to come, nevertheless, and from my own country—from Arkansaw.

She was a brand-new bride, innocent, girlish, happy in herself and her grave and worshiping stripling of a husband. She was about eighteen, just out of school, free from affections, unconscious of that passionless multitude around her. And the very first time she smote that old wreck one recognized that it had met its destiny. Her stripling brought an armful of aged sheet-music from their room—for this bride went "heeled," as you might say—and bent himself lovingly over and got ready to turn the pages.

The bride fetched a swoop with her fingers from one end of the keyboard to the other just to get her bearings, as it were, and you could see the congregation set their teeth with the agony of it. Then without any more preliminaries she turned on all the horrors of the "Battle of Prague," that venerable shivaree, and waded chin-deep in the blood of the slain. She made a fair and honorable average of two false notes in every five but her soul was in arms and she never stopped to correct. The audience stood it with pretty fair grit for a while but when the cannonade waxed hotter and fiercer and the discord average rose to four in five the procession began to move. A few stragglers held their ground ten minutes longer but when the girl began to wring the true inwardness out of the "cries of the wounded" they struck their colors and retired in a kind of panic.

There never was a completer victory. I was the only noncombatant left on the field. I would not have deserted my countrywoman anyhow, but indeed I had no desires in that direction. None of us like mediocrity but we all reverence perfection. This girl's music was perfection in its way. It was the worst music that had ever been achieved on our planet by a mere human being.

I moved up close and never lost a strain. When she got through I asked her to play it again. She did it with a pleased alacrity and a heightened enthusiasm. She made it *all* discords this time. She got an amount of anguish into the cries of the wounded that shed a new light on human suffering. She was on the war-path all the evening. All the time, crowds of people gathered on the porches and pressed their noses against the windows to look and marvel but the bravest never ventured in. The bride went off satisfied and happy with her young fellow when her appetite was finally gorged, and the tourists swarmed in again.

In the morning when we looked out of our windows we saw a wonderful sight. Across the valley and apparently quite neighborly and close at hand, the giant form of the Jungfrau rose cold and white into the clear sky beyond a gateway in the nearer highlands. It reminded me somehow of one of those colossal billows which swells suddenly up beside one's ship at sea, sometimes, with its crest and shoulders snowy white and the rest of its noble proportions streaked downward with creamy foam.

I took out my sketch-book and made a little picture of the Jungfrau merely to get the shape.

I do not regard this as one of my finished works, in fact I do not rank it among my Works at all. It is only a study. It is hardly more than what one might call a sketch. Other artists have done me the grace to admire it but I am severe in my judgments of my own pictures and this one does not move me.

It was hard to believe that that lofty wooded rampart on the left which so overtops the Jungfrau was not actually the

higher of the two but it was not, of course. It is only two or three thousand feet high and of course has no snow upon it in summer, whereas the Jungfrau is not much short of fourteen thousand feet high and therefore that lowest verge of snow on her side, which seems nearly down to the valley level, is really about seven thousand feet higher up in the air than the summit of that wooded rampart. It is the distance that makes the deception. The wooded height is but four or five miles removed from us but the Jungfrau is four or five times that distance away.

The beautiful Giesbach Fall is near Interlaken, on the other side of the lake of Brienz, and is illuminated every night with those gorgeous theatrical fires whose name I cannot call just at this moment. This was said to be a spectacle which the tourist ought by no means to miss. I was strongly tempted but I could not go there with propriety, because one goes in a boat. The task which I had set myself was to walk over Europe on foot, not skim over it in a boat. I had made a tacit contract with myself. It was my duty to abide by it. I was willing to make boat trips for pleasure but I could not conscientiously make them in the way of business.

It cost me something of a pang to lose that fine sight but I lived down the desire and gained in my self-respect through the triumph. I had a finer and a grander sight, however, where I was. This was the mighty dome of the Jungfrau softly outlined against the sky and faintly silvered by the starlight. There was something subduing in the influence of that silent and solemn and awful presence. One seemed to meet the immutable, the indestructible, the eternal, face to face, and to feel the trivial and fleeting nature of his own existence the more sharply by the contrast. One had the sense of being under the brooding contemplation of a spirit, not an inert mass of rocks and ice—a spirit which had looked down through the slow drift of the ages upon a million vanished races of men and judged them and would judge a million more—and still be there, watching, unchanged and unchangeable, after all life should be gone and the earth have become a vacant desolation.

While I was feeling these things I was groping without knowing it toward an understanding of what the spell is which people find in the Alps and in no other mountains—that strange, deep, nameless influence which, once felt, cannot be forgotten—once felt, leaves always behind it a restless longing to feel it again—a longing which is like homesickness, a grieving, haunting yearning which will plead, implore and persecute till it has its will. I met dozens of people, imaginative and unimaginative, cultivated and uncultivated, who had come from far countries and roamed through the Swiss Alps year after year—they could not explain why. They had come first, they said, out of idle curiosity because everybody talked about it. They had come since because they could not help it, and they should keep on coming, while they lived, for the same reason. They had tried to break their chains and stay away but it was futile. Now, they had no desire to break them. Others came nearer formulating what they felt: they said they could find perfect rest and peace nowhere else when they were troubled. All frets and worries and chafings sank to sleep in the presence of the benignant serenity of the Alps. The Great Spirit of the Mountain breathed his own peace upon their hurt minds and sore hearts and healed them. They could not think base thoughts or do mean and sordid things here before the visible throne of God.

Down the road a piece was a Kursaal—whatever that may be—and we joined the human tide to see what sort of enjoyment it might afford. It was the usual open-air concert in an ornamental garden, with wines, beer, milk, whey, grapes, etc.—the whey and the grapes being necessaries of life to certain invalids whom physicians cannot repair and who only continue to exist by the grace of whey or grapes. One of these departed spirits told me in a sad and lifeless way that there was no way for him to live but by whey. Never drank anything now but whey, and dearly, dearly loved whey. He didn't know whey he did but he did. After making this pun he died—that is the whey it served him.

Some other remains, preserved from decomposition by the grape system, told me that the grapes were of a peculiar breed highly medicinal in their nature and that they were counted out and administered by the grape-doctors as methodically as if they were pills. The new patient, if very feeble, began with one grape before breakfast, took three during breakfast, a couple between meals, five at luncheon, three in the afternoon, seven at dinner, four for supper, and part of a grape just before going to bed, by way of a general regulator. The quantity was gradually and regularly increased according to the needs and capacities of the patient until by and by you would find him disposing of his one grape per second all the day long, and his regular barrel per day.

He said that men cured in this way and enabled to discard the grape system never afterward got over the habit of talking as if they were dictating to a slow amanuensis, because they always made a pause between each two words while they sucked the substance out of an imaginary grape. He said these were tedious people to talk with. He said that men who had been cured by the other process were easily distinguished from the rest of mankind because they always tilted their heads back between every two words and swallowed a swig of imaginary whey. He said it was an impressive thing to observe two men who had been cured by the two processes engaged in conversation—said their pauses and accompanying movements were so continuous and regular that a stranger would think himself in the presence of a couple of automatic machines. One finds out a great many wonderful things by traveling if he stumbles upon the right person.

I did not remain long at the Kursaal. The music was good enough but it seemed rather tame after the cyclone of that Arkansaw expert. Besides, my adventurous spirit had conceived a formidable enterprise—nothing less than a trip from Interlaken by the Gemmi and Visp clear to Zermatt on foot!

So it was necessary to plan the details and get ready for an early start. The courier thought that the portier of the hotel would be able to tell us how to find our way. And so it turned out. He showed us the whole thing on a relief-map and we could see our route with all its elevations and depressions, its villages and its rivers, as clearly as if we were sailing over it in a balloon. A relief-map is a great thing. The portier also wrote down each day's journey and the nightly hotel on a piece of paper and made our course so plain that we should never be able to get lost without high-priced outside help.

I put the courier in the care of a gentleman who was going to Lausanne and then we went to bed after laying out the walking-costumes and putting them into condition for instant occupation in the morning.

However, when we came down to breakfast at 8 A.M. it looked so much like rain that I hired a two-horse top-buggy for the first third of the journey. For two or three hours we jogged along the level road which skirts the beautiful lake of Thun, with a dim and dreamlike picture of watery expanses and spectral Alpine forms always before us, veiled in a mellowing mist. Then a steady downpour set in and hid everything but the nearest objects. We kept the rain out of our faces with umbrellas and away from our bodies with the leather apron of the buggy but the driver sat unsheltered and placidly soaked the weather in and seemed to like it. We had the road all to ourselves and I never had a pleasanter excursion.

The weather began to clear while we were driving up a valley called the Kienthal, and presently a vast black cloud-bank in front of us dissolved away and uncurtained the grand proportions and the soaring loftiness of the Blumis Alp. It was a sort of breathtaking surprise, for we had not supposed there was anything behind that low-hung blanket of sable cloud but level valley. What we had been mistaking for fleeting glimpses of sky away aloft there were really patches of the Blumis's snowy crest caught through shredded rents in the drifting pall of vapor.

We dined in the inn at Frutigen, and our driver ought to have dined there too but he would not have had time to dine and get drunk both, so he gave his mind to making a masterpiece of the latter and succeeded. A German gentleman and his two young-lady daughters had been taking their nooning at the inn, and when they left just ahead of us it was plain that their driver was as drunk as ours and as happy and good-natured too, which was saying a good deal. These rascals overflowed with attentions and information for their guests and with brotherly love for each other. They tied their reins and took off their coats and hats so that they might be able to give unencumbered attention to conversation and to the gestures necessary for its illustration.

The road was smooth. It led up and over and down a continual succession of hills. But it was narrow, the horses were used to it and could not well get out of it anyhow, so why shouldn't the drivers entertain themselves and us? The noses of our horses projected sociably into the rear of the forward carriage, and as we toiled up the long hills our driver stood up and talked to his friend, and his friend stood up and talked back to him, with his rear to the scenery. When the top was reached and we went flying down the other side, there was no change in the program. I carry in my memory yet the picture of that forward driver on his knees on his high seat, resting his elbows on its back, and beaming down on his passengers with happy eye and flying hair and jolly red face, and offering his card to the old German gentleman while he praised his hack and horses, and both teams were whizzing down a long hill with nobody in a position to tell whether we were bound to destruction or an undeserved safety.

Toward sunset we entered a beautiful green valley dotted with chalets, a cozy little domain hidden away from the busy world in a cloistered nook among giant precipices topped with snowy peaks that seemed to float like islands above the curling surf of the sea of vapor that severed them from the lower world. Down from vague and vaporous heights little ruffled zigzag milky currents came crawling and found their way to the verge of one of those tremendous overhanging walls whence they plunged, a shaft of silver shivered to atoms in mid-descent and turned to an airy puff of luminous dust. Here and there in grooved depressions among the snowy desolations of the upper altitudes one glimpsed the extremity of a glacier, with its seagreen and honeycombed battlements of ice.

Up the valley, under a dizzy precipice, nestled the village of Kandersteg, our halting-place for the night. We were soon there and housed in the hotel. But the waning day had such an inviting influence that we did not remain housed many moments but struck out and followed a roaring torrent of ice-water up to its far source in a sort of little grass-carpeted parlor, walled in all around by vast precipices and overlooked by clustering summits of ice. This was the snuggest little croquet-ground imaginable. It was perfectly level and not more than a mile long by half a mile wide. The walls around it were so gigantic and everything about it was on so mighty a scale that it was belittled by contrast to what I have likened it to—a cozy and carpeted parlor. It was so high above the Kandersteg valley that there was nothing between it and the snow-peaks. I had never been in such intimate relations with the high altitudes before. The snow-peaks had always been remote and unapproachable grandeurs hitherto but now we were hob-a-nob—if one may use such a seemingly irreverent expression about creations so august as these.

We could see the streams which fed the torrent we had followed issuing from under the greenish ramparts of glaciers. But two or three of these, instead of flowing over the precipices, sank down into the rock and sprang in big jets out of holes in the mid-face of the walls.

The green nook which I have been describing is called the Gasternthal. The glacier streams gather and flow through it in a broad and rushing brook to a narrow cleft between lofty precipices. Here the rushing brook becomes a mad torrent and goes booming and thundering down toward Kandersteg, lashing and thrashing its way over and among monster boulders and hurling chance roots and logs about like straws. There was no lack of cascades along this route. The path by the side of the torrent was so narrow that one had to look sharp, when he heard a cow-bell, and hunt for a place that was wide enough to accommodate a cow and a Christian side by side, and such places were not always to be had at an instant's notice. The cows wear church-bells and that is a good idea in the cows, for where that torrent is you couldn't hear an ordinary cow-bell any further than you could hear the ticking of a watch.

I needed exercise, so I employed my agent in setting stranded logs and dead trees adrift, and I sat on a boulder and watched them go whirling and leaping head over heels down the boiling torrent. It was a wonderfully exhilarating spectacle. When I had had exercise enough I made the agent take some by running a race with one of those logs. I made a trifle by betting on the log.

After dinner we had a walk up and down the quiet Kandersteg valley in the soft gloaming, with the spectacle of the dying lights of day playing about the crests and pinnacles of the still and solemn upper realm for contrast, and text for talk. There were no sounds but the dulled complaining of the torrent and the occasional tinkling of a distant bell. The spirit of the place was a sense of deep, pervading peace. One might dream his life tranquilly away there and not miss it or mind it when it was gone.

The summer departed with the sun, and winter came with the stars. It grew to be a bitter night in that little hotel backed up against a precipice that had no visible top to it but we kept warm, and woke in time in the morning to find that everybody else had left for the Gemmi three hours before— so our little plan of helping that German family (principally the old man) over the pass was a blocked generosity.

29. The End of the World

We hired the only guide left, to lead us on our way. He was over seventy but he could have given me nine-tenths of his strength and still had all his age entitled him to. He shouldered our satchels, overcoats and alpenstocks and we set out up the steep path. It was hot work. The old man soon begged us to hand over our coats and waistcoats to him to carry too and we did it. One could not refuse so little a thing to a poor old man like that. He should have had them if he had been a hundred and fifty.

When we began that ascent we could see a microscopic chalet perched away up against heaven on what seemed to be the highest mountain near us. It was on our right across the narrow head of the valley. But when we got up abreast it on its own level, mountains were towering high above on every hand and we saw that its altitude was just about that of the little Gasternthal which we had visited the evening before. Still it seemed a long way up in the air in that waste and lonely wilderness of rocks. It had an unfenced grass-plot in front of it which seemed about as big as a billiard-table, and this grass-plot slanted so sharply downward and was so brief and ended so exceedingly soon at the verge of the absolute precipice that it was a shuddery thing to think of a person's venturing to trust his foot on an incline so situated at all. Suppose a man stepped on an orange peel in that yard. There would be nothing for him to seize. Nothing could keep him from rolling. Five revolutions would bring him to the edge and over he would go. What a frightful distance he would fall!

—for there are very few birds that fly as high as his starting-point. He would strike and bounce two or three times on his way down but this would be no advantage to him. I would as soon take an airing on the slant of a rainbow as in such a front yard. I would rather, in fact, for the distance down would be about the same and it is pleasanter to slide than to bounce. I could not see how the peasants got up to that chalet —the region seemed too steep for anything but a balloon.

As we strolled on, climbing up higher and higher, we were continually bringing neighboring peaks into view and lofty prominence which had been hidden behind lower peaks before. So by and by, while standing before a group of these giants, we looked around for the chalet again. There it was, away down below us, apparently on an inconspicuous ridge in the valley! It was as far below us now as it had been above us when we were beginning the ascent.

After a while the path led us along a railed precipice and we looked over—far beneath us was the snug parlor again, the little Gasternthal, with its water jets spouting from the face of its rock walls. We could have dropped a stone into it. We had been finding the top of the world all along—and always finding a still higher top stealing into view in a disappointing way just ahead. When we looked down into the Gasternthal we felt pretty sure that we had reached the genuine top at last but it was not so. There were much higher altitudes to be scaled yet. We were still in the pleasant shade of forest trees, we were still in a region which was cushioned with beautiful mosses and aglow with the many-tinted luster of innumerable wild flowers.

We found indeed more interest in the wild flowers than in anything else. We gathered a specimen or two of every kind which we were unacquainted with, so we had sumptuous bouquets. But one of the chief interests lay in chasing the seasons of the year up the mountain and determining them by the presence of flowers and berries which we were acquainted with. For instance, it was the end of August at the level of the sea. In the Kandersteg valley at the base of the pass we found flowers which would not be due at the sea-level for two or three weeks. Higher up we entered October and gathered fringed gentians. I made no notes and have forgotten the details but the construction of the floral calendar was very entertaining while it lasted.

In the high regions we found rich store of the splendid red flower called the Alpine rose but we did not find any examples of the ugly Swiss favorite called Edelweiss. Its name seems to indicate that it is a noble flower and that it is white. It may be noble enough but it is not attractive and it is not white. The fuzzy blossom is the color of bad cigar ashes and appears to be made of a cheap quality of gray plush. It has a noble and distant way of confining itself to the high altitudes but that is probably on account of its looks. It apparently has no monopoly of those upper altitudes, however, for they are sometimes intruded upon by some of the loveliest of the valley families of wild flowers. Everybody in the Alps wears a sprig of Edelweiss in his hat. It is the native's pet and also the tourist's.

All the morning as we loafed along, having a good time, other pedestrians went staving by us with vigorous strides and with the intent and determined look of men who were walking for a wager. These wore loose knee-breeches, long yarn stockings and hobnailed high-laced walking-shoes. They were gentlemen who would go home to England or Germany and tell how many miles they had beaten the guidebook every day. But I doubted if they ever had much real fun outside of the mere magnificent exhilaration of the tramp through the green valleys and the breezy heights, for they were almost always alone, and even the finest scenery loses incalculably when there is no one to enjoy it with.

All the morning an endless double procession of mulemounted tourists filed past us along the narrow path—the one procession going, the other coming. We had taken a good deal of trouble to teach ourselves the kindly German custom of saluting all strangers with doffed hat and we resolutely clung to it that morning although it kept us bareheaded most of the time and was not always responded to. Still we found an interest in the thing, because we naturally liked to know who were English and Americans among the passers-by. All continental natives responded, of course. So did some of the English and Americans but as a general thing these two races gave no sign. Whenever a man or a woman showed us cold neglect we spoke up confidently in our own tongue and asked for such information as we happened to need and we always got a reply in the same language. The English and American folk are not less kindly than other races, they are only more reserved, and that comes of habit and education. In one dreary, rocky waste, away above the line of vegetation, we met a procession of twenty-five mounted young men, all from America. We got answering bows enough from these, of course, for they were of an age to learn to do in Rome as Rome does, without much effort.

At one extremity of this patch of desolation, overhung by bare and forbidding crags which husbanded drifts of everlasting snow in their shaded cavities, was a small stretch of thin and discouraged grass, and a man and a family of pigs were actually living here in some shanties. Consequently this place could be really reckoned as "property." It had a money value and was doubtless taxed. I think it must have marked the limit of real estate in this world. It would be hard to set a money value upon any piece of earth that lies between that spot and the empty realm of space. That man may claim the distinction of owning the end of the world, for if there is any definite end to the world he has certainly found it.

From here forward we moved through a stormswept and smileless desolation. All about us rose gigantic masses, crags and ramparts of bare and dreary rock, with not a vestige or semblance of plant or tree or flower anywhere or glimpse of any creature that had life. The frost and the tempests of unnumbered ages had battered and hacked at these cliffs with a deathless energy, destroying them piecemeal. So all the region about their bases was a tumbled chaos of great fragments which had been split off and hurled to the ground.

Soiled and aged banks of snow lay close about our path. The
ghastly desolation of the place was as tremendously complete
as if Doré had furnished the working-plans for it. But every
now and then through the stern gateways around us we
caught a view of some neighboring majestic dome sheathed
with glittering ice and displaying its white purity at an elevation compared to which ours was groveling and plebeian,
and this spectacle always chained one's interest and admiration at once and made him forget there was anything ugly in
the world.

I have just said that there was nothing but death and desolation in these hideous places but I forgot. In the most forlorn
and arid and dismal one of all, where the racked and splin-
tered debris was thickest, where the ancient patches of snow
lay against the very path, where the winds blew bitterest and
the general aspect was mournfulest and dreariest and furthest from any suggestion of cheer or hope, I found a solitary
wee forget-me-not flourishing away, not a droop about it
anywhere, but holding its bright blue star up with the petti-
est and gallantest air in the world, the only happy spirit, the
only smiling thing, in all that grisly desert. She seemed to say,
"Cheer up!—as long as we are here, let us make the best of
it." I judged she had earned a right to a more hospitable
place, so I plucked her up and sent her to America to a friend
who would respect her for the fight she had made all by her
small self to make a whole vast despondent Alpine desolation
stop breaking its heart over the unalterable and hold up its
head and look at the bright side of things for once.

We stopped for a nooning at a strongly built little inn called
the Schwarenbach. It sits in a lonely spot among the peaks,
where it is swept by the trailing fringes of the cloud-rack and
is rained on, snowed on and pelted and persecuted by the
storms nearly every day of its life. It was the only habitation
in the whole Gemmi Pass.

Close at hand now was a chance for a blood-curdling Alpine adventure. Close at hand was the snowy mass of the
Great Altels cooling its topknot in the sky and daring us to

an ascent. I was fired with the idea and immediately made up my mind to procure the necessary guides, ropes, etc., and undertake it. I instructed Harris to go to the landlord of the inn and set him about our preparations. Meantime I went diligently to work to read up and find out what this much-talked-of mountain-climbing was like, and how one should go about it—for in these matters I was ignorant.

After about an hour Harris burst into the room in a noble excitement and said the ropes and the guides were secured and asked if I was ready. I said I believed I wouldn't ascend the Altels this time. I said Alp-climbing was a different thing from what I had supposed it was and so I judged we had better study its points a little more before we went definitely into it. But I told him to retain the guides and order them to follow us to Zermatt, because I meant to use them there. I said I could feel the spirit of adventure beginning to stir in me and was sure that the fell fascination of Alp-climbing would soon be upon me. I said he could make up his mind to it that we would do a deed before we were a week older which would make the hair of the timid curl with fright.

This made Harris happy and filled him with ambitious anticipations. He went at once to tell the guides to follow us to Zermatt and bring all their paraphernalia with them.

30. A New Interest

A great and priceless thing is a new interest! How it takes possession of a man! How it clings to him, how it rides him! I strode onward from the Schwarenbach hostelry a changed man, a reorganized personality. I walked in a new world, I saw with new eyes. I had been looking aloft at the giant snow-peaks only as things to be worshiped for their grandeur and magnitude and their unspeakable grace of form. I looked up at them now as also things to be conquered and climbed. My sense of their grandeur and their noble beauty was neither lost nor impaired. I had gained a new interest in the mountains without losing the old ones. I followed the steep lines up inch by inch with my eye and noted the possibility or impossibility of following them with my feet. When I saw a shining helmet of ice projecting above the clouds I tried to imagine I saw files of black specks toiling up it roped together with a gossamer thread.

We skirted the lonely little lake called the Daubensee and presently passed close by a glacier on the right—a thing like a great river frozen solid in its flow and broken square off like a wall at its mouth. I had never been so near a glacier before.

Here we came upon a new board shanty and found some men engaged in building a stone house, so the Schwarenbach was soon to have a rival. We bought a bottle or so of beer here. At any rate they called it beer but I knew by the price that it was dissolved jewelry and I perceived by the taste that dissolved jewelry is not good stuff to drink.

We were surrounded by a hideous desolation. We stepped forward to a sort of jumping-off place and were confronted by a startling contrast: we seemed to look down into fairyland. Two or three thousand feet below us was a bright green level with a pretty town in its midst and a silvery stream winding among the meadows. The charming spot was walled in on all sides by gigantic precipices clothed with pines, and over the pines, out of the softened distances, rose the snowy domes and peaks of the Monte Rosa region. How exquisitely green and beautiful that little valley down there was! The distance was not great enough to obliterate details, it only made them little and mellow and dainty, like landscapes and towns seen through the wrong end of a spy-glass.

Right under us a narrow ledge rose up out of the valley, with a green, slanting, bench-shaped top, and grouped about

upon this green-baize bench were a lot of black and white
sheep which looked merely like oversized worms. The bench
seemed lifted well up into our neighborhood but that was a
deception—it was a long way down to it.

We began our descent now by the most remarkable road
I have ever seen. It wound in corkscrew curves down the
face of the colossal precipice—a narrow way, with always the
solid rock wall at one elbow and perpendicular nothingness
at the other. We met an everlasting procession of guides,
porters, mules, litters and tourists climbing up this steep and
muddy path, and there was no room to spare when you had
to pass a tolerably fat mule. I always took the inside when I
heard or saw the mule coming, and flattened myself against
the wall. I preferred the inside, of course, but I should have
had to take it anyhow because the mule prefers the outside.
A mule's preference—on a precipice—is a thing to be respected. Well, his choice is always the outside. His life is
mostly devoted to carrying bulky panniers and packages
which rest against his body—therefore he is habituated to
taking the outside edge of mountain paths to keep his bundles from rubbing against rocks or banks on the other. When
he goes into the passenger business he absurdly clings to his
old habit and keeps one leg of his passenger always dangling
over the great deeps of the lower world while that passenger's heart is in the highlands, so to speak. More than once
I saw a mule's hind foot cave over the outer edge and send
earth and rubbish into the bottomless abyss and I noticed
that upon these occasions the rider, whether male or female,
looked tolerably unwell.

There was one place where an eighteen-inch breadth of
light masonry had been added to the verge of the path, and
as there was a very sharp turn here a panel of fencing had
been set up there at some ancient time as a protection. This
panel was old and gray and feeble, and the light masonry had
been loosened by recent rains. A young American girl came
along on a mule, and in making the turn the mule's hind foot
caved all the loose masonry and one of the fence-posts over-

board. The mule gave a violent lurch inboard to save himself and succeeded in the effort but that girl turned as white as the snows of Mont Blanc for a moment.

The path here was simply a groove cut into the face of the precipice. There was a four-foot breadth of solid rock under the traveler and a four-foot breadth of solid rock just above his head, like the roof of a narrow porch. He could look out from this gallery and see a sheer summitless and bottomless wall of rock before him across a gorge or crack a biscuit's toss in width—but he could not see the bottom of his own precipice unless he lay down and projected his nose over the edge. I did not do this, because I did not wish to soil my clothes.

Every few hundred yards, at particularly bad places, one came across a panel or so of plank fencing but they were always old and weak and they generally leaned out over the chasm and did not make any rash promises to hold up people who might need support. There was one of these panels which had only its upper board left. A pedestrianizing English youth came tearing down the path, was seized with an impulse to look over the precipice, and without an instant's thought he threw his weight upon that crazy board. It bent outward a foot! I never made a gasp before that came so near suffocating me. The English youth's face simply showed a lively surprise but nothing more. He went swinging along valleyward again as if he did not know he had just swindled a coroner by the closest kind of a shave.

The Alpine litter is sometimes like a cushioned box made fast between the middles of two long poles and sometimes it is a chair with a back to it and a support for the feet. It is carried by relays of strong porters. The motion is easier than that of any other conveyance. We met a few men and a great many ladies in litters. It seemed to me that most of the ladies looked pale and nauseated. Their general aspect gave me the idea that they were patiently enduring a horrible suffering. As a rule they looked at their laps and left the scenery to take care of itself.

But the most frightened creature I saw was a led horse that

overtook us. Poor fellow, he had been born and reared in the grassy levels of the Kandersteg valley and had never seen anything like this hideous place before. Every few steps he would stop short, glance wildly out from the dizzy height and then spread his red nostrils wide and pant as violently as if he had been running a race, and all the while he quaked from head to heel as with a palsy. He was a handsome fellow and he made a fine statuesque picture of terror but it was pitiful to see him suffer so.

This dreadful path has had its tragedy. Baedeker, with his customary overterseness, begins and ends the tale thus:

"The descent on horseback should be avoided. In 1861 a Comtesse d'Herlincourt fell from her saddle over the precipice and was killed on the spot."

We looked over the precipice there and saw the monument which commemorates the event. It stands in the bottom of the gorge in a place which has been hollowed out of the rock to protect it from the torrent and the storms. Our old guide never spoke but when spoken to, and then limited himself to a syllable or two, but when we asked him about this tragedy he showed a strong interest in the matter. He said the Countess was very pretty and very young—hardly out of her girlhood, in fact. She was newly married and was on her bridal tour. The young husband was riding a little in advance. One guide was leading the husband's horse, another was leading the bride's. The old man continued:

"The guide that was leading the husband's horse happened to glance back, and there was that poor young thing sitting up staring out over the precipice, and her face began to bend downward a little and she put up her two hands slowly and met it—so—and put them flat against her eyes—so—and then she sunk out of the saddle with a sharp shriek, and one caught only the flash of a dress and it was all over."

Then after a pause:

"Ah yes, that guide saw these things—yes, he saw them all. He saw them all, just as I have told you."

After another pause:

"Ah yes, he saw them all. My God, that was *me*. I was that guide!"

This had been the one event of the old man's life, so one may be sure he had forgotten no detail connected with it. We listened to all he had to say about what was done and what happened and what was said after the sorrowful occurrence, and a painful story it was.

When we had wound down toward the valley until we were about on the last spiral of the corkscrew, Harris's hat blew over the last remaining bit of precipice—a small cliff a hundred or hundred and fifty feet high—and sailed down toward a steep slant composed of rough chips and fragments which the weather had flaked away from the precipices. We went leisurely down there, expecting to find it without any trouble but we had made a mistake as to that. We hunted during a couple of hours—not because the old straw hat was valuable but out of curiosity to find out how such a thing could manage to conceal itself in open ground where there was nothing left for it to hide behind. When one is reading in bed and lays his paper-knife down, he cannot find it again if it is smaller than a saber. That hat was as stubborn as any paper-knife could have been, and we finally had to give it up. But we found a fragment that had once belonged to an opera-glass, and by digging around and turning over the rocks we gradually collected all the lenses and the cylinders and the various odds and ends that go to make up a complete opera-glass. We afterward had the thing reconstructed, and the owner can have his adventurous long-lost property by submitting proofs and paying costs of rehabilitation. We had hopes of finding the owner there, distributed around amongst the rocks, for it would have made an elegant paragraph, but we were disappointed. Still, we were far from being disheartened, for there was a considerable area which we had not thoroughly searched. We were satisfied he was there somewhere, so we resolved to wait over a day at Leuk and come back and get him.

Then we sat down to polish off the perspiration and ar-

range about what we would do with him when we got him.
Harris was for contributing him to the British Museum but
I was for mailing him to his widow. That is the difference
between Harris and me: Harris is all for display, I am all for
the simple right, even though I lose money by it. Harris
argued in favor of his proposition and against mine, I argued
in favor of mine and against his. The discussion warmed into
a dispute. The dispute warmed into a quarrel. I finally said,
very decidedly:

"My mind is made up. He goes to the widow."

Harris answered sharply:

"And *my* mind is made up. He goes to the Museum."

I said calmly:

"The Museum may whistle when it gets him."

Harris retorted:

"The widow may save herself the trouble of whistling, for
I will see that she never gets him."

After some angry bandying of epithets I said:

"It seems to me that you are taking on a good many airs
about these remains. I don't quite see what *you've* got to say
about them?"

"*I?* I've got *all* to say about them. They'd never have been
thought of if I hadn't found their opera-glass. The corpse
belongs to me and I'll do as I please with him."

I was leader of the Expedition, and all discoveries achieved
by it naturally belonged to me. I was entitled to these remains and could have enforced my right. But rather than
have bad blood about the matter, I said we would toss up for
them. I threw heads and won but it was a barren victory, for
although we spent all the next day searching, we never found
a bone. I cannot imagine what could ever have become of
that fellow.

The town in the valley is called Leuk or Leukerbad. We
pointed our course toward it down a verdant slope which was
adorned with fringed gentians and other flowers and presently entered the narrow alleys of the outskirts and waded
toward the middle of the town through liquid "fertilizer."

They ought to either pave that village or organize a ferry.

Harris's body was simply a chamois-pasture. His person was populous with the little hungry pests. His skin, when he stripped, was splotched like a scarlet-fever patient's. So, when we were about to enter one of the Leukerbad inns and he noticed its sign, "Chamois Hotel," he refused to stop there. He said the chamois was plentiful enough without hunting up hotels where they made a specialty of it. I was indifferent, for the chamois is a creature that will neither bite me nor abide with me: but to calm Harris we went to the Hôtel des Alpes.

At the table d'hôte we had this for an incident. A very grave man—in fact his gravity amounted to solemnity and almost to austerity—sat opposite us and he was "tight" but doing his best to appear sober. He took up a *corked* bottle of wine, tilted it over his glass awhile, then set it out of the way with a contented look and went on with his dinner.

Presently he put his glass to his mouth and of course found it empty. He looked puzzled and glanced furtively and suspiciously out of the corner of his eye at a benignant and unconscious old lady who sat at his right. Shook his head, as much as to say, "No, she couldn't have done it." He tilted the corked bottle over his glass again, meantime searching around with his watery eye to see if anybody was watching him. He ate a few mouthfuls, raised his glass to his lips and of course it was still empty. He bent an injured and accusing side-gaze upon that unconscious old lady, which was a study to see. She went on eating and gave no sign. He took up his glass and his bottle with a wise private nod of his head and set them gravely on the left-hand side of his plate—poured himself another imaginary drink—went to work with his knife and fork once more—presently lifted his glass with good confidence and found it empty as usual.

This was almost a petrifying surprise. He straightened himself up in his chair and deliberately and sorrowfully inspected the busy old ladies at his elbows, first one and then the other. At last he softly pushed his plate away, set his glass directly in front of him, held on to it with his left hand and proceeded to pour with his right. This time he observed that nothing came. He turned the bottle clear upside down. Still nothing issued from it. A plaintive look came into his face and he said as if to himself, *"'ic! They've got it all!"* Then he set the bottle down resignedly and took the rest of his dinner dry.

It was at that table d'hôte, too, that I had under inspection the largest lady I have ever seen in private life. She was over seven feet high and magnificently proportioned. What had first called my attention to her was my stepping on an outlying flange of her foot and hearing, from up toward the ceiling, a deep "Pardon, m'sieu, but you encroach!"

That was when we were coming through the hall and the place was dim and I could see her only vaguely. The thing which called my attention to her the second time was that at a table beyond ours were two very pretty girls, and this great lady came in and sat down between them and me and blotted out the view. She had a handsome face and she was very finely formed—perfectly formed, I should say. But she made everybody around her look trivial and commonplace. Ladies near her looked like children, and the men about her looked mean. They looked like failures. And they looked as if they felt so, too. She sat with her back to us. I never saw such a back in my life. I would have so liked to see the moon rise over it. The whole congregation waited under one pretext or another till she finished her dinner and went out. They wanted to see her at her full altitude and they found it worth tarrying for. She filled one's idea of what an empress ought to be when she rose up in her unapproachable grandeur and moved superbly out of that place.

We were not at Leuk in time to see her at her heaviest weight. She had suffered from corpulence and had come there to get rid of her extra flesh in the baths. Five weeks of soaking—five uninterrupted hours of it every day—had accomplished her purpose and reduced her to the right proportions.

Those baths remove fat and also skin-diseases. The patients

remain in the great tanks for hours at a time. A dozen gentlemen and ladies occupy a tank together and amuse themselves with rompings and various games. They have floating desks and tables and they read or lunch or play chess in water that is breast-deep. The tourist can step in and view this novel spectacle if he chooses. There's a poor-box and he will have to contribute. There are several of these big bathinghouses and you can always tell when you are near one of them by the romping noises and shouts of laughter that proceed from it. The water is running water and changes all the time, else a patient with a ringworm might take the bath with only a partial success, since, while he was ridding himself of his ringworm, he might catch the itch.

The next morning we wandered back up the green valley leisurely, with the curving walls of those bare and stupendous precipices rising into the clouds before us. I had never seen a clean, bare precipice stretching up five thousand feet above me before and I never shall expect to see another one. They exist perhaps but not in places where one can easily get close to them. This pile of stone is peculiar. From its base to the soaring tops of its mighty towers all its lines and all its details vaguely suggest human architecture. There are rudimentary bow-windows, cornices, chimneys, demarcations of stories, etc. One could sit and stare up there and study the features and exquisite graces of this grand structure bit by bit and day after day and never weary his interest. The termination, toward the town, observed in profile, is the perfection of shape. It comes down out of the clouds in a succession of rounded, colossal, terracelike projections—a stairway for the gods. At its head spring several lofty storm-scarred towers one above another, with faint films of vapor curling always about them like spectral banners. If there were a king whose realms included the whole world, here would be the palace meet and proper for such a monarch. He would only need to hollow it out and put in the electric light. He could give audience to a nation at a time under its roof.

Our search for those remains having failed, we inspected

with a glass the dim and distant track of an old-time avalanche that once swept down from some pine-grown summits behind the town and swept away the houses and buried
the people. Then we struck down the road that leads toward
the Rhone, to see the famous Ladders. These perilous things
are built against the perpendicular face of a cliff two or three
hundred feet high. The peasants of both sexes were climbing
up and down them with heavy loads on their backs. I ordered
Harris to make the ascent so I could put the thrill and horror
of it in my book, and he accomplished the feat successfully
through a subagent for three francs, which I paid. It makes
me shudder yet when I think of what I felt when I was
clinging there between heaven and earth in the person of
that proxy. At times the world swam around me and I could
hardly keep from letting go, so dizzying was the appalling
danger. Many a person would have given up and descended
but I stuck to my task and would not yield until I had accomplished it. I felt a just pride in my exploit but I would not have
repeated it for the wealth of the world. I shall break my neck
yet with some such foolhardy performance, for warnings
never seem to have any lasting effect upon me. When the
people of the hotel found that I had been climbing those
crazy Ladders it made me an object of considerable attention.

Next morning early we drove to the Rhone valley and took
the train for Visp. There we shouldered our knapsacks and
things and set out on foot in a tremendous rain up the winding gorge toward Zermatt. Hour after hour we slopped along
by the roaring torrent and under noble Lesser Alps which
were clothed in rich velvety green all the way up and had
little atomy Swiss homes perched upon grassy benches along
their mist-dimmed heights.

The rain continued to pour and the torrent to boom and
we continued to enjoy both. At the one spot where this torrent tossed its white mane highest and thundered loudest
and lashed the big boulders fiercest the canton had done
itself the honor to build the flimsiest wooden bridge that

exists in the world. While we were walking over it, along with a party of horsemen, I noticed that even the larger raindrops made it shake. I called Harris's attention to it and he noticed it too. It seemed to me that if I owned an elephant that was a keepsake and I thought a good deal of him I would think twice before I would ride him over that bridge.

We climbed up to the village of St. Nicholas about half past four in the afternoon, waded ankle-deep through the fertilizer-juice and stopped at a new and nice hotel close by the little church. We stripped and went to bed and sent our clothes down to be baked. All the horde of soaked tourists did the same. That chaos of clothing got mixed in the kitchen and there were consequences. I did not get back the same drawers I sent down, when our things came up at six-fifteen. I got a pair on a new plan. They were merely a pair of white ruffle-cuffed absurdities hitched together at the top with a narrow band, and they did not come quite down to my knees. They were pretty enough but they made me feel like two people, and disconnected at that. The man must have been an idiot that got himself up like that to rough it in the Swiss mountains. The shirt they brought me was shorter than the drawers and hadn't any sleeves to it—at least it hadn't anything more than what Mr. Darwin would call "rudimentary" sleeves. These had "edging" around them but the bosom was ridiculously plain. The knit silk undershirt they brought me was on a new plan and was really a sensible thing. It opened behind and had pockets in it to put your shoulder-blades in but they did not seem to fit mine and so I found it a sort of uncomfortable garment. They gave my bobtail coat to somebody else and sent me an ulster suitable for a giraffe. I had to tie my collar on, because there was no button behind on that foolish little shirt which I described a while ago.

When I was dressed for dinner at six-thirty I was too loose in some places and too tight in others, and altogether I felt slovenly and ill-conditioned. However, the people at the table d'hôte were no better off than I was. They had everybody's clothes but their own on. A long stranger recognized his ulster as soon as he saw the tail of it following me in but nobody claimed my shirt or my drawers though I described them as well as I was able. I gave them to the chambermaid that night when I went to bed and she probably found the owner, for my own things were on a chair outside my door in the morning.

There was a lovable English clergyman who did not get to the table d'hôte at all. His breeches had turned up missing and without any equivalent. He said he was not more particular than other people but he had noticed that a clergyman at dinner without any breeches was almost sure to excite remark.

31. Fault Finding by Harris

We did not oversleep at St. Nicholas. The church-bell began to ring at four-thirty in the morning, and from the length of time it continued to ring I judged that it takes the Swiss sinner a good while to get the invitation through his head.

We took a tolerably early breakfast and tramped off toward Zermatt through the reeking lanes of the village, glad to get away from that bell. By and by we had a fine spectacle on our right. It was the wall-like butt end of a huge glacier, which looked down on us from an Alpine height which was well up in the blue sky. It was an astonishing amount of ice to be compacted together in one mass. We ciphered upon it and decided that it was not less than several hundred feet from the base of the wall of solid ice to the top of it—Harris believed it was really twice that. We judged that if St. Paul's, St. Peter's, the Great Pyramid, the Strasburg Cathedral and the Capitol at Washington were clustered against that wall, a man sitting on its upper edge could not hang his hat on the top of any one of them without reaching down three or four hundred feet—a thing which, of course, no man could do.

To me that mighty glacier was very beautiful. I did not imagine that anybody could find fault with it but I was mistaken. Harris had been snarling for several days. He was a rabid Protestant and he was always saying:

"In the Protestant cantons you never see such poverty and dirt and squalor as you do in this Catholic one. You never see the lanes and alleys flowing with foulness. You never see such wretched little sties of houses. You never see an inverted tin turnip on top of a church for a dome. And as for a church-bell, why, you never hear a church-bell at all."

All this morning he had been finding fault, straight along. First it was with the mud. He said, "It ain't muddy in a Protestant canton when it rains." Then it was with the dogs: "They don't have those lop-eared dogs in a Protestant canton." Then it was with the roads: "They don't leave the roads to make themselves in a Protestant canton, the people make them—and they make a road that *is* a road, too." Next it was the goats: "You never see a goat shedding tears in a Protestant canton—a goat there is one of the cheerfulest objects in nature." Next it was the chamois: "You never see a Protestant chamois act like one of these—they take a bite or two and go. But these fellows camp with you and stay." Then it was the guide-boards: "In a Protestant canton you couldn't get lost if you wanted to, but you never see a guide-board in a Catholic canton." Next, "You never see any flower-boxes in the windows here—never anything but now and then a cat—a torpid one. But you take a Protestant canton: windows perfectly lovely with flowers—and as for cats, there's just acres of them. These folks in this canton leave a road to make itself and then fine you three francs if you 'trot' over it—as if a horse could trot over such a sarcasm of a road." Next about the goiter: "*They* talk about goiter! I haven't seen a goiter in this whole canton that I couldn't put in a hat."

He had growled at everything but I judged it would puzzle him to find anything the matter with this majestic glacier. I intimated as much but he was ready and said with surly discontent: "You ought to see them in the Protestant cantons."

This irritated me. But I concealed the feeling and asked: "What is the matter with this one?"

"Matter? Why, it ain't in any kind of condition. They never take any care of a glacier here. The moraine has been spilling gravel around it and got it all dirty."

"Why, man, *they* can't help that."

"They? You're right. That is, they *won't.* They could if they wanted to. You never see a speck of dirt on a Protestant glacier. Look at the Rhone glacier. It is fifteen miles long and seven hundred feet thick. If this was a Protestant glacier you wouldn't see it looking like this, I can tell you."

"That is nonsense. What would they do with it?"

"They would whitewash it. They always do."

I did not believe a word of this but rather than have trouble I let it go, for it is a waste of breath to argue with a bigot. I even doubted if the Rhone glacier *was* in a Protestant canton but I did not know, so I could not make anything by contradicting a man who would probably put me down at once with manufactured evidence.

About nine miles from St. Nicholas we crossed a bridge over the raging torrent of the Visp and came to a long strip of flimsy fencing which was pretending to secure people from tumbling over a perpendicular wall forty feet high and into the river. Three children were approaching. One of them, a little girl about eight years old, was running. When pretty close to us she stumbled and fell, and her feet shot under the rail of the fence and for a moment projected over the stream. It gave us a sharp shock, for we thought she was gone, sure, for the ground slanted steeply, and to save herself seemed a sheer impossibility. But she managed to scramble up and ran by us laughing.

We went forward and examined the place and saw the long

tracks which her feet had made in the dirt when they darted over the verge. If she had finished her trip she would have struck some big rocks in the edge of the water and then the torrent would have snatched her down-stream among the half-covered boulders and she would have been pounded to pulp in two minutes. We had come exceedingly near witnessing her death.

And now Harris's contrary nature and inborn selfishness were strikingly manifested. He has no spirit of self-denial. He began straight off and continued for an hour to express his gratitude that the child was not destroyed. I never saw such a man. That was the kind of person he was. Just so *he* was gratified, he never cared anything about anybody else. I had noticed that trait in him over and over again. Often, of course, it was mere heedlessness, mere want of reflection. Doubtless this may have been the case in most instances but it was not the less hard to bear on that account—and after all, its bottom, its groundwork, was selfishness. There is no avoiding that conclusion. In the instance under consideration I did think the indecency of running on in that way might occur to him. But no, the child was saved and he was glad, that was sufficient—he cared not a straw for *my* feelings, or my loss of such a literary plum, snatched from my very mouth at the instant it was ready to drop into it. His selfishness was sufficient to place his own gratification in being spared suffering clear before all concern for me, his friend. Apparently he did not once reflect upon the valuable details which would have fallen like a windfall to me: fishing the child out—witnessing the surprise of the family and the stir the thing would have made among the peasants—then a Swiss funeral—then the roadside monument to be paid for by us and have our names mentioned in it. And we should have gone into Baedeker and been immortal. I was silent. I was too much hurt to complain. If he could act so and be so heedless and so frivolous at such a time and actually seem to glory in it after all I had done for him, I would have cut my hand off before I would let him see that I was wounded.

We were approaching Zermatt. Consequently we were approaching the renowned Matterhorn. A month before, this mountain had been only a name to us but latterly we had been moving through a steadily thickening double row of pictures of it, done in oil, water, chromo, wood, steel, copper, crayon and photography, and so it had at length become a shape to us—and a very distinct, decided and familiar one, too. We were expecting to recognize that mountain whenever or wherever we should run across it. We were not deceived. The monarch was far away when we first saw him but there was no such thing as mistaking him. He has the rare peculiarity of standing by himself. He is peculiarly steep, too, and is also most oddly shaped. He towers into the sky like a colossal wedge, with the upper third of its blade bent a little to the left. The broad base of this monster wedge is planted upon a grand glacier-paved Alpine platform whose elevation is ten thousand feet above sea-level. As the wedge itself is some five thousand feet high, it follows that its apex is about fifteen thousand feet above sea-level. So the whole bulk of this stately piece of rock, this sky-cleaving monolith, is above the line of eternal snow. Yet while all its giant neighbors have the look of being built of solid snow from their waists up, the Matterhorn stands black and naked and forbidding the year round, or merely powdered or streaked with white in places, for its sides are so steep that the snow cannot stay there. Its strange form, its august isolation and its majestic unkinship with its own kind make it—so to speak—the Napoleon of the mountain world. "Grand, gloomy and peculiar," is a phrase which fits it as aptly as it fitted the great captain.

A walk from St. Nicholas to Zermatt is a wonderful experience. Nature is built on a stupendous plan in that region. One marches continually between walls that are piled into the skies, with their upper heights broken into a confusion of sublime shapes that gleam white and cold against the background of blue. And here and there one sees a big glacier displaying its grandeurs on the top of a precipice, or a graceful cascade leaping and flashing down the green declivities.

There is nothing tame or cheap or trivial—it is all magnificent. That short valley is a picture-gallery of a notable kind,
for it contains no mediocrities. From end to end the Creator
has hung it with His masterpieces.

We made Zermatt at three in the afternoon, nine hours out
from St. Nicholas. Distance by guide-book twelve miles, by
pedometer seventy-two. We were in the heart and home of
the mountain-climbers now, as all visible things testified. The
snow-peaks did not hold themselves aloof in aristocratic reserve, they nestled close around in a friendly, sociable way.
Guides, with the ropes and axes and other implements of
their fearful calling slung about their persons, roosted in a
long line upon a stone wall in front of the hotel and waited
for customers. Sunburnt climbers in mountaineering costume and followed by their guides and porters arrived from
time to time from breakneck expeditions among the peaks
and glaciers of the High Alps. Male and female tourists on
mules filed by in a continuous procession, hotelward-bound
from wild adventures which would grow in grandeur every
time they were described at the English or American fireside
and at last outgrow the possible itself.

We were not dreaming. This was not a make-believe home
of the Alp-climber created by our heated imaginations. No,
for here was Mr. Girdlestone himself, the famous Englishman who hunts his way to the most formidable Alpine summits without a guide. I was not equal to imagining a Girdlestone. It was all I could do to even realize him while looking
straight at him at short range. I would rather face whole
Hyde Parks of artillery than the ghastly forms of death which
he has faced among the peaks and precipices of the mountains. There is probably no pleasure equal to the pleasure of
climbing a dangerous Alp but it is a pleasure which is
confined strictly to people who can find pleasure in it. I have
not jumped to this conclusion. I have traveled to it per grav-
el-train, so to speak. I have thought the thing all out and am
quite sure I am right. A born climber's appetite for climbing
is hard to satisfy. When it comes upon him he is like a starving

man with a feast before him. He may have other business on hand but it must wait. Mr. Girdlestone had had his usual summer holiday in the Alps and had spent it in his usual way, hunting for unique chances to break his neck. His vacation was over and his luggage packed for England, but all of a sudden a hunger had come upon him to climb the tremendous Weisshorn once more, for he had heard of a new and utterly impossible route up it. His baggage was unpacked at once and now he and a friend, laden with knapsacks, ice-axes, coils of rope and canteens of milk, were just setting out. They would spend the night high up among the snows somewhere and get up at two in the morning and finish the enterprise. I had a strong desire to go with them but forced it down— a feat which Mr. Girdlestone with all his fortitude could not do.

Even ladies catch the climbing mania and are unable to throw it off. A famous climber of that sex had attempted the Weisshorn a few days before our arrival, and she and her guides had lost their way in a snow-storm high up among the peaks and glaciers and been forced to wander around a good while before they could find a way down. When this lady reached the bottom she had been on her feet twenty-three hours!

Our guides, hired on the Gemmi, were already at Zermatt when we reached there. So there was nothing to interfere with our getting up an adventure whenever we should choose the time and the object. I resolved to devote my first evening in Zermatt to studying up the subject of Alpine climbing by way of preparation.

I read several books, and here are some of the things I found out. One's shoes must be strong and heavy and have pointed hobnails in them. The alpenstock must be of the best wood, for if it should break, loss of life might be the result. One should carry an ax to cut steps in the ice with on the great heights. There must be a ladder, for there are steep bits of rock which can be surmounted with this instrument—or this utensil—but could not be surmounted without it. Such an obstruction has compelled the tourist to waste hours hunting another route when a ladder would have saved him all trouble. One must have from one hundred and fifty to five hundred feet of strong rope to be used in lowering the party down steep declivities which are too steep and smooth to be traversed in any other way. One must have a steel hook on another rope—a very useful thing, for when one is ascending and comes to a low bluff which is yet too high for the ladder, he swings this rope aloft like a lasso, the hook catches at the top of the bluff and then the tourist climbs the rope hand over hand—being always particular to try and forget that if the hook gives way he will never stop falling till he arrives in some part of Switzerland where they are not expecting him. Another important thing—there must be a rope to tie the whole party together with, so that if one falls from a mountain or down a bottomless chasm in a glacier the others may brace back on the rope and save him. One must have a silk veil to protect his face from snow, sleet, hail and gale, and colored goggles to protect his eyes from that dangerous enemy, snow-blindness. Finally, there must be some porters to carry provisions, wine and scientific instruments, and also blanket bags for the party to sleep in.

32. Ascending the Riffelberg

After I had finished my readings I was no longer myself. I was tranced, uplifted, intoxicated by the almost incredible perils and adventures I had been following my authors through, and the triumphs I had been sharing with them. I sat silent some time, then turned to Harris and said:

"My mind is made up."

Something in my tone struck him and when he glanced at my eye and read what was written there, his face paled perceptibly. He hesitated a moment, then said:

"Speak."

I answered with perfect calmness:

"I WILL ASCEND THE RIFFELBERG."

If I had shot my poor friend he could not have fallen from his chair more suddenly. If I had been his father he could not have pleaded harder to get me to give up my purpose. But I turned a deaf ear to all he said. When he perceived at last that nothing could alter my determination he ceased to urge, and for a while the deep silence was broken only by his sobs. I sat in marble resolution with my eyes fixed upon vacancy, for in spirit I was already wrestling with the perils of the mountains, and my friend sat gazing at me in adoring admiration through his tears. At last he threw himself upon me in a loving embrace and exclaimed in broken tones:

"Your Harris will never desert you. We will die together!"

I cheered the noble fellow with praises, and soon his fears were forgotten and he was eager for the adventure. He wanted to summon the guides at once and leave at two in the morning, as he supposed the custom was, but I explained that nobody was looking at that hour and that the start in the dark was not usually made from the village but from the first night's resting-place on the mountainside. I said we would leave the village at 3 or 4 P.M. on the morrow. Meantime he could notify the guides and also let the public know of the attempt which we proposed to make.

I went to bed but not to sleep. No man can sleep when he is about to undertake one of these Alpine exploits. I tossed feverishly all night long and was glad enough when I heard the clock strike half past eleven and knew it was time to get up for dinner. I rose jaded and rusty and went to the noon meal, where I found myself the center of interest and curiosity, for the news was already abroad. It is not easy to eat calmly when you are a lion but it is very pleasant, nevertheless.

As usual at Zermatt when a great ascent is about to be undertaken, everybody, native and foreign, laid aside his own projects and took up a good position to observe the start. The expedition consisted of 198 persons, including the mules, or 205, including the cows. As follows:

CHIEFS OF SERVICE		SUBORDINATES	
	Myself	1	Veterinary Surgeon
	Mr. Harris	1	Butler
17	Guides	12	Waiters
4	Surgeons	1	Footman
1	Geologist	1	Barber
1	Botanist	1	Head Cook
3	Chaplains	9	Assistants
2	Draftsmen	4	Pastry Cooks
15	Barkeepers	1	Confectionery Artist
1	Latinist		

TRANSPORTATION, ETC.

27	Porters	3	Coarse Washers and Ironers
44	Mules	1	Fine ditto
44	Muleteers	7	Cows
		2	Milkers

Total, 154 men, 51 animals. Grand Total, 205.

RATIONS, ETC.		APPARATUS	
16	Cases Hams	25	Spring Mattresses
2	Barrels Flour	2	Hair ditto
22	Barrels Whisky		Bedding for same
1	Barrel Sugar	2	Mosquito-nets
1	Keg Lemons	29	Tents
2,000	Cigars		Scientific Instruments
1	Barrel Pies	97	Ice-axes
1	Ton of Pemmican	5	Cases Dynamite
143	Pair Crutches	7	Cans Nitroglycerin
2	Barrels Arnica	22	40-foot Ladders
1	Bale of Lint	2	Miles of Rope
27	Kegs Paregoric	154	Umbrellas

It was full four o'clock in the afternoon before my caval-
cade was entirely ready. At that hour it began to move. In
point of numbers and spectacular effect it was the most imposing expedition that had ever marched from Zermatt.

I commanded the chief guide to arrange the men and
animals in single file twelve feet apart and lash them all
together on a strong rope. He objected that the first two
miles was a dead level, with plenty of room, and that the rope
was never used except in very dangerous places. But I would
not listen to that. My reading had taught me that many serious accidents had happened in the Alps simply from not
having the people tied up soon enough. I was not going to
add one to the list. The guide then obeyed my order.

When the procession stood at ease, roped together and
ready to move, I never saw a finer sight. It was 3,122 feet long
—over half a mile. Every man but Harris and me was on foot
and had on his green veil and his blue goggles and his white
rag around his hat and his coil of rope over one shoulder and
under the other and his ice-ax in his belt and carried his
alpenstock in his left hand, his umbrella (closed) in his right
and his crutches slung at his back. The burdens of the pack-
mules and the horns of the cows were decked with the Edelweiss and the Alpine rose.

I and my agent were the only persons mounted. We were
in the post of danger in the extreme rear and tied securely
to five guides apiece. Our armor-bearers carried our ice-axes,
alpenstocks and other implements for us. We were mounted
upon very small donkeys as a measure of safety. In time of
peril we could straighten our legs and stand up and let the
donkey walk from under. Still, I cannot recommend this sort
of animal—at least for excursions of mere pleasure—because
his ears interrupt the view. I and my agent possessed the
regulation mountaineering costumes but concluded to leave
them behind. Out of respect for the great numbers of tourists
of both sexes who would be assembled in front of the hotels
to see us pass, and also out of respect for the many tourists
whom we expected to encounter on our expedition, we de-

cided to make the ascent in evening dress.

At fifteen minutes past four I gave the command to move, and my subordinates passed it along the line. The great crowd in front of the Monte Rosa hotel parted in twain with a cheer as the procession approached, and as the head of it was filing by I gave the order—"Unlimber—make ready—HOIST!"—and with one impulse up went my half-mile of umbrellas. It was a beautiful sight and a total surprise to the spectators. Nothing like that had ever been seen in the Alps before. The applause it brought forth was deeply gratifying to me and I rode by with my plug hat in my hand to testify my appreciation of it. It was the only testimony I could offer, for I was too full to speak.

We watered the caravan at the cold stream which rushes down a trough near the end of the village, and soon afterward left the haunts of civilization behind us. About half past five o'clock we arrived at a bridge which spans the Visp, and after throwing over a detachment to see if it was safe the caravan crossed without accident. The way now led by a gentle ascent, carpeted with fresh green grass, to the church at Winkelmatten. Without stopping to examine this edifice, I executed a flank movement to the right and crossed the bridge over the Findelenbach after first testing its strength. Here I deployed to the right again and presently entered an inviting stretch of meadowland which was unoccupied save by a couple of deserted huts toward its furthest extremity. These meadows offered an excellent camping-place. We pitched our tents, supped, established a proper guard, recorded the events of the day and then went to bed.

We rose at two in the morning and dressed by candle-light. It was a dismal and chilly business. A few stars were shining but the general heavens were overcast and the great shaft of the Matterhorn was draped in a sable pall of clouds. The chief guide advised a delay. He said he feared it was going to rain. We waited until nine o'clock and then got away in tolerably clear weather.

Our course led up some terrific steeps densely wooded

with arches and cedars and traversed by paths which the rains had guttered and which were obstructed by loose stones. To add to the danger and inconvenience, we were constantly meeting returning tourists on foot or horseback and as constantly being crowded and battered by ascending tourists who were in a hurry and wanted to get by.

Our troubles thickened. About the middle of the afternoon the seventeen guides called a halt and held a consultation. After consulting an hour they said their first suspicion remained intact—that is to say, they believed they were lost. I asked if they did not *know* it? No, they said, they *couldn't* absolutely know whether they were lost or not because none of them had ever been in that part of the country before. They had a strong instinct that they were lost but they had no proofs—except that they did not know where they were. They had met no tourists for some time and they considered that a suspicious sign.

Plainly we were in an ugly fix. The guides were naturally unwilling to go alone and seek a way out of the difficulty, so we all went together. For better security we moved slow and cautiously, for the forest was very dense. We did not move up the mountain but around it, hoping to strike across the old trail. Toward nightfall, when we were about tired out, we came up against a rock as big as a cottage. This barrier took all the remaining spirit out of the men, and a panic of fear and despair ensued. They moaned and wept and said they should never see their homes and their dear ones again. Then they began to upraid me for bringing them upon this fatal expedition. Some even muttered threats against me.

Clearly it was no time to show weakness. So I made a speech in which I said that other Alp-climbers had been in as perilous a position as this and yet by courage and perserverance had escaped. I promised to stand by them, I promised to rescue them. I closed by saying we had plenty of provisions to maintain us for quite a siege—and did they suppose Zermatt would allow half a mile of men and mules to mysteriously disappear during any considerable time right above their noses and make no inquiries? No, Zermatt would send out searching-expeditions and we should be saved.

This speech had a great effect. The men pitched the tents with some little show of cheerfulness and we were snugly under cover when the night shut down. I now reaped the reward of my wisdom in providing one article which is not mentioned in any book of Alpine adventure but this. I refer to the paregoric. But for that beneficent drug not one of those men would have slept a moment during that fearful night. But for that gentle persuader they must have tossed, unsoothed, the night through. For the whisky was for me. Yes, they would have risen in the morning unfitted for their heavy task. As it was, everybody slept but my agent and me —only we two and the barkeepers. I would not permit myself to sleep at such a time. I considered myself responsible for all those lives. I meant to be on hand and ready in case of avalanches. I am aware now that there were no avalanches up there but I did not know it then.

We watched the weather all through that awful night and kept an eye on the barometer to be prepared for the least change. There was not the slightest change recorded by the instrument during the whole time. Words cannot describe the comfort that that friendly, hopeful, steadfast thing was to me in that season of trouble. It was a defective barometer and had no hand but the stationary brass pointer but I did not know that until afterward. If I should be in such a situation again I should not wish for any barometer but that one.

All hands rose at two in the morning and took breakfast, and as soon as it was light we roped ourselves together and went at that rock. For some time we tried the hook-rope and other means of scaling it but without success—that is, without perfect success. The hook caught once and Harris started up it hand over hand but the hold broke and if there had not happened to be a chaplain sitting underneath at the time, Harris would certainly have been crippled. As it was, it was the chaplain. He took to his crutches and I ordered the hook-rope to be laid aside. It was too dangerous an implement where so many people were standing around.

We were puzzled for a while. Then somebody thought of the ladders. One of these was leaned against the rock, and the men went up it tied together in couples. Another ladder was sent up for use in descending. At the end of half an hour everybody was over and that rock was conquered. We gave our first grand shout of triumph. But the joy was short-lived, for somebody asked how we were going to get the animals over.

This was a serious difficulty. In fact, it was an impossibility. The courage of the men began to waver immediately. Once more we were threatened with a panic. But when the danger was most imminent we were saved in a mysterious way. A mule which had attracted attention from the beginning by its disposition to experiment tried to eat a five-pound can of nitroglycerin. This happened right alongside the rock. The explosion threw us all to the ground and covered us with dirt and debris. It frightened us extremely, too, for the crash it made was deafening and the violence of the shock made the ground tremble. However, we were grateful, for the rock was gone. Its place was occupied by a new cellar about thirty feet across by fifteen feet deep. The explosion was heard as far as Zermatt and an hour and a half afterward many citizens of that town were knocked down and quite seriously injured by descending portions of mule meat frozen solid. This shows better than any estimate in figures how high the experimenter went.

We had nothing to do now but bridge the cellar and proceed on our way. With a cheer the men went at their work. I attended to the engineering myself. I appointed a strong detail to cut down trees with ice-axes and trim them for piers to support the bridge. This was a slow business, for ice-axes are not good to cut wood with. I caused my piers to be firmly set up in ranks in the cellar, and upon them I laid six of my forty-foot ladders side by side, and laid six more on top of them. Upon this bridge I caused a bed of boughs to be spread, and on top of the boughs a bed of earth six inches deep. I stretched ropes upon either side to serve as railings, and then my bridge was complete. A train of elephants could have crossed it in safety and comfort. By nightfall the caravan was on the other side and the ladders taken up.

Next morning we went on in good spirits for a while though our way was slow and difficult, by reason of the steep and rocky nature of the ground and the thickness of the forest. But at last a dull despondency crept into the men's faces and it was apparent that not only they but even the guides were now convinced that we were lost. The fact that we still met no tourists was a circumstance that was but too significant. Another thing seemed to suggest that we were not only lost but very badly lost, for there must surely be searching-parties on the road before this time, yet we had seen no sign of them.

Demoralization was spreading. Something must be done and done quickly too. Fortunately I am not unfertile in expedients. I contrived one now which commended itself to all, for it promised well. I took three-quarters of a mile of rope and fastened one end of it around the waist of a guide and told him to go and find the road while the caravan waited. I instructed him to guide himself back by the rope in case of failure. In case of success he was to give the rope a series of violent jerks, whereupon the Expedition would go to him at once. He departed, and in two minutes had disappeared among the trees. I payed out the rope myself while everybody watched the crawling thing with eager eyes. The rope crept away quite slowly at times, at other times with some briskness. Twice or thrice we seemed to get the signal, and a shout was just ready to break from the men's lips when they perceived it was a false alarm. But at last, when over half a mile of rope had slidden away, it stopped gliding and stood absolutely still—one minute—two minutes—three—while we held our breath and watched.

Was the guide resting? Was he scanning the country from some high point? Was he inquiring of a chance mountaineer? Stop—had he fainted from excess of fatigue and anxiety?

This thought gave us a shock. I was in the very act of

detailing an Expedition to succor him, when the cord was assailed with a series of such frantic jerks that I could hardly keep hold of it. The huzza that went up, then, was good to hear. "Saved! saved!" was the word that rang out all down the long rank of the caravan.

We rose up and started at once. We found the route to be good enough for a while but it began to grow difficult by and by and this feature steadily increased. When we judged we had gone half a mile we momentarily expected to see the guide but no, he was not visible anywhere. Neither was he waiting, for the rope was still moving, consequently he was doing the same. This argued that he had not found the road yet but was marching to it with some peasant. There was nothing for us to do but plod along—and this we did. At the end of three hours we were still plodding. This was not only mysterious but exasperating. And very fatiguing too, for we had tried hard, along at first, to catch up with the guide but had only fagged ourselves in vain, for although he was traveling slowly he was yet able to go faster than the hampered caravan over such ground.

At three in the afternoon we were nearly dead with exhaustion—and still the rope was slowly gliding out. The murmurs against the guide had been growing steadily, and at last they were become loud and savage. A mutiny ensued. The men refused to proceed. They declared that we had been traveling over and over the same ground all day in a kind of circle. They demanded that our end of the rope be made fast to a tree so as to halt the guide until we could overtake him and kill him. This was not an unreasonable requirement, so I gave the order.

As soon as the rope was tied, the Expedition moved forward with that alacrity which the thirst for vengeance usually inspires. But after a tiresome march of almost half a mile we came to a hill covered thick with a crumbly rubbish of stones, and so steep that no man of us all was now in a condition to climb it. Every attempt failed and ended in crippling somebody. Within twenty minutes I had five men

on crutches. Whenever a climber tried to assist himself by
the rope it yielded and let him tumble backward. The frequency of this result suggested an idea to me. I ordered the
caravan to 'bout face and form in marching order. I then
made the tow-rope fast to the rear mule and gave the command:

"Mark time—by the right flank—forward—march!"

The procession began to move to the impressive strains of
a battle-chant and I said to myself, "Now, if the rope don't
break I judge *this* will fetch that guide into the camp." I
watched the rope gliding down the hill, and presently when
I was all fixed for triumph I was confronted by a bitter disappointment. There was no guide tied to the rope, it was only
a very indignant old black ram. The fury of the baffled Expedition exceeded all bounds. They even wanted to wreak their
unreasoning vengeance on this innocent dumb brute. But I
stood between them and their prey, menaced by a bristling
wall of ice-axes and alpenstocks, and proclaimed that there
was but one road to this murder, and it was directly over my
corse. Even as I spoke I saw that my doom was sealed except
a miracle supervened to divert these madmen from their fell
purpose. I see that sickening wall of weapons now. I see that
advancing host as I saw it then. I see the hate in those cruel
eyes. I remember how I drooped my head upon my breast.
I feel again the sudden earthquake shock in my rear, administered by the very ram I was sacrificing myself to save. I hear
once more the typhoon of laughter that burst from the as-
saulting column as I clove it from van to rear like a Sepoy shot
from a Rodman gun.

I was saved. Yes, I was saved, and by the merciful instinct
of ingratitude which nature had planted in the breast of that
treacherous beast. The grace which eloquence had failed to
work in those men's hearts had been wrought by a laugh. The
ram was set free and my life was spared.

We lived to find out that that guide had deserted us as soon
as he had placed a half-mile between himself and us. To avert
suspicion, he had judged it best that the line should continue

to move, so he caught that ram, and at the time that he was sitting on it making the rope fast to it, we were imagining that he was lying in a swoon, overcome by fatigue and distress. When he allowed the ram to get up it fell to plunging around, trying to rid itself of the rope, and this was the signal which we had risen up with glad shouts to obey. We had followed this ram round and round in a circle all day—a thing which was proven by the discovery that we had watered the Expedition seven times at one and the same spring in seven hours. As expert a woodman as I am, I had somehow failed to notice this until my attention was called to it by a hog. This hog was always wallowing there, and as he was the only hog we saw, his frequent repetition, together with his unvarying similarity to himself, finally caused me to reflect that he must be the same hog, and this led me to the deduction that this must be the same spring also—which indeed it was.

I made a note of this curious thing, as showing in a striking manner the relative difference between glacial action and the action of the hog. It is now a well-established fact that glaciers move. I consider that my observations go to show with equal conclusiveness that a hog in a spring does not move. I shall be glad to receive the opinions of other observers upon this point.

To return, for an explanatory moment, to that guide, and then I shall be done with him. After leaving the ram tied to the rope, he had wandered at large a while and then happened to run across a cow. Judging that a cow would naturally know more than a guide, he took her by the tail, and the result justified his judgment. She nibbled her leisurely way downhill till it was near milking-time, then she struck for home and towed him into Zermatt.

33. An American Grandson

We went into camp on that wild spot to which that ram had brought us. The men were greatly fatigued. Their conviction that we were lost was forgotten in the cheer of a good supper, and before the reaction had a chance to set in I loaded them up with paregoric and put them to bed.

Next morning I was considering in my mind our desperate situation and trying to think of a remedy, when Harris came to me with a Baedeker map which showed conclusively that the mountain we were on was still in Switzerland—yes, every part of it was in Switzerland. So we were not lost after all. This was an immense relief. It lifted the weight of two such mountains from my breast. I immediately had the news disseminated and the map exhibited. The effect was wonderful. As soon as the men saw with their own eyes that they knew where they were and that it was only the summit that was lost and not themselves they cheered up instantly and said with one accord, let the summit take care of itself, they were not interested in its troubles.

Our distresses being at an end, I now determined to rest the men in camp and give the scientific department of the Expedition a chance. First I made a barometric observation to get our altitude but I could not perceive that there was any result. I knew by my scientific reading that either thermometers or barometers ought to be boiled to make them accurate. I did not know which it was, so I boiled both. There was still no result, so I examined these instruments and discovered that they possessed radical blemishes: the barometer had no hand but the brass pointer, and the ball of the theromometer was stuffed with tin-foil. I might have boiled those things to rags and never found out anything.

I hunted up another barometer. It was new and perfect. I boiled it half an hour in a pot of bean soup which the cooks were making. The result was unexpected. The instrument was not affected at all but there was such a strong barometer taste to the soup that the head cook, who was a most conscientious person, changed its name in the bill of fare. The dish was so greatly liked by all that I ordered the cook to have barometer soup every day. It was believed that the barometer might eventually be injured but I did not care for that. I had demonstrated to my satisfaction that it could not tell how high a mountain was, therefore I had no real use for it. Changes of the weather I could take care of without it. I did not wish to know when the weather was going to be good, what I wanted to know was when it was going to be bad, and this I could find out from Harris's corns. Harris had had his corns tested and regulated at the government observatory in Heidelberg, and one could depend upon them with confidence. So I transferred the new barometer to the cooking department, to be used for the official mess. It was found that even a pretty fair article of soup could be made with the defective barometer, so I allowed that one to be transferred to the subordinate messes.

I next boiled the thermometer and got a most excellent result. The mercury went up to about 200 degrees Fahrenheit. In the opinion of the other scientists of the Expedition this seemed to indicate that we had attained the extraordinary altitude of two hundred thousand feet above sea-level. Science places the line of eternal snow at about ten thousand feet above sea-level. There was no snow where we were, consequently it was proven that the eternal snow-line ceases somewhere above the ten-thousand-foot level and does not begin any more. This was an interesting fact and one which had not been observed by any observer before. It was as valuable as interesting, too, since it would open up the deserted summits of the highest Alps to population and agriculture. It was a proud thing to be where we were, yet it caused us a pang to reflect that but for that ram we might just as well have been two hundred thousand feet higher.

The success of my last experiment induced me to try an experiment with my photographic apparatus. I got it out and boiled one of my cameras but the thing was a failure: it made the wood swell up and burst, and I could not see that the lenses were any better than they were before.

I now concluded to boil a guide. It might improve him, it could not impair his usefulness. But I was not allowed to proceed. Guides have no feeling for science, and this one would not consent to be made uncomfortable in its interest.

In the midst of my scientific work one of those needless accidents happened which are always occurring among the ignorant and thoughtless. A porter shot at a chamois and missed it and crippled the Latinist. This was not a serious matter to me, for a Latinist's duties are as well performed on crutches as otherwise—but the fact remained that if the Latinist had not happened to be in the way a mule would have got that load. That would have been quite another matter, for when it comes down to a question of value there is a palpable difference between a Latinist and a mule. I could not depend on having a Latinist in the right place every time. So, to make things safe, I ordered that in the future the chamois must not be hunted within limits of the camp with any other weapon than the forefinger.

My nerves had hardly grown quiet after this affair when they got another shake-up—one which utterly unmanned me for a moment: a rumor swept suddenly through the camp that one of the barkeepers had fallen over a precipice!

However, it turned out that it was only a chaplain. I had laid in an extra force of chaplains purposely to be prepared for emergencies like this, but by some unaccountable oversight had come away rather short-handed in the matter of barkeepers.

On the following morning we moved on well refreshed

and in good spirits. I remember this day with peculiar pleasure because it saw our road restored to us. Yes, we found our road again and in quite an extraordinary way. We had plodded along some two hours and a half, when we came up against a solid mass of rock about twenty feet high. I did not need to be instructed by a mule this time. I was already beginning to know more than any mule in the Expedition. I at once put in a blast of dynamite and lifted that rock out of the way. But to my surprise and mortification I found that there had been a chalet on top of it.

I picked up such members of the family as fell in my vicinity, and subordinates of my corps collected the rest. None of these poor people were injured, happily, but they were much annoyed. I explained to the head chaleteer just how the thing happened and that I was only searching for the road and would certainly have given him timely notice if I had known he was up there. I said I had meant no harm and hoped I had not lowered myself in his estimation by raising him a few rods in the air. I said many other judicious things, and finally when I offered to rebuild his chalet and pay for the breakages and throw in the cellar he was mollified and satisfied. He hadn't any cellar at all before. He would not have as good a view now as formerly but what he had lost in view he had gained in cellar, by exact measurement. He said there wasn't another hole like that in the mountains—and he would have been right if the late mule had not tried to eat up the nitroglycerin.

I put a hundred and sixteen men at work, and they rebuilt the chalet from its own debris in fifteen minutes. It was a good deal more picturesque than it was before, too. The man said we were now on the Feli-Stutz, above the Schwegmatt —information which I was glad to get, since it gave us our position to a degree of particularity which we had not been accustomed to for a day or so. We also learned that we were standing at the foot of the Riffelberg proper and that the initial chapter of our work was completed.

We had a fine view from here of the energetic Visp as it

makes its first plunge into the world from under a huge arch of solid ice, worn through the foot-wall of the great Gorner Glacier. And we could also see the Furggenbach, which is the outlet of the Furggen Glacier.

The mule-road to the summit of the Riffelberg passed right in front of the chalet, a circumstance which we almost immediately noticed, because a procession of tourists was filing along it pretty much all the time.* The chaleteer's business consisted in furnishing refreshments to tourists. My blast had interrupted this trade for a few minutes by breaking all the bottles on the place but I gave the man a lot of whisky to sell for Alpine champagne, and a lot of vinegar which would answer for Rhine wine, consequently trade was soon as brisk as ever.

Leaving the Expedition outside to rest, I quartered myself in the chalet with Harris, purposing to correct my journals and scientific observations before continuing the ascent. I had hardly begun my work when a tall, slender, vigorous American youth of about twenty-three, who was on his way down the mountain, entered and came toward me with that breezy self-complacency which is the adolescent's idea of the well-bred ease of the man of the world. His hair was short and parted accurately in the middle and he had all the look of an Amercan person who would be likely to begin his signature with an initial and spell his middle name out. He introduced himself, smiling a smirky smile borrowed from the courtiers of the stage, extended a fair-skinned talon, and while he gripped my hand in it he bent his body forward three times at the hips as the stage-courtier does and said in the airiest and most condescending and patronizing way—I quote his exact language:

"Very glad to make your acquaintance, 'm sure. Very glad indeed, assure you. I've read all your little efforts and greatly admired them, and when I heard you were here, I . . ."

---

*"Pretty much" may not be elegant English but it is high time it was. There is no elegant word or phrase which means just what it means.

I indicated a chair and he sat down. This grandee was the grandson of an American of considerable note in his day and not wholly forgotten yet—a man who came so near being a great man that he was quite generally accounted one while he lived.

I slowly paced the floor, pondering scientific problems, and heard this conversation:

Grandson. First visit to Europe?

Harris. Mine? Yes.

G.S. (With a soft reminiscent sigh suggestive of bygone joys that may be tasted in their freshness but once.) Ah, I know what it is to you. A first visit!—ah, the romance of it! I wish I could feel it again.

H. Yes, I find it exceeds all my dreams. It is enchantment. I go . . .

G. S. (With a dainty gesture of the hand signifying "Spare me your callow enthusiasms, good friend.") Yes, *I* know, I know. You go to cathedrals and exclaim. And you drag through league-long picture-galleries and exclaim. And you stand here and there and yonder upon historic ground and continue to exclaim. And you are permeated with your first crude conceptions of Art and are proud and happy. Ah yes, proud and happy—that expresses it. Yes-yes, enjoy it—it is right—it is an innocent revel.

H. And you? Don't you do these things now?

G. S. I! Oh, that is *very* good! My dear sir, when you are as old a traveler as I am you will not ask such a question as that. *I* visit the regulation gallery, moon around the regulation cathedral, do the worn round of the regulation sights, *yet?* Excuse me!

H. Well, what *do* you do then?

G. S. Do? I flit—and flit—for I am ever on the wing—but I avoid the herd. To-day I am in Paris, to-morrow in Berlin, anon in Rome. But you would look for me in vain in the galleries of the Louvre or the common resorts of the gazers in those other capitals. If you would find me you must look in the unvisited nooks and corners where others never think of going. One day you will find me making myself at home in some obscure peasant's cabin, another day you will find me in some forgotten castle worshiping some little gem of art which the careless eye has overlooked and which the unexperienced would despise. Again you will find me a guest in the inner sanctuaries of palaces while the herd is content to get a hurried glimpse of the unused chambers by feeing a servant.

H. You are a *guest* in such places?

G. S. And a welcome one.

H. It is surprising. How does it come?

G. S. My grandfather's name is a passport to all the courts in Europe. I have only to utter that name and every door is open to me. I flit from court to court at my own free will and pleasure and am always welcome. I am as much at home in the palaces of Europe as you are among your relatives. I know every titled person in Europe, I think. I have my pockets full of invitations all the time. I am under promise now to go to Italy, where I am to be the guest of a succession of the noblest houses in the land. In Berlin my life is a continued round of gaiety in the imperial palace. It is the same wherever I go.

H. It must be very pleasant. But it must make Boston seem a little slow when you are at home.

G. S. Yes, of course it does. But I don't go home much. There's no life there—little to feed a man's higher nature. Boston's very narrow, you know. She doesn't know it and you couldn't convince her of it—so I say nothing when I'm there: where's the use? Yes, Boston is very narrow but she has such a good opinion of herself that she can't see it. A man who has traveled as much as I have and seen as much of the world, sees it plain enough but he can't cure it, you know, so the best way is to leave it and seek a sphere which is more in harmony with his tastes and culture. I run across there, once a year, perhaps, when I have nothing important on hand but I'm very soon back again. I spend my time in Europe.

H. I see. You map out your plans and . . .

G. S. No, excuse me. I don't map out any plans. I simply follow the inclination of the day. I am limited by no ties, no requirements, I am not bound in any way. I am too old a traveler to hamper myself with deliberate purposes. I am simply a traveler—an inveterate traveler—a man of the world, in a word—I can call myself by no other name. I do not say, "I am going here or I am going there"—I say nothing at all, I only act. For instance, next week you may find me the guest of a grandee of Spain or you may find me off for Venice or flitting toward Dresden. I shall probably go to Egypt presently. Friends will say to friends, "He is at the Nile cataracts" —and at that very moment they will be surprised to learn that I'm away off yonder in India somewhere. I am a constant surprise to people. They are always saying, "Yes, he was in Jerusalem when we heard of him last but goodness knows where he is now."

Presently the Grandson rose to leave—discovered he had an appointment with some Emperor, perhaps. He did his graces over again: gripped me with one talon, at arm's-length, pressed his hat against his stomach with the other, bent his body in the middle three times, murmuring:

"Pleasure, 'm sure. Great pleasure, 'm sure. Wish you much success."

Then he removed his gracious presence. It is a great and solemn thing to have a grandfather.

I have not purposed to misrepresent this boy in any way, for what little indignation he excited in me soon passed and left nothing behind it but compassion. One cannot keep up a grudge against a vacuum. I have tried to repeat the lad's very words. If I have failed anywhere I have at least not failed to reproduce the marrow and meaning of what he said. He and the innocent chatterbox whom I met on the Swiss lake are the most unique and interesting specimens of Young America I came across during my foreign tramping. I have made honest portraits of them, not caricatures. The Grandson of twenty-three referred to himself five or six times as an "old traveler," and as many as three times (with a serene complacency which was maddening) as a "man of the world." There was something very delicious about his leaving Boston to her "narrowness," unreproved and uninstructed.

I formed the caravan in marching order presently, and after riding down the line to see that it was properly roped together gave the command to proceed. In a little while the road carried us to open, grassy land. We were above the troublesome forest now and had an uninterrupted view, straight before us, of our summit—the summit of the Riffelberg.

We followed the mule-road, a zigzag course now to the right, now to the left but always up and always crowded and incommoded by going and coming files of reckless tourists who were never in a single instance tied together. I was obliged to exert the utmost care and caution, for in many places the road was not two yards wide, and often the lower side of it sloped away in slanting precipices eight and even nine feet deep. I had to encourage the men constantly to keep them from giving way to their unmanly fears.

We might have made the summit before night but for a delay caused by the loss of an umbrella. I was for allowing the umbrella to remain lost but the men murmured and with reason, for in this exposed region we stood in peculiar need of protection against avalanches. So I went into camp and detached a strong party to go after the missing article.

The difficulties of the next morning were severe but our courage was high, for our goal was near. At noon we conquered the last impediment—we stood at last upon the summit and without the loss of a single man except the mule that ate the glycerin. Our great achievement was achieved—the possibility of the impossible was demonstrated, and Harris and I walked proudly into the great dining-room of the Riffelberg Hotel and stood our alpenstocks up in the corner.

Yes, I had made the grand ascent. But it was a mistake to do it in evening dress. The plug hats were battered, the swallow-tails were fluttering rags, mud added no grace, the general effect was unpleasant and even disreputable.

There were about seventy-five tourists at the hotel—mainly ladies and little children—and they gave us an admiring welcome which paid us for all our privations and sufferings. The ascent had been made, and the names and dates now stand recorded on a stone monument there to prove it to all future tourists.

I boiled a thermometer and took an altitude, with a most curious result: *the summit was not as high as the point on the mountainside where I had taken the first altitude.* Suspecting that I had made an important discovery, I prepared to verify it. There happened to be a still higher summit (called the Gorner Grat) above the hotel, and notwithstanding the fact that it overlooks a glacier from a dizzy height and that the ascent is difficult and dangerous, I resolved to venture up there and boil a thermometer. So I sent a strong party with some borrowed hoes in charge of two chiefs of service to dig a stairway in the soil all the way, and this I ascended, roped to the guides. This breezy height was the summit proper—so I accomplished even more than I had originally purposed to do. This foolhardy exploit is recorded on another stone monument.

I boiled my thermometer, and sure enough this spot, which purported to be two thousand feet higher than the locality of the hotel, turned out to be nine thousand feet *lower.* Thus the fact was clearly demonstrated that *above a certain point, the higher a point seems to be, the lower it actually is.* Our ascent itself was a great achievement but this contribution to science was an inconceivably greater matter.

Cavilers object that water boils at a lower and lower temperature the higher and higher you go and hence the apparent anomaly. I answer that I do not base my theory upon what the boiling water does but upon what a boiled thermometer says. You can't go behind the thermometer.

I had a magnificent view of Monte Rosa and apparently all the rest of the Alpine world from that high place. All the circling horizon was piled high with a mighty tumult of snowy crests. One might have imagined he saw before him the tented camps of a beleaguering host of Brobdingnagians.

But lonely, conspicuous and superb rose that wonderful upright wedge, the Matterhorn.* Its precipitous sides were powdered over with snow, and the upper half hidden in thick clouds which now and then dissolved to cobweb films and gave brief glimpses of the imposing tower as through a veil. A little later the Matterhorn took to himself the semblance of a volcano. He was stripped naked to his apex—around this circled vast wreaths of white cloud which strung slowly out and streamed away slantwise toward the sun, a twenty-mile stretch of rolling and tumbling vapor, and looking just as if it were pouring out of a crater. Later again, one of the mountain's sides was clean and clear, and another side densely clothed from base to summit in thick smokelike cloud which feathered off and blew around the shaft's sharp edge like the smoke around the corners of a burning building. The Matterhorn is always experimenting, and always gets up fine effects, too. In the sunset, when all the lower world is palled in gloom, it points toward heaven out of the pervading blackness like a finger of fire. In the sunrise—well, they say it is very fine in the sunrise.

Authorities agree that there is no such tremendous "layout" of snowy Alpine magnitude, grandeur and sublimity to be seen from any other accessible point as the tourist may see from the summit of the Riffelberg. Therefore, let the tourist rope himself up and go there, for I have shown that with nerve, caution and judgment the thing can be done.

I wish to add one remark here—in parentheses, so to speak —suggested by the word "snowy," which I have just used.

---

*I had the very unusual luck to catch one little momentary glimpse of the Matterhorn wholly unencumbered by clouds. I leveled my photographic apparatus at it without the loss of an instant and should have got an elegant picture if my donkey had not interfered. It was my purpose to draw this photograph all by myself for my book but I was obliged to put the mountain part of it into the hands of the professional artist because I found I could not do landscape well.

We have all seen hills and mountains and levels with snow on
them and so we think we know all the aspects and effects
produced by snow. But indeed we do not until we have seen
the Alps. Possibly mass and distance add something—at any
rate, something *is* added. Among other noticeable things,
there is a dazzling, intense whiteness about the distant Alpine snow, when the sun is on it, which one recognizes as
peculiar and not familiar to the eye. The snow which one is
accustomed to has a tint to it—painters usually give it a bluish
cast—but there is no perceptible tint to the distant Alpine
snow when it is trying to look its whitest. As to the unimaginable splendor of it when the sun is blazing down on it—well,
it simply *is* unimaginable.

34. Traveling by Glacier

A guide-book is a queer thing. The reader has just seen what
a man who undertakes the great ascent from Zermatt to the
Riffelberg Hotel must experience. Yet Baedeker makes these
strange statements concerning this matter:

1. Distance—3 hours.
2. The road cannot be mistaken.
3. Guide unnecessary.
4. Distance from Riffelberg Hotel to the Gorner Grat, one
hour and a half.
5. Ascent simple and easy. Guide unnecessary.
6. Elevation of Zermatt above sea-level, 5,315 feet.
7. Elevation of Riffelberg Hotel above sea-level, 8,429 feet.
8. Elevation of the Gorner Grat above sea-level, 10,289
feet.

I have pretty effectually throttled these errors by sending him the following demonstrated facts:

1. Distance from Zermatt to Riffelberg Hotel, 7 days.

2. The road *can* be mistaken. If I am the first that did it, I want the credit of it too.

3. Guides *are* necessary, for none but a native can read those finger-boards.

4. The estimate of the elevation of the several localities above sea-level is pretty correct—for Baedeker. He only misses it about a hundred and eighty or ninety thousand feet.

I found my arnica invaluable. My men were suffering excruciatingly from the friction of sitting down so much. During two or three days not one of them was able to do more than lie down or walk about, yet so effective was the arnica that on the fourth all were able to sit up. I consider that more than to anything else I owe the success of our great undertaking to arnica and paregoric.

My men being restored to health and strength, my main perplexity now was how to get them down the mountain again. I was not willing to expose the brave fellows to the perils, fatigues and hardships of that fearful route again if it could be helped. First I thought of balloons but of course I had to give that idea up, for balloons were not procurable. I thought of several other expedients but upon consideration discarded them, for cause. But at last I hit it. I was aware that the movement of glaciers is an established fact, for I had read it in Baedeker, so I resolved to take passage for Zermatt on the great Gorner Glacier.

Very good. The next thing was, how to get down to the glacier comfortably—for the mule-road to it was long and winding and wearisome. I set my mind at work and soon thought out a plan. One looks straight down upon the vast frozen river called the Gorner Glacier, from the Gorner Grat, a sheer precipice twelve hundred feet high. We had one hundred and fifty-four umbrellas—and what is an umbrella but a parachute?

I mentioned this noble idea to Harris with enthusiasm and

was about to order the Expedition to form on the Gorner Grat with their umbrellas and prepare for flight by platoons, each platoon in command of a guide, when Harris stopped me and urged me not to be too hasty. He asked me if this method of descending the Alps had ever been tried before. I said, no, I had not heard of an instance. Then, in his opinion, it was a matter of considerable gravity. In his opinion it would not be well to send the whole command over the cliff at once. A better way would be to send down a single individual first and see how he fared.

I saw the wisdom of this idea instantly. I said as much and thanked my agent cordially and told him to take his umbrella and try the thing right away and wave his hat when he got down, if he struck in a soft place, and then I would ship the rest right along.

Harris was greatly touched with this mark of confidence and said so in a voice that had a perceptible tremble in it but at the same time he said he did not feel himself worthy of so conspicuous a favor, that it might cause jealousy in the command, for there were plenty who would not hesitate to say he had used underhanded means to get the appointment, whereas his conscience would bear him witness that he had not sought it at all nor even in his secret heart desired it.

I said these words did him extreme credit but that he must not throw away the imperishable distinction of being the first man to descend an Alp per parachute, simply to save the feelings of some envious underlings. No, I said, he *must* accept the appointment—it was no longer an invitation, it was a command.

He thanked me with effusion and said that putting the thing in this form removed every objection. He retired and soon returned with his umbrella, his eyes flaming with gratitude and his cheeks pallid with joy. Just then the head guide passed along. Harris's expression changed to one of infinite tenderness and he said:

"That man did me a cruel injury four days ago and I said in my heart he should live to perceive and confess that the only noble revenge a man can take upon his enemy is to return good for evil. I resign in his favor. Appoint him."

I threw my arms around the generous fellow and said:

"Harris, you are the noblest soul that lives. You shall not regret this sublime act, neither shall the world fail to know of it. You shall have opportunities far transcending this one, too, if I live—remember that."

I called the head guide to me and appointed him on the spot. But the thing aroused no enthusiasm in him. He did not take to the idea at all. He said:

"Tie myself to an umbrella and jump over the Gorner Grat! Excuse me, there are a great many pleasanter roads to the devil than that."

Upon a discussion of the subject with him, it appeared that he considered the project distinctly and decidedly dangerous. I was not convinced, yet I was not willing to try the experiment in any risky way—that is, in a way that might cripple the strength and efficiency of the Expedition. I was about at my wits' end when it occurred to me to try it on the Latinist.

He was called in. But he declined on the plea of inexperience, diffidence in public, lack of curiosity and I don't know what all. Another man declined on account of a cold in the head. Thought he ought to avoid exposure. Another could not jump well—never *could* jump well—did not believe he could jump so far without long and patient practice. Another was afraid it was going to rain, and his umbrella had a hole in it. Everybody had an excuse. The result was what the reader has by this time guessed: the most magnificent idea that was ever conceived had to be abandoned from sheer lack of a person with enterprise enough to carry it out. Yes, I actually had to give that thing up—while doubtless I should live to see somebody use it and take all the credit from me.

Well, I had to go overland—there was no other way. I marched the Expedition down the steep and tedious mule-path and took up as good a position as I could upon the middle of the glacier—because Baedeker said the middle part travels the fastest. As a measure of economy, however, I put some of the heavier baggage on the shoreward parts, to go as slow freight.

I waited and waited but the glacier did not move. Night was coming on, the darkness began to gather—still we did not budge. It occurred to me then that there might be a time-table in Baedeker. It would be well to find out the hours of starting. I called for the book—it could not be found. Bradshaw would certainly contain a time-table. But no Bradshaw could be found.

Very well, I must make the best of the situation. So I pitched the tents, picketed the animals, milked the cows, had supper, paregoricked the men, established the watch and went to bed—with orders to call me as soon as we came in sight of Zermatt.

I awoke about half past ten next morning and looked around. We hadn't budged a peg! At first I could not understand it. Then it occurred to me that the old thing must be aground. So I cut down some trees and rigged a spar on the starboard and another on the port side and fooled away upward of three hours trying to spar her off. But it was no use. She was half a mile wide and fifteen or twenty miles long and there was no telling just whereabouts she *was* aground. The men began to show uneasiness, too, and presently they came flying to me with ashy faces, saying she had sprung a leak.

Nothing but my cool behavior at this critical time saved us from another panic. I ordered them to show me the place. They led me to a spot where a huge boulder lay in a deep pool of clear and brilliant water. It did look like a pretty bad leak but I kept that to myself. I made a pump and set the men to work to pump out the glacier. We made a success of it. I perceived then that it was not a leak at all. This boulder had descended from a precipice and stopped on the ice in the middle of the glacier, and the sun had warmed it up every day and consequently it had melted its way deeper and deeper into the ice until at last it reposed as we had found it, in a deep pool of the clearest and coldest water.

Presently Baedeker was found again and I hunted eagerly for the time-table. There was none. The book simply said the glacier was moving all the time. This was satisfactory, so I shut up the book and chose a good position to view the scenery as we passed along. I stood there some time enjoying the trip but at last it occurred to me that we did not seem to be gaining any on the scenery. I said to myself, "This confounded old thing's aground again, sure"—and opened Baedeker to see if I could run across any remedy for these annoying interruptions. I soon found a sentence which threw a dazzling light upon the matter. It said, "The Gorner Glacier travels at an average rate of a little less than an inch a day." I have seldom felt so outraged. I have seldom had my confidence so wantonly betrayed. I made a small calculation. One inch a day, say thirty feet a year. Estimated distance to Zermatt, three and one-eighteenth miles. Time required to go by glacier, *a little over five hundred years!* I said to myself, "I can *walk* it quicker—and before I will patronize such a fraud as this, I will do it."

When I revealed to Harris the fact that the passenger part of this glacier—the central part—the lightning-express part, so to speak—was not due in Zermatt till the summer of 2378 and that the baggage, coming along the slow edge, would not arrive until some generations later, he burst out with:

"That is European management all over! An inch a day— think of that! Five hundred years to go a trifle over three miles! But I am not a bit surprised. It's a Catholic glacier. You can tell by the look of it. And the management."

I said, no, I believed nothing but the extreme end of it was in a Catholic canton.

"Well, then, it's a government glacier," said Harris. "It's all the same. Over here the government runs everything—so everything's slow. Slow and ill-managed. But with us everything's done by private enterprise—and then there ain't much lolling around, you can depend on it. I wish Tom Scott could get his hands on this torpid old slab once—you'd see it take a different gait from this."

I said I was sure he would increase the speed if there was trade enough to justify it.

"He'd *make* trade," said Harris. "That's the difference between governments and individuals. Governments don't care, individuals do. Tom Scott would take all the trade. In two years Gorner stock would go to two hundred, and inside of two more you would see all the other glaciers under the hammer for taxes." After a reflective pause Harris added, "A little less than an inch a day. A little less than an *inch*, mind you. Well, I'm losing my reverence for glaciers."

I was feeling much the same way myself. I have traveled by canal-boat, ox-wagon, raft and by the Ephesus and Smyrna railway. But when it comes down to good solid honest slow motion, I bet my money on the glacier. As a means of passenger transportation I consider the glacier a failure but as a vehicle for slow freight I think she fills the bill. In the matter of putting the fine shades on that line of business, I judge she could teach the Germans something.

I ordered the men to break camp and prepare for the land journey to Zermatt. At this moment a most interesting find was made. A dark object, bedded in the glacial ice, was cut out with the ice-axes, and it proved to be a piece of the undressed skin of some animal—a hair trunk, perhaps. But a close inspection disabled the hair-trunk theory, and further discussion and examination exploded it entirely—that is, in the opinion of all the scientists except the one who had advanced it. This one clung to his theory with the affectionate fidelity characteristic of originators of scientific theories, and afterward won many of the first scientists of the age to his view by a very able pamphlet which he wrote, entitled, "Evidences going to show that the hair trunk, in a wild state, belonged to the early glacial period and roamed the wastes of chaos in company with the cave-bear, primeval man and the other Oölitics of the Old Silurian family."

Each of our scientists had a theory of his own and put forward an animal of his own as a candidate for the skin. I sided with the geologist of the Expedition in the belief that this patch of skin had once helped to cover a Siberian elephant in some old forgotten age—but we divided there, the geologist believing that this discovery proved that Siberia had formerly been located where Switzerland is now, whereas I held the opinion that it merely proved that the primeval Swiss was not the dull savage he is represented to have been but was a being of high intellectual development who liked to go to the menagerie.

We arrived that evening, after many hardships and adventures, in some fields close to the great ice-arch where the mad Visp boils and surges out from under the foot of the great Gorner Glacier, and here we camped, our perils over and our magnificent undertaking successfully completed. We marched into Zermatt the next day and were received with the most lavish honors and applause. A document, signed and sealed by all the authorities, was given to me which established and indorsed the fact that I had made the ascent of the Riffelberg. This I wear around my neck, and it will be buried with me when I am no more.

35. Mont Blanc and Its Neighbors

Switzerland is simply a large humpy solid rock with a thin skin of grass stretched over it. Consequently they do not dig graves, they blast them out with powder and fuse. They cannot afford to have large graveyards, the grass skin is too circumscribed and too valuable. It is all required for the support of the living.

The graveyard in Zermatt occupies only about one-eighth of an acre. The graves are sunk in the living rock and are very permanent but occupation of them is only temporary. The occupant can only stay till his grave is needed by a later subject. He is removed then, for they do not bury one body on top of another. As I understand it, a family owns a grave just as it owns a house. A man dies and leaves his house to his son—and at the same time this dead father succeeds to his own father's grave. He moves out of the house and into the grave, and his predecessor moves out of the grave and into the cellar of the chapel. I saw a black box lying in the churchyard with skull and cross-bones painted on it and was told that this was used in transferring remains to the cellar.

In that cellar the bones and skulls of several hundreds of former citizens were compactly corded up. They made a pile eighteen feet long, seven feet high and eight feet wide. I was told that in some of the receptacles of this kind in the Swiss villages the skulls were all marked, and if a man wished to find the skulls of his ancestors for several generations back he could do it by these marks, preserved in the family records.

An English gentleman who had lived some years in this region said it was the cradle of compulsory education. But he said that the English idea that compulsory education would reduce bastardy and intemperance was an error—it has not that effect. He said there was more seduction in the Protestant than in the Catholic cantons because the confessional protected the girls. I wonder why it doesn't protect married women in France and Spain?

This gentleman said that among the poorer peasants in the Valais it was common for the brothers in a family to cast lots to determine which of them should have the coveted privilege of marrying. Then the lucky one got married, and his brethren—doomed bachelors—heroically banded themselves together to help support the new family.

We left Zermatt in a wagon—and in a rain-storm, too—for St. Nicholas about ten o'clock one morning. Again we passed between those grass-clad, prodigious cliffs specked with wee dwellings peeping over at us from velvety green walls ten and twelve hundred feet high. It did not seem possible that the imaginary chamois even could climb those precipices. Lovers on opposite cliffs probably kiss through a spy-glass and correspond with a rifle.

In Switzerland the farmer's plow is a wide shovel which scrapes up and turns over the thin earthy skin of his native rock—and there the man of the plow is a hero. Now here, by our St. Nicholas road, was a grave and it had a tragic story. A plowman was skinning his farm one morning—not the steepest part of it but still a steep part—that is, he was not skinning the front of his farm but the roof of it, near the eaves —when he absent-mindedly let go of the plow-handles to moisten his hands in the usual way. He lost his balance and fell out of his farm backward. Poor fellow, he never touched anything till he struck bottom fifteen hundred feet below.* We throw a halo of heroism around the life of the soldier and the sailor because of the deadly dangers they are facing all the time. But we are not used to looking upon farming as a heroic occupation. This is because we have not lived in Switzerland.

From St. Nicholas we struck out for Visp—or Vispach—on foot. The rain-storms had been at work during several days and had done a deal of damage in Switzerland and Savoy. We came to one place where a stream had changed its course and plunged down the mountain in a new place, sweeping everything before it. Two poor but precious farms by the roadside were ruined. One was washed clear away and the bed-rock exposed. The other was buried out of sight under a tumbled chaos of rocks, gravel, mud and rubbish. The resistless might of water was well exemplified. Some saplings which had stood in the way were bent to the ground, stripped clean of their bark and buried under rocky debris. The road had been swept away too.

In another place, where the road was high up on the moun-

*This was on a Sunday.

tain's face and its outside edge protected by flimsy masonry, we frequently came across spots where this masonry had caved off and left dangerous gaps for mules to get over. And with still more frequency we found the masonry slightly crumbled, and marked by mule-hoofs, thus showing that there had been danger of an accident to somebody. When at last we came to a badly ruptured bit of masonry, with hoof-prints evidencing a desperate struggle to regain the lost foothold, I looked quite hopefully over the dizzy precipice. But there was nobody down there.

They take exceedingly good care of their rivers in Switzerland and other portions of Europe. They wall up both banks with slanting solid stone masonry—so that from end to end of these rivers the banks look like the wharves at St. Louis and other towns on the Mississippi River.

It was during this walk from St. Nicholas in the shadow of the majestic Alps that we came across some little children amusing themselves in what seemed at first a most odd and original way—but it wasn't. It was in simply a natural and characteristic way. They were roped together with a string, they had mimic alpenstocks and ice-axes, and were climbing a meek and lowly manure-pile with a most blood-curdling amount of care and caution. The "guide" at the head of the line cut imaginary steps in a laborious and painstaking way, and not a monkey budged till the step above him was vacated. If we had waited we should have witnessed an imaginary accident, no doubt, and we should have heard the intrepid band hurrah when they made the summit and looked around upon the "magnificent view," and seen them throw themselves down in exhausted attitudes for a rest in that commanding situation.

In Nevada I used to see the children play at silvermining. Of course, the great thing was an accident in a mine, and there were two "star" parts: that of the man who fell down the mimic shaft and that of the daring hero who was lowered into the depths to bring him up. I knew one small chap who always insisted on playing *both* of these parts—and he carried his point. He would tumble into the shaft and die, and then come to the surface and go back after his own remains.

It is the smartest boy that gets the hero part everywhere. He is head-guide in Switzerland, head miner in Nevada, head bull-fighter in Spain, etc. But I knew a preacher's son seven years old who once selected a part for himself compared to which those just mentioned are tame and unimpressive. Jimmy's father stopped him from driving imaginary horse-cars one Sunday—stopped him from playing captain of an imaginary steamboat next Sunday—stopped him from leading an imaginary army to battle the following Sunday—and so on. Finally the little fellow said:

"I've tried everything and they won't any of them do. What *can* I play?"

"I hardly know, Jimmy, but you *must* play only things that are suitable to the Sabbath-day."

Next Sunday the preacher stepped softly to a backroom door to see if the children were rightly employed. He peeped in. A chair occupied the middle of the room, and on the back of it hung Jimmy's cap. One of the little sisters took the cap down, nibbled at it, then passed it to another small sister and said, "Eat of this fruit, for it is good." The Reverend took in the situation—alas, they were playing the Expulsion from Eden! Yet he found one little crumb of comfort. He said to himself, "For once Jimmy has yielded the chief role—I have been wronging him, I did not believe there was so much modesty in him. I should have expected him to be either Adam or Eve." This crumb of comfort lasted but a very little while. He glanced around and discovered Jimmy standing in an imposing attitude in a corner, with a dark and deadly frown on his face. What that meant was very plain—*he was impersonating the Deity!* Think of the guileless sublimity of that idea.

We reached Vispach at 8 P.M., only about seven hours out from St. Nicholas. So we must have made fully a mile and a half an hour, and it was all downhill, too, and very muddy at that. We stayed all night at the Hôtel du Soleil. I remember it because the landlady, the portier, the waitress and the chambermaid were not separate persons but were all contained in one neat and chipper suit of spotless muslin, and she was the prettiest young creature I saw in all that region. She was the landlord's daughter. And I remember that the only native match to her I saw in all Europe was the young daughter of the landlord of a village inn in the Black Forest. Why don't more people in Europe marry and keep hotel?

Next morning we left with a family of English friends and went by train to Brevet and thence by boat across the lake to Ouchy (Lausanne).

Ouchy is memorable to me, not on account of its beautiful situation and lovely surroundings—although these would make it stick long in one's memory—but as the place where I caught the London *Times* dropping into humor. It was not aware of it, though. It did not do it on purpose. An English friend called my attention to this lapse and cut out the reprehensible paragraph for me. Think of encountering a grin like this on the face of that grim journal:

ERRATUM.—We are requested by Reuter's Telegram Company to correct an erroneous announcement made in their Brisbane telegram of the 2d inst., published in our impression of the 5th inst., stating that "Lady Kennedy had given birth to twins, the eldest being a son." The Company explain that the message they received contained the words "Governor of Queensland, *twins first son.*" Being, however, subsequently informed that Sir Arthur Kennedy was unmarried and that there must be some mistake, a telegraphic repetition was at once demanded. It has been received to-day (11th inst.) and shows that the words really telegraphed by Reuter's agent were "Governor Queensland *turns first sod,*" alluding to the Maryborough-Gympic Railway in course of construction. The words in italics were mutilated by the telegraph in transmission from Australia, and reaching the company in the form mentioned above gave rise to the mistake.

I had always had a deep and reverent compassion for the sufferings of the "prisoner of Chillon," whose story Byron has told in such moving verse, so I took the steamer and made pilgrimage to the dungeons of the Castle of Chillon to see the place where poor Bonnivard endured his dreary captivity three hundred years ago. I am glad I did that, for it took away some of the pain I was feeling on the prisoner's account. His dungeon was a nice cool roomy place and I cannot see why he should have been so dissatisfied with it. If he had been imprisoned in a St. Nicholas private dwelling, where the fertilizer prevails and the goat sleeps with the guest and the chickens roost on him and the cow comes in and bothers him when he wants to muse, it would have been another matter altogether. But he surely could not have had a very cheerless time of it in that pretty dungeon. It has romantic window-slits that let in generous bars of light, and it has tall noble columns carved apparently from the living rock. And what is more, they are written all over with thousands of names: some of them—like Byron's and Victor Hugo's—of the first celebrity. Why didn't he amuse himself reading these names? Then there are the couriers and tourists—swarms of them every day—what was to hinder him from having a good time with them? I think Bonnivard's sufferings have been overrated.

Next we took the train and went to Martigny, on the way to Mont Blanc. Next morning we started about eight o'clock on foot. We had plenty of company in the way of wagon-loads and mule-loads of tourists—and dust. This scattering procession of travelers was perhaps a mile long. The road was uphill —interminably uphill—and tolerably steep. The weather was blistering hot, and the man or woman who had to sit on a creeping mule or in a crawling wagon and broil in the beating sun was an object to be pitied. We could dodge among the bushes and have the relief of shade but those people could not. They paid for a conveyance, and to get their money's worth they rode.

We went by the way of the Tête Noir and after we reached

high ground there was no lack of fine scenery. In one place the road was tunneled through a shoulder of the mountain. From there one looked down into a gorge with a rushing torrent in it, and on every hand was a charming view of rocky buttresses and wooded heights. There was a liberal allowance of pretty waterfalls, too, on the Tête Noir route.

About half an hour before we reached the village of Argentière a vast dome of snow with the sun blazing on it drifted into view and framed itself in a strong V-shaped gateway of the mountains, and we recognized Mont Blanc, the "monarch of the Alps." With every step after that this stately dome rose higher and higher into the blue sky and at last seemed to occupy the zenith.

Some of Mont Blanc's neighbors—bare, light-brown, steeplelike rocks—were very peculiarly shaped. Some were whittled to a sharp point and slightly bent at the upper end, like a lady's finger. One monster sugar-loaf resembled a bishop's hat. It was too steep to hold snow on its sides but had some in the division.

While we were still on very high ground and before the descent toward Argentière began we looked up toward a neighboring mountain-top and saw exquisite prismatic colors playing about some white clouds which were so delicate as to almost resemble gossamer webs. The faint pinks and greens were peculiarly beautiful. None of the colors were deep, they were the lightest shades. They were bewitchingly commingled. We sat down to study and enjoy this singular spectacle. The tints remained during several minutes—flitting, changing, melting into each other, paling almost away for a moment, then reflushing—a shifting, restless, unstable succession of soft opaline gleams shimmering over that airy film of white cloud and turning it into a fabric dainty enough to clothe an angel with.

By and by we perceived what those super-delicate colors and their continuous play and movement reminded us of. It is what one sees in a soap-bubble that is drifting along, catching changes of tint from the objects it passes. A soap-bubble is the most beautiful thing and the most exquisite in nature. That lovely phantom fabric in the sky was suggestive of a soap-bubble split open and spread out in the sun. I wonder how much it would take to buy a soap-bubble if there was only one in the world? One could buy a hatful of Koh-i-Noors with the same money, no doubt.

We made the tramp from Martigny to Argentière in eight hours. We beat all the mules and wagons. We didn't usually do that. We hired a sort of open baggage-wagon for the trip down the valley to Chamonix and then devoted an hour to dining. This gave the driver time to get drunk. He had a friend with him, and this friend also had had time to get drunk.

When we drove off, the driver said all the tourists had arrived and gone by while we were at dinner. "But," said he impressively, "be not disturbed by that—remain tranquil—give yourselves no uneasiness—their dust rises far before us, you shall see it fade and disappear far behind us—rest you tranquil, leave all to me—I am the king of drivers. Behold!"

Down came his whip and away we clattered. I never had such a shaking up in my life. The recent flooding rains had washed the road clear away in places but we never stopped, we never slowed down for anything. We tore right along over rocks, rubbish, gullies, open fields—sometimes with one or two wheels on the ground but generally with none. Every now and then that calm good-natured madman would bend a majestic look over his shoulder at us and say, "Ah, you perceive? It is as I have said—I am the king of drivers." Every time we just missed going to destruction he would say with tranquil happiness, "Enjoy it, gentlemen, it is very rare, it is very unusual—it is given to few to ride with the king of drivers—and observe, it is as I have said, *I* am he."

He spoke in French and punctuated with hiccoughs. His friend was French too but spoke in German—using the same system of punctuation, however. The friend called himself the "Captain of Mont Blanc" and wanted us to make the ascent with him. He said he had made more ascents than any other man—forty-seven—and his brother had made thirty-seven. His brother was the best guide in the world except, himself—but he, yes, observe him well—he was the "Captain of Mont Blanc"—that title belonged to none other.

The "king" was as good as his word—he overtook that long procession of tourists and went by it like a hurricane. The result was that we got choicer rooms at the hotel in Chamonix than we should have done if his majesty had been a slower artist—or rather, if he hadn't most providentially got drunk before he left Argentière.

36. Of Various Cities

Mr. Harris and I took some guides and porters and ascended to the Hôtel des Pyramides, which is perched on the high moraine which borders the Glacier des Bossons. The road led sharply uphill all the way through grass and flowers and woods and was a pleasant walk, barring the fatigue of the climb.

From the hotel we could view the huge glacier at very close range. After a rest we followed down a path which had been made in the steep inner frontage of the moraine, and stepped upon the glacier itself. One of the shows of the place was a tunnel-like cavern which had been hewn in the glacier. The proprietor of this tunnel took candles and conducted us into it. It was three or four feet wide and about six feet high. Its walls of pure and solid ice emitted a soft and rich blue light that produced a lovely effect and suggested enchanted caves and that sort of thing. When we had proceeded some yards and were entering darkness we turned about and had a dainty sunlit picture of distant woods and heights framed in the strong arch of the tunnel and seen through the tender blue radiance of the tunnel's atmosphere.

The cavern was nearly a hundred yards long, and when we reached its inner limit the proprietor stepped into a branch tunnel with his candles and left us buried in the bowels of the glacier and in pitch-darkness. We judged his purpose was murder and robbery, so we got out our matches and prepared to sell our lives as dearly as possible by setting the glacier on fire if the worst came to the worst—but we soon perceived that this man had changed his mind. He began to sing in a deep melodious voice and woke some curious and pleasing echoes. By and by he came back and pretended that that was what he had gone behind there for. We believed as much of that as we wanted to.

Thus our lives had been once more in imminent peril but by the exercise of the swift sagacity and cool courage which had saved us so often we had added another escape to the long list. The tourist should visit that ice-cavern by all means, for it is well worth the trouble, but I would advise him to go only with a strong and well-armed force. I do not consider artillery necessary, yet it would not be unadvisable to take it along if convenient. The journey going and coming is about three miles and a half, three of which are on level ground. We made it in less than a day but I would counsel the unpractised—if not pressed for time—to allow themselves two. Nothing is gained in the Alps by over-exertion. Nothing is gained by crowding two days' work into one for the poor sake of being able to boast of the exploit afterward. It will be found much better in the long run to do the thing in two days and then subtract one of them from the narrative. This saves fatigue, and does not injure the narrative. All the more thoughtful among the Alpine tourists do this.

We now called upon the Guide-in-Chief and asked for a squadron of guides and porters for the ascent of the Montanvert. This idiot glared at us and said:

"You don't need guides and porters to go to the Montanvert."

"What do we need, then?"

"Such as *you?*—an ambulance!"

I was so stung by this brutal remark that I took my custom
elsewhere.

Betimes, next morning, we had reached an altitude of five
thousand feet above the level of the sea. Here we camped
and breakfasted. There was a cabin there—the spot is called
the Caillet—and a spring of ice-cold water. On the door of
the cabin was a sign in French to the effect that "One may
here see a living chamois for fifty centimes." We did not
invest. What we wanted was to see a dead one.

A little after noon we ended the ascent and arrived at the
new hotel on the Montanvert and had a view of six miles
right up the great glacier, the famous Mer de Glace. At this
point it is like a sea whose deep swales and long, rolling swells
have been caught in mid-movement and frozen solid. But
further up it is broken up into wildly tossing billows of ice.

We descended a ticklish path in the steep side of the moraine and invaded the glacier. There were tourists of both
sexes scattered far and wide over it everywhere and it had
the festive look of a skating-rink.

The Empress Josephine came this far, once. She ascended
the Montanvert in 1810—but not alone. A small army of men
preceded her to clear the path—and carpet it, perhaps—and
she followed under the protection of *sixty-eight* guides.

Her successor visited Chamonix later but in far different
style. It was seven weeks after the first fall of the Empire, and
poor Marie Louise, ex-Empress, was a fugitive. She came at
night and in a storm, with only two attendants, and stood
before a peasant's hut, tired, bedraggled, soaked with rain,
"the red print of her lost crown still girdling her brow," and
implored admittance—and was refused! A few days before,
the adulations and applauses of a nation were sounding in her
ears, and now she was come to this!

We crossed the Mer de Glace in safety but we had misgivings. The crevices in the ice yawned deep and blue and mysterious and it made one nervous to traverse them. The huge round waves of ice were slippery and difficult to climb, and the chances of tripping and sliding down them and darting into a crevice were too many to be comfortable.

In the bottom of a deep swale between two of the biggest of the ice-waves we found a fraud who pretended to be cutting steps to insure the safety of tourists. He was "soldiering" when we came upon him but he hopped up and chipped out a couple of steps about big enough for a cat and charged us a franc or two for it. Then he sat down again to doze till the next party should come along. He had collected blackmail from two or three hundred people already that day but had not chipped out ice enough to impair the glacier perceptibly. I have heard of a good many soft sinecures but it seems to me that keeping toll-bridge on a glacier is the softest one I have encountered yet.

That was a blazing hot day and it brought a persistent and persecuting thirst with it. What an unspeakable luxury it was to slake that thirst with the pure and limpid ice-water of the glacier! Down the sides of every great rib of ice poured limpid rills in gutters carved by their own attrition. Better still, wherever a rock had lain there was now a bowl-shaped hole with smooth white sides and bottom of ice, and this bowl was brimming with water of such absolute clearness that the careless observer would not see it at all but would think the bowl was empty. These fountains had such an alluring look that I often stretched myself out when I was not thirsty and dipped my face in and drank till my teeth ached. Everywhere among the Swiss mountains we had at hand the blessing—not to be found in Europe *except* in the mountains—of water capable of quenching thirst. Everywhere in the Swiss highlands brilliant little rills of exquisitely cold water went dancing along by the roadsides, and my comrade and I were always drinking and always delivering our deep gratitude.

But in Europe everywhere except in the mountains the water is flat and insipid beyond the power of words to describe. It is served lukewarm. But no matter, ice could not help it. It is incurably flat, incurably insipid. It is only good to wash with. I wonder it doesn't occur to the average inhabitant to try it for that. In Europe the people say contemptuously, "Nobody drinks water here." Indeed they have a sound and sufficient reason. In many places they even have what may be called prohibitory reasons. In Paris and Munich, for instance, they say, "Don't drink the water, it is simply poison."

Either America is healthier than Europe, notwithstanding her "deadly" indulgence in ice-water, or she does not keep the run of her death-rate as sharply as Europe does. I think we do keep up the death statistics accurately, and if we do, our cities are healthier than the cities of Europe. Every month the German government tabulates the death-rate of the world and publishes it. I scrap-booked these reports during several months and it was curious to see how regular and persistently each city repeated its same death-rate month after month. The tables might as well have been stereotyped, they varied so little. These tables were based upon weekly reports showing the average of deaths in each 1,000 of population for a year. Munich was always present with her 33 deaths in each 1,000 of her population (yearly average), Chicago was as constant with her 15 or 17, Dublin with her 48— and so on.

Only a few American cities appear in these tables but they are scattered so widely over the country that they furnish a good general average of *city* health in the United States, and I think it will be granted that our towns and villages are healthier than our cities.

Here is the average of the only American cities reported in the German tables:

Chicago, deaths in 1,000 of population annually, 16; Philadelphia, 18; St. Louis, 18; San Francisco, 19; New York (the Dublin of America), 23.

See how the figures jump up as soon as one arrives at the transatlantic list:

Paris, 27; Glasgow, 27; London, 28; Vienna, 28; Augsburg, 28; Braunschweig, 28; Königsberg, 29; Cologne, 29; Dresden, 29; Hamburg, 29; Berlin, 30; Bombay, 30; Warsaw, 31; Breslau, 31; Odessa, 32; Munich, 33; Strasburg, 33; Pesth, 35; Cassel, 35; Lisbon, 36; Liverpool, 36; Prague, 37; Madras, 37; Bucharest, 39; St. Petersburg, 40; Trieste, 40; Alexandria (Egypt), 43; Dublin, 48; Calcutta, 55.

Edinburgh is as healthy as New York—23. But there is no *city* in the entire list which is healthier except Frankfort-on-the-Main—20. But Frankfort is not as healthy as Chicago, San Francisco, St. Louis or Philadelphia.

Perhaps a strict average of the world might develop the fact that where one in 1,000 of America's population dies, two in 1,000 of the other populations of the earth succumb.

I do not like to make insinuations but I do think the above statistics darkly suggest that these people over here drink this detestable water "on the sly."

We climbed the moraine on the opposite side of the glacier and then crept along its sharp ridge a hundred yards or so in pretty constant danger of a tumble to the glacier below. The fall would have been only one hundred feet but it would have closed me out as effectually as one thousand, therefore I respected the distance accordingly and was glad when the trip was done. A moraine is an ugly thing to assault head-first. At a distance it looks like an endless grave of fine sand accurately shaped and nicely smoothed but close by it is found to be made mainly of rough boulders of all sizes, from that of a man's head to that of a cottage.

By and by we came to the Mauvais Pas, or the Villainous Road, to translate it feelingly. It was a breakneck path around the face of a precipice forty or fifty feet high, and nothing to hang on to but some iron railings. I got along slowly, safely and uncomfortably and finally reached the middle. My hopes began to rise a little but they were quickly blighted, for there I met a hog—a long-nosed, bristly fellow that held up his snout and worked his nostrils at me inquiringly. A hog on a pleasure excursion in Switzerland—think of it! It is striking and unusual. A body might write a poem about it. He could not retreat if he had been disposed to do it. It would have been foolish to stand upon our dignity in a place where there was hardly room to stand upon our feet, so we did nothing of the sort. There were twenty or thirty ladies and gentlemen behind us. We all turned about and went back and the hog followed behind. The creature did not seem set up by what he had done. He had probably done it before.

We reached the restaurant on the height called the Chapeau at four in the afternoon. It was a memento-factory and the stock was large, cheap and varied. I bought the usual paper-cutter to remember the place by and had Mont Blanc, the Mauvais Pas and the rest of the region branded on my alpenstock. Then we descended to the valley and walked home without being tied together. This was not dangerous, for the valley was five miles wide and quite level.

We reached the hotel before nine o'clock. Next morning we left for Geneva on top of the diligence, under shelter of a gay awning. If I remember rightly, there were more than twenty people up there. It was so high that the ascent was made by ladder. The huge vehicle was full everywhere, inside and out. Five other diligences left at the same time, all full. We had engaged our seats two days beforehand, to make sure, and paid the regulation price, five dollars each, but the rest of the company were wiser. They had trusted Baedeker and waited. Consequently some of them got their seats for one or two dollars. Baedeker knows all about hotels, railway and diligence companies and speaks his mind freely. He is a trustworthy friend of the traveler.

We never saw Mont Blanc at his best until we were many miles away. Then he lifted his majestic proportions high into the heavens, all white and cold and solemn, and made the rest of the world seem little and plebeian and cheap and trivial.

As he passed out of sight at last, an old Englishman settled himself in his seat and said:

"Well, I am satisfied, I have seen the principal features of Swiss scenery—Mont Blanc and the goiter—now for home!"

37. American Manners

We spent a few pleasant restful days at Geneva, that delightful city where accurate time-pieces are made for all the rest of the world but whose own clocks never give the correct time of day by any accident.

Geneva is filled with pretty shops, and the shops are filled with the most enticing gimcrackery, but if one enters one of these places he is at once pounced upon and followed up and so persecuted to buy this, that and the other thing that he is very grateful to get out again and is not at all apt to repeat his experiment. The shopkeepers of the smaller sort in Geneva are as troublesome and persistent as are the salesmen of that monster hive in Paris, the Grands Magasins du Louvre —an establishment where ill-mannered pestering, pursuing and insistence have been reduced to a science.

In Geneva prices in the smaller shops are very elastic— that is another bad feature. I was looking in at a window at a very pretty string of beads suitable for a child. I was only admiring them. I had no use for them. I hardly ever wear beads. The shopwoman came out and offered them to me for thirty-five francs. I said it was cheap but I did not need them.

"Ah, but monsieur, they are so beautiful!"

I confessed it but said they were not suitable for one of my age and simplicity of character. She darted in and brought them out and tried to force them into my hands, saying:

"Ah, but only see how lovely they are! Surely monsieur will take them. Monsieur shall have them for thirty francs. There, I have said it—it is a loss but one must live."

I dropped my hands and tried to move her to respect my unprotected situation. But no, she dangled the beads in the sun before my face, exclaiming, "Ah, monsieur *cannot* resist them!" She hung them on my coat button, folded her hand resignedly and said: "Gone—and for thirty francs, the lovely things—it is incredible!—but the good God will sanctify the sacrifice to me."

I removed them gently, returned them and walked away, shaking my head and smiling a smile of silly embarrassment while the passers-by halted to observe. The woman leaned out of her door, shook the beads and screamed after me:

"Monsieur shall have them for twenty-eight!"

I shook my head.

"Twenty-seven! It is a cruel loss, it is ruin—but take them, only take them."

I still retreated, still wagging my head.

"Mon Dieu, they shall even go for twenty-six! There, I have said it. Come!"

I wagged another negative. A nurse and a little English girl had been near me and were following me now. The shopwoman ran to the nurse, thrust the beads into her hands and said:

"Monsieur shall have them for twenty-five! Take them to the hotel—he shall send me the money to-morrow—next day—when he likes." Then to the child: "When thy father sends me the money, come thou also, my angel, and thou shalt have something oh so pretty!"

I was thus providentially saved. The nurse refused the beads squarely and firmly and that ended the matter.

The "sights" of Geneva are not numerous. I made one attempt to hunt up the houses once inhabited by those two disagreeable people, Rousseau and Calvin, but had no success. Then I concluded to go home. I found it was easier to propose to do that than to do it, for that town is a bewildering place. I got lost in a tangle of narrow and crooked streets and stayed lost for an hour or two. Finally I found a street which looked somewhat familiar and said to myself, "Now I am at home, I judge." But I was wrong. This was *"Hell* street." Presently I found another place which had a familiar look and said to myself, "Now I am at home, sure." It was another error. This was *"Purgatory* street." After a little I said, *"Now* I've got the right place, anyway . . . no, this is *'Paradise* street.' I'm further from home than I was in the beginning." Those were queer names—Calvin was the author of them, likely. "Hell" and "Purgatory" fitted those two streets like a glove but the "Paradise" appeared to be sarcastic.

I came out on the lake-front at last and then I knew where I was. I was walking along before the glittering jewelry shops when I saw a curious performance. A lady passed by, and a trim dandy lounged across the walk in such an apparently carefully timed way as to bring himself exactly in front of her when she got to him. He made no offer to step out of the way. He did not apologize. He did not even notice her. She had to stop still and let him lounge by. I wondered if he had done that piece of brutality purposely. He strolled to a chair and seated himself at a small table. Two or three other males were sitting at similar tables sipping sweetened water. I waited. Presently a youth came by, and this fellow got up and served him the same trick. Still, it did not seem possible that anyone could do such a thing deliberately. To satisfy my curiosity I went around the block and, sure enough, as I approached, at a good round speed, he got up and lounged lazily across my path, fouling my course exactly at the right moment to receive all my weight. This proved that his previous performances had not been accidental but intentional.

I saw that dandy's curious game played afterward in Paris but not for amusement, not with a motive of any sort, indeed, but simply from a selfish indifference to other people's comfort and rights. One does not see it as frequently in Paris as he might expect to, for there the law says in effect, "It is the business of the weak to get out of the way of the strong." We fine a cabman if he runs over a citizen. Paris fines the citizen for being run over. At least so everybody says—but I saw something which caused me to doubt. I saw a horseman run over an old woman one day—the police arrested him and took him away. That looked as if they meant to punish him.

It will not do for me to find merit in American manners— for are they not the standing butt for the jests of critical and polished Europe? Still, I must venture to claim one little matter of superiority in our manners. A lady may traverse our streets all day, going and coming as she chooses, and she will never be molested by any man. But if a lady unattended walks abroad in the streets of London even at noonday she will be pretty likely to be accosted and insulted—and not by drunken sailors but by men who carry the look and wear the dress of gentlemen. It is maintained that these people are not gentlemen but are a lower sort disguised as gentlemen. The case of Colonel Valentine Baker obstructs that argument, for a man cannot become an officer in the British army except he hold the rank of gentleman. This person, finding himself alone in a railway compartment with an unprotected girl— but it is an atrocious story and doubtless the reader remembers it well enough. London must have been more or less accustomed to Bakers and the ways of Bakers, else London would have been offended and excited. Baker was "imprisoned"—in a parlor. And he could not have been more visited or more overwhelmed with attentions if he had committed six murders and then—while the gallows was preparing— "got religion"—after the manner of the holy Charles Peace of saintly memory. Arkansaw—it seems a little indelicate to be trumpeting forth our own superiorities, and comparisons are always odious, but still—Arkansaw would certainly have hanged Baker. I do not say she would have tried him first but she would have hanged him, anyway.

Even the most degraded woman can walk our streets unmolested, her sex and her weakness being her sufficient protection. She will encounter less polish than she would in the

old world but she will run across enough humanity to make
up for it.

The music of a donkey awoke us early in the morning and
we rose up and made ready for a pretty formidable walk—
to Italy. But the road was so level that we took the train. We
lost a good deal of time by this but it was no matter, we were
not in a hurry. We were four hours going to Chambèry. The
Swiss trains go upward of three miles an hour in places but
they are quite safe.

That aged French town of Chambèry was as quaint and
crooked as Heilbronn. A drowsy reposeful quiet reigned in
the back streets, which made strolling through them very
pleasant, barring the almost unbearable heat of the sun. In
one of these streets, which was eight feet wide, gracefully
curved, and built up with small antiquated houses, I saw
three fat hogs lying asleep, and a boy (also asleep) taking care
of them. From queer old-fashioned windows along the curve
projected boxes of bright flowers, and over the edge of one
of these boxes hung the head and shoulders of a cat—asleep.
The five sleeping creatures were the only living things visible
in that street. There was not a sound. Absolute stillness pre-
vailed. It was Sunday. One is not used to such dreamy Sun-
days on the continent. In our part of the town it was different
that night. A regiment of brown and battered soldiers had
arrived home from Algiers and I judged they got thirsty on
the way. They sang and drank till dawn in the pleasant open
air.

We left for Turin at ten the next morning by a railway
which was profusely decorated with tunnels. We forgot to
take a lantern along, consequently we missed all the scenery.
Our compartment was full. A ponderous tow-headed Swiss
woman, who put on many fine-lady airs but was evidently
more used to washing linen than wearing it, sat in a corner
seat and put her legs across into the opposite one, propping
them intermediately with her up-ended valise. In the seat
thus pirated sat two Americans greatly incommoded by that
woman's majestic coffin-clad feet. One of them begged her

politely to remove them. She opened her wide eyes and gave him a stare but answered nothing. By and by he preferred his request again, with great respectfulness. She said in good English and in a deeply offended tone that she had paid her passage and was not going to be bullied out of her "rights" by ill-bred foreigners, even if she *was* alone and unprotected.

"But I have rights, also, madam. My ticket entitles me to a seat but you are occupying half of it."

"I will not talk with you, sir. What right have you to speak to me? I do not know you. One would know you came from a land where there are no gentlemen. No *gentleman* would treat a lady as you have treated me."

"I come from a region where a lady would hardly give me the same provocation."

"You have insulted me, sir! You have intimated that I am not a lady—and I hope I am *not* one, after the pattern of your country."

"I beg that you will give yourself no alarm on that head, madam. But at the same time I must insist—always respect-fully—that you let me have my seat."

Here the fragile laundress burst into tears and sobs.

"I never was so insulted before! Never, never! It is shame-ful, it is brutal, it is base, to bully and abuse an unprotected lady who has lost the use of her limbs and cannot put her feet to the floor without agony!"

"Good heavens, madam, why didn't you say that at first! I offer a thousand pardons. And I offer them most sincerely. I did not know—I *could* not know—anything was the matter. You are most welcome to the seat, and would have been from the first if I had only known. I am truly sorry it all happened, I do assure you."

But he couldn't get a word of forgiveness out of her. She simply sobbed and snuffled in a subdued but wholly unappea-sable way for two long hours, meantime crowding the man more than ever with her undertaker-furniture and paying no sort of attention to his frequent and humble little efforts to do something for her comfort. Then the train halted at the

Italian line and she hopped up and marched out of the car with as firm a leg as any washerwoman of all her tribe! And how sick I was, to see how she had fooled me.

Turin is a very fine city. In the matter of roominess it transcends anything that was ever dreamed of before, I fancy. It sits in the midst of a vast dead-level, and one is obliged to imagine that land may be had for the asking and no taxes to pay, so lavishly do they use it. The streets are extravagantly wide, the paved squares are prodigious, the houses are huge and handsome, and compacted into uniform blocks that stretch away as straight as an arrow into the distance. The sidewalks are about as wide as ordinary European *streets* and are covered over with a double arcade supported on great stone piers or columns. One walks from one end to the other of these spacious streets under shelter all the time, and all his course is lined with the prettiest of shops and the most inviting dining-houses.

There is a wide and lengthy court, glittering with the most wickedly enticing shops, which is roofed with glass, high aloft overhead, and paved with soft-toned marbles laid in graceful figures. And at night when this place is brilliant with gas and populous with a sauntering and chatting and laughing multitude of pleasure-seekers, it is a spectacle worth seeing.

Everything is on a large scale. The public buildings, for instance—and they are architecturally imposing, too, as well as large. The big squares have big bronze monuments in them. At the hotel they gave us rooms that were alarming, for size, and parlor to match. It was well the weather required no fire in the parlor, for I think one might as well have tried to warm a park. The place would have a warm look, though, in any weather, for the window-curtains were of red silk damask and the walls were covered with the same fire-hued goods—so, also, were the four sofas and the brigade of chairs. The furniture, the ornaments, the chandeliers, the carpets were all new and bright and costly. We did not need a parlor at all but they said it belonged to the two bedrooms and we might use it if we chose. Since it was to cost nothing we were not averse to using it, of course.

Turin must surely read a good deal, for it has more book-stores to the square rod than any other town I know of. And it has its own share of military folk. The Italian officers' uniforms are very much the most beautiful I have ever seen. And, as a general thing, the men in them were as handsome as the clothes. They were not large men but they had fine forms, fine features, rich olive complexions and lustrous black eyes.

For several weeks I had been culling all the information I could about Italy from tourists. The tourists were all agreed upon one thing—one must expect to be cheated at every turn by the Italians. I took an evening walk in Turin and presently came across a little Punch and Judy show in one of the great squares. Twelve or fifteen people constituted the audience. This miniature theater was not much bigger than a man's coffin stood on end. The upper part was open and displayed a tinseled parlor—a good-sized handkerchief would have answered for a drop-curtain. The footlights consisted of a couple of candle-ends an inch long. Various mani-kins the size of dolls appeared on the stage and made long speeches at each other, gesticulating a good deal, and they generally had a fight before they got through. They were worked by strings from above, and the illusion was not per-fect, for one saw not only the strings but the brawny hand that manipulated them—and the actors and actresses all talked in the same voice, too. The audience stood in front of the theater and seemed to enjoy the performance heartily.

When the play was done a youth in his shirtsleeves started around with a small copper saucer to make a collection. I did not know how much to put in but thought I would be guided by my predecessors. Unluckily I only had two of these and they did not help me much because they did not put in anything. I had no Italian money, so I put in a small Swiss coin worth about ten cents. The youth finished his collection trip and emptied the result on the stage. He had some very ani-mated talk with the concealed manager, then he came work-

ing his way through the little crowd—seeking me, I thought.
I had a mind to slip away but concluded I wouldn't. I would
stand my ground and confront the villainy, whatever it was.
The youth stood before me and held up that Swiss coin, sure
enough, and said something. I did not understand him but I
judged he was requiring Italian money of me. The crowd
gathered close to listen. I was irritated and said—in English,
of course:

"I know it's Swiss but you'll take that or none. I haven't any
other."

He tried to put the coin in my hand and spoke again. I
drew my hand away and said:

"*No*, sir. I know all about you people. You can't play any
of your fraudful tricks on me. If there is a discount on that
coin, I am sorry, but I am not going to make it good. I noticed
that some of the audience didn't pay you anything at all. You
let them go without a word but you come after me because
you think I'm a stranger and will put up with an extortion
rather than have a scene. But you are mistaken this time—
you'll take that Swiss money or none."

The youth stood there with the coin in his fingers, non-
plussed and bewildered. Of course he had not understood a
word. An English-speaking Italian spoke up now and said:

"You are misunderstanding the boy. He does not mean any
harm. He did not suppose you gave him so much money
purposely, so he hurried back to return you the coin lest you
might get away before you discovered your mistake. Take it
and give him a penny—that will make everything smooth
again."

I probably blushed then, for there was occasion. Through
the interpreter I begged the boy's pardon but I nobly refused
to take back the ten cents. I said I was accustomed to squand-
ering large sums in that way—it was the kind of person I was.
Then I retired to make a note to the effect that in Italy
persons connected with the drama do not cheat.

The episode with the showman reminds me of a dark chapter in my history. I once robbed an aged and blind beggar-

woman of four dollars—in a church. It happened in this way. When I was out with the Innocents Abroad, the ship stopped in the Russian port of Odessa and I went ashore with others to view the town. I got separated from the rest and wandered about alone until late in the afternoon, when I entered a Greek church to see what it was like. When I was ready to leave I observed two wrinkled old women standing stiffly upright against the inner wall, near the door, with their brown palms open to receive alms. I contributed to the nearer one and passed out. I had gone fifty yards, perhaps, when it occurred to me that I must remain ashore all night, as I had heard that the ship's business would carry her away at four o'clock and keep her away until morning. It was a little after four now. I had come ashore with only two pieces of money, both about the same size but differing largely in value—one was a French gold piece worth four dollars, the other a Turkish coin worth two cents and a half. With a sudden and horrified misgiving I put my hand in my pocket now and, sure enough, I fetched out that Turkish penny!

Here was a situation. A hotel would require pay in advance —I must walk the street all night and perhaps be arrested as a suspicious character. There was but one way out of the difficulty—I flew back to the church and softly entered. There stood the old woman yet, and in the palm of the nearest one still lay my gold piece. I was grateful. I crept close, feeling unspeakably mean. I got my Turkish penny ready and was extending a trembling hand to make the nefarious exchange when I heard a cough behind me. I jumped back as if I had been accused, and stood quaking while a worshiper entered and passed up the aisle.

I was there a year trying to steal that money. That is, it seemed a year though of course it must have been much less. The worshipers went and came. There were hardly ever three in the church at once but there was always one or more. Every time I tried to commit my crime somebody came in or somebody started out, and I was prevented. But at last my opportunity came. For one moment there was nobody in the church but the two beggar-women and me. I whipped the gold piece out of the poor old pauper's palm and dropped my Turkish penny in its place. Poor old thing, she murmured her thanks—they smote me to the heart. Then I sped away in a guilty hurry, and even when I was a mile from the church I was still glancing back every moment to see if I was being pursued.

That experience has been of priceless value and benefit to me, for I resolved then that as long as I lived I would never again rob a blind beggar-woman in a church, and I have always kept my word. The most permanent lessons in morals are those which come not of booky teaching but of experience.

38. The Old Masters

In Milan we spent most of our time in the vast and beautiful Arcade or Gallery or whatever it is called. Blocks of tall new buildings of the most sumptuous sort, rich with decoration and graced with statues, the streets between these blocks roofed over with glass at a great height, the pavements all of smooth and variegated marble arranged in tasteful patterns —little tables all over these marble streets, people sitting at them, eating, drinking or smoking—crowds of other people strolling by—such is the Arcade. I should like to live in it all the time. The windows of the sumptuous restaurants stand open and one breakfasts there and enjoys the passing show.

We wandered all over the town, enjoying whatever was going on in the streets. We took one omnibus ride, and as I did not speak Italian and could not ask the price, I held out some copper coins to the conductor and he took two. Then he went and got his tariff card and showed me that he had taken only the right sum. So I made a note—Italian omnibus conductors do not cheat.

Near the Cathedral I saw another instance of probity. An old man was peddling dolls and toy fans. Two small American children bought fans, and one gave the old man a franc and three copper coins, and both started away. But they were called back, and the franc and one of the coppers were restored to them. Hence it is plain that in Italy parties connected with the drama and with the omnibus and toy interests do not cheat.

The stocks of goods in the shops were not extensive, generally. In the vestibule of what seemed to be a clothing store we saw eight or ten wooden dummies grouped together, clothed in woolen business suits and each marked with its price. One suit was marked forty-five francs—nine dollars. Harris stepped in and said he wanted a suit like that. Nothing easier. The old merchant dragged in the dummy, brushed him off with a broom, stripped him and shipped the clothes to the hotel. He said he did not keep two suits of the same kind in stock, but manufactured a second when it was needed to reclothe the dummy.

In another quarter we found six Italians engaged in a violent quarrel. They danced fiercely about, gesticulating with their heads, their arms, their legs, their whole bodies. They would rush forward occasionally in a sudden access of passion and shake their fists in each other's very faces. We lost half an hour there, waiting to help cord up the dead, but they finally embraced each other affectionately and the trouble was all over. The episode was interesting but we could not have afforded all that time to it if we had known nothing was going to come of it but a reconciliation. Note made—in Italy, people who quarrel cheat the spectator.

We had another disappointment afterward. We approached a deeply interested crowd, and in the midst of it found a fellow wildly chattering and gesticulating over a box on the ground which was covered with a piece of old blanket. Every little while he would bend down and take hold of the edge of the blanket with the extreme tips of his fingers, as if to show there was no deception—chattering away all the while—but always, just as I was expecting to see a wonderful feat of legerdemain, he would let go the blanket and rise to explain further. However, at last he uncovered the box and got out a spoon with a liquid in it, and held it fair and frankly around for people to see that it was all right and he was taking no advantage—his chatter became more excited than ever. I supposed he was going to set fire to the liquid and swallow it, so I was greatly wrought up and interested. I got a cent ready in one hand and a florin in the other, intending to give him the former if he survived and the latter if he killed himself—for his loss would be my gain in a literary way and I was willing to pay a fair price for the item—but this impostor ended his intensely moving performance by simply adding some powder to the liquid and polishing the spoon! Then he held it aloft, and he could not have shown a wilder exultation if he had achieved an immortal miracle. The crowd applauded in a gratified way, and it seemed to me that history speaks the truth when it says these children of the south are easily entertained.

We spent an impressive hour in the noble cathedral, where long shafts of tinted light were cleaving through the solemn dimness from the lofty windows and falling on a pillar here, a picture there and a kneeling worshiper yonder. The organ was muttering, censers were swinging, candles were glinting on the distant altar and robed priests were filing silently past them. The scene was one to sweep all frivolous thoughts away and steep the soul in a holy calm. A trim young American lady paused a yard or two from me, fixed her eyes on the mellow sparks flecking the far-off altar, bent her head reverently a moment, then straightened up, kicked her train into the air with her heel, caught it deftly in her hand and marched briskly out.

We visited the picture-galleries and the other regulation

"sights" of Milan—not because I wanted to write about them again but to see if I had learned anything in twelve years. I afterward visited the great galleries of Rome and Florence for the same purpose. I found I had learned one thing. When I wrote about the Old Masters before, I said the copies were better than the originals. That was a mistake of large dimensions. The Old Masters were still unpleasing to me but they were truly divine contrasted with the copies. The copy is to the original as the pallid, smart, inane new wax-work group is to the vigorous, earnest, dignified group of living men and women whom it professes to duplicate. There is a mellow richness, a subdued color, in the old pictures which is to the eye what muffled and mellowed sound is to the ear. That is the merit which is most loudly praised in the old picture and is the one which the copy most conspicuously lacks and which the copyist must not hope to compass. It was generally conceded by the artists with whom I talked that that subdued splendor, that mellow richness, is imparted to the picture by *age*. Then why should we worship the Old Master for it, who didn't impart it, instead of worshiping Old Time, who did? Perhaps the picture was a clanging bell until Time muffled it and sweetened it.

In conversation with an artist in Venice I asked: "What is it that people see in the Old Masters? I have been in the Doge's palace and I saw several acres of very bad drawing, very bad perspective and very incorrect proportions. Paul Veronese's dogs do not resemble dogs. All the horses look like bladders on legs. One man had a *right* leg on the left side of his body. In the large picture where the Emperor (Barbarossa?) is prostrate before the Pope, there are three men in the foreground who are over thirty feet high, if one may judge by the size of a kneeling little boy in the center of the foreground. And according to the same scale, the Pope is seven feet high and the Doge is a shriveled dwarf of four feet."

The artist said:

"Yes, the Old Masters often drew badly. They did not care

much for truth and exactness in minor details. But after all, in spite of bad drawing, bad perspective, bad proportions and a choice of subjects which no longer appeal to people as strongly as they did three hundred years ago, there is a *something* about their pictures which is divine—a something which is above and beyond the art of any epoch since—a something which would be the despair of artists but that they never hope or expect to attain it and therefore do not worry about it."

That is what he said—and he said what he believed, and not only believed but felt.

Reasoning—especially reasoning without technical knowledge—must be put aside in cases of this kind. It cannot assist the inquirer. It will lead him, in the most logical progression, to what in the eyes of artists would be a most illogical conclusion. Thus: bad drawing, bad proportion, bad perspective, indifference to truthful detail, color which gets its merit from time and not from the artist—these things constitute the Old Master. Conclusion, the Old Master was a bad painter, the Old Master was not an Old Master at all but an Old Apprentice. Your friend the artist will grant your premises but deny your conclusion. He will maintain that notwithstanding this formidable list of confessed defects, there is still a something that is divine and unapproachable about the Old Master and that there is no arguing the fact away by any system of reasoning whatever.

I can believe that. There are women who have an indefinable charm in their faces which makes them beautiful to their intimates, but a cold stranger who tried to reason the matter out and find this beauty would fail. He would say of one of these women: This chin is too short, this nose is too long, this forehead is too high, this hair is too red, this complexion is too pallid, the perspective of the entire composition is incorrect. Conclusion, the woman is not beautiful. But her nearest friend might say, and say truly, "Your premises are right, your logic is faultless, but your conclusion is wrong nevertheless. She is an Old Master—she is beautiful but only to such as know her. It is a beauty which cannot be formulated but it is there just the same."

I found more pleasure in contemplating the Old Masters this time than I did when I was in Europe in former years but still it was a calm pleasure. There was nothing overheated about it. When I was in Venice before I think I found no picture which stirred me much but this time there were two which enticed me to the Doge's palace day after day and kept me there hours at a time. One of these was Tintoretto's three-acre picture in the Great Council Chamber. When I saw it twelve years ago I was not strongly attracted to it—the guide told me it was an insurrection in heaven—but this was an error.

The movement of this great work is very fine. There are ten thousand figures and they are all doing something. There is a wonderful "go" to the whole composition. Some of the figures are diving headlong downward with clasped hands, others are swimming through the cloud-shoals—some on their faces, some on their backs—great processions of bishops, martyrs and angels are pouring swiftly centerward from various outlying directions—everywhere is enthusiastic joy, there is rushing movement everywhere. There are fifteen or twenty figures scattered here and there with books but they cannot keep their attention on their reading—they offer the books to others but no one wishes to read now. The Lion of St. Mark is there with his book. St. Mark is there with his pen uplifted. He and the Lion are looking each other earnestly in the face, disputing about the way to spell a word—the Lion looks up in rapt admiration while St. Mark spells. This is wonderfully interpreted by the artist. It is the master-stroke of this incomparable painting.

I visited the place daily and never grew tired of looking at that grand picture. As I have intimated, the movement is almost unimaginably vigorous. The figures are singing, hosannahing, and many are blowing trumpets. So vividly is noise suggested that spectators who become absorbed in the picture almost always fall to shouting comments in each

The Lion of St. Mark

other's ears, making ear-trumpets of their curved hands, fearing they may not otherwise be heard. One often sees a tourist, with the eloquent tears pouring down his cheeks, funnel his hands at his wife's ear, and hears him roar through them, "OH, TO BE THERE AND AT REST!"

None but the supremely great in art can produce effects like these with the silent brush.

Twelve years ago I could not have appreciated this picture. One year ago I could not have appreciated it. My study of Art in Heidelberg has been a noble education to me. All that I am to-day in Art I owe to that.

The other great work which fascinated me was Bassano's immortal Hair Trunk. This is in the Chamber of the Council of Ten. It is in one of the three forty-foot pictures which decorate the walls of the room. The composition of this picture is beyond praise. The Hair Trunk is not hurled at the stranger's head—so to speak—as the chief feature of an immortal work so often is. No, it is carefully guarded from prominence, it is subordinated, it is restrained, it is most deftly and cleverly held in reserve, it is most cautiously and ingeniously led up to by the master, and consequently when the spectator reaches it at last he is taken unawares, he is unprepared and it bursts upon him with a stupefying surprise.

One is lost in wonder at all the thought and care which this elaborate planning must have cost. A general glance at the picture could never suggest that there was a hair trunk in it. The Hair Trunk is not mentioned in the title even—which is, "Pope Alexander III and the Doge Ziani, the Conqueror of the Emperor Frederick Barbarossa." You see, the title is actually utilized to help divert attention from the Trunk. Thus, as I say, nothing suggests the presence of the Trunk by any hint, yet everything studiedly leads up to it step by step. Let us examine into this and observe the exquisitely artful artlessness of the plan.

At the extreme left end of the picture are a couple of women, one of them with a child looking over her shoulder at a wounded man sitting with bandaged head on the ground. These people seem needless, but no, they are there for a purpose. One cannot look at them without seeing the gorgeous procession of grandees, bishops, halberdiers and banner-bearers which is passing along behind them. One cannot see the procession without feeling a curiosity to follow it and learn whither it is going. It leads him to the Pope in the center of the picture, who is talking with the bonnet-less Doge—talking tranquilly, too, although within twelve feet of them a man is beating a drum, and not far from the drummer two persons are blowing horns, and many horsemen are plunging and rioting about—indeed, twenty-two feet of this great work is all a deep and happy holiday serenity and Sunday-school procession, and then we come suddenly upon eleven and one-half feet of turmoil and racket and insubordination. This latter state of things is not an accident, it has its purpose. But for it, one would linger upon the Pope and the Doge, thinking them to be the motive and supreme feature of the picture, whereas one is drawn along almost unconsciously to see what the trouble is about. Now at the very *end* of this riot, within four feet of the end of the picture and full thirty-six feet from the beginning of it, the Hair Trunk bursts with an electrifying suddenness upon the spectator in all its matchless perfection, and the great master's triumph is sweeping and complete. From that moment no other thing in those forty feet of canvas has any charm. One sees the Hair Trunk and the Hair Trunk only—and to see it is to worship it. Bassano even placed objects in the immediate vicinity of the Supreme Feature whose pretended purpose was to divert attention from it yet a little longer and thus delay and augment the surprise. For instance, to the right of it he has placed a stooping man with a cap so red that it is sure to hold the eye for a moment—to the left of it, some six feet away, he has placed a red-coated man on an inflated horse, and that coat plucks your eye to that locality the next moment—then, between the Trunk and the red horseman he has intruded a man naked to his waist, who is carrying a fancy floursack on the middle of his back instead of on his shoulder—this admirable feat interests you, of course—keeps you at bay a little longer, like a sock or a jacket thrown to the pursuing wolf—but at last, in spite of all distractions and detentions, the eye of even the most dull and heedless spectator is sure to fall upon the World's Masterpiece, and in that moment he totters to his chair or leans upon his guide for support.

Descriptions of such a work as this must necessarily be imperfect, yet they are of value. The top of the Trunk is arched. The arch is a perfect half-circle, in the Roman style of architecture, for in the then rapid decadence of Greek art the rising influence of Rome was already beginning to be felt in the art of the Republic. The Trunk is bound or bordered with leather all around where the lid joins the main body. Many critics consider this leather too cold in tone but I consider this its highest merit, since it was evidently made so to emphasize by contrast the impassioned fervor of the hasp. The high lights in this part of the work are cleverly managed, the *motif* is admirably subordinated to the ground tints, and the technique is very fine. The brass nail-heads are in the purest style of the early Renaissance. The strokes here are very firm and bold—every nail-head is a portrait. The handle on the end of the Trunk has evidently been retouched—I think with a piece of chalk—but one can still see the inspiration of the Old Master in the tranquil, almost too tranquil, hang of it. The hair of this Trunk is *real* hair—so to speak—white in patches, brown in patches. The details are finely worked out. The repose proper to hair in a recumbent and inactive attitude is charmingly expressed. There is a feeling about this part of the work which lifts it to the highest altitudes of art. The sense of sordid realism vanishes away—one recognizes that there is *soul* here.

View this Trunk as you will, it is a gem, it is a marvel, it is a miracle. Some of the effects are very daring, approaching even to the boldest flights of the rococo, the sirocco and the Byzantine schools—yet the master's hand never falters—it moves on, calm, majestic, confident—and, with that art which conceals art, it finally casts over the *tout ensemble* by mysterious methods of its own a subtle something which refines, subdues, etherealizes the arid components and endues them with the deep charm and gracious witchery of poesy.

Among the art-treasures of Europe there are pictures which approach the Hair Trunk—there are two which may be said to equal it, possibly—but there is none that surpasses it. So perfect is the Hair Trunk that it moves even persons who ordinarily have no feeling for art. When an Erie baggagemaster saw it two years ago he could hardly keep from checking it. And once when a customs inspector was brought into its presence, he gazed upon it in silent rapture for some moments, then slowly and unconsciously placed one hand behind him with the palm uppermost and got out his chalk with the other. These facts speak for themselves.

39. American and European Meals

One lingers about the Cathedral a good deal in Venice. There is a strong fascination about it—partly because it is so old and partly because it is so ugly. Too many of the world's famous buildings fail of one chief virtue—harmony. They are made up of a methodless mixture of the ugly and the beautiful. This is bad. It is confusing, it is unrestful. One has a sense of uneasiness, of distress, without knowing why. But one is calm before St. Mark's, one is calm within it, one would be calm on top of it, calm in the cellar, for its details are masterfully ugly, no misplaced and impertinent beauties are intruded anywhere, and the consequent result is a grand harmonious whole of soothing, entrancing, tranquilizing, soul-satisfying ugliness. One's admiration of a perfect thing always grows, never declines, and this is the surest evidence to him that it *is* perfect. St. Mark's is perfect. To me it soon grew to be so nobly, so augustly ugly that it was difficult to stay away from it even for a little while. Every time its squat domes disappeared from my view I had a despondent feeling. Whenever they reappeared I felt an honest rapture—I have not known any happier hours than those I daily spent in front of Florian's, looking across the Great Square at it. Propped on its long row of low thick-legged columns, its back knobbed with domes, it seemed like a vast warty bug taking a meditative walk.

St. Mark's is not the oldest building in the world, of course, but it seems the oldest and looks the oldest—especially inside. When the ancient mosaics in its walls become damaged, they are repaired but not altered. The grotesque old pattern is preserved. Antiquity has a charm of its own, and to smarten it up would only damage it. One day I was sitting on a red marble bench in the vestibule looking up at an ancient piece of apprentice-work, in mosaic, illustrative of the command to "multiply and replenish the earth." The Cathedral itself had seemed very old but this picture was illustrating a period in history which made the building seem young by comparison. But I presently found an antique which was older than either the battered Cathedral or the date assigned to that piece of history. It was a spiral-shaped fossil as large as the crown of a hat. It was embedded in the marble bench and had been sat upon by tourists until it was worn smooth. Contrasted with the inconceivable antiquity of this modest fossil, those other things were flippantly modern—jejune—mere matters of day-before-yesterday. The sense of the oldness of the Cathedral vanished away under the influence of this truly venerable presence.

St. Mark's is monumental. It is an imperishable remembrancer of the profound and simple piety of the Middle Ages. Whoever could ravish a column from a pagan temple did it and contributed his swag to this Christian one. So this fane is upheld by several hundred acquisitions procured in that peculiar way. In our day it would be immoral to go on the highway to get bricks for a church, but it was no sin in the old times. St. Mark's was itself the victim of a curious robbery once. The thing is set down in the history of Venice but it might be smuggled into the Arabian Nights and not seem out of place there:

Nearly four hundred and fifty years ago a Candian named Stammato, in the suite of a prince of the house of Este, was allowed to view the riches of St. Mark's. His sinful eye was dazzled and he hid himself behind an altar with an evil purpose in his heart but a priest discovered him and turned him out. Afterward he got in again—by false keys, this time. He went there night after night and worked hard and patiently, all alone, overcoming difficulty after difficulty with his toil, and at last succeeded in removing a great block of the marble paneling which walled the lower part of the treasury. This block he fixed so that he could take it out and put it in at will. After that, for weeks he spent all his midnights in his magnificent mine, inspecting it in security, gloating over its marvels at his leisure, and always slipping back to his obscure lodgings before dawn, with a duke's ransom under his cloak. He did not need to grab haphazard and run—there was no hurry. He could make deliberate and well-considered selections. He could consult his esthetic tastes. One comprehends how undisturbed he was and how safe from any danger of interruption when it is stated that he even carried off a unicorn's horn —a mere curiosity—which would not pass through the egress entire but had to be sawn in two—a bit of work which cost him hours of tedious labor. He continued to store up his treasures at home until his occupation lost the charm of novelty and became monotonous. Then he ceased from it, contented. Well he might be, for his collection, raised to modern values, represented nearly fifty million dollars!

He could have gone home much the richest citizen of his country, and it might have been years before the plunder was missed, but he was human—he could not enjoy his delight alone, he must have somebody to talk about it with. So he exacted a solemn oath from a Candian noble named Crioni, then led him to his lodgings and nearly took his breath away with a sight of his glittering hoard. He detected a look in his friend's face which excited his suspicion, and was about to slip a stiletto into him when Crioni saved himself by explaining that that look was only an expression of supreme and happy astonishment. Stammato made Crioni a present of one of the state's principal jewels—a huge carbuncle, which afterward figured in the Ducal cap of state—and the pair parted. Crioni went at once to the palace, denounced the criminal and handed over the carbuncle as evidence. Stammato was arrested, tried and condemned, with the old-time

Venetian promptness. He was hanged between the two great columns in the Piazza—with a gilded rope out of compliment to his love of gold, perhaps. He got no good of his booty at all—it was *all* recovered.

In Venice we had a luxury which very seldom fell to our lot on the continent—a home dinner with a private family. If one could always stop with private families when traveling, Europe would have a charm which it now lacks. As it is, one must live in the hotels, of course, and that is a sorrowful business. A man accustomed to American food and American domestic cookery would not starve to death suddenly in Europe but I think he would gradually waste away and eventually die.

He would have to do without his accustomed morning meal. That is too formidable a change altogether. He would necessarily suffer from it. He could get the shadow, the sham, the base counterfeit of that meal but that would do him no good, and money could not buy the reality.

To particularize: the average American's simplest and commonest form of breakfast consists of coffee and beefsteak. Well, in Europe coffee is an unknown beverage. You can get what the European hotel-keeper thinks is coffee but it resembles the real thing as hypocrisy resembles holiness. It is a feeble, characterless, uninspiring sort of stuff, and almost as undrinkable as if it had been made in an American hotel. The milk used for it is what the French call "Christian" milk—milk which has been baptized.

After a few months' acquaintance with European "coffee" one's mind weakens, and his faith with it, and he begins to wonder if the rich beverage of home, with its clotted layer of yellow cream on top of it, is not a mere dream after all and a thing which never existed.

Next comes the European bread—fair enough, good enough, after a fashion, but cold. Cold and tough and unsympathetic. And never any change, never any variety—always the same tiresome thing.

Next, the butter—the sham and tasteless butter. No salt in it, and made of goodness knows what.

Then there is the beefsteak. They have it in Europe but they don't know how to cook it. Neither will they cut it right. It comes on the table in a small, round, pewter platter. It lies in the center of this platter, in a bordering bed of grease-soaked potatoes. It is the size, shape and thickness of a man's hand with the thumb and fingers cut off. It is a little over-done, is rather dry, it tastes pretty insipid, it rouses no enthusiasm.

Imagine a poor exile contemplating that inert thing. And imagine an angel suddenly sweeping down out of a better land and setting before him a mighty porterhouse steak an inch and a half thick, hot and sputtering from the griddle. Dusted with fragrant pepper. Enriched with little melting bits of butter of the most unimpeachable freshness and genuineness. The precious juices of the meat trickling out and joining the gravy, archipelagoed with mushrooms. A township or two of tender, yellowish fat gracing an outlying district of this ample county of beefsteak. The long white bone which divides the sirloin from the tenderloin still in its place. And imagine that the angel also adds a great cup of American home-made coffee, with the cream a-froth on top, some real butter, firm and yellow and fresh, some smoking-hot biscuits, a plate of hot buckwheat cakes with transparent syrup—could words describe the gratitude of this exile?

The European dinner is better than the European breakfast but it has its faults and inferiorities. It does not satisfy. He comes to the table eager and hungry. He swallows his soup—there is an undefinable lack about it somewhere. Thinks the fish is going to be the thing he wants—eats it and isn't sure. Thinks the next dish is perhaps the one that will hit the hungry place—tries it and is conscious that there was a something wanting about it also. And thus he goes on from dish to dish like a boy after a butterfly which just misses getting caught every time it alights but somehow doesn't get caught after all. And at the end the exile and the boy have fared about alike. The one is full but grievously unsatisfied, the other has had plenty of exercise, plenty of interest and a fine lot of hopes but he hasn't got any butterfly. There is here and there an American who will say he can remember rising from a European table d'hôte perfectly satisfied but we must not overlook the fact that there is also here and there an American who will lie.

The number of dishes is sufficient but then it is such a monotonous variety of *unstriking* dishes. It is an inane dead-level of "fair-to-middling." There is nothing to *accent* it. Perhaps if the roast of mutton or of beef—a big, generous one —were brought on the table and carved in full view of the client, that might give the right sense of earnestness and reality to the thing. But they don't do that, they pass the sliced meat around on a dish, and so you are perfectly calm, it does not stir you in the least. Now a vast roast turkey stretched on the broad of his back, with his heels in the air and the rich juices oozing from his fat sides . . . but I may as well stop there, for they would not know how to cook him. They can't even cook a chicken respectably. And as for carving it, they do that with a hatchet.

This is about the customary table d'hôte bill in summer:

Soup (characterless).

Fish—sole, salmon or whiting—usually tolerably good.

Roast—mutton or beef—tasteless—and some last year's potatoes.

A pâte or some other made dish—usually good—"considering."

One vegetable—brought on in state and all alone—usually insipid lentils or string-beans or indifferent asparagus.

Roast chicken, as tasteless as paper.

Lettuce-salad—tolerably good.

Decayed strawberries or cherries.

Sometimes the apricots and figs are fresh but this is no advantage, as these fruits are of no account anyway.

The grapes are generally good, and sometimes there is a tolerably good peach by mistake.

The variations of the above bill are trifling. After a fortnight one discovers that the variations are only apparent, not real. In the third week you get what you had the first, and in the fourth week you get what you had the second. Three or four months of this weary sameness will kill the robustest appetite.

It has now been many months, at the present writing, since I have had a nourishing meal but I shall soon have one—a modest, private affair, all to myself. I have selected a few dishes and made out a little bill of fare which will go home in the steamer that precedes me and be hot when I arrive—as follows:

Radishes. Baked apples with cream.

Fried oysters. Stewed oysters. Frogs.

American coffee, with real cream.

American butter.

Fried chicken, Southern style.

Porterhouse steak.

Saratoga potatoes.

Broiled chicken, American style.

Hot biscuits, Southern style.

Hot wheat-bread, Southern style.

Hot buckwheat cakes.

American toast. Clear maple syrup.

Virginia bacon, broiled.

Blue points on the half shell.

Cherry-stone clams.

San Francisco mussels, steamed.

Oyster soup. Clam soup.

Philadelphia Terrapin soup.

Oysters roasted in shell—Northern style.

Soft-shell crabs. Connecticut shad.

Baltimore perch.

Brook-trout from Sierra Nevadas.

Lake-trout from Tahoe.

Sheepshead and croakers from New Orleans.

Black-bass from the Mississippi.

American roast beef.

Roast turkey, Thanksgiving style.

Cranberry sauce. Celery.

Roast wild turkey. Woodcock.

Canvasback-duck from Baltimore.

Prairie-hens from Illinois.

Missouri partridges, broiled.

Possum. Coon.

Boston bacon and beans.

Bacon and greens, Southern style.

Hominy. Boiled onions. Turnips.

Pumpkin. Squash. Asparagus.

Butter-beans. Sweet-potatoes.

Lettuce. Succotash. String-beans.

Mashed potatoes. Catsup.

Boiled potatoes in their skins.

New potatoes, minus the skins.

Early Rose potatoes, roasted in the ashes, Southern style, served hot.

Sliced tomatoes with sugar or vinegar. Stewed tomatoes.

Green corn cut from the ear and served with butter and pepper.

Green corn on the ear.

Hot corn-pone with chitlings, Southern style.

Hot hoe-cake, Southern style.

Hot egg-bread, Southern style.

Hot light-bread, Southern style.

Buttermilk. Iced sweet milk.

Apple dumplings with real cream.

Apple pie. Apple fritters.

Apple puffs, Southern style.

Peach cobbler, Southern style.

Peach pie. American mince pie.

Pumpkin pie. Squash pie.

All sorts of American pastry.

Fresh American fruits of all sorts, including strawberries, which are not to be doled out as if they were jewelry, but in a more liberal way.

Ice-water—not prepared in the ineffectual goblet but in the sincere and capable refrigerator.

Americans intending to spend a year or so in European hotels will do well to copy this bill and carry it along. They will find it an excellent thing to get up an appetite with in the dispiriting presence of the squalid table d'hôte.

Foreigners cannot enjoy our food, I suppose, any more than we can enjoy theirs. It is not strange. For tastes are made, not born. I might glorify my bill of fare until I was tired. But after all, the Scotchman would shake his head and say, "Where's your haggis?" and the Fijian would sigh and say, "Where's your missionary?"

I have a neat talent in matters pertaining to nourishment. This has met with professional recognition. I have often furnished recipes for cook-books. Here are some designs for pies and things which I recently prepared for a friend's projected cook-book, but as I forgot to furnish diagrams and perspectives, they had to be left out, of course.

Recipe for an Ash-Cake

Take a lot of water and add to it a lot of coarse Indian-meal and about a quarter of a lot of salt. Mix well together, knead into the form of a "pone" and let the pone stand awhile—not on its edge but the other way. Rake away a place among the embers, lay it there and cover it an inch deep with hot ashes. When it is done, remove it. Blow off all the ashes but one layer. Butter that one and eat.

N. B.—No household should ever be without this talisman. It has been noticed that tramps never return for another ash-cake.

Recipe for New England Pie

To make this excellent breakfast dish, proceed as follows: Take a sufficiency of water and a sufficiency of flour and construct a bullet-proof dough. Work this into the form of a disk, with the edges turned up some three-fourths of an inch. Toughen and kiln-dry it a couple of days in a mild but unvarying temperature. Construct a cover for this redoubt in the same way and of the same material. Fill with stewed dried apples. Aggravate with cloves, lemon-peel and slabs of citron. Add two portions of New Orleans sugar, then solder on the lid and set in a safe place till it petrifies. Serve cold at breakfast and invite your enemy.

Recipe for German Coffee

Take a barrel of water and bring it to a boil. Rub a chicory berry against a coffee berry, then convey the former into the water. Continue the boiling and evaporation until the intensity of the flavor and aroma of the coffee and chicory has been diminished to a proper degree. Then set aside to cool. Now unharness the remains of a once cow from the plow, insert them in a hydraulic press, and when you shall have acquired a teaspoonful of that pale-blue juice which a German superstition regards as milk, modify the malignity of its strength in a bucket of tepid water and ring up the breakfast. Mix the beverage in a cold cup, partake with moderation and keep a wet rag around your head to guard against over-excitement.

To Carve Fowls in the German Fashion

Use a club and avoid the joints.

40. Titian's Venus

I wonder why some things are? For instance, Art is allowed as much indecent license today as in earlier times—but the privileges of Literature in this respect have been sharply curtailed within the past eighty or ninety years. Fielding and Smollett could portray the beastliness of their day in the beastliest language. We have plenty of foul subjects to deal with in our day but we are not allowed to approach them very near, even with nice and guarded forms of speech. But not so with Art. The brush may still deal freely with any subject, however revolting or indelicate. It makes a body ooze sarcasm at every pore to go about Rome and Florence and see what this last generation has been doing with the statues. These works, which had stood in innocent nakedness for ages, are all fig-leaved now. Yes, every one of them. Nobody noticed their nakedness before, perhaps. Nobody can help noticing it now, the fig-leaf makes it so conspicuous. But the comical thing about it all is that the fig-leaf is confined to cold and pallid marble, which would be still cold and unsuggestive without this sham and ostentatious symbol of modesty, whereas warm-blooded paintings which do really need it have in no case been furnished with it.

At the door of the Uffizzi, in Florence, one is confronted by statues of a man and a woman, noseless, battered, black with accumulated grime—they hardly suggest human beings —yet these ridiculous creatures have been thoughtfully and conscientiously fig-leaved by this fastidious generation. You enter and proceed to that most-visited little gallery that exists in the world—the Tribune—and there, against the wall, without obstructing rag or leaf, you may look your fill upon the foulest, the vilest, the obscenest picture the world possesses—Titian's Venus. It isn't that she is naked and stretched out on a bed—no, it is the attitude of one of her arms and hand. If I ventured to describe that attitude there would be a fine howl—but there the Venus lies, for anybody to gloat over that wants to—and there she has a right to lie, for she is a work of art and Art has its privileges. I saw young girls stealing furtive glances at her. I saw young men gaze long and absorbedly at her. I saw aged, infirm men hang upon her charms with a pathetic interest. How I should like to describe her—just to see what a holy indignation I could stir up in the world—just to hear the unreflecting average man deliver himself about my grossness and coarseness and all that. The world says that no worded description of a moving spectacle is a hundredth part as moving as the same spectacle seen with one's own eyes—yet the world is willing to let its son and its daughter and itself look at Titian's beast but won't stand a description of it in words. Which shows that the world is not as consistent as it might be.

There are pictures of nude women which suggest no impure thought—I am well aware of that. I am not railing at such. What I am trying to emphasize is the fact that Titian's Venus is very far from being one of that sort. Without any question it was painted for a bagnio and it was probably refused because it was a trifle too strong. In truth it is too strong for any place but a public Art Gallery. Titian has two Venuses in the Tribune. Persons who have seen them will easily remember which one I am referring to.

In every gallery in Europe there are hideous pictures of blood, carnage, oozing brains, putrefaction—pictures portraying intolerable suffering—pictures alive with every conceivable horror, wrought out in dreadful detail—and similar pictures are being put on the canvas every day and publicly exhibited—without a growl from anybody—for they are innocent, they are inoffensive, being works of art. But suppose a literary artist ventured to go into a painstaking and elaborate description of one of these grisly things—the critics would skin him alive. Well, let it go, it cannot be helped. Art retains her privileges. Literature has lost hers. Somebody else may cipher out the whys and the wherefores and the consistencies of it—I haven't got time.

Titian's Venus defiles and disgraces the Tribune, there is no softening that fact, but his "Moses" glorifies it. The simple truthfulness of this noble work wins the heart and the applause of every visitor, be he learned or ignorant. After wearying one's self with the acres of stuffy, sappy, expressionless babies that populate the canvases of the Old Masters of Italy it is refreshing to stand before this peerless child and feel that thrill which tells you you are at last in the presence of the real thing. This is a human child, this is genuine. You have seen him a thousand times—you have seen him just as he is here —and you confess without reserve that Titian *was* a Master. The doll-faces of other painted babes may mean one thing, they may mean another, but with the "Moses" the case is different. The most famous of all the art-critics has said, "There is no room for doubt here—plainly this child is in trouble."

I consider that the "Moses" has no equal among the works of the Old Masters except it be the divine Hair Trunk of Bassano. I feel sure that if all the other Old Masters were lost and only these two preserved, the world would be the gainer by it.

My sole purpose in going to Florence was to see this immortal "Moses," and by good fortune I was just in time, for

they were already preparing to remove it to a more private
and better-protected place because a fashion of robbing the
great galleries was prevailing in Europe at the time.

We took a turn to Rome and some other Italian cities—
then to Munich and thence to Paris—partly for exercise but
mainly because these things were in our projected program
and it was only right that we should be faithful to it.

From Paris I branched out and walked through Holland
and Belgium, procuring an occasional lift by rail or canal
when tired, and I had a tolerably good time of it "by and
large." I worked Spain and other regions through agents to
save time and shoe-leather.

We crossed to England and then made the homeward passage in the Cunarder *Gallia,* a very fine ship. I was glad to
get home—immeasurably glad. So glad, in fact, that it did not
seem possible that anything could ever get me out of the
country again. I had not enjoyed a pleasure abroad which
seemed to me to compare with the pleasure I felt in seeing
New York harbor again. Europe has many advantages which
we have not but they do not compensate for a good many still
more valuable ones which exist nowhere but in our own
country. Then we are such a homeless lot when we are over
there! So are Europeans themselves, for that matter. They
live in dark and chilly vast tombs—costly enough, maybe, but
without conveniences. To be condemned to live as the average European family lives would make life a pretty heavy
burden to the average American family.

On the whole, I think that short visits to Europe are better
for us than long ones. The former preserve us from becoming
Europeanized. They keep our pride of country intact and at
the same time they intensify our affection for our country
and our people. Whereas long visits have the effect of dulling
those feelings—at least in the majority of cases. I think that
one who mixes much with Americans long resident abroad
must arrive at this conclusion.